Ritual Abuse – Spring

Spiritual Warfare

Lynda L. Irons

Irons Quill

Lynda L. Irons

This is a work of fiction that is loosely based on some actual events from the author's life. Names, characters, places, and incidents that resemble that of any actual persons, living or dead, business establishments, locales, churches, and so on, is purely coincidental and are the product of the author's wild imagination.

This story is not for everyone. It contains some very disturbing information. Unfortunately, while this book is purely fictional, it depicts the tormented lives of far too many ritual abuse survivors who live in our communities. The representative characters in this book give voice to these amazing survivors in a way that only hints at the horrors that they have experienced day in and day out. This narrative is not meant to be sensational, rather to raise awareness that these people exist and desperately need the help of the Church.

WARNING: If you are a Satanic or Witchcraft Ritual Abuse survivor, please be aware that some of the content of this book could trigger unresolved programming.

Cover by H. Gene Irons

Lynda L. Irons

TABLE OF CONTENTS

Lynda L. Irons

Key people from previous books and final paragraphs from Ritual Abuse - Winter

This is the third in a four-book series. The following are some of the key characters that were introduced in the first two books. Ritual Abuse – Summer follows.

Abigail Steele, a pastoral counselor, started her life over after the deaths of her husband and three sons by purchasing a small ten-acre farm in a remote area.

Earl and Jan Milner are Abigail's elderly neighbors. Earl, a World War II sharpshooter, taught Abigail how to shoot.

Carrie Sue Wagner was born to Satanist parents, Susan and Ron. He recently died of cancer. Carrie Sue had been programmed and fragmented into multiple personalities by Satanists. She had been working with Abigail Steele for several years. Her brother, Danny, died at age 25 in a traffic accident. Their other brother, Billy, was recently killed by the cult.

F. Amy Bolton, another SRA survivor, works with Abigail as well. Her very closed and secretive internal system resembles a prison complex.

Prinz, a regional master, resided in the capital of the state and had risen to power over the decades. He was reputed to be over a century old.

Daggett and Darod are area masters and subject to Prinz until they could rise in power and overthrow him.

Zorroz and Herrak are local masters who reign under Daggett and Darod respectively. Carrie Sue fell under Daggett's jurisdiction while Amy fell under Darod's jurisdiction.

Xerxes, an influential congressman who was being groomed for the American presidency, reigned above this region.

Gary and Cindy McCord are good friends of Abigail Steele and parents of little Traci and Bryan. Cindy and Abigail are prayer partners and attend the Springfield Baptist church where Daniel Spalding is the pastor.

Gary's cousin, Lee Norris, recently moved back east from Montana to be near his extended family. He sold his ranch and purchased a farm across the road from the Milners and Abigail.

David and Martha York are Abigail's neighbors to the south.

Final paragraphs of Ritual Abuse – Winter:

Flipping the cap off the scope and loading the cartridges, Earl brought the rifle up to his cheek just as the man at the end of Abigail's property did the same. Abigail was just mounting the steps when the first shot rang out. Another one followed a split second later.

Lee heard the two shots and knew that they had come from the other side of the road. Leaping into his truck, he peeled down his driveway, barely watching for traffic and headed for Abigail's house. He had a feeling. "Lord, no! Lord. Please don't let anything happen to Abigail!" He prayed desperately.

Seeing no one in front, leaving the truck running, Lee sprinted in a crouch around the back as he pulled his handgun. His heart sank when he saw the blown-out glass and Abigail curled in a fetal position on the deck.

1

Monday, March 19

Adrenaline was coursing through Lee's system making it possible to assess the situation from all angles within a matter of seconds. Lee heard the man at the end of the pasture cursing as he tried to remount his spooked horse and determined that he was no longer a threat. He heard Earl yelling something from his home on the next hill. He took in what was left of the panel of glass with the irregular spider-web pattern of cracks radiating from the eye-level hole.

"Abigail!" Lee shouted as he holstered his gun and leaped up the steps to her side.

Uncurling from the protective position that she instinctively took, Abigail finally dared to open her eyes and looked quickly from Lee to the shattered door and back again. "Oh, man! I heard the shots and I thought I heard Earl yelling at me to stay down so I hit the deck and didn't move!"

"That guy tried to shoot you. I heard two heavy-duty shots and came running." Lee was looking at Abigail and assessing her as if he was still a paramedic.

"You saw someone?" Abigail's heart was back in her throat. "I looked around like I usually do and didn't see anyone."

"He was probably hiding until the last minute."

Abigail did not want to think about the implications and looked with disdain at the damage. "Great! Now I have to replace my door." Locating the keys that she had dropped, she started to get up.

Lynda L. Irons

Lee stood first and helped her up. Wrapping her in his arms, and hugging her to his chest, Lee whispered, "I thought I'd lost you."

The reality of how close she had come to being killed abruptly hit Abigail. Legs suddenly weak, she dropped the keys again, and began to shake and sob. Lee held her closer.

Hearing a vehicle come up the driveway, Lee released Abigail and had her lean against the house. Gun in hand, he peeked around the corner. "It's your neighbors."

Holstering his gun, Lee stepped out and gave Earl and Jan a thumbs-up sign and then went back to Abigail. He picked up the keys that she had dropped and unlocked the door.

"Careful."

Earl stopped to turn off Lee's truck and then he and Jan were right behind them. Bustling into the living room, talking over each other, asking questions, and telling the others what they had seen and thought, they finally lapsed into silence. Earl automatically analyzed the shot, both before and after he pulled the trigger and believed that since he shot from roughly twice the distance that the other shooter did, Earl probably hit the man just as he got the shot off.

"He had a scope. He should have nailed you," Earl said.

"I think I must have a pretty roughed up guardian angel." The shock was wearing off and Abigail said, "I need to stoke up this fire."

"I need to do something with that door," Lee said. "Where's your duct tape? Do you have some plastic sheeting?"

"Uh, yeah, the duct tape should be on the workbench downstairs. Humph! The last time I had to use it was with Billy's break in. This has got to stop. Oh, and check by the painting supplies for some plastic."

Lee went to the basement, flipping on lights as he went. Quickly collecting the items, he hurried back upstairs. "Earl, would you mind taping what's left of the door. I'll help with the plastic when I get back. I want to see if there's anything to see down there before we completely lose daylight."

"You should find some of his rifle stock. I was aiming for his hand."

"I believe you winged him judging by the way he was trying to get on that big horse of his."

"You be careful!" Jan instructed.

"Don't worry, I will. I don't think he's still down there. I heard the horse gallop off."

With that, Lee carefully walked out the back door and briskly strode down to the end of the pasture. It did not take him long to locate the exact place where the man had stood when the shots rang out. To his satisfaction, there were pieces of a broken stock as well as a casing nearby. Photographing them with his cell phone before picking them up with his handkerchief, Lee quickly looked around before heading over to Abigail's security camera. He removed the SD card, added it to his pocket of evidence and made his way back up the pasture, glancing back over his shoulder and stopping to listen from time to time.

By the time Lee returned to the house, Earl had taped the crazed glass ensuring that no more shards would drop out. He and Lee finished putting a layer of plastic over the temporary repair.

"Oh, by the way," Abigail said, "this is Lee Norris, our across-the-road neighbor with the two trucks."

"Well, we are pleased to meet you," Jan said.

"Yes, and welcome to the neighborhood. We think highly of our Abigail here. I'm glad we have someone else to help keep an eye on her – she can be a handful!" Earl grinned at Abigail as he shook Lee's hand.

"Hey!" Abigail protested.

Lee retrieved the SD card from his pocket and asked, "Do you want to look at this now?"

"Yes. Come on, everyone, let's move the party into my office."

Earl and Jan were intrigued by the technology and stood looking over Abigail's shoulder as she pulled images up on her computer screen. She scrolled through them until she came to one that clearly showed the rider with the braided hair.

"There he is again," Abigail commented. "I wish I knew who he was. He's got to live somewhere around here."

Earl squinted and leaned forward. "He does. He lives down the road a couple miles."

"I knew it! On the other side, right?"

"Yep. Looks like Charlie Fletcher. I knew he was a mean S.O.B..."

"Earl Ray!" Jan reserved the use of his middle name for occasions such as this.

"... but I didn't think that snake would stoop this low! I should have shot him instead of his rifle!" Earl was angry. "Why, I oughta go over there and finish the job!"

"Now, Earl, don't you get yourself all worked up! You stopped him and that's enough." Jan shook her finger at him and chided him. "This is a spiritual battle. We need to keep praying."

"Yeah, and keep our powder dry, too."

"Earl," Lee said, "you might want to look at these." He pulled out the shards of the rifle stock and the empty casing.

Earl turned them over and grunted with satisfaction. "He won't be using that rifle any time soon. Looks like a little blood there."

Eventually, Earl calmed down because they were finally assured that Abigail was safe. For now. They were ready to head back home. They left through the front door and soon their taillights were seen going down the driveway.

———————

After hearing the gunshots, David and Martha York warily watched out the kitchen windows at the back of their house.

"There's that horse," Martha reported.

"Seems like every time there's a ruckus next door, that horse is close by," David commented.

"Did you see who's riding him this time?"

"No, I'm just glad they leave us alone."

"Maybe when Richard comes home we can have him do some checking."

———————

The large horse had followed these trails numerous times under the guidance of various riders and followed the path home without much direction from

13

his rider. Charlie Fletcher clutched his left hand to his chest under his coat. The stunned man did not want to look at his hand. It was mostly numb, but he could feel the warm ooze of blood running down his arm and soaking through his shirt. Cursing his pain, cursing his luck, cursing Max for not being there to do the petty dirty work, he slid off the horse and led him into the barn where he left him in a stall.

In the house, he carefully pulled the blood-slick glove off. He let it drop to the kitchen floor and was sickened at the sound of the soggy thud. Forcing himself to look at his shaking hand, he was shocked to see that the web of flesh between his thumb and palm was gone along with the tattoo of the upside-down cross. Charlie slowly turned his trembling hand over as if another view would render another result. He let out another stream of curses. Gone!

Lee and Abigail had gone back to Lee's place to stow the tools he had dropped earlier and to check on the horses. They were soon settled back at Abigail's house eating their dinner when they saw the flash of blue lights coming down the road.

"Oh dear, I hope that doesn't have anything to do with the shooting!" Abigail was alarmed until the car blew past her driveway. "What'll happen to Earl if Charlie Fletcher reports this?"

"I was wondering what the legal ramifications of this thing might be. After all, Earl shot the man. He could press charges. But then we have evidence that he shot at you."

"What good would that do? They don't believe any of our evidence. Besides, he's one of them."

A few minutes later, the blue lights streamed past them going in the other direction. Sheriff Bynum and Charlie Fletcher unleashed curses and vowed vengeance as they passed by. Zorroz had helped Viper wrap his hand and pack it in ice. Dr. Bacchus would be attending to yet another casualty of this war. Mastiff died of pancreatic cancer. Zorroz' windpipe was damaged. Max was in that wreck. Prinz was weakening. And now this.

It took Abigail a long time to fall asleep that night. Despite declarations that no weapon formed against her would prosper, she startled at any foreign sound. She scrolled through the events of the day in her mind trying to make sense of it all. She thought about replacing the door and that eventually brought her to the five words Lee had said when they were standing by that door – "I thought I'd lost you." The way he said it, the tone of his voice; what were the implications? She finally fell into a fitful sleep.

Lee was also tossing and turning. He poured out his heart in prayer. "Lord, I just met her in September and I'm afraid to move too fast, but today... Oh, God! I don't want to lose her. I don't want to sound selfish, but I need her. I thought I was fine being alone, but I just love being with her..."

Just as he drifted off to sleep, he heard the familiar words, "It is not good for man to be alone."

2

March 20, Spring Equinox

Ah, the first day of spring! Lee was excited that the excavators had arrived promptly at seven o'clock. The plans for his house had been revised, but that did not affect the starting date. Lee was initially going to build a simple one-story home with three bedrooms and a bath and a half. After his first kiss, he decided that he needed more than a bachelor pad. After meeting with his daughter, he decided that he should add guest rooms as well.

Going over the final plans with his contractor, he was satisfied that the two-level home would be more than adequate for a family. He had casually asked Abigail about the kinds of features she liked and disliked in a kitchen as well as a house in general. He did not want to admit it then, but he had already made up his mind that he would pursue this woman and marry her, that is, with the Lord's blessing. After last night, Lee felt the pleasure of God's approval.

Abigail was busy on the phone that morning. The building and supply company that had originally installed her back door assured her that they could order and replace the damaged glass. Jan called and checked on her and assured her that she and Earl would remain vigilant. She commented that they had noticed the sheriff's car that went by last night and prayed that it would keep going. Abigail called Cindy and filled her in on the latest drama.

"Abigail! You could have been killed!"

16

"It was close," Abigail conceded. "But the guy still didn't get onto the property."

"Yeah, but his bullet sure did."

"I don't understand why bullets and packs of poison can get across, but not the people."

"Well, maybe those legalistic demons are saying that you prayed against people, but not things."

"You might be right! Duh! Why didn't I think of that? Let's pray!"

Cindy and Abigail prayed that not only would the human opponents be banned from the property, but that any tangible or intangible thing – poison, curses, bullets, vehicles, animals, demons, and so on – would also be prohibited from crossing the boundary lines. They prayed for protection for Earl and Jan. They prayed for protection over Abigail's vehicle and her office. They prayed for Lee and his property. They prayed for Carrie Sue and Amy. They appealed to the heavenly court for righteousness and justice to prevail so that the defendants, especially Charlie Fletcher, would be brought to justice. They prayed that Jesus would complete and correct anything they prayed inadequately.

"Well, I'm not going to take this laying down," Abigail stated flatly.

"What do you mean?"

"I'm going to call Carrie Sue and see if we can meet today. She's got something funky going on and I want to see if we can head off any more problems."

Across town, Dorkas, Susan Wagner's cult-loyal personality, was ecstatic. She was finally able to access

17

a part of Carrie Sue that would comply with the cult and, more importantly, get her off the hook. She had been under intense pressure by Daggett to bring her daughter back into compliance.

Carrie Sue, the Christian host, was trapped inside. Her main protectors, David and Titus, had been ambushed, too. All they could do was pray and listen to the conversations between the imposter host, Mirror, and their mother.

"Well, it's about time you got here!" Dorkas reprimanded the impostor host. "I've had hell to pay since you were gone."

"That's not my fault. I tried, but that goody-two-shoes and her counselor kept blocking me."

"You're expected to show tonight and renounce God."

"No problem. I don't *do* God."

God, no! Don't let that impostor undo everything You have done! O God, You said You'd set the captives free. Carrie Sue was co-conscious and prayed fervently, desperately.

David and Titus were praying as well. *Contend, O Lord, with those who contend with us.* They prayed all the prayers they knew using some of the warring Scriptures that they had learned. They knew what was at stake. This was the spring equinox and it was a ritual day. At least the Equinox Quints were taken care of last fall; maybe it wouldn't be so bad.

They were relieved when Dorkas hung up. They became hopeful when Abigail called. *God, please make that impostor cooperate!*

"Carrie Sue?"

"Yes," the impostor answered dryly.

"Hey, I was thinking about you and wondered if you would be up for a session today."

"Why? So that you can trick me into letting that lame host take over again?"

"I don't think I could trick you into anything; I just want to talk. This is a ritual day and I'd hate to see you or anyone else get hurt again."

"Aww. Aren't you sweet?" The impostor was trying to goad Abigail.

"No, I'm just doing what I believe God wants me to do. I'm as dedicated to my God as you are to yours."

"I told you before," she huffed, "I don't do God."

"Maybe you don't do my God or Carrie Sue's God, but you are serving a god."

"I am not! I do what I please."

"I don't want to argue the point, but I beg to differ with you there. Can we please get together today and talk about this some more?"

"Sure. I have nothing better to do. This could be entertaining. What time?"

"How about one o'clock?"

"See ya then."

After they hung up, Abigail busied herself with straightening the house and eating a light lunch. Emerging from the house, she took a quick glance around the front of the property. She scanned the woods and the pasture as she walked to the truck. "Oh, Lord, sometimes I wish I wasn't doing this work and I could just go to Lee's and mess with the horses or watch the construction. But I know this is what You've called me to do. Please bless this time with that impostor part and let the system be purged of all cult-loyal personalities."

19

Abigail was already set up and waiting for several minutes before Mirror, the impostor host, came in and sat down crossing her arms and legs.

Defensive body language... Oh, Lord grant me favor. "Thanks for coming."

"Start the entertainment."

"Do you mind if I ask some questions so I can understand you a bit better?"

"Sure. You have fun with that."

"When you say that you don't do God, does that mean that you don't believe that He exists or that you just won't have anything to do with Him?"

"I see God and Satan in a chess game. They're equals. One's just as bad as the other."

"If they're in a chess game, does that make you the chess board?"

"Huh," she sneered a laugh, "something like that. They each make their moves and I align myself with whoever can protect me. So far, your God hasn't done much."

"Protect you from what?"

"I went to the E-risk-o-palian church."

Catching the pun, Abigail asked, "Why was it so risky to go to that church?"

"Because God sure didn't protect me."

"Protect you from what?"

"From them! From Father Littleton, from all his Erisk-o-pals – the elders and the stupid shrink and even my grandfather!" Mirror was getting worked up.

Carrie Sue was not unlike so many of the SRA survivors who were admitted to the psych ward in certain hospitals after going to the emergency room for suicidal thoughts or attempts, for panic attacks or any of a variety of mysterious physical symptoms. The test results of these survivors consistently recorded false negatives or false positives. The mystified medical professionals eventually referred them for a psychological evaluation.

Once in the psych ward, they were assigned to a secret inner department that was run by the Satanists. Dr. Alexander Kammad was the head of the psychiatric department. The majority of the personnel on the ward were totally unaware of this special unit. The "patients" were often subjected to operations that implanted devices or removed organs. Their minds were altered by drugs. They were programmed through torture and hypnosis. Like clock-work, several times a year, the tormented souls would make their way to the hospital because of the programming.

"Okay, I think I'm beginning to get the picture. You were taken to a church that was led by someone who hurt you. You expected God to protect you, but instead you got abused, so you got mad at God. And you had to play the part, act like a so-called Christian to protect yourself from other religious people."

"You got that right! And I'm not going anywhere until I see a Warrior who can protect us now. I don't care about the Father's love. I have no relationship with God and I'm not going to until He meets me half way."

"You have a problem, then."

"What do you mean?"

"You got brought to this church by your parents. You thought – you hoped – that there really was a good, protective God that you could appeal to, but instead you basically got Satanism. The church looked like a real church to the community, but in reality, it was a demon-driven place. And you, the Mirror image of the Christian host, are just like that."

"What do you mean?" she demanded indignantly.

"You can do all the right religious things, say all the right things, fake a prayer, and so on. But in reality, you are demon-driven." Abigail held her hands up, "Now, don't get all excited. Think about it a minute. Father Littleton abuses you in church. Your grandfather abuses you and is associated with church. I wouldn't want anything to do with any father, let alone a heavenly Father either. So, I'd make a boatload of vows, too."

Mirror was silent for several minutes. "I have no relationship with God and Carrie Sue needs me to find the God who can make us feel safe. I just don't think He exists. If He does, He's too busy to help me out."

"What if we can find a way through this so you can quit the chess game and have a relationship with the true Father?"

"I'm listening."

"You know that the last thing your parents and grandparents and all the other cult people want is for you to have a relationship with the true Father God. They set you up. This is no slam against your intelligence, it's just a fact that you were up against adults who fine-tuned their ways. They manipulated your world so that you would see things from their perspective, so you would not trust God or any genuine Christian. They probably set up all kinds of scenarios in which you were jeopardized and the real God did not show up. They put you in double-binds."

"It was real."

"I'm not saying it wasn't real. But that reality was designed to embitter you against God and to have you make those vows that would guarantee that you *wouldn't* come near God."

"What vows?"

Abigail flipped back in her notes. "Let's see... you said, 'I'm not going anywhere until I see a Warrior who can protect us now' and 'I don't care about the Father's love' and 'I have no relationship with God and I'm not going to until He meets me half way.'"

"So?"

"Vows bind your soul with an oath. They put up a fence, a wall. You can't get past them until you renounce them. So, you have put yourself into double-binds, too. The very thing you really, really want – security with the protective Warrior God – is the thing you keep yourself from." Abigail looked at the distressed personality with compassion.

"We, and I include myself in this, we want to create God in our image. That's not the way it works. He is God. I mean, I hate to say this but I think the Satanists respect Satan more than Christians respect Christ. Too many demand that God draws near to them, that God proves Himself to them, makes the first concession and *then* they will come to Him. Like it or not, I have to go by His laws."

Mirror said nothing, but it was evident that she was turning these things over in her mind.

Abigail continued to press. "You respect God's natural laws, right?"

"Sure, who doesn't?"

"So, if I jump off a roof and demand that God suspends the law of gravity for me for that time and

23

place, wouldn't that be about as presumptuous as trying to by-pass His spiritual laws?"

"I guess so."

"Do you want to try it God's way instead of Father Littleton's way?"

"What do I have to do?"

"We could start by getting you free of anything they imposed on you like programming and demons."

"I was listening in when you were working with the others," she said with a sigh of resignation. "Just go for the whole thing. I'm done."

Abigail was thrilled. She was not expecting Mirror to give up without a bigger fight. She prayed the comprehensive prayer for healing and deliverance. She led Mirror in a prayer of renunciation of the vows and for forgiveness towards her persecutors. She checked with Mirror to be sure that there was nothing that remained and then prayed for her integration.

"Hallelujah!" Carrie Sue exclaimed. "I'm back! Thank you, thank you, thank you!"

"Praise God!" Abigail joined in the happy celebration.

"That was close. We were supposed to go to the equinox ritual tonight and she was going to renounce God. Mom's been at our apartment all the time since Mirror showed up and all we could do was fuss and pray."

"Well, your prayers were answered. Do you think there are any more in there programmed for the ritual?"

"Yes, I think so."

They prayed for the Spring Equinox Quints and they were soon integrated as well. They both sensed that Carrie Sue would be safe so they finished their session and each went their own way.

Carrie Sue's heart dropped when she pulled into her parking spot and saw her mother sitting in her truck outside of her apartment. "Oh, Lord, please don't let Dorkas show up. I'm exhausted already."

"Ah, there you are, you ungrateful wretch."

"Nice to see you, too, Mom."

"Where have you been? We have to get ready for tonight."

"I'm not going anywhere tonight."

Dorkas realized that Mirror was no longer in executive control and had been replaced by that Christian host. She began to curse and swear at Carrie Sue.

Carrie Sue nudged her way past her mother and opened the door to her apartment. Standing resolutely in the doorway, Carrie Sue said firmly, "Go home. I'm done with Satanism. When you are too, then you are welcome."

Dorkas was uncharacteristically flabbergasted. She faded to the background leaving Martyr Mom to handle the situation.

Martyr Mom wailed, "Carrie Sue, why do you treat your momma like this? What have I done to deserve a daughter like you?"

"Go home, Mom." Carrie Sue softly closed the door behind her and prayed for her mother.

Charlie Fletcher's hand was throbbing despite having had it elevated and on ice packs all day. Tiny shards of bone and metal and wood could not be removed surgically. They would have to make their way to the surface and be removed eventually. His curses echoed through his desolate house.

He did not relish going to the ritual tonight, but he would be expected to be there – or else. It would be held at the regional site at the pavilion in the state park and he did not even want to drive there much less participate. He was a Satanist, but he knew that he was not being groomed to be a master. He enjoyed the perks that his limited powers gave him, but he was beginning to question whether or not it was worth it. He was beginning to feel a weakening of his powers as well and had an increased sense of foreboding ever since he was shot. He knew it was Earl Milner. He'd bide his time and get even.

He and Sheriff Bynum had had an indirect discussion on that drive to the hospital about the rash of injuries and deaths and losses of powers. Zorroz also suggested that maybe Prinz would heal his hand at the ritual like he healed his damaged throat, but he did not dare mention how the healing had been reversed in that damnable church and Dr. Bacchus had to patch that one up, too. Zorroz seemed edgier since the recent sacrifice of his own daughter. There was a paternal part of him buried somewhere deep underneath the satanic parts.

They agreed that it would not be worth arresting Earl, but they would take care of him unofficially. After all, any friend of Abigail Steele was *not* a friend of theirs. They did not voice their secret fears that Earl had that same mysterious Power.

There was a new moon tonight. It would be very dark. As darkness stole over the region the faithful began their covert journeys to the state park. Drawn by internal forces, they obeyed the will of their masters. The van filled with furniture and other supplies arrived early enough to set up for the festivities. Sacrifices had been properly prepared. Blood-thirsty demons goaded their hosts to gratify their lusts and by doing so, ensured their descent into depravity and deprived them of any hope of redemption. After all, they had done too much for too long. They knew the ordinance of God, that those who practice such things are worthy of death. But they not only did these things, they gave hearty approval to others who also practiced the dark arts.

The frown lines etched into Prinz' face were deeper and more distinct making him look older and yet more formidable. Fierce. He assessed the condition of his weakening flock. His highest-level masters, Daggett and Darod, were weakening in some ways but also looking hungrily at him, assessing his strength as they readied themselves for a coup. He, himself, was both looking over his shoulder at them and looking greedily at Xerxes.

Although Xerxes was a congressman in a mostly agricultural state, it was rumored that he was being groomed for the presidency. Xerxes came from money; lots of money. His lineage went back to the Merovingian line. And he would not be the first Satanist to be sworn in on a Bible, of all things, as the president of the United States of America.

Prinz sighed. After the fiasco last month when he and Xerxes were humiliated by that woman's superior powers, he was not so sure about his own future. He shook his head. He did not want to think about that sudden hail storm and the iced-up road. Xerxes would be here tonight. That was not a good omen.

When one gets kicked, one looks for someone else to kick. Prinz was no exception. "Viper!" he barked out. "Where are you?

There was a quiet shuffling in the darkness and soon Viper stood reverently like an altar boy in front of a priest before Prinz. Prinz stepped close to him and in a low voice, Prinz rasped out his fear-driven fury, "Why couldn't you nail that woman?" Vaguely aware of his own hypocrisy, he continued to press Viper for details. *Just what powers did that woman possess?*

By three o'clock in the morning, Satan had been somewhat appeased by the pitiful sacrifices. Curses had been sent out all over the inhabited world, and like a meteor shower flashing through the atmosphere, they were snuffed out before doing much damage. The shields of faith of their intended targets kept them sleeping peacefully through the night.

3

Friday, March 30

Sheriff Bynum and his wife had already moved to their new house near the southern end of the county close to Hillsdale. There was a small Baptist church there that they could join. Their remaining daughter was crying that morning. "I miss my sister," she wailed inconsolably.

"You don't have a sister," her mother calmly said. "You never did."

"Yes, I did," she insisted with less conviction.

"You made her up. You've always been an only child," her father reinforced. "Look around this house. Do you see anything? No clothes. No toys. No furniture. Now go to your room!"

She snuffled and wiped her nose on the back of her sleeve as she shuffled down the hall with dread. She knew that it was dangerous to make her daddy mad. He was always mad. But she also knew that she had a miniature princess figurine hidden in her room. *My sister gave it to me and I did not make it up!*

As her father entered her room, she turned and saw the malevolent glint in his eyes and knew what was coming. Losing her remaining strength, she slid down the wall and stared at the tiny figurine that was under her bed. While her father ravaged her body, her mind took her deep inside, into her secret place. It was a place her daddy could never find.

Carrie Sue was eager for her appointment with Abigail. She was starting to believe that she was getting very close to full integration. She was not losing time, that is, she was not being displaced by other personalities and not knowing what those personalities had been up to. At least she thought she was not losing any time. There was no evidence, but then, there was always the possibility of cover up programs and other schemes that the cult had developed over the millennia. She and Abigail had uncovered several programmed stragglers recently and each time she hoped it was the last. *Just how many layers of insurance did the cult need?* It was as if they were privy to information about who would encounter a liberator like Abigail Steele.

"You don't know how much I appreciate you meeting with me on Tuesday. I just know Mom would have gotten me to that ritual somehow."

"I was glad to do it. It's kind of like the more I can help you get better, the more satisfaction I get that they aren't getting away with anything."

"What do you mean?"

Abigail did not want to go into all the attacks against her, especially not the recent shooting by her Satanist neighbor, Charlie Fletcher. "Oh, you know, like Dude being poisoned and stuff they've done to you." Changing the subject, Abigail suggested that they open with prayer.

"What are you sensing?" Abigail asked.

"I think we need to work with the core person."

"Anything specific?"

"I think she wants to integrate everyone we know of – the protectors and me."

"Seriously?"

"Yeah, she says she's ready."

"Are you ready?"

"Yes and no." Carrie Sue rocked her head slightly from side to side demonstrating her ambivalence.

"What about the protectors?"

"They feel about like I do, but they're willing to try it."

"Well, what if you do a trial integration for a week and when we get back together, let me know if you guys want to keep it that way or if you need to back off for a while."

They continued to discuss various scenarios and possible problems. The protectors' greatest fear was that the original Carrie Sue would not have the fortitude to face the mother. The host's greatest fear was that she would not be able to handle the day-to-day affairs of their life.

"I mean, what if she forgets to pay the rent?"

"You'll be a part of her, you'll be inside of her. She will have all your information."

"Yeah, you're right. It's only a week."

"Hey, aren't you the person who wanted to be fully integrated within the first month?"

"Boy, was I ever an idiot! I had no idea."

They laughed for a moment before finally coming to a consensus. They prayed for everyone that they knew of and even those that they might not be aware of. They prayed for them to be integrated into the original Carrie Sue Wagner and then waited.

Carrie Sue Wagner looked up at Abigail with a look of wonder. "Wow! I didn't realize there were so many still in hiding. It was like someone opened a gate and they all came rushing in. Then there was a flash of light and, poof, they were gone."

"Interesting."

"Yeah, it feels empty now. Totally empty. It's a bit shocking, I mean, it's just weird to close my eyes and it's dark... empty... like the whole internal world just collapsed."

"That's very similar to what I've heard from other survivors. I can only imagine that after a life-time of being dissociated and having an elaborate inner world, how huge this change must be."

"I'm not sure what to do with it."

"Accept it. Celebrate it. How does it feel to be normal?"

"*That* was normal. I'm not sure what *this* is. I'm not sure if I can handle this. I mean, I feel so alone. It's so quiet inside."

"I promise; you will get used to it. Give it a week and if we need to, we can ask God to pull some key players back out for you."

"All right," Carrie Sue sighed.

They finished their session with prayer. Carrie Sue headed home and Abigail took a short break. Amy Bolton was waiting for her when she got back to her office.

"Hey there!" Abigail greeted her.

"Hey," Amy replied with a subdued voice.

Frowning and looking at her askance, "What's the matter?"

"I'm not feeling that great – a little crampy and, um, I spotted last night." Amy was very uncomfortable talking about gynecological matters.

It always amazed Abigail that these survivors who had been exposed to every kind of perverse sexual experience for most of their lives would be so hesitant to speak about normal female issues and functions.

"Have you seen a doctor yet?"

"Nope. You know how I hate doctors."

"I know, but you need to be checked and start on vitamins and stuff like that."

"Yes, Mother." Amy's sarcastic humor surfaced.

"Can I give you the name of my doctor? She's good and she's also a Christian."

"Sure."

They opened with prayer and Head Honcho immediately replaced host Amy. "I'm worried about that baby. There's something not quite right about it."

"Because of the spotting?"

"No, it's more than that. It's like it's some kind of parasite or something. It's so little, but it feels like it's kicking the crap out of us. There's something evil about it."

"Well considering that the father is one of those masters…" Abigail did not need to finish the thought.

"Yeah, that."

"I think we need to pray about that again."

"Good idea."

Abigail launched into a prayer that covered the generational curses and familial spirits that would have come down through the father's lineage. She prayed about all the strongholds that were created by the violence that surrounded the conception, and all the spiels, hexes, chants, and other verbal assaults that were poured onto both Amy and the child that was developing in her womb. "And Father, we pray that

You would complete and correct anything that we may have prayed inadequately, amen."

"Amen." Head Honcho echoed. "It seems a little calmer inside. Now what?"

"Let's see what the Lord wants us to do today."

Head Honcho shook his head. "Okay, here's what I'm getting: we're supposed to do something like Mayor did with his town."

"Completely remove it?"

"No, more like remodel it. I don't think we're all supposed to integrate yet, but the prison is mostly empty and there are too many places in it for the subterranean level guys to hide. We've captured a few who were trying to sneak out through the prison now that their other tunnels were messed up."

"What have you done with them?" Abigail had a pretty good idea, but she wanted to hear it from Head Honcho. She loved the way they had taken the initiative in continuing the internal work.

"We isolated them in some of our holding rooms. We treated them real nice after we stripped all their demons and programming away. Most of them were willing to defect to God's kingdom and get healed and integrated. There are a couple of hold outs."

"Could you tell what level they came from?"

"We've gotten some from every level except for Apollyon's level. Apparently, the seal is still keeping them locked down. The ones who are holding out are mostly from Judas' level. He's level five, you remember, and they're still calling us traitors."

"Good job!" Abigail was pleased with the report. "Are you ready to pray about the remodeling job?"

"I'll alert everyone." With that, Head Honcho blinked and then refocused on Abigail. "We're ready."

"Lord, we're not exactly sure what You have in mind. As we submit to Your will, we ask that You would remodel the prison in whatever way You deem necessary for this stage of Amy's healing." Abigail finished her prayer and waited for the report from Head Honcho.

"Okay," Head Honcho began his debriefing in his typical military style. "We no longer have six buildings; we have one. It's no longer six stories high; it's one story. As far as we can tell, it's on a slab. Anyone wanting to get in would have to drill through the floor. There are rooms off the main meeting room. A couple of them are holding the guys from the subterranean levels. The rest are for our use."

"That sounds a lot simpler."

"Yes. And taking down the previous structure exposed a bunch more victims and a couple more of the lower level spies. Our guards captured them right away and they've joined the others in the new holding cells."

"Very good!"

"We're hearing some strange buzzing noise that's coming from way below. I'm not sure what that's all about."

"Do you think Nicholai might know?"

"Good idea. I'll check with him and be right back."

Moments later he came back with a report from Nicholai. Nicholai and his first subterranean level personalities were experts at infiltration as well. They had plenty of practice before they defected to God's

Lynda L. Irons

kingdom. He related the vital information to Head Honcho who passed it on to Abigail.

"It sounds like buzzing and it's definitely coming from Apollyon's level. Apparently, they're getting pretty upset with being sealed in and somehow they're getting intel on what just happened up here."

"Very interesting." Abigail pondered and prayed silently.

"How would they be able to find out anything if they're sealed up?"

"My best guess is that might they have demonic messengers. Why don't we ask God to make sure that outside demons can't communicate with the demons attached to Apollyon's people?"

They prayed together about that and Head Honcho reported that the buzzing increased. "I think God did something just now and they're really not pleased." He briefly smiled showing his approval.

They concluded the session after praying about the upcoming rituals – the thirty-first, Palm Sunday, Passover, Maundy Thursday, and Good Friday. It was going to be a busy week for the Satanists. There would be a mighty clash between the demons and the angelic hosts as well. The prayers of the saints and the curses of the sinners would crisscross the heavens. The sweet aroma of the incense of the prayers would contrast with the sulfuric road-kill snake stench of the curses.

Abigail stopped at Lee's farm on the way home. She was as excited as he was about the construction of his new house. The excavation had been finished and the forms for the foundation had been taken off already. Lee had an engineering degree and he was a stickler for doing things right. As much as he wanted the

36

construction crew to come in and start building, he insisted that they waited at least a week to ten days so that the concrete was at least at seventy-five per cent strength. After all, it would have to support a two-story house.

Lee's broad smile lit up his face when he saw Abigail's truck coming up his lane. He walked over to her truck and opened the door for her. "Hello. How was your day?"

"Good. Got some good break throughs with the ladies. How was your day?"

"Oh, busy as usual. Too much to do and too little time and energy to finish everything on my list. I don't get quite as much done as I used to when I was younger."

"I know what you mean. What will it be like when we're over fifty?"

"Listen to us talking like old people! Come on, let me show you how far we got. The county inspector was here yesterday so the construction crew will be here Monday."

Abigail tried to match Lee's enthusiasm, but all she saw was a foundation with piles of dirt and stacks of forms around it. They walked down to the horses and laughed as the four mares and Buster vied for their attention. Lee grabbed Abigail's hand as they walked back up to the foundation.

"Can you come over for supper?" Abigail asked. "Nothing special, just some burgers – not on the grill – and maybe a salad or something."

"Sounds great. I was hoping we could get together. I have a couple more things to do here and then I'll head over."

Abigail drove the short distance to her house and unloaded her groceries. It was still chilly enough that she wanted to keep a low fire going. The house somehow seemed cozier. Turning her attention to making their supper, Abigail busied herself with making the burger patties, preparing a salad, and setting the dining room table. She made a quick trip to the basement and retrieved a jar of green beans and one jar of applesauce.

Lee arrived shortly after she started the burgers. She greeted him at the door and they hugged briefly; their demonstrations of affection were no longer awkward. After they were finished eating and cleaning up the kitchen and dining room, Lee took Abigail by the hand and led her to the couch in the living room.

Nervously clearing his throat, he said, "Abigail, I've known you for six months now and I really, really like you."

"Thanks, Lee, I really like you, too."

"Abigail," Lee continued softly, "I need to say something to you." He paused as he held her hand in his. "When I thought that you had been killed, I realized how much I didn't want to be without you." He picked up the tempo of his proposal. "I've been praying and I believe that God has given me a second chance with you. I might be about to make a colossal mistake here because I don't know if you're ready for another relationship yet or not, but I would really like to court you."

Tears welled up in Abigail's eyes unbidden. "Oh, Lee, yes. Yes, I'd be honored. I've been praying like crazy, too, and wrestling with moving on. I think I'm finally ready."

Lee broke into a huge smile and then wrapped Abigail in his arms.

Laughing and crying at the same time, Abigail looked up into his moist eyes and asked, "Now what?"

"I don't know. I'm not good at this courting thing, but I do know this – I love you. There I said it."

Abigail frowned. "Lee, are you sure about being with me? I mean, look at all the crazy stuff that has been going on with the cult. I don't want you to be hurt."

"Abigail, I know enough to know that it's a serious business, but I also know that if God can keep you safe, He can keep me safe, too. And maybe the cowards will back off when you're with me in our new home."

"Or maybe they'll attack you and the horses, too. Oh, Lee, I don't want anything to happen to you or them on account of me."

"What are you always saying?" He raised his eyebrows in a mock scolding, "'No weapon formed against us will prosper?' I'm choosing this knowing that there are risks."

"Okay. I just want to be sure. Don't say I didn't warn you." She giggled mischievously.

They prayed and planned, laughed and talked long into the night. Finally, Lee reluctantly stood and got ready to leave. "See you tomorrow?"

4

Sunday, April 1, Palm Sunday

Abigail desperately ran through her back yard and up the steps. Shots rang out and she could see pock marks puncturing the side of her house, each one getting closer to hitting her. It was as if the shooter was playing with her. She reversed her course, ducked around the corner, and ran past her truck but shots rang out from the woods on that side of the house. She was surrounded, trapped. There was no place to run. There was no place to hide. They were going to kill her. Another shot rang out. She spun and dropped into a fetal position, waiting for them to come and finish her off. The pain in her shoulder and numbness in her left arm caused her to groan.

The muffled sound of her own voice woke Abigail out of her nightmare. Sitting up in her bed, nightgown drenched with sweat, breaths coming in rapid pants, Abigail finally realized that she had been dreaming. She realized that she had been laying on her left side and had somehow impinged the shoulder joint causing the arm to go numb. The vivid nightmare left her shaken. Getting out of bed, shaking her arm and rubbing her shoulder, Abigail stood resolutely and declared, "No weapon formed against me will prosper! I plead the blood of Jesus Christ over me and everything that belongs to me."

Breathing a deep, cleansing breath, Abigail began to calm down. She turned on her radio station and sang along with the music. The songs seemed to have been customized for her situation. *Lord, I have to admit that I was traumatized. Please come right now and soothe my spirit, soul, and body with Your healing balm.* Abigail continued to pray and soon she was calmly going through her Sunday morning routine.

Lee picked Abigail up for church as had become their habit over the last several weeks. Abigail looked at him with new eyes today. It was one thing to be comfortable in a friendship with this man, but quite another to realize that he was on a quest to marry her. *Mrs. Norris. God, is this totally, one hundred per cent Your will?* She knew deep in her spirit that it was.

She slid into the pew next to Cindy and gave her a brief hug.

"What's going on?" Cindy asked.

"What do you mean?"

"You look different. Happy. Kind of glowing."

"We'll talk later."

The worship team had begun to play the introduction to the first song and summoned the congregation to join them in praise and worship. They had chosen some contemporary songs and included some traditional Easter songs as well. Soon they returned to their seats and Pastor Spalding mounted the steps to the stage with his customary vim and vigor.

"Good morning!"

Getting a weak response, he reiterated his greeting, "I said, 'Good morning!'"

"Good morning!" The congregation responded more heartily.

"That's better," he teased. "This morning I want to draw attention to some of the events that occurred just

41

before Palm Sunday. Let's look at Mark chapter ten. It describes a hodge-podge of encounters with people that typified Jesus' ministry." He went on to talk about Jesus' response to Pharisees who tried to trip Him up with religious questions, reprimands for the disciples, an encounter with a seeker, teaching the disciples, and healing a blind man.

"Let's focus on the young fellow who was seeking assurance about inheriting eternal life. He had followed all the commandments and yet, he felt as if something was still lacking. In the other gospels he's described as the rich, young ruler. It says here that Jesus felt a love for him; He had compassion for the young man. He told this wealthy young man who lacked nothing in the natural world that he lacked one thing in the spiritual world – he needed to sell everything he owned, to give it to the poor, and follow Jesus. He had to abandon all his earthly wealth in order to inherit a heavenly treasure."

After letting that sink in for a moment, Pastor Spalding continued, "Now, I have a theory. Let's turn to Mark fifteen. Check out verses fifty-one and two. '*And a certain young man was following Him, wearing nothing but a linen sheet over his naked body; and they seized him. But he left the linen sheet behind, and escaped naked.*' Now why would this little side note be included in the middle of this very dramatic and moving account of Judas' betrayal of Jesus? I mean, it just doesn't fit with the flow of the story."

He let them puzzle over his question before continuing. "I propose that this streaker is the rich young ruler that was mentioned in chapter ten. None of the twelve disciples would have dared to show up at a Passover dinner wearing nothing but a sheet. A linen sheet. Did you know that linen was expensive in those days? Only rich people bought them. And linen is symbolic of righteousness. I'd just like to think and hope, that that young man who went away sad a few days before did some soul searching. He decided that he was all in. He sold everything except for a sheet – literally – and followed Jesus."

Nodding to the worship team, he concluded his sermon. "Let me ask you this: Are you like that young man who followed all the commandments, but you just have a nagging suspicion that there's something that's still standing in your way? Is it stuff? Is it position? Is it your house or car? Your children or grandchildren? Is there anyone or anything that comes between you and God? Folks, would you do it? Would you sell everything and give it all away to gain a heavenly inheritance? Come and pray with someone if you need to get something right with God. Come down if you need prayer for healing or anything else."

The musicians played softly as he stepped down and prayed with a young couple. The prayer team was ministering to others while most of the people shuffled up the aisles talking softly as they made their way to the parking lot. Cindy and Abigail were among them. Lee had dropped back to talk to Gary.

"So, what is going on with you?" Cindy was bursting with curiosity.

"I guess Lee and I are officially an item. Last night he told me that after Charlie Fletcher almost killed me he realized how much he wanted me in his life. He asked if he could court me."

Covering her mouth to stifle a yip, Cindy did an excited hop and then hugged Abigail. "Oh, I was hoping you two would get together!" She stopped and asked in mock horror, "you did say it was okay?"

"Yes, yes. I kind of like the idea of having him in my life, too."

Soon Cindy and Gary paired up and went to pick Traci and Bryan up from their respective classes. Lee joined Abigail and they went to Lee's truck. They spent the rest of the afternoon together; lunch at Abigail's, then looking at the construction site, and tending the horses at Lee's.

Monday's sky was gray with low-lying clouds writhing in the gusts and threatening to wring out their moisture. Lee was praying against rain; he was doubly anxious to get this house built. He breathed a prayer of thanks for all his blessings. "God, You've given me a fresh start and a new beginning. Thank You! Thank You! Thank You!"

Abigail was getting ready for the Ministerial Alliance meeting. This month Rev. Paul Overton was hosting the meeting in his United Methodist church. She pulled into the parking lot a few minutes before noon. There were a dozen vehicles already there.

She had never been here before, but followed the sound of voices and tantalizing aromas down the stairs. She began to greet some of the clergymen that she had met at the last meeting and was introduced to Pastor Clara Bardwell, pastor of a non-denominational church near the southern county line road. Several more came in after her and before long, Rev. Overton got everyone's attention and had them find a seat. He opened with prayer and several ladies from his congregation brought soup, salad, and sandwiches to the tables.

Pastor Don Wilmore from the Hillsdale Baptist church was sitting across from Pastor Spalding. "Daniel, I stole some of your sheep."

"Oh?" Pastor Spalding responded. "Who might that be?"

"It's Sheriff Bynum and his family."

Abigail perked up at the mention of his name.

"I wondered why I hadn't seen them recently. They usually just came on Sunday mornings and the two girls always sat with them in the balcony." Pastor Spalding wondered if Pastor Wilmore suspected that Roger Bynum was a Satanist.

"Did you say girls?"

"Yes, they homeschool them. One's probably about six or seven and the other one is maybe four or five."

"I've only seen one girl. Mrs. Bynum... I don't remember her name... Mrs. Bynum is very shy and never looks directly at me. The little girl is the same way."

"I wonder what happened to the other girl." Pastor Spalding mused.

Abigail suddenly had a sinking feeling. *Oh, Lord, surely he didn't sacrifice his own daughter.* But she knew that these Satanists would sacrifice anything and anyone to please their king. It never ceased to amaze her to see the dedication of the Satanists. She remembered Pastor Spalding's sermon of the previous day and his question – Would you be willing to sell, leave, give away anything for the sake of inheriting eternal rewards? Christians actually had to think about it while Satanists acted on it. *What's wrong with this picture?*

Pastor Spalding gave Abigail a questioning look. When she slowly nodded, he took a deep breath and said, "Don, you need to know something. Actually, I think this whole group needs to know something."

Paul Overton had been listening and took the cue. "Hey, everyone, I hate to interrupt you, but we have a point of discussion that we all need to hear." Turning their attention to him, he nodded to Pastor Spalding.

"It's come to my attention that Sheriff Bynum and his family have started to attend Pastor Wilmore's church here in Hillsdale. They used to go to my church until a couple of weeks ago. Here's what you need to know: Sheriff Bynum is a Satanist."

The shocked silence in the room was palpable. It lasted several minutes as they processed this information.

"What do I do?" Pastor Wilmore asked with alarm.

Pastor Spalding looked at Abigail and nodded.

It was her turn to take a deep breath. "Let's start with some of the practical thoughts. Like we said last time, our enemies are not flesh and blood, but principalities and powers. The enemy is the enemy. That being said, this might be a good time to let you know that there are several high-level officials in this county that are also Satanists."

She paused as she let this sobering information sink in. "I have several SRA survivors that I counsel. One of them picked Sheriff Bynum's picture out of our directory. His cult name is Zorroz."

"Excuse me," Rev. George Bordman of the Hawville Presbyterian Church said. "Did you say, 'cult name'? Zorroz?"

"Yes, apparently the Satanists are given a cult name. I'm not always aware of what they are, but many of them are the names of ancient gods or have some occult meaning. Likely, it's the name of one of their personal demons."

She could hear some gasps, but she continued, "I know this is shocking to most of you, but you can look in the Bible and see Satanism described quite accurately there."

"Exactly where?" George Bordman said more out of curiosity than as a challenge.

"I don't know the passage off hand, but it's somewhere in Kings and Chronicles. Look at King Manasseh. He sacrificed his son, he practiced witchcraft, used divination, and used spiritists and mediums, and filled Jerusalem with blood. And then there's the last part of Romans one. If that doesn't describe Satanists, I don't know what does."

She saw some thoughtful nods and continued. "We need to be wise as serpents and innocent as doves. I do *not* confront or challenge them. I pretty much act as if I am clueless about their involvement in Satanism. However, if they get in my face, I will war back. Not directly, but through prayer. I think that last month's testimony by Pastor Spalding is a good example. After Max Berryman threatened a young man in our church, he and Pastor Spalding got together and prayed for God to do what He needed to do to protect Jason and his little sister. Max got into a life-threatening accident

47

within the hour. He's in rehab now and we're praying that he will be transformed."

Abigail had their attention so she continued. "I have reason to believe that Judge Roberts is a Satanist as well."

She heard breaths being sucked in by the astonished clergy. Some of them knew him. Some of them had voted for him. "This is not unusual. We have had presidents and congressmen who were and are Satanists."

She could sense that they were curious but neither she nor they wanted to discuss the details right now. Now they wanted to have a sound strategy for dealing with their local situation.

Looking around the table at the clergy, she continued, "As leaders, your congregations and churches are under your jurisdiction. As long as you exercise proper jurisdiction, you'll be safe. But if you shrink back, the enemy will encroach. If you go beyond your jurisdiction, you'll find another kind of trouble."

Rev. Benjamin Morgan raised his hand and cleared his throat. "Can you give us some specifics about what you mean about jurisdiction? I have an idea, but I want to be sure."

Nods from the others indicated that they wanted a little help with this as well.

"Okay, I'll give you an example of what I do both personally and professionally. I was getting sick and tired of all the cars and trucks that were coming up my driveway on a daily basis. When I finally figured out that there just weren't that many lost people turning around and that it was cult people, I asked God to station a couple of warring angels at the foot of my driveway and have them strip off any demonic hitchhikers that might come with them or even me. Sometimes I get slimed when I work with these highly demonized folks, you know. After I prayed that, they stopped coming up the driveway. In fact, if they do pull in, I notice that they quickly back out and leave. I believe that they sense that they lost their powers."

These were new concepts to some who did not have much exposure to spiritual warfare and deliverance ministries.

"Now, I don't think God would station His angels all over the road that runs by my property no matter how hard I pray because that road doesn't fall under my jurisdiction. So, what I'm saying is that 'we have not because we ask not' in some cases and sometimes 'we ask amiss.' Each of you has both natural and God-given jurisdiction – personally and as the leader of your church. Prayerfully consider your jurisdiction and then pray bold prayers."

Don Wilmore asked, "Could you give me an idea of how I should pray in light of Sheriff Bynum coming here?"

"Sure," Abigail said, "Why don't I pray and then you pray in agreement? Remember the enemy is a legalist and a squatter. We don't want them saying, 'Abigail prayed, but he didn't so we don't have to budge.'"

"Makes sense."

"Holy Father, we come to Your throne of grace in the name of Jesus the Christ. We are asking that You would cover the entire property that falls under the jurisdiction of Pastor Wilmore with the cleansing blood of Jesus. Let that holy blood extend to the heavens above it, every molecule of the structures, and the ground below it however far You deem necessary. We ask that You would remove every foul spirit from that property and demolish every stronghold that has been established during the present and the past administrations. Send those spirits to a place where they will never afflict anyone again. Heal and seal any breaches or broken places that may remain with Your Holy Spirit and Your blessings. You said that every place that we put the soles of our feet belong to us. We are claiming what is rightfully ours and ask that no so-called trespassers – human or demonic – be allowed to do any damage. We pray for Your will to be done on earth as it is in heaven. In heaven, there is no fear, no harassment, no conflict. May Your peace which passes all understanding pervade that church. May Sheriff Bynum be attracted to you and be transformed. We pray these things in the name of Jesus the Christ, amen."

"Father, I pray in agreement. I pray for wisdom and discernment, too. I pray that You would let me know who the godly and like-minded people are in my congregation. I pray for the sheriff to be saved in Jesus' name, amen."

Amens echoed softly from the thoughtful clergy. They continued to eat and carry on discussions about Satanists in positions of political authority. They each wondered how many Satanists might be in their respective churches. How many did they run into on a daily basis in their everyday encounters in the marketplace?

By the end of the meeting, they had decided on a strategy that they could agree upon. They would pray and fast weekly for all the churches in the county. They would pray for more like-minded pastors and parishioners. They scheduled the next meeting in May at Benjamin Morgan's United Methodist Church in Kingston.

"Excuse me," Dennis Walsh stopped Abigail. "I have a lady who attends my church who needs some counseling. Would it be all right if I have her contact you? I think her issues are beyond me and I think she'd open up to a woman better."

"Sure," Abigail reached into her date book and pulled out a business card. "Have her give me a call. I work on Fridays."

Once again the heavens were stirred up because of the conflict between the kingdom of darkness and the kingdom of Light. Urdang was furious. Those clay freaks were starting to unite. They were starting to pay attention to the real world, the invisible realm. He and his cohorts would have to distract them, divide them. Divide and conquer. That blasted woman was responsible!

Abigail got home and was excited about getting into her play clothes and heading over to Lee's. Construction was coming along steadily with the favorable weather. The first inspection was completed and the rough framing was coming along nicely. Lee thought that the shell would be done by the end of the week. Then Abigail would have a better idea of what the house would look like. She was not good at interpreting the blueprints and looked forward to being able to see walls and windows, floors and doors.

Glancing at the phone, she noticed the flashing light. After putting her coat in the closet she listened to the voice mail. A husky woman's voice said, "Hello, I'm Loretta Evans. My pastor, Dennis Walsh, gave me your number. I, uh, I need some counseling and he recommended you. My number is 354-1015. I'd appreciate it if you'd call me back. Thanks."

Abigail pecked at the keys and waited for Loretta to answer. She picked up on the third ring and they arranged to meet on Friday at two o'clock at the church.

Abigail could hear the faint sound of hammering that echoed softly between the hills and she was anxious to get over there. She had been making a habit of using her four-wheeler and the path between their properties was becoming well-defined. On a whim, she called Jan. She wanted to apprise her of Lee's intentions to court her.

"Come on up, I've always got a minute for you!" Jan's hearty reply warmed Abigail's heart. She missed her mother even though they had never really been very close. Jan helped fill that gap.

Torqueing the throttle, Abigail drove out of the barn, up the slope to the wide-open gate, and down the driveway. Instead of cutting across the road, she veered to the left and took Earl's jeep trail that paralleled the road and was soon at the top of their hill. They often joked about being next-hill neighbors.

Bounding up the steps, Abigail was greeted with a warm hug by Jan. "Come in, come in. Do you have time for a quick cup of tea?"

"Do we ever have a quick cup?"

"Well, no, and I have a hunch that you want to get over to Lee's place. We're not spying on you, but it's kind of obvious that the two of you are spending a lot of time together."

"That's what I wanted to talk to you about."

"Oh?"

"Remember that night Charlie Fletcher shot at me?" Abigail did not give Jan time to reply, but gushed, "Well, Lee said that he thought he'd lost me and decided that he didn't like that idea and he asked if he could court me."

"Well?"

"Well, I said yes. I kind of like the idea of him being in my life, too. I just wanted to let you two know that we're taking that next step. Maybe it takes the thought of almost dying to make you really want to live, I mean, not just exist somewhere between the past and some nebulous future."

"That's good news. For both of you. We both think Lee is a fine man." Jan gave Abigail another hug. "Now you scoot! I know you want to get over there to see him."

Earl got out of his easy chair and ambled over to Abigail and gave her a hug, too. "You watch your back, now."

"I thought you were watching it. But you, too. Charlie Fletcher isn't just a snake, he's a Satanist. You'll be a target now. You know what they're capable of."

"No weapon!"

"No weapon!" With that Abigail fired up the four-wheeler again and headed down their driveway. It was not exactly legal, but she gunned her four-wheeler up the road the short distance to Lee's driveway, made the right-hand turn, and followed it to a clear space in front of the barn.

What she did not know was that Charlie Fletcher had taken up a position not far from where Max Berryman used to park. He had been studying her habits and knew that she would come along that trail that she was burning between her house and Lee Norris' property. His assignment was an annoyance before Earl Milner shot his weapon out of his hand. Now he wanted revenge. He looked ruefully at his swollen, deformed hand.

Lee heard her coming up the driveway and made his way to the barn. He gave her a hug as he greeted her. "Why did you come up the driveway?"

"Oh, I wanted to stop by Earl and Jan's and let them know our good news."

He smiled. *Our good news.* "We still have some daylight, are you up for a ride for a change?"

"You mean you don't need me to supervise the construction?"

"Not today. What do you say? The horses need a little change of scenery."

"Let's do it."

They went to the barn and gathered the tack that they'd need. Of course, Abigail was going to ride Buster. Lee chose Sparkles. Lee's four-wheeler was larger and would hold both of them with one saddle lashed onto the front and one on the back. Within thirty minutes, they were astride their horses and heading toward York Creek. They had a general plan to cross the road and follow the creek on Abigail's side of the road and explore some of the trails that went to the south.

Suddenly Lee pulled up and looked intently at the ground. "Look here, Abigail." He pointed to the ground.

She nosed Buster up to where she could see what he was pointing at. Larger than usual hoof prints. She felt a stab of fear impale her mid-section. "Those look fresh."

"I'd say that they were made within the hour," Lee confirmed. "Let's follow them."

"Can we pray first?"

"Good idea. You got a round chambered?"

"Good idea." Abigail unholstered Walther and chambered a round as Lee did the same.

"Lord," he prayed, "we need Your wisdom and protection. We're not sure where this guy is, but he's definitely been on my property. I ask that You would send more warring angels here and evict any trespassers that may have been left behind."

"Yes, Lord. And God, we need a strategy. Should we even follow him?"

After a few moments of listening, Lee asked, "What are you thinking?"

"I'm not sure what we'd do if we catch up with him. I mean, he could be setting an ambush. He could be watching us right now. I'm sensing that we need to see where he's been on your property and maybe we can figure out if he's done something or is planning something."

"That sits right with me." Lee looked at the tracks again and then pointed to his right. "It looks like he came from up there. See the bent grasses? He came down this way, but I wonder how he got up there." Lee's tracking skills quickly resurfaced and he was factoring in all the data that he already had as well as other probabilities. Looking around the area, Lee surmised that Charlie would not want to be seen. That would mean that he would want to ride in the stand of trees that lay between the road and the horses' pasture.

"Let's backtrack him." Lee clucked to Sparkles and gently nudged her.

Abigail followed on Buster. It was not long before Lee stopped in a thick patch of brush in the stand of trees and motioned for Abigail to come forward. "Look. He stood here for a while."

"That reminds me of that hiding place in the field behind Buster's pasture where he or someone on that horse had a spot trampled down from watching me so much. I think Max borrowed his horse and did most of that, but we caught Charlie on camera, too."

"What do you see ahead?" Lee asked the question almost like a scout master quizzing his scout.

Abigail stood up in her stirrups and craned her neck. "I don't see anything. Wait. That's the trail I usually come up." Suddenly the implications hit her. "Oh, Lord."

"I guess we know why you came up the driveway today. God sure is looking out for you."

Abigail was almost speechless as she remembered what she thought was an impulsive decision to visit Earl and Jan on the way over to Lee's today. "No weapon formed against us will prosper."

"No weapon."

Charlie groomed his horse after his failed attempt to ambush that woman. Did she know? How did she know? Was it just a fluke that she went a different way today? He was beginning to fear her uncanny power. Would he end up crippled like Max? Or dead like Nathan or Billy or Ron Wagner? He could feel the shift in the atmosphere. Charlie Fletcher was not anxious to give his report at the ritual later that night. He looked down at his deformed left hand and cursed Earl and Abigail. It was still raw where the bullet had struck it, effectively removing the tattoo of the upside-down cross that had been in the web between the thumb and index finger.

The full moon fell on Passover making tonight's ritual extra special. It would be celebrated at the regional meeting place with Prinz and other dignitaries. What a prize she would have been. Viper's status would have been elevated immensely. He cursed his bad luck. He did not want to admit that he was getting tired of this, but there was no way out. He signed a blood covenant so he was committed. *Unless.* Unless he could provide a substitute. His son or daughter? *Not yet.* He resigned himself to be there for tomorrow's ritual on the third of the month. There was a one-day break and then a crescendo of rituals for Maundy Thursday, Good Friday, Holy Saturday, and finally Easter.

5

April 6, Good Friday

The stormy weather seemed to reflect the squall in the spiritual realm. Although the eternal outcome had been settled over two thousand years ago, the snake with the crushed skull continued to writhe. The fury of the ones who had been disarmed, publicly displayed, and who had been triumphed over was boundless, inexhaustible.

Lee was disappointed that the construction would have to be halted until the storm system moved further east. It was under roof, but the OSB sheathing had not been fully applied to the exterior walls. There was still much to do with installing doors and windows after that as well as installing the house wrap. He wanted this place to be snug. Lee frowned as he listened to the weather report that predicted rain continuing through Monday. He resigned himself to working on some of his projects inside the barn.

Abigail was looking forward to seeing how things were going with Carrie Sue and Amy. She was also curious about the new lady. Driving past Lee's driveway, she breathed a prayer for his safety and for a good day. She shuddered involuntarily as she remembered that she narrowly escaped another attack by Charlie Fletcher. If he shot at her one time, surely, he would try it again. "Lord, those angels you assigned to me are sure getting a workout!"

Carrie Sue was waiting for Abigail at the church. They entered together, set up the office, and opened with prayer.

"Well?" Abigail asked. "How did the great experiment go?"

Carrie Sue smiled and with a voice that sounded much like the host Carrie Sue's voice and yet slightly softer, she said, "I think I like it. It feels a little bit strange, though. It's like I've taken over living someone else's life but it feels like it's mine, too. I don't quite know how to explain it."

"I think I understand. Lots of other people that I've worked with have had difficulty explaining it, too."

"Like when I went home last week and was just wandering around the apartment – my apartment – it was familiar but it didn't seem like mine. I mean, I didn't even know where she, er, we, um, I kept the spices, but as I started cooking it was like I just knew where they were. And then it seemed like it was my kitchen and like I always knew how to cook. At least I knew how to make spaghetti."

"That's very similar to what I've heard from others. As you walk through your life, you begin to own it."

"Yeah." Carrie Sue seemed relieved to know that she was not crazy or weird. "So where do we go from here? When I first started working with you, I thought that once I was all the way integrated I'd be done."

"I know what I think, but what do you think still needs to be worked on before you're done?"

She puffed out a quick breath and said, "Probably how to be normal. Get off this disability and maybe get a job. Figure out how to deal with my mom. I don't know, stuff like that."

Lynda L. Irons

"That sounds pretty much like my thoughts. Remember that we still need to monitor things for at least another calendar year just to be sure that there are no more latent programs, triggers, or even some stragglers that haven't been integrated for whatever reason."

Carrie Sue huffed at that last thought. "I just want to be normal. Whatever that is."

"I'm not sure what normal is for you. I just know that the authentic Carrie Sue – the Carrie Sue that God intended for you to be – is going to be normal for you. When your spiritual gifts and talents, desires and temperament, purpose and destiny all overlap in whatever you are doing, then life is going to be sweet!"

"That's what I want."

They continued to talk and pray about some of these issues. Carrie Sue said that she was not visited by her mother at all the last week and she had no urges or restlessness on the ritual nights. She was so encouraged and yet so intimidated.

"It's so quiet inside my head. It's dark, too."

"That's a good sign and confirmation that integration was pretty thorough. Let me ask you a question." Abigail's eyes twinkled mischievously as she asked, "Do you want to undo what we prayed last week and split everyone back out again?"

"No way!" Carrie Sue shot out her answer almost before Abigail completed the question.

"Are you sure? You hesitated a whole nano-second."

They laughed together and made plans to meet again the following week. Walking out the door together, they met Amy coming in a little early. It was the first time the two of them had crossed paths but Abigail noticed that they both hesitated slightly, making her wonder if they had been at rituals together at some point. It was a distinct possibility. Interesting.

After getting settled, she and Amy got down to business.

"Have you made an appointment to see the doctor?" Abigail asked.

"Yeah. I'll see her Monday. It was the soonest she could see me. They said that if I had any more bleeding I need to go to the emergency room."

"We'll pray that it doesn't come to that. Let's ask God what's next for today."

As expected, Head Honcho replaced the host and began to fill Abigail in on the status of their internal world. "Nicholai came up with an interesting question. He wondered if it would be a good idea to ask God if the subterranean levels could or should be remodeled, too."

"That's a good question. Is he thinking about his level or all the other ones, too?" Abigail had been given a general description of the subterranean levels and she was trying to visualize what she had been told. Each level was six-sided with a central hub that had a shaft which connected the various levels. She was picturing a bicycle tire with six spokes that connected the central area with the outside edges. There were various rooms off the spokes and numerous tunnels and mazes that connected different areas as well as connecting each level to other levels. It was complex and afforded many secret passages and hiding places. No one knew how many personalities were entrapped on the various levels.

Lynda L. Irons

"I think that's part of his question. He's got jurisdiction over level one, but we're not sure what, if anything, can be done with two through six."

"Let's pray about it and see what the Lord says." Abigail led the prayer and waited for a response.

"I'm sensing that the Lord wants us to remodel Nicholai's level first and then He'll let us know what else after that."

"Is Nicholai okay with coming up front and center? I know he likes to keep a low profile, but I think it would be better if he prayed with me. Jurisdiction."

"He's willing." With that Head Honcho faded into the background and Nicholai surfaced.

"Good to see you again. You've been doing some amazing work down there. I'm proud of you."

"Thanks," Nicholai replied squinting through his somewhat light-sensitive eyes. "I'll just be glad when all this is over. We've had a bunch of guys from the lower levels come up waving white flags. We helped them defect and get integrated. Some of them are afraid of whatever is going on with level six and Apollyon. They're afraid that those guys will find a way out and whoever is in their path…"

"Yeah, they were mean enough before getting sealed in. They'll vent their frustration on anyone and everyone. You ready to pray?"

"Let's do it."

Abigail led their prayer asking God to remodel level one. She waited a couple of very long minutes for Nicholai to give her a report.

"Okay, here's what happened: First of all, it was like someone slowly reversed a dimmer switch and gradually made the whole level bright without hurting our eyes. Then all the walls came down. There are still pillars, but no more walls. It's one big room. All the triangle-shaped areas between the spokes are cleaned out." Nicholai looked down uncomfortably. "That's where we held and prepared some of the parts before the rituals."

"Hey, that's past and forgiven."

"I know, but there's still consequences." He paused a moment before he continued to describe the changes on his level. "We still have a holding room, but it's for the ones who might come up and will need a place to think about defecting... if you know what I mean."

"I think so."

"It looks like all the tunnels and other secret passages have been sealed up and the central shaft has glass walls around it and a door with a mechanism that allows us to open it up if we want to let someone in or out. Looks like we won't have to worry about being infiltrated."

"What about your people? A couple months ago Joktan allowed the pre-verbal little ones to integrate. There must still be a bunch of kids around." Joktan was the leader of all six of the subterranean levels.

"Yes, now that the walls are down and they lost their hiding places, I'm seeing quite a few of them. They're scared of wide open spaces. This might be a good time to take care of them but I still need my crew."

"You make the call."

"Let's integrate all the females, uh, no offense, and all the teens and younger."

"Is there anything that still needs to be healed for any of them?"

"Ah, they're just scared without the hiding places."

"Okay, then. Why don't you pray them in?"

"Me? Oh, uh, sure," Nicholai stammered. He awkwardly prayed and then reported that as far as he could tell, only adult males were left on his level. He thanked Abigail and receded into the background.

Head Honcho's presence was evident by the ramrod posture that was now assumed. "That was quite interesting," he commented.

"Yes. Now we have five more levels to work on. I wonder what Joktan is thinking about this new development."

"I think he's a little uneasy about it. He's not real happy that Apollyon has been sealed in. He might not be very happy with Nicholai right now."

"We'll leave it alone for today, but maybe next time, if Joktan is willing, we can touch base."

"We can touch base right now, lady! Who do you think you are rearranging my turf?"

"I'm sorry, Joktan, I wasn't trying to by-pass you. I was under the impression that Nicholai had the authority to make that decision about his level."

"You have just effectively sealed off levels two, three, four, and five!" Joktan was furious. "I should never have let you talk me into that first manipulation of yours. You think Satanists are bad? You're just as bad. You just trapped all my people! You better fix this and you better do it right now!"

"I'm sorry. That was not my intention at all."

"Well, that's the end result! Fix it lady!"

"Can I ask you a question?" Abigail ventured cautiously.

"Fire away."

"If they can't get up through the first level and Apollyon's people can't get out; how did you get here?"

"I have my own place which you are going to know nothing about!"

"I don't want to know. I'm just thinking about your predicament."

"It's *your* predicament. Now you fix it!"

"Is the top Fuchsya putting pressure on you?"

His head snapped back in surprise. "How would you know about that?"

"My Leader lets me know things I need to know. Besides, it makes sense that she would react to the things that are going on in her jurisdiction." Abigail paused and looked sympathetically at him. "Look, I know that you're in a double-bind right now. You got pressure from the top and the bottom; pressure from the inside and the outside. I'm going to pray and ask my God to give us a strategy that will satisfy everyone."

"We want it back the way it was. You've stolen too many of our people already."

"Nobody went anywhere. All of your people integrated into some of your other people and strengthened them in the process." Abigail was not going to put up with him twisting the facts. "Besides, you agreed to it. I laid it out and gave you the option to step in and stop it at any point that you were uncomfortable. Right?"

She got a short huff in response.

"I am going to ask my Leader for a strategy which I will lay out to you and you can decide if it's acceptable or not."

"Fine."

Abigail launched into her prayer, "Holy Father, we have a situation here that is causing problems for Joktan. Would you please give us a strategy that will be acceptable for all concerned parties?" Abigail continued to pray silently, pleading for a clear communication from God. She was totally blank and had no idea how to resolve this impasse. She waited silently for another minute.

"Okay, here's what I'm getting," Abigail said slowly. "God said that He would establish exit routes that bypass level one so that those on levels two through five could come and go as they need to."

"What about level six?" Joktan demanded.

"He said that stays sealed up for now."

Joktan let a stream of expletives loose under his breath.

"Hey, take it up with Him. I'm just the messenger."

"Fine!"

"But there's something else you need to know."

"What?" he snapped suspiciously.

"He said that you have to be aware that by opening up those routes you are opening yourselves up to increased infiltration by the Satanists and demons."

"And just why will it be increased?"

"They have fewer targets because Mayor and his people are integrated, Head Honcho's prison is consolidated, and now Nicholai's level is inaccessible to them. They'll continue to send as many as they ever have. They'll just have your levels to focus on."

"It's all your fault. You need to fix it."

"Whoa! Wait a minute. You're the Satanist. You're the one who likes demons and other Satanists to run your life. What's the problem?" Abigail knew that she was provoking him, but she wanted him to reason this out.

"Who says I like it?"

"Oh, you don't like it?" Abigail countered.

"Lady! You're making me nuts. Stop twisting my words."

"You're the one that's giving me the mixed messages. On one hand you say you are on the side of the Satanists and demons and like their company and their agenda and you want to be just like them. On the other hand, you are saying that it's a problem that more of them are going to infiltrate your turf and that I have to fix it. Which is it? I'm confused." She could see that he was about to explode with frustration. She was using his own words to prove her point and he did not like it.

"It's just the way it is. We're just doing our job," he said through gritted teeth.

"Your job," Abigail said flatly. "Who gave you that job?"

"I don't know! That's just the way it's always been and I want it back the way it was."

"You don't know who gave you your job? You just blindly follow whatever they say and do their bidding?"

"Yes. No!" He reversed himself. "I don't do anything blindly."

"So then, you chose to be like your parents and grandparents. You like serving Satan and sacrificing innocent people?"

"No. Yes! You're confusing me."

More gently, Abigail said, "Joktan, you have been assigned and programmed to do their bidding generations ago. You have not had a chance to make any real decisions until now."

"No, I don't. You don't understand."

"Oh, I understand more than you think. You've been able to think outside the box a bit today. You've always thought that you had one choice and only one choice. They never wanted or expected you to meet someone like me that could tell you otherwise."

"Lady, I'm on dangerous ground here."

"I know. You're being pressured by your demons. You're stuck in your programming and you don't want to even hope that you could be set free because you're beginning to see that they have given you a bunch of empty promises."

He began to sputter his protest but settled for a familiar string of curses, maligning her heritage, and demanding that she perform some anatomically impossible feats. "I gotta go."

Head Honcho came back shaking his head. "He's flustered."

"I hope he's not in too much hot water."

"He'll be okay. You gave him a lot to think about. He's not used to *not* being able to intimidate people."

"It'll be interesting to see where we go from here."

"I'll keep you posted." With that, Head Honcho disappeared and Amy emerged once again.

"Whew! I have a headache! I was able to catch most of that. He wanted to kill you, but the good guys wouldn't let him out of our chair."

"Thanks," Abigail replied. She knew that it was a very real possibility. "You feeling okay otherwise?"

"I'm fine. I'll keep you posted."

"Call me if you need to."

They concluded their session and Amy left after tossing a few crumpled dollars on the desk. Abigail took a deep breath and prayed for Amy's protection as she waited for the new counselee to arrive. *What was her name again?* Abigail looked at her date book. Loretta Evans.

"Hello?" a husky voice called out.

Abigail walked to the doorway and greeted her. "Hi, I'm Abigail, you must be Loretta Evans."

"That's me."

Abigail handed her a clipboard with the information and disclaimer papers. Loretta quickly filled them out and brought them to Abigail. Slumping into the chair, Loretta looked expectantly at Abigail who quickly scanned the information.

"I'm glad you're here. Can you tell me what you need help with?"

"Pastor Walsh said that he thought you would be able to help me with my issues better than he could." She looked directly at Abigail with a slight tilt to her chin, as if she were defying or challenging Abigail. "I had a gastric by-pass done a few years ago and as you can see, I by-passed the by-pass."

"I see," Abigail acknowledged. She estimated that the woman was well over three hundred pounds. "Why don't you tell me your story? What was your childhood like? What kinds of traumas have you gone through?"

Loretta took a deep breath and nodded. "All right. I'm the oldest of three kids and, well, three's a crowd, ya know? I was the black sheep of the family. My sister was pretty and smart and popular. My brother was athletic and got scholarships to college. I had to work my way through college on my own. My father wouldn't even sign a Parents' Confidential Statement. He signed one for my sister, but not for me." Her resentment was becoming very evident.

"It just seemed like I could never do anything right, so why try?" Loretta continued. "They called me pudge. I look at my pictures and I wasn't that fat, but kids at school made fun of me. My parents and even my emaciated brother and sister called me names. I couldn't wait to get out of that house. Huh!" she huffed. "I'd do the exact opposite of what they said just to make them mad. Dad would whip me, but I'd die before I'd let them see me cry. I thought college would be better. It was in some ways, but when I got free I went wild. Drank. Tried marijuana. I slept around because the guys made me feel pretty and acceptable." She stopped and looked at Abigail wondering if she should go on.

"Sounds like you have a lot of anger and resentment built up in there."

"You betcha!" Loretta stormed. "I hate my family. I don't count. Like when I turned thirty, I didn't even get so much as a phone call. What do you think happened when the prince and princess turned thirty? Ha! Big birthday bashes."

"Was it like that even when you were kids?"

"Yeah. Want to hear a good one? When I was a senior in high school and my brother was a junior and my sister was a freshman, I had a job and I saved enough to buy a sweet Mustang convertible. But I got grounded because I was dating a guy that my parents didn't approve of. Dad took away my keys. So, one night I'm working the drive-through and who comes through? My brother and sister in *my* car! Dad gave him the keys!"

"Wow. I think I'd be out the window smacking them."

"Yeah, and asking if they wanted fries with that!" Loretta almost smiled at the thought.

Abigail chuckled gently. "I'm sorry. That's awful. I've heard a lot of black-sheep-of-the-family stories, but this one ranks right up there near the top. So, tell me; how does that make you feel? What emotions are attached to these memories?"

"Anger... resentment... pain... hurt... unworthy... rejected... shame," she rattled off, paused and then added, "neglected and betrayed."

"On a scale of zero to ten which ones of these rate a nine or ten?"

"Probably unworthy and rejection."

"Okay, if you work with me, we can get you a lot of relief from all of this. This is all very fixable. Let me talk to you a little bit about verbal assaults first." Abigail went on to explain about deceptions and vows, curses and judgments. She explained the Greek and Hebrew meanings of the words and the unintended consequences of embracing them.

Loretta was hungrily tracking with her.

"So, for instance, when you get called pudge and you've already made a vow – you've bound your soul with an oath; you've built that fence, that enclosure – when you said, 'I'll do the opposite of what you say just to make you mad', you've locked yourself into obesity because they want you skinny like your sister

71

and you're saying, 'hey, you think this is pudgy? Watch me blimp out!' You have this war going on inside between really wanting to maintain a healthy weight and the vow that says that you'll make them mad by being fat. You get a by-pass and you by-pass the by-pass because of the vow."

The blood drained out of Loretta's face as she pondered the implication Abigail's words. "I did it to myself. I cut off my nose to spite their faces." Loretta let her tough-gal mask down a little and tears welled up in her eyes. Blinking furiously, she said, "So what do I need to do?"

"What do you really want?"

"I want to lose this stupid weight. I want to quit living *at* them."

"Let's renounce the vows." Abigail explained the principles of putting off the old and putting on the new. She explained about tormenting spirits that operate from the strongholds that have been created because of sins committed by or against us. When she thought that Loretta understood, she asked if she was ready to pray.

"Yes I am. I'm tired of this old mess."

"Okay, do some business with the Lord and use active verbs – Lord, I confess... Lord I renounce – and then I'll pray in agreement with you."

Loretta prayed a simple prayer confessing her pride, her self-protection, her willfulness. She renounced the vows and Abigail prayed when she finished.

"I feel lighter, like a weight's been lifted off my chest," Loretta reported. "Whew! I'm tired."

Abigail smiled. She loved being able to participate with the Lord. They wrapped up the session and made plans for another appointment on the following week.

Abigail was closing up her office when she heard Pastor Spalding whistling tunelessly as he came down the hall. *Why do men whistle?*

"Abigail! I'm glad I caught you."

"What's up?"

"I just got word that Max is coming home from the rehab facility next week. It's been almost two months since the accident."

"What condition is he in? Can he walk?"

"Haven't you heard? They fused his spine and he's walking with a walker and a brace as I understand it."

"I gotta confess that I'm not sure if I want him running around town again. I mean, he's done a lot of damage to me and Carrie Sue."

"Well, we'll keep praying that God will get a hold of that young man. His parents want him to come see you for counseling."

Abigail tried not to choke. But she thought of the implications. "Actually, that would be amazing if God got a hold of him and he got out of Satanism. I'll be praying. And of course, if he comes, you'll be right there with us, right?"

"I wouldn't miss it!"

6

Sunday, April 8, Easter

"He is risen!" Pastor Spalding boomed.

"He is risen indeed!" the congregation responded.

"He is risen!" Pastor Spalding boomed again.

"He is risen indeed!"

The pastor and congregation gave a traditional Easter greeting that went back to the early Church. After singing several Easter-focused hymns and worship songs, Pastor Spalding gave some opening remarks and then launched into his sermon.

"Turn to Colossians two, please. We're going to look at verses thirteen and fourteen. Now I know that this is not a traditional Easter message, but I wanted to emphasize the practical and personal impact that the resurrection has on those of us who are Christians. I see that we have a number of visitors with us today and I hope that you are here because you're also believers, but if not, I am praying that this message will clearly lay out why Easter is such a big deal."

Pages ruffled, mint wrappers crackled, and people expectantly settled in their places as Pastor Spalding talked a little bit about the context of the passage before wrapping up his final points.

"Folks, every last one of us was born with a sin nature. Every last one of us has sinned. That's what it means when it says that we were dead in our transgressions and uncircumcision of our flesh. And because God loved us so much He sent His Son, Jesus Christ, to pay that debt. It says that the certificate of debt which was filled with hostile decrees against us was taken care of by Jesus. Back then, when someone was crucified, a certificate was nailed above his head. Thief. Adulterer. Murderer. Shall I get more personal? Glutton. Selfish. Liar. Cheater. We all have sins we're ashamed of." He paused as he looked at the congregation with compassion.

"Picture this. Picture yourself in a long line of people each of whom is standing in front of a cross. And there you are in front of your own cross with a certificate of debt that you owe because of your sins. And there I am a couple of crosses down from you and you look the other way and see friends and family each with a cross and a certificate. We deserved it. We sinned. Right?" He saw the nods of most of the congregation.

"And then, just when we felt hopeless and condemned, and the soldiers were getting ready to nail us up, Jesus Christ came down the lineup of all humanity and said that He would take every certificate and pay the debt. He would nail all of our certificates onto His cross and He would pay it so that we would not have to." He had their attention and he was praying that some unbelievers would respond.

"Let me just ask another question." He walked down to the front of the auditorium as the worship team went back up on the stage. "How proud would someone have to be to say, 'no thanks, I'd rather be crucified and pay the debt myself. I will choose eternity in hell rather than let Jesus pay my debt.'? Or how resentful would someone be if no one told them the Good News that they can ask Jesus to take their certificate of debt for them? Please, please," he

75

pleaded. "If you have never heard about how to be saved or if you've heard but are holding back – please come down today and let us pray with you."

He turned and nodded to the worship leader who began to play softly. The members of the prayer team made their way to the front and began to pray with some who had come for prayer. Abigail and her friends did the "church shuffle" toward the exits.

Carrie Sue had come and joined them. She noticed that Lee had moved from his former place on the other side of Gary to a place next to Abigail. She initially felt a little bit awkward as she sat between Abigail and Cindy, but soon felt comfortable. Normal.

Cindy caught Carrie Sue's elbow. "Hey, we're having Easter dinner at our house. There's always room for one more. If you don't have any plans, we'd love to have you."

Carrie Sue looked from Cindy to Gary to Abigail to Lee. They were all smiling and nodding. How could she say no? How could she say yes? Strangers. Crowds.

"Come on," Abigail goaded her. "This is part of your 'normal' training."

"Oh, all right. I'd love to come."

The driveway was packed with cars. Grandpa and Grandma McVeigh were there. Scott, Jill, and their teenagers had picked up his parents, Mike and Cora Bradley. Gary's parents, Ben and Esther McCord were there. Lee's parents were the only ones missing. They had both succumbed to cancer too early in life. It was a mini family reunion. Baked ham, vegetables, sweet potatoes, and more were squeezed onto all available surfaces.

"Have a seat, everyone." It did not take long for Gary to get everyone's attention. "Grandpa, would you ask a blessing on the food?"

"I'd be honored," he replied. He prayed a prayer that everyone could have recited with him because it was the same one he had prayed before meals as long as they could remember. He prayed with the same sincerity that he had the first time he prayed it.

Dishes were passed and the happy chatter of family members ebbed and flowed around the tables. After the meal was over the ladies shooed the men out of the room, promising that they would be called when the desserts were ready. The men retreated to the family room, the ladies cleaned up the kitchen and dining room.

"So, Lee, how long before you move into that house of yours?" Grandpa asked.

"It's under roof already. Windows and doors are in. I think they'll be able to finish the house wrap by next week and then start with the plumbing, water, electric, and all the ductwork for the heat and air. Once that's done and it passes inspection, they can finish the siding and roofing and we can start on the drywall."

In the next room, Cindy cornered Abigail and grilled her, much to the amusement of Carrie Sue. "So, is Lee your new chauffeur?" she teased with a twinkle in her eye. "I noticed that you don't drive yourself to church much anymore." She knew that Lee and Abigail were unofficially but officially an item, and she wanted to make sure that the rest of the relatives were in on the not-so-secret secret.

"Well, we are just being patriotic, saving gas and reducing pollution by car-pooling." Abigail tried to joke back and hoped that the subject would be dropped. She was not entirely sure what this courting thing meant yet.

Grandma McVeigh was quick to jump into the conversation. "Child, is that Lee asking you to join this family?"

Suddenly all eyes were on Abigail. *Hoo boy!* "Um, well, Lee asked me if he could court me."

That really started the questions. Abigail managed to give Cindy a thanks-for-putting-me-on-the-spot look in the midst of it.

"So, when's the date?"

"No wonder he wants to build that nice big house."

"Lee's momma and daddy would have loved to have met you."

"Have you met Lisa yet?"

They were excited. Abigail was squirming inside but happy with the approval and acceptance. Carrie Sue loved feeling normal. She really loved seeing Abigail on the hot seat for a change and laughed out loud with the ladies.

Soon enough, the desserts were laid out and the men and children were called back into the dining room. Of course, Lee's aunts had to congratulate him.

"What's this?" Grandpa McVeigh asked looking from Lee to Abigail with his bushy eyebrows held in suspension over his inquisitive eyes.

Lee looked at Abigail who raised her palms up and slowly shook her head from side to side as if to say, "I didn't start this mess."

"Okay, everyone." Lee stood, and good-naturedly held his hands up in surrender. He walked over to Abigail and slid an arm around her waist and said, "I have asked this woman if I could court her and she has said yes. That's as far as we have gotten."

Dessert was forgotten momentarily as another round of congratulations were expressed. The whole family was delighted. Abigail had been considered a member of their family for years anyway because of her friendship with Cindy. Oh, yes, they approved and were ready to rush the happy couple to the altar of matrimony immediately.

Prinz was dissatisfied with the latest crescendo of rituals that marked the Lenten season. He was always dissatisfied. There was a hunger deep in his soul that he could never placate. On top of that he could feel the pressure coming from the ranks below him. He felt the pressure coming from Xerxes above him and, no doubt, the powers that ruled over him. The hierarchy of human and demonic beings was established according to rank, but was always in flux. Anyone could be overthrown at any time. Treachery and duplicity reigned amongst them.

Daggett and Darod had the uneasy understanding that eventually one of them could ascend to the regional post that Prinz currently held. There were others of their rank under Prinz that could usurp the regional position as well. Unless, of course Levi became ambitious. They, too, had to watch above and below, to the left and to the right. It was impossible to distinguish the parasite from the host. They needed each other. They despised each other. They worked together. They were wary of each other.

Zorroz, still trying to curry favor, was able to supply the male sacrifice for Good Friday. The unfortunate man was thirty-three according to his driver's license. Perfect. As the sheriff/Satanist, Roger Bynum/Zorroz was able to detain the out-of-state man who had gone just slightly over the speed limit in the wrong county at the wrong time shortly after making a gas purchase with his credit card.

Zorroz had a system for procuring victims for the rituals. After handcuffing them in the back seat of his squad and drugging them, he'd drive them over to the windowless building where they would be prepared by other Satanists. He would have the victim's car impounded and taken to the local junk yard. The owner was a loyal comrade and he would dismantle the vehicle chop-shop style. All evidence of the man's appearance in the county would vanish leaving friends and family with unanswered questions.

It was nearly two months since Max rolled his truck on that icy Sunday morning. The doctors were pleased with his progress and were making plans to discharge him from the rehab facility in the next few days. He had some residual weakness in his left leg which necessitated a brace that would keep his knee from hyper-extending. The fractures in his ribs and sternum were well healed. His left arm was out of the cast.

He was doing well in physical therapy after the spinal surgery. The first time he was put up on the tilt-table, he nearly passed out before they got him to forty-five degrees. Soon enough he tolerated standing upright. He progressed to the parallel bars and eventually to a walker. He was a subdued young man. He had had plenty of time to think about his life and about how close he had come to death. He did not want to think too much about weighty things because it made his head hurt worse. He did not want to face the futility of life. He did not want to think about how much he grieved his mother and disappointed his father. Maybe it wasn't too late.

Maybe it was.

"Where's your favorite place around here?" Lee asked Abigail as they drove home together after the Easter gathering.

"Oh, let me think a minute," Abigail replied. "I have several favorite places. One is my back deck. I just love to watch the sunsets. Another is pretty much any trail out there with Buster. And then there's the beach. I haven't been there in quite some time."

"Why don't we take some time tomorrow and ride? I'd like to get a couple of steaks. Are you up to grilling them at your place? Around sundown?"

"I'd like that."

They made their plans on their way to Lee's farm. They checked on the horses as usual and then Lee brought Abigail home.

"I'd love to spend the rest of the day with you, but I have things to do at the apartment and I need to call Lisa to let her know about us. I have to beat my aunts and cousins to the draw if it isn't too late already." They shared another laugh as they envisioned their aunts hustling to be the first.

Amy opened her eyes on Monday morning and smiled contentedly. Despite the internal turmoil, she did not end up at an Easter ritual for the first time in her life. *Praise God!* She was beginning to feel hopeful that she would be able to escape Satanism eventually. The biggest challenge that she faced right now was the pregnancy. She had so many mixed feelings. Who was the father? How could she support a child when she could barely support herself? She sighed and rolled out of bed feeling slightly queasy.

She reluctantly kept her appointment with Dr. Weaver. Because of the spotting, she was sent for an ultrasound and despite the friendly technician's attempts to point out the baby's features, the only thing that was recognizable to Amy was the tiny curled spinal column that made it look like she was carrying a seahorse. She was relieved to get a good report. Eight weeks down, at least thirty to go.

Lee loved to hear the sounds coming from the construction site. Every phase of construction meant he was closer to getting out of that apartment in town and settling into his own house in the country. He was not a city boy. He was picturing life with Abigail by his side and smiled.

Soon enough, it was time to pick up Abigail and stow the steaks in her refrigerator. Abigail had packed some sandwiches and snacks for their ride.

She was riding Buster and Lee was on Lady. Crossing the road, riding up Abigail's driveway, they entered the pasture and rode down to the far end.

They took the time to exchange the SD cards in the cameras. There had been no noticeable activity since the shooting, but it would be wise to remain vigilant.

The spring weather was mild, but the recent rains had left puddles in the saturated trails. Sometimes they sloshed through them, sometimes they went around them. The rhythmic sounds of the sucking and squelching of the hooves was soothing. Abigail missed Dude. He would have scared up every rabbit and squirrel, every bird and deer in the vicinity by now.

They rode for about an hour before stopping for lunch at the old bridge. The one lane rusted bridge was seldom used. It may not have been safe for a vehicle to cross it, but four-wheelers and horses crossed it almost daily. Abigail told Lee about the time that she crossed the bridge while two old guys were there shooting at something in the river. "It was very wet and Dude had just jumped into a puddle that was deeper than he thought. He trotted up behind those men and shook off on them just like he used to do to Buster. I thought they were going to shoot him!" Abigail laughed at the memory.

Lee told Abigail stories about his dog, Bullet, and they laughed together. She teared up when he told her that he had to put Bullet down just before he brought the rest of his belongings here. The rest of the afternoon was spent exploring trails, laughing and talking. They finally turned around and headed back. The horses quickened their paces knowing that there would be a treat at the end of the ride.

After grooming the horses and making a quick check on the progress of the construction, they drove back up to Abigail's house. Lee manned the grill while

83

Abigail prepared the potatoes and salad. The temperature was balmy and they sat quietly on the deck as the sun began its slide over the horizon. Spikes of gold and peach, orange and red decorated the rims of the cottony clouds.

Reaching into his pocket, kneeling down in front of Abigail's chair, Lee took her hands. Abigail gave him a quizzical look. "Abigail," he said slowly in a quiet, low voice, "I love you. Will you be my wife?"

Abigail sucked in her breath. She was not expecting this so soon. "Yes, yes! I'd be honored to be your wife."

He slid the slender golden ring with the diamond chip onto her finger. "This is just a pre-engagement ring," he said. "I want us to pick out the engagement ring and wedding bands together."

Max's head still hurt from the concussion. He spent the majority of his days in his room alternately sleeping and playing mindless video games which did not help his headaches. Nothing satisfied his restless spirit. He wanted to smoke a joint. He wanted to find his stash of pills. He was feeling the urges to get to the rituals, but his body was not healed enough to go anywhere. Besides, his father had not yet replaced his totaled truck. His mother had to drive him to physical therapy appointments. His parents were so relieved to have him home, but his mother's constant hovering was getting annoying.

"I'm not a kid anymore! Just leave me alone!"

Barbara retreated from his room in tears. She slumped in her rocker and hugged her Bible to her chest. "Oh, God, please help my son. I know You didn't spare him just so that he could go back to his old ways." She sobbed for a while and then decided to call the church to see if Pastor Spalding was available.

"Sure, sure," he answered her with a soothing tone. "Let me just tidy up a couple of things here and I'll be over within the hour." He hung up and started his own string of prayers. He sounded competent and comforting as a pastor would, but he was not entirely sure of what he should do or say. After that difficult conversation with Ted and Barbara outside of the ICU in which he disclosed his strong suspicions that Max was involved in the cult, the Berryman's seemed to be avoiding him.

Barbara had called Ted and he came home early from the dealership and he ushered Pastor Spalding into their family room. Barbara came equipped with a box of tissue. Her nose was red. Her eyes were bloodshot. Most of her mascara had already been dabbed and smeared into the wad of tissues that were on the bottom of the nearby waste basket.

"Tell me what's going on," Pastor Spalding said as he sat on the sofa and accepted a cup of coffee.

Barbara's tensed vocal cords and raised palate made her voice high-pitched as she resisted the sobs that were crouched like a panther waiting to pounce. "I just don't know what to do. He won't talk to us. He's rude and mean one minute and then he's sweet and thoughtful the next."

"Has he always been like that? I mean, shifting between, um," Pastor Spalding was trying to be tactful while navigating relatively new territory. "Well, like a Dr. Jekyll and Mr. Hyde maybe?"

"That would be a good description," Ted affirmed. "I'm not sure if he's always been like that." He pursed his lips and looked at the floor to his side.

"It seems like he changed after his bout with leukemia," Barbara said. "Of course, he was only five and it's hard to tell about kids. He'd just come through the terrible two's and three's when he got sick."

"I didn't know he had leukemia."

"We don't talk about it much. It was so scary to think we could lose our little boy. Maybe we spoiled him too much," Barbara mused.

Ted was not one to avoid the hard questions. "Did we create this monster?"

"I don't think you created a monster," Pastor Spalding replied. "Your response is perfectly natural. The enemy would have taken full advantage of the situation. Trauma affects people. And you have to remember that Max has made many choices along the road."

"I suppose so," Ted conceded. "So where do we go from here?"

"I think we need to keep praying for Max. I also think it would be a good idea for you to meet with Abigail Steele and work through some of your guilt and pain. She can really help you with the spiritual warfare aspects. It seems like the enemy wants him dead but God keeps him alive. And, we really need for Max to meet with Abigail and myself. I suspect that he's torn between wanting to be that sweet son that you know and the wild child that is involved with the cult."

They continued to discuss possibilities and then prayed together. There were fewer sniffles as Barbara calmed down. Pastor Spalding left them with a final admonition, "Don't let this tear you two apart. You have to present a united front to Max and that unity is only going to come from pressing in to God harder than you ever did when his life was in the balance."

As they walked him to the door, he had another thought. "Would you mind if I spoke to Abigail Steele about this situation? I have to admit that she has much more expertise in these matters than I do and it would be helpful to me when I get a chance to talk to Max."

They had no problem with his request. "Anything that will help Max." Ted shook Pastor Spalding's hand and closed the door softly behind him. Then he gathered his wife in his arms and kissed the top of her head. "We'll get through this, too, hon."

7

Friday, April 13

Fair weather buoyed Lee's already high spirits. The construction was coming along on time. With the thawed ground, he was able to run more fence lines, effectively creating three fair-sized pastures. Each one had access to creek or pond water. Through a contact at the feed store, he found a breeder who gave him a good price on seven heifers.

Across the road, Abigail was getting ready for her day of counseling. She was glad to be able to wear a lighter weight jacket again. Taking a precautionary look out the back door, she scanned the pasture that was beginning to grow. Without Buster to graze it, it would need to be bush hogged. She chose not to worry about that today. "This is the day that You have made, Lord. I will rejoice and be glad in it." She continued her prayers as she drove down the driveway and past her neighbors' houses. She felt a stab of excitement in her belly as she thought about Lee and their future together.

Carrie Sue was waiting for her with a big smile. "So, how's the future Mrs. Norris doing today?"

"You enjoyed yourself way too much on Sunday."

"Yep. I sure did. I really like this normal stuff."

"Come on. We have work to do," Abigail laughed good-naturedly.

They set up the office together as they had so many weeks for several years. They had been through thick and thin and had come to respect and like each other.

"So, what are we working on today?"

"I think I need to deal with, um," Carrie Sue paused awkwardly, "with normal relationships. I guess when I saw you and Lee and all the couples last Sunday, I started thinking that I really want that, but it terrifies me, too. I mean, what guy would want me? I've been so... so used. And I want to have kids but after all I've been through, I'm just not sure if God would let me."

"Why wouldn't God let you have kids?"

"Because I didn't save my babies."

"And *why* didn't you save them?" Abigail pressed Carrie Sue to think about the truth of those circumstances.

"I don't know. I should have been able to get away. To run. To stop it somehow. I should have seen it coming."

"Let's review," Abigail said gently. "You were impregnated against your will when you were barely a teenager, surrounded by a menacing crowd of Satanists, held down, drugged – need I go on?"

"But I should have known. I should have seen it coming." Carrie Sue was deeply distressed and was unaccustomed to bearing the full weight of all the emotions that she was feeling now that she was integrated. "I don't like feeling this way."

"Sorry, this is part of being normal."

"I'm not sure I want to be normal then." Carrie Sue's tears were threatening to cascade down her cheeks.

"Can we take this to the Lord?"

Carrie Sue nodded her consent and reached for a tissue.

"Lord, Carrie Sue is feeling a lot of intense emotions right now. We ask that You would salve these wounds with Your healing balm. Lord, what do You have to say about letting Carrie Sue have babies someday? Is she undeserving?" Abigail sat quietly, expectantly.

Carrie Sue snuffled and blew her nose. When she looked up, she had a soft smile on her face. "He said, 'It's not your fault.' I feel like a load has been lifted from my shoulders."

"Isn't that amazing? I can tell you that until I'm blue in the face, but when He tells you, the Truth really will set you free. Praise God!" Abigail never tired of watching God work.

Soon Carrie Sue was on her way home and Amy was seated in Abigail's office.

"How's it going? What did the doctor say?"

"She says that everything looks normal, but if I spot again, I need to call her. If it's after hours, I need to go to the emergency room. Thanks for the referral. She's nice."

"Good. And if worst case scenario happens, call me. Even if it's the middle of the night. Seriously."

"Thanks, but I don't want to bother you."

"Who else do you have around here?"

"Nobody."

"Call me if you need to."

"Okay, okay. I promise."

"Good, let's open with prayer."

Head Honcho showed up and gave her a report about the status of their internal world. Joktan was still upset because Abigail's warning about increased demonic pressure had the personalities on the various levels more stirred up than usual. They were already edgy because of the vibes coming from Apollyon's level. The internal tensions were building and if something was not done, there was no telling what would happen. Head Honcho said that he was feeling the tension as well.

Nicholai had told Head Honcho that many of the lower level personalities were banging on his doors and wanted to come in. He was pleased to report that once they were in the tranquility of his newly revamped level one, they wanted peace. There were many who got saved and healed, delivered and integrated.

"Is there any sense of who they are integrating into?" Abigail was curious. She suspected that they would be integrated into the original F. Amy Bolton, but sometimes God had a different plan.

"We're pretty sure that they are not integrating into anyone that's still on the other levels. It seems like the ones who come in groups are related to each other in some way and they consolidate and then the one they integrate into will either defect to Nicholai's level or join my people. Sometimes they all integrate, but no one up here feels anything so maybe they're going into the original."

"What's going on with Apollyon's level? Has that quieted down any?"

"Actually, it seems like when they get loud we get a bunch more coming up to defect and integrate and then they get even louder."

"It makes me wonder if they're integrating into the original F. Amy and she's getting stronger and aging. They would notice those changes. If they can't harm her, it would explain a lot of their reaction."

"Makes sense."

"Time will tell."

"Is Joktan around?"

"He's waiting to have a word with you." Head Honcho backed off and was immediately displaced.

"Okay, lady, I'm here and I'm still not happy with what you did," Joktan snarled.

"Under more attack?"

"You could say that."

"I have a solution that can take care of that."

"Not on your life, lady! I don't want anything to do with your bright ideas."

"Then what do you propose? Besides putting everything back to square one because that isn't going to happen even if I prayed about it."

"I want my guys to stop being harassed. More of them are disappearing and that's got to stop." He was angry and frustrated.

"I can't blame them for wanting to bail."

"Shut up!"

"It sounds like we have an impasse. Maybe I need to talk to Fuchsya." She was the cult-loyal leader over the whole system.

"You're nuts! It's your life." With that he disappeared and Fuchsya replaced him.

"And just why have you summoned me?" Fuchsya demanded in an icy tone.

"I'm just trying to negotiate some peace in the system."

"What do you have in mind?"

"I don't have an agenda. I'd like to pray and ask God for an answer. It seems that the last time you were involved in a decision, the integrations that occurred benefited each sector."

"It did. But I can't afford to lose any more people."

"Why not?"

"Because they have jobs to do."

"Do you know what's going on in Apollyon's level?" Abigail completely changed the subject.

"Yes. No. What difference does it make?"

"How old is the original Fuchsya?"

Fuchsya swore under her breath. "You're nothing but a meddling fool! What right do you have to mess with us?"

"I take it that she's aging and you can't stop the defections and integrations that are strengthening her."

Fuchsya gave Abigail a hard stare that had a demonic edge to it. The left side of her lip curled upward and Abigail fully expected to hear a snarl at any moment or maybe even a full manifestation of the demon. Abigail prayed silently in the spirit and neither happened. She watched as the flatness disappeared and the natural human eye reappeared.

Abigail said gently, "Fuchsya, I'm not the enemy. You're in a tough spot now and it's only going to get tougher. Please let me help you. Please. There is a way through this."

"Lady, you don't know what we've done. It's impossible. There's no way back. We were on track until you showed up."

"Can you honestly look back and find one instance in which they didn't renege on their promises?"

"If they did, it was because we failed."

"No. If you failed, it was because they put you in a no-win situation. They are masters of the double-bind. Think about it. When you failed, wasn't it because they withheld some critical piece of information or instruction and they convinced you that they *did* tell you but you didn't remember?"

Fuchsya scowled and reluctantly scrolled through her memory banks. "All right, maybe that happened sometimes. What does that prove?"

"I'm just saying that you have aligned yourself with someone who doesn't have your best interests in mind."

"We can handle it."

"You've done an amazing job of handling stuff I would crumble under." Abigail truly admired these survivors. Even the obnoxious ones. Actually, they were her favorites because they were so real.

Fuchsya was not expecting a compliment. "Keep your sympathies to yourself." She did not know what to do with encouragement. She only knew that her hostilities kept people at bay. *Why wasn't this lady intimidated? What did she really want?*

"Would you think about what I've been saying and the positive things that have been going on for Head Honcho and Nicholai since they defected? It's available for everyone. Including you."

"Whatever." It was too much for Fuchsya. Trying to save face, she disappeared into her dark world that swirled with sulfuric fumes from her demonic companions.

Amy resurfaced. "Whew!"

"You okay?"

"Yeah, but you really shook up Fuchsya."

They continued to talk awhile. Abigail used the chitchat about Amy's work and Abigail's garden plans to help Amy settle down after the intense session. They closed in prayer and made an appointment for the following Friday.

Loretta came in and Abigail was amazed at the difference in her. She looked like she had lost some weight and she wore make-up today. There was something in her bearing and mannerisms that hinted at improved self-worth.

"So, how was your week?" Abigail asked.

"Actually, it was one of the most peaceful weeks I can remember. Maybe ever."

"Wonderful! Let's open with prayer and see where the Lord wants to start today."

Loretta's shoulders sagged as she opened her eyes and looked briefly at Abigail. "Okay, I was hoping that I wouldn't have to talk about this, but I guess I have to."

Abigail chuckled softly, "I think I'm unshockable by now. You can't tell me anything that will make me think less of you."

"I don't know about that, but I do know I have to talk about it." Loretta kept her eyes averted. "Okay, I have a girlfriend." She stated it abruptly and then looked for Abigail's reaction.

"How much of a conflict is that for you since you're a Christian and probably know all the Bible verses that are against it better than I do?"

"I just try not to think about it. Maybe that's why I don't have much of a relationship with God. I mean, He can't possibly approve of me."

"Kind of like your father?"

"Yeah, exactly like that," she said with an edge of bitterness.

"Why don't we talk a little bit about the Heavenly Father slash earthly father association?"

"Okay," she replied warily.

"God originally intended for a mom and a dad to give a kid a tangible image of Him when He said, 'Let Us create mankind in Our image – male and female He created them.' So, if our parents are a perfect, sinless representation of God, we'll have a pretty good image of Him. But since none of our parents were perfect, we all got a skewed image of God. Right?"

"Yeah, that makes sense."

"If you were to ask me what I thought of God when I was your age, I would have said He was a perfectionist and expected me to be one, too, and He'd point out all my mistakes. Well, that was my dad. Now, Dad's a great guy and he's mellowed over the years, but that was my image of God."

"How do we fix this?"

"Let's pray and ask God to sever the connection, the association between the Heavenly Father and your earthly father."

Loretta nodded her assent and Abigail led her in a prayer. "Heavenly Father, we ask that You would cut in two the cords of the wicked and sever any false connection or association between You and her dad. Your Word says that if, or since my father and mother have let me down, the Lord would lift us up. Father, would You re-parent Loretta in those places where her parents have let her down? And God, would You address that thought that You do not approve of

Loretta because of her lifestyle? We ask this in the name of Jesus the Christ, amen."

"Amen," Loretta echoed. She sat thinking for a few moments and then said, "That made a difference. I think I heard the words, 'I'll always love you.'" She wept openly and reached for a tissue. After blowing her nose she laughed and said, "I never cry and that's all I do in here!"

"Hey, tears are the pressure valve of the heart. Are you ready to look at the relationship you have with that girlfriend now? I'm kind of sensing that you know that it's not God's best for either of you."

"Yeah."

"When did it start and what attracted you to her. You said last time that you went wild with guys in college. I don't want to pigeon-hole you, but do you consider yourself bi-sexual?"

"Actually, I ruined a lot of relationships with guys. I think I'm seeing now that I was mad at Dad and was taking it out on them. You might not believe it, but when I was in college and I was really only about twenty pounds overweight, I was attractive. I would have sex with a guy and get all the pleasure out of him the first time we were together and then the next time he wanted to have sex, I'd refuse and just get rid of him. They were really frustrated." She paused thoughtfully and continued, "I guess I was getting even with my parents again."

"Ah, sounds like another vow."

"Oh, yes. I will rebel against everything you say. If you think I should be a virgin, watch me!"

"Were you conflicted again between wanting to be good and to be a virgin and wanting to spite them?"

Lynda L. Irons

"Yep. I did it to myself again. What's wrong with me? I don't even know why I went with a girlfriend."

"Let's ask God to take us to the root of that. Let me know what thought or memory comes up."

After the prayer, Loretta opened her eyes and looked at Abigail. "Humph. I'm remembering a family gathering. I was in my twenties. I told my mom that I was going to bring my boyfriend and she said, 'Will he be an embarrassment?'"

"What did you say or think in response to that?"

"I remember thinking, 'if you think this decent guy is an embarrassment, wait until you see who I bring to the next gathering!' Right about that time I broke up with him and she – we worked together – she was comforting and it felt like she loved me. I ate it up."

"So, she was there at a vulnerable time and you had just made another vow to bring someone even more unacceptable to the family gatherings. You could kill two birds with one stone."

"Something like that. Oh, crap! I did it to myself again. I spent my whole dog-gone life getting even with them and they don't even care. I'm the one being destroyed. I'm done. I'm just done with her. I'm done with binge eating. I'm done with trying to get even. I'm going to live my own life the way I need to; the way God wants me to."

"Sounds like a bunch of good vows."

"What now?"

"Do you think you need to confess and repent of that relationship?"

"Yeah," Loretta said penitently and did not wait for a prompt. "God, I really screwed up my life being so mad at my parents. Please forgive me for all the sexual

98

sins, for the way I treated those guys, for the relationship with Roberta, for all my anger and rebellion against my parents. God, I still don't like them, but I'm done with getting even. Amen."

"Amen," Abigail echoed. "How are you feeling?"

"I can breathe a lot deeper now. A big weight has been lifted. I need to go break off that relationship right now." Loretta came to a stand.

"Okay, then. Do you want to meet again next week?"

"Yes, please. Same time, same station?"

"Works."

Just as the majority of the people in the communities in the region were settling down for sleep, a minority of people were being drawn to various ritual sites. Charlie Fletcher was resigned to the invasion of his property tonight. He was feeling the pressure. He knew that he was not master material. He was just a lackey, a flunky.

He had started out much like Max Berryman had when he was a cocky high school kid decades ago. Too smart for his own good, he had been seduced by promises of money, sex, and power. It was not long before he had been duped into participating in a ritual. His hand gripped the ceremonial dagger. His tongue tasted the blood. He was guilty. Damned. Doomed. All he could hope for was atonement. There had to be someone he could bring as a substitute that would release him from the grip of the cult. But was he in too far to get out?

99

He put on his game face as he donned his robe and gingerly tugged the hood over his head with his left hand. There were still some splinters in the flesh. Dr. Bacchus was not sure if they were fragments of bone, splinters of the gun stock, or particles of the shell casing. They would have to wait for them to work themselves out. He could only do so much surgery at one time. Tonight's gathering would be small since just the local group would be meeting. Zorroz would officiate as the highest local master.

Zorroz was still seething. His deeply rooted fear was driving his anger. As he drove over to Charlie Fletcher's farm he reviewed some of the events of the past several months. Carrie Sue had broken the hyoid bone and cartilage in his throat. Prinz healed it, but then it was reversed in church. He recalled the loss of power when he was on Abigail Steele's property. He remembered the sacrifice of his daughter. Honor or punishment? At one time he felt invincible with a bright future. Now he felt an ominous dread. Somehow, he had to redeem himself. It was, after all, do or die.

8

Saturday, April 14

The gray skies confirmed the weather report. Abigail had hoped that she could work on her latest outdoor project without having to dodge rain drops but it looked like she would have to work indoors. She had decided that she would turn the tack room into a chicken coop now that she did not have Buster anymore. Stopping by the bank for extra cash, she made her way to the lumber store in Springfield. She had researched what she needed to make nesting boxes and decided that she could put them together with one sheet of plywood, some two by two's, and whatever scrap wood she had laying around the barn. She also picked up some corner brackets and a small box of wood screws.

Coming home down the back roads with the tarp-wrapped wood, she shuddered involuntarily as she passed Charlie Fletcher's driveway. *There must have been a ritual there last night.* Throwing up a quick prayer, Abigail continued to cruise down the road to her driveway. She did not dare to back the truck all the way down to the tack room because of the rain-slicked mud so she parked at the gate and got the four-wheeler with the trailer to take the bulky wood the rest of the way down.

Trekking up the hill and across the back yard, she went down to her basement shop and picked up her circular saw and battery powered drill. Slinging two fifty-foot power cords over her shoulder, she trudged back up the stairs and out to the tack room. Some day she wanted to run a line to the barn and tack room, but for now she used extension cords that she could plug into the outlet on the yard light pole.

By noon she had put together a unit of four nesting boxes and a shelf that was four feet off the floor to set them on. She stepped back and looked at it with satisfaction. The tack room was roughly eight feet by twelve feet and would be plenty big. Her next project was to remove everything else from the tack room. Those chickens would roost on anything and there would be droppings everywhere.

Since the rain had stopped, she decided to scour the woods for hickory saplings to make roosts. They needed to be at least eight feet long and two inches in diameter. Finding two suitable trees, she quickly cut them down, trimmed the branches, and dragged them back to the tack room where she installed one roost four feet off the floor and the other one two feet away that was two feet off the floor. Except for the wood shavings and straw, it was ready for her chicks. She had ordered twenty red comet chicks from a contact at the feed store. They should be hatching out in about ten days. She planned to keep them in the utility room in a large tote box until they were a little bit older. The medicated starter feed and dispensers for both feed and water were ready.

Lee was going to pick up his heifers today after having lunch with Abigail. She heard the soft toots of his horn as he approached her house even though he was driving the white truck. They were both excited about getting the heifers. Lee missed his cattle ranch. This was not going to be like Montana, but it would be satisfying. He would miss the long trail rides to check on the cattle who ranged over a fairly large spread, but with only eighty acres, it would be less time intensive so he would be able to devote his energy to other pursuits – a part time job and time with Abigail.

Lee smiled at Abigail as her chatter brought him back to the present. "Are you about ready to go? We just need to run by my place and pick up the trailer. I've got it hitched to the diesel. I figure seven heifers can fit in there as easily as four horses."

"I'm ready."

After switching vehicles, they were on their way. Abigail was fairly familiar with the main roads in the neighboring county and they were soon pulling up the lane of a large, well-kept farm that specialized in breeding Black Angus cattle. The owner came out of one of the barns and waved them over with his hat in his hand.

Lee greeted the man with a handshake and introduced Abigail. They went into the barn where Luke Riley led them to a pen that held seven brown-eyed heifers who stared curiously at the newcomers. "They're just over six months old and they're all about four hundred fifty pounds give or take. They're all up to date on their vaccinations and such."

Lee had a good eye for cattle and sized them up quickly. "Oh, they're some pretty gals. They'll make good mommas." He slowly walked up to the pen and let one of them sniff and blow on his extended hand. "I think they'll do just fine."

The men loaded the heifers into Lee's trailer and secured it. Lee paid Luke and soon they were on their way to Lee's farm. Winding through the low hills,

Lynda L. Irons

they talked about the heifers and Abigail's chicken coop among other things. Soon enough, he was backing the trailer expertly through the open gate of one of the grazing fields.

"We'll just let the ladies get used to standing still for a few minutes. I don't want them to panic after their first ride." He talked gently to them in soothing tones and within twenty minutes he began to slowly open the back doors after he pulled out the ramp. "Come on, ladies. Fresh grass. We got to fatten you up."

Eventually they braved the ramp, lowered their heads to the grass and began to nibble as they walked away still clustered together.

"I don't think they'll try to come out the gate when I move the truck, but just to be safe, why don't you close it once I get clear?"

"No problem." Abigail moved over to the gate. Lee parked the truck, secured the gate and then looked with satisfaction at his young herd. Abigail smiled at the man that she had come to love. *Oh, Lord, life sure is interesting!*

"Come on, I'll show you the house. It's starting to look like something we can live in." He opened the front door with his key and they walked slowly though the rooms, their voices echoing softly in the empty structure.

The thought startled Abigail. She always thought of it as Lee's house. *Duh! I'll be living here, too, once we're married.* "We," Abigail said. "Has a nice ring to it."

"Yes, it does," Lee agreed. "Abigail, I know I've just given you a pre-engagement ring, but I think we need to start talking about a date." His voice lifted as if he were asking a question.

"What do you have in mind?"

"How about yesterday?" he teased.

"I'm not ready. I'd like to get a new dress at least. I'll make that my annual-wear-a-dress day."

"Your what?"

"My annual-wear-a-dress day. I make it a point to wear a dress just one day every year."

"Why?"

"Well, I just hated wearing dresses as a kid – tomboy, you know – but I want to remember that I'm a lady so I make sure that I wear a dress at least once a year."

"Okay," Lee said slowly and smiled one of his I-don't-understand-but-I'll-pretend-I-do smiles. What do you think would work for you?"

"I'll think about it and pray about it, but you haven't passed all the tests yet," she said with a twinkle in her eyes.

"What tests?"

"Well you passed the friends and church people test with flying colors, but you haven't passed the dad or brother test yet."

"Oh," Lee said knowingly. "Those tests. When do you want to introduce me to your family?"

"Since they all live about six or seven hours away, maybe we can head up there Memorial Day weekend or something. They usually get together."

"You plan it and we'll do it. Meanwhile, do you want to go with me to the big city and buy some rings?"

"Let's do it!" *Hoo boy! This is getting real!*

Lynda L. Irons

Amy groaned on her bed. After the optimism of the last couple of weeks, her world quaked and then settled back into a familiar old pattern. Levi paid her another visit. This time he came with reinforcements. While they did not rape her, they did rough her up once again. Her lips were swollen. Her eyes were puffy. Bruises were beginning to mark the places that the kicks and punches landed. Oh, she got in a few licks herself, but there were three of them and Michael and the other protectors were no match.

She felt the familiar moisture and knew that she was spotting again. Wild thoughts raced through her mind. *They want me to carry this baby. If I lose it now, then neither one of us will have it. I won't have to worry about what might happen to the baby. It'll be safe with Jesus in heaven and maybe they'll leave me alone.* Maternal drives tugged at her heart. *But, God, I really want this baby.* Cramping confirmed her worst fears.

She did not want to bother Abigail, but Abigail did tell her to call if she needed to. She needed to call. She got the answering machine and left a message with a shaky voice.

Lee brought Abigail home so she could change her clothes before they went shopping. He would stop at his place in town on the way and change into nicer clothes as well. Abigail looked at the phone as was her habit when she entered the living room and noticed the flashing light. Punching the buttons, she retrieved her messages. The first one was a sales call. The second one was from Amy.

"Uh, Abigail, I'm sorry to bother you, but I'm spotting again. I need to get to the E.R. and I was

106

hoping you could take me if you get this message pretty soon. It's, uh, three-thirty."

Abigail looked at the clock. It was four o'clock.

"Lee, we might have to postpone our shopping trip. Amy needs a ride to the E.R. She's spotting again. She doesn't sound too good."

"Let's go. I'll drive. There's plenty of room in my truck."

Abigail immediately called Amy's cell phone and found out that Amy was already driving herself to the hospital in Springfield. "I'll meet you there with Lee." They hastily headed back out the door and down the driveway and made it in record time because the traffic was light and Lee's foot was slightly heavy.

Amy had already registered and was taken back to the triage area. After she was assessed, she was taken back to a curtained area and instructed to put on a patient gown. Amy was hoping that she could stay in executive control. *Please, God, no kids or hostile ones tonight.* She prayed silently, desperately, and then made an internal announcement: *Okay, everyone, this is for adults only. God is with us. Abigail is coming and we're going to be safe. Just stay put.*

The nurse looked at her face suspiciously and asked about her other injuries.

"Oh, it's nothing. I fell. I'm just here because of the spotting. My doctor told me to come here if I started spotting again." Amy knew it was a lie and knew that the nurse knew that it was a lie.

The nurse had worked the E.R. too many years to buy her flimsy excuse. She did not press the issue, but continued her preliminary examination, asking about her medical history, asking about the pregnancy. Soon the doctor came in and told her that they would send her for an ultrasound and then he would need to do an exam.

The nurse had also talked to her supervisor and she agreed that Amy's injuries would need to be reported to the authorities. After all, it was obvious to both of them that there had been an assault.

Lee dropped Abigail off at the E.R. entrance and parked the truck. Abigail inquired about Amy and was allowed to go back to the curtained area.

"Amy!" Abigail was not prepared to see the battered woman. "Oh, my! What happened?"

"Levi and two other guys broke in around four o'clock this morning. Michael got in some good licks, but he didn't stand a chance. At least they didn't rape us."

By the time Amy was wheeled back to the E.R. area from the ultrasound department on the gurney, a uniformed deputy was waiting just outside of the curtain. Amy's heart lurched. The hair on Abigail's arms and the back of her neck stood up. *Crap! Another Satanist.*

"Are you Fuchsya Bolton?" he asked gruffly as he walked up to the gurney and towered over her.

"Yeah."

"I need to see your identification."

"What for?"

"I need to fill out a report about an alleged assault."

"I didn't call you. There's nothing to report."

He glared at her and Abigail could see that Amy was feeling very vulnerable under the thin sheet and the even thinner patient gown. "Sir, do you think you could step back a little? She's already very upset about her medical condition. You're making her very nervous." Abigail reached for Amy's hand that gripped the sheet.

He looked to the other side of the gurney and as his gaze shifted to Abigail, he said. "I need to see your identification, too."

"Why? I'm just here with my friend."

"Identification! Now!" He looked as if he were ready to slap cuffs on her and haul her to jail.

Abigail reached into her pocket, reluctantly took her license out of her wallet, walked around to the foot of the gurney, and placed it into his outstretched hand. That effectively forced him to retract the arm that was extended over Amy. He wrote her information on his report and handed it back to Abigail.

Abigail pressed him, "And are you accusing Amy of assaulting someone or are you trying to investigate an assault against her?"

Looking down at his clipboard to get her name, he said, "Ms. Steele, I ask the questions here."

"All I'm saying is that if she's already been assaulted, she doesn't need to be intimidated by you, too. I know you're just trying to do your job, but I'm asking you to be a little sensitive here."

He glared at her and then at Amy. He turned on his heels and abruptly left the room.

"Holy cow!" Amy exclaimed. "What a jerk! I'm so glad that you were here."

"Me, too. Humph! He never even got your identification. He gave me the creeps; do you think he's a Satanist?"

"I've never seen him, but then, a lot of them wear hoods and it's dark and all. But he sure gave me the willies, too."

They kept their voices low and continued talking until a young doctor swept the curtain aside and stepped in with the chart. "Fuchsya, we got your ultrasound report and everything looks okay for now. I won't do an exam today so we don't stir things up any more than we need to, but you need to follow up with your OB/GYN as soon as possible. Meanwhile, you need to be on bedrest. Lay flat and only get up to use the bathroom."

Amy's mouth dropped open as she thought about being on bedrest. *What about work?* "For how long?"

"Let your doctor answer that question. You're at a critical stage in this pregnancy. I'll be honest with you. If a woman were to miscarry, it's usually in the first trimester, so go home and rest."

"Yes, sir." Amy was troubled about the prospect. "Okay, I'll discharge you, then. Good luck." He signed his note, handed the chart to the nurse and moved on to the next patient.

The nurse took over discharging her and making sure that she understood everything. She had a kind face and a gentle manner. "I'm sorry about that deputy. I can't believe they didn't send a female officer," she apologized. In a very low voice she added, "Look, I know someone assaulted you by your injuries and defensive wounds. Please don't be mad at me for calling in the law, I have to report things or I can lose my license."

"I understand."

"You take care, honey."

Abigail went to the waiting room and apprised Lee of Amy's new situation. She also told him about the deputy. "I'm going to take her home with me," she said decisively.

"I'll follow you and make sure you get there safely," Lee said equally decisively.

Levi was patrolling the parking lot waiting for Amy to return to her car. He and his companions would follow her home and finish the job. They had already located her car and were just cruising slowly up and down the rows of parked cars, too restless to just park and watch.

The orderly wheeled Amy to the exit while Lee walked out to the parking lot to retrieve Amy's old car. Abigail waited with Amy.

"Abigail!" Amy tugged on Abigail's sleeve and pointed. "That's Levi in that black car! Looks like someone's with him." The sun had already set, but the lights in the parking lot were bright enough to distinguish details.

"Well, I tell you what. I'm going to pray that we become invisible to him." Sometimes Abigail was surprised at the things that came out of her own mouth. She squatted down next to Amy, took her hand, and prayed, "Lord, we ask that You would make us invisible to Levi and anyone else that might be lurking out there. Confuse them and keep them occupied until we get out of here, amen."

"Amen."

They could see Levi circling the parking lot as Lee pulled up in Amy's car. Levi even drove right past them and looked their way. It was as if he looked through them. It was definitely Levi. Amy figured

111

that the men that were with him were the same ones who had helped Levi beat her up.

Lee came around the front of the car and helped Amy into the passenger seat while Abigail took over the driver's seat. She told Lee about Levi.

"I'll follow you."

She and Amy drove right past Levi unnoticed and giggled as they praised the Lord for His intervention.

The ride to Abigail's house was uneventful other than Amy protesting about the arrangements. "I can't impose on you like this. I don't have any clothes." Every once in a while, she would come up with another argument. "I have to call work."

"You can use my phone. What alternative do you have? Your family is toxic. You'd be a sitting duck in your trailer, you know? Besides, I can lend you a pair of jammies and tomorrow I'll go over to your place and get some stuff if you want. You can stay as long as you need to."

"What about work? I'll get fired." Amy was scrolling through a long list of catastrophes that would begin to domino when the long-term-bed-rest domino toppled.

"Amy, let's just see what the doctor says when you call her Monday. Try not to worry because that won't help you or your baby."

Abigail found a set of sweats and a tee shirt for Amy to wear until she could go to her mobile home and bring back some clothing and toiletries. She and Lee put together a quick supper. It was nearly ten o'clock before they finally got to eat. Amy was settled in the back bedroom and Lee said that he was going to stop by his place to check on the horses and the heifers and then head home. Abigail enjoyed a hot shower after a very eventful day and headed to bed herself.

Levi and his companion were astounded that Amy's car had disappeared from the parking lot right under their noses. They swore and then decided to go to Amy's trailer to see if they could intercept her there. Their humiliation fueled their anger and they vowed revenge.

9

Sunday, April 15

Removing his helmet and wiping sooty grime off his sweaty forehead, the fireman commented to his partner, "I sure hope no one was in there when this thing started, he wouldn't have stood a chance."

"These old trailers are tinder boxes all right," the other one agreed. "Probably an electrical short. That's what usually happens."

They were volunteer fire fighters who responded to the neighbors' calls to 911. As they sifted through the glowing rubble hoping that they would not find a body, they shook their heads at the utter loss. Nothing survived the intense blaze. If it were not for some of the alert neighbors hosing down neighboring trailers, there would have been more than one home destroyed. The whole park could have been destroyed.

No one really knew Amy. Except for her last name on the mailbox and an occasional exchange, Amy had kept to herself. No one knew her family. No one knew where she worked. No one knew where she was. They were hoping that she would not be found in the ashes. No one deserved that.

———————————

Lee was satisfied that his heifers were making themselves at home in the newly fenced pasture. They had plenty of grass and access to the creek-fed pond. Glancing at his watch, he hurried back to his truck and headed over to pick up Abigail. She had fussed over

Amy, brought her breakfast in bed, moved the radio/CD player into her room in case she wanted to listen to music, and made her promise to stay in bed.

"Lee and I will drive over to your place after church and get this stuff on your list so we should be back by about one-thirty or two o'clock at the latest. I have a roast and stuff in the crock pot so we can have a late lunch."

"Okay, Mommy," Amy could not resist teasing Abigail. "I'll be a good girl." Amy was incredibly grateful but she was afraid that she would weep if she said anything seriously.

"I'm not kidding. Don't worry about anything except that baby right now. Do you mind if I ask for prayers at church?"

"No problem; I'd like that. Thanks, Abigail."

"My privilege. See ya soon."

Abigail scooted into the pew and gave Cindy a brief hug. "Miss you, lady, we haven't gotten together lately."

"I know. Do I dare ask you what's new?"

"Why, Cindy, you know I have a perfectly dull and predictable life," Abigail said with mock seriousness.

"What's going on?"

"One of my SRA ladies called me last night. She got beat up. She's pregnant and is spotting. Needs to be on bedrest. So, I took her home."

"Not Carrie Sue?"

"No, a different one." The music started playing so Abigail whispered, "I'll tell you more later."

They turned their attention to worship and soon Pastor Spalding was preaching his sermon. "Acts twelve is filled with a lot of death. The early church

115

underwent a lot of persecution. Herod had just killed James. He saw that it pleased the Jews who hated the Christ-followers. The Jews. How deep their hatred of the Christians must have been for disrupting their religion! Let me ask you a question. Was God sovereign in that situation in which James was killed?"

He paused to let them think a moment. "Now he wanted to go after Peter, too, and really please the Jews. So, Peter was put in prison with four squads of soldiers to guard him. Four squads. That was sixteen soldiers to guard a fisherman. Apparently, this Herod had heard about someone else who had escaped from Roman guards." He paused again as chuckles rippled through the congregation.

"Now, I ask again: Was God sovereign in this situation with Peter? Peter certainly must have thought so. Here he was chained in a stinking, rat-infested prison between two guards. No television, no bed, no heat. And we find him sleeping. Maybe he's thinking that he was heading to heaven and wanted to be good and rested before he got there. After all, one Herod killed all the baby boys when Jesus was born and another Herod took out John the Baptist." Pastor Spalding watched the thoughtful expressions on their faces.

"Meanwhile, the church is praying all night for his deliverance. And when the answer to their prayers is knocking on the door, they didn't believe it. They thought the servant was out of her mind and that she saw Peter's ghost. Obviously, their theology wasn't well developed at that time." He gave them a wink and a broad smile before he continued to develop his teaching.

"Here's the bottom line: when God permits someone to die and then delivers another one; when God appears to let one Herod get away with murder but this Herod is eaten by worms, is God still sovereign? Is He still God when people and demons appear to be getting away with something? If you haven't settled this yet, I urge you to settle it because life is filled with the good, the bad, and the ugly." He saw the nods of his attentive congregation and invited anyone who wanted to do business with the Lord about this or any other thing to come down for prayer.

Abigail got Cindy caught up on Amy and the chicken coop while Lee got Gary caught up on the heifers and the house. Eventually, Gary and Cindy went to pick up the children. As they approached the doorway to the foyer, they could hear Pastor Spalding greeting people as they were leaving. It was a slow-moving crowd today, but Abigail wanted Pastor Spalding to be in prayer for Amy as well.

"Well, Abigail and Lee! How are you two doing?" He asked it as if he knew all the details of their pre-engagement. Of course, every woman in the place, including his wife, would have noticed the ring so it would not have taken long for their engagement to become public knowledge.

"Great!" Abigail replied squeezing Lee's hand and lowering her voice. "I just have a prayer request for you. One of my SRA survivors will be staying with me for some time. She's pregnant and needs to be on bed rest. We'll see her doctor tomorrow and find out if it's temporary or long term. She got beat by three thugs early Saturday morning so we were in the E.R. last night with her."

117

"Oh my! I definitely will be praying. Can I put her on the prayer list?"

"Yes. She said it was okay. Her first name is Amy. The guys were definitely cult goons and they followed her to the hospital."

"Are you going to be safe?" he raised his eyebrows in concern.

"No weapon formed against us shall prosper."

"No weapon. Keep me posted."

Lee and Abigail left the building and got into Lee's truck. She gave him directions to Amy's mobile home park and it was not long before she pointed to the sign and directed him to turn right at the first corner. Lee navigated the ill-kept narrow lane that was crossed with speed bumps and dotted with pot holes.

"Uh, oh, looks like there was a fire here," Lee said as he pointed ahead at the yellow tape that sagged between poles and trees.

"Lee! That's Amy's place!" Abigail exclaimed. "Oh my. Yes," she affirmed as she looked at the mailbox. "Bolton. 166 Shady Lane. Oh, poor Amy!"

"Looks like nothing but ashes. Wow!" Lee stopped the truck and they got out and quietly surveyed the ruins of Amy's home. A few wisps of smoke curled from the debris. The stench of the acrid rubble was pungent. Lee took out his cell phone and snapped a couple of pictures. "She may not want to see this but at least she's alive to see it."

"Our portfolio of pictures of fires, dead dogs, and break-ins is getting bigger," Abigail said pensively.

There was nothing left to do but go back to Abigail's house and break the news to Amy. The ride back was quiet with each of them deeply immersed in thought.

"Are you sure you want to be a part of my crazy life?"

"Absolutely!"

"Okay, then, don't say that I never warned you."

A few minutes later they drove up Abigail's driveway. Both of them were extra alert and scanned the woods and fields for any sign of trouble. Neither one of them wanted to think that someone might have attacked Amy while they were gone.

"Let's wait and tell her after we have some lunch."

"Good idea."

Abigail called out to Amy as she unlocked the front door and came into the living room. She heard Amy's hello and felt relief. Checking on Amy, she told her that she would be serving lunch in about five minutes. Amy was clearly uncomfortable with all the attention but she was too tired and sore to attempt joking around today.

After lunch, Lee and Abigail cleared their dishes. Abigail retrieved Amy's tray as well. Lee went into the living room and Abigail went to Amy's room.

"Hey, lady, we need to talk about something. I'm afraid I have some bad news."

A worried frown formed on Amy's forehead. "Uh, oh, what did I do wrong?"

"You didn't do anything. It's what was done to you. I won't beat around the bush. Your trailer has been burned to the ground. There's nothing left but a bunch of rubble."

"You're not smiling."

"No. This is not a joke. Lee took pictures with his cell camera if you want to see."

Lynda L. Irons

"Yeah!" The implications of what Abigail said were beginning to swirl around in Amy's head.

Abigail got Lee's phone and brought it to the bedroom. "Here it is." She handed the phone to Amy who scrolled through the pictures a couple of times.

"Holy cow! I can't believe it's gone. Everything. My clothes... my stuff... all my important papers... Humph! Well, at least I got my taxes filed. Oh, joy, my mailbox is still standing. I can still get my refunds." Amy's mind was rapidly scrolling through the myriad of problems that she was facing.

Abigail knelt down by the side of the bed and looked Amy in the face. "Well, for now, you have a place to stay. As long as you need to. We'll figure out how to get copies of your papers. At least you still have your car and driver's license. We can have your mail forwarded to my address. I know this is a shock, but try to stay calm and rest."

"Yeah. Calm. That's me. Calm. Real calm. I'll just rest here all calm and stuff."

"I'm so sorry." Abigail patted her forearm and stood up again. "No weapon formed against us will prosper! It might look bleak right now, but God isn't finished with this story yet. He won't let them triumph. I'll let you rest. Calmly. Call me if you need anything."

"Thanks, Abigail, I, I really don't know what I'd do without you." She was on the verge of tears and fought to maintain her composure.

Abigail left so that Amy could process her losses in private.

"How's she doing?"

"She's tough. She's been through worse."

"Do you think they'll figure out that she's here and come after her again?"

"Eventually."

"You don't seem concerned."

"No weapon!"

"No weapon," Lee sighed in agreement. He admired the grit that he saw in these ladies.

At nine o'clock in the morning Amy was waiting on hold for the receptionist to connect her to the nurse. After several minutes, Amy heard her cheerful voice. Amy filled her in on her visit to the E.R. and let her know that she was still spotting and how often she had to change her pads. The nurse would check with the doctor and call Amy back with instructions.

After waiting nearly an hour, the nurse called back, apologizing for the delay. "Amy, the doctor says that she wants you to stay on bedrest and call us again on Friday morning to let us know if there has been any change. Of course, if it gets much worse, get to the E.R. right away."

Amy called Abigail to her room. "Looks like I'm going to be in bed for the rest of the week. I need to call them on Friday, but if it gets worse, it's back to the hospital."

"Okay, we can handle that." Abigail gave her a smile. "Amy, God is knitting that child together in your womb. That child is God's idea, not some Satanist's." She paused for a moment and then her practical side kicked in.

"Now, I'm sure you're going to want to change your clothes sometime this week. What size do you wear?

121

Grab that pen and paper and write down what size bra, panties, socks, shoes, pants, and tops you wear. I'll pick some stuff up for you when I run to town."

Amy groaned and blushed slightly but did as she was told. "I don't have any money. I'll probably lose my job, too. I'd better call them."

"Ah, don't you worry about that. You can be my indentured servant, I mean, I'm getting those chickens next week and that coop will have to be cleaned out. I have a garden to till and lawns to mow. Yeah, I think this will work out quite nicely."

She finally got a smile out of Amy.

Abigail stopped at Lee's farm on her way to Springfield. "Hey," he said. "I have an idea. Why don't we go together so we can finish that shopping that we didn't get done last week?"

"Are you sure? It may take me awhile to hunt down all these things for Amy."

"I'm sure. I can find a toothbrush and tooth paste and shoes and socks while you're getting the undies and other stuff. And," he lifted his chin a little, "I'll have you know that I've done some shopping for my daughter a time or two. I know how to put stripes and plaids together. She'll look sharp."

"All right then," Abigail laughed. "Hop in. I'll drive."

They stopped at the jewelry store first and ordered their rings. Then they split up the list and went their separate ways. Finally, laden with their purchases, they met for a bite to eat at a little sandwich shop. Three hours later, Abigail was back home again after dropping Lee off at his farm.

Zorroz looked like he was on patrol, but he was on the prowl. The twenty-first through the twenty-sixth of the month marked the abduction and ceremonial preparation and holding of the sacrificial victim who was to be a female up to age twenty-five. The Grand Climax would be celebrated from the twenty-sixth through May first. He would need more than one female to fulfill the blood-thirsty assemblies that would gather in various places around the region.

He pulled up to the Berryman's house and knocked on the door. Barbara answered the door and looked shocked to see Sheriff Bynum standing there in uniform. "Oh, dear," she said. "Is anything wrong?"

"No, no," he said gently. "Nothing like that. I was just in the neighborhood and thought I'd see how Max is doing. I haven't seen him since the accident and since my family moved and we're going to a different church, well, I haven't had an opportunity to check on him. Is he here?"

"That's so thoughtful of you. Yes, yes, he's in his room. I'll go get him." She turned quickly, nervously, and went down the hall to Max's room.

Soon the sound of a cane rhythmically tapping the tiles became louder as Max neared the living room. "Hi, Sheriff." Max was clearly nervous.

"Max! So good to see you getting around. How long will you need that cane?"

"Oh, I'm not sure. The P.T. says I'm making good progress, but I still have a lot of weakness in this left leg. I might have to wear the brace the rest of my life."

"When will you be able to get back to work?" Both Sheriff Bynum and Max knew what he was asking, but

Barbara did not pick up the double meanings that were carefully woven into their conversation.

"I'm not sure. Um, soon, I hope."

"Well, I need to get back to work. I hope you can get back to your pre-accident life pretty soon. The weather's nice and there's so much to do." He tipped his hat, flashing the goat sign in the process, and said a cordial goodbye to Barbara and Max.

An internal cult-loyal part of Max responded to Zorroz' sign. Max felt the impact immediately and went back to his room. He was confused. He was dangling between hope and despair. Could it be that Pastor Spalding and that counselor were right? Or had he gone too far?

Praying to his powers, Zorroz continued his prowling. Sometimes he had to drive to the larger towns and cities to procure his prizes. Junkies and prostitutes. Run-aways and hitch-hikers. Inattentive parents with toddlers who want to see the puppy or just someone being in the wrong place at the wrong time. It did not matter because this part of Sheriff Bynum had no conscience and was fully cult and demon-loyal.

Demons swooped and cursed in the upper atmosphere. They could see the pattern that was beginning to develop in this region. If they could see it, their superiors could. Eventually Satan himself would be notified and then there would be far more trouble than their miserable existences already experienced. Yes, these self-serving demons would aid their depraved human charges.

10

Friday, April 20

Amy was becoming more relaxed as the days progressed. She was pleased with the clothing selection. She and Abigail fell into a comfortable routine that included many hours of alone time for Amy. She was glad that Abigail had called Jan and let her and Earl know that she had a house guest for a while. Jan immediately volunteered her services to stay with Amy should the need arise.

"She's one of my SRA survivors. She's pregnant and on bedrest."

"You make sure she has our phone number in case you're gone and she needs something. And we'll keep an eye out for Charlie or whoever!"

"Thanks, I'll let her know."

The spotting only increased after she got up to do necessary things in the bathroom. She became an expert at taking quick showers. By Friday, she was becoming a bit more nervous wondering what the doctor would say. She was both disappointed and relieved that the doctor put her on extended bedrest.

"I'd have you come in, but there's really nothing we can do so I don't want to risk causing more bleeding. I think this latest bout is a reaction to your recent trauma. I checked the ultrasounds from the other night and I don't see anything to worry about, but if this doesn't settle down pretty soon, we'll have you come in for a hormone panel to see if those levels are within normal limits."

Abigail told Amy that she could stay for the entire duration of the pregnancy if she needed to. There was a fiercely independent part of Amy that resisted the notion, but there were plenty of others who relished the sense of security and of having someone actually take care of her without requiring anything. Not a thing.

"I'm heading to town to meet with my other ladies. Call Jan if you need to. I'll stop by the post office and get a change-of-address card for you, too. Meanwhile, why don't you call your local post office and see if they'll hold your mail?"

"Good idea. I'm not good at thinking about all this stuff. I don't know how I'll ever be able to pay you back."

"I already told you – chickens... lawn... garden. And if you don't like outdoor work, I have lots of dust bunnies. Oh, and I can't remember the last time the basement was cleaned."

"Get outta here." Amy grinned.

Abigail headed down the road and made it to the church just a couple of minutes late. Carrie Sue was already there. They went in, got settled, and opened with prayer after a little small-talk.

"I think I need to deal with my mom issues some more."

"Like forgiveness issues?"

"No, more like where-was-she-and-why-didn't-she-protect-me issues."

"Ah, the absence-of-good traumas. Do you need to forgive her for her sins of omission?"

"Yeah, I think that's part of it. And I guess I just need to let go of my expectations. After all, like you said, this is Mom and this is the way she is until God changes her."

Carrie Sue confessed her long-held grudges for her mother's negligence and lack of mothering. She reported that she felt a weight lift off of her.

"What else?"

"I think I'm finally ready to get out into the world and get a job. I checked with social security disability and they told me how much I can make a month before I lose my benefits. I think I can start out part time and see how it goes and then get off the disability. I'm tired of being a drain on society and feeling like a loser. Besides, my old shrink called and said that I needed to come in for a complete evaluation in order to keep the disability."

"I didn't know you still saw a shrink."

"Well, I haven't seen him in about a year. I needed someone to vouch for the disability and prescribe the anti-depressants and anti-anxiety meds."

"Hey, you needed it and now you're transitioning. How can I help?"

"Can I use you as a referral?"

"Absolutely! I'll let them know that you can take out a sheriff and that you have exceptional survival skills and…"

"Abigail!"

"Where are you thinking of putting in applications?"

"You know that thrift store that the Methodist church runs across from the court house? I get some of my stuff there and I was talking to the manager. She told me that they needed someone a couple days a week and invited me to fill out an app."

They continued to talk about other things. There were fewer and fewer SRA issues to address. Carrie Sue was pleased to report that there was no indication that there were any stragglers surfacing. She also was tickled that when her mother did show up or call, Dorkas did not switch in. All in all, she was making a successful transition from a highly fragmented survivor to a so-called normal person with ordinary problems.

Loretta was on time and looked even better than she had the previous week. She had lost some more weight and she seemed eager to wade through more issues.

"You look great," Abigail said. "Content."

"I am. I don't know how to thank you. People at church and at work are asking me about the changes. I told them that I found a good counselor. Oh, by the way, do you have some business cards? Some of them were asking."

"Sure," Abigail said and pushed the little card holder towards Loretta. "Take as many as you want. But, you know, I can't be an effective counselor unless the counselee cooperates. You've grabbed a hold of the principles and applied them. You humbled yourself before God and dumped a load. That makes it a lot easier for me to work my way out of a job."

"I think I have one more issue for today. Nothing real big like the last two times, but just something that I want to work through. I guess I just don't know how to make friends or to keep friends. My relationships have been... well, difficult or, or complicated. I don't know."

"Let's pray and ask the Lord to take us to the root of the issue."

"Sure." Loretta had quickly learned that what seemed illogical in the natural was sensible in the spiritual realm.

"Lord, would You go back through Loretta's history and take us to the root of this friendship/relationship issue?" She waited for a minute and then asked, "What are you sensing?"

"Huh, I had a friend who lived down the street when we lived on Crandall Ave."

"What happened?"

Loretta looked sadly at the floor. "She got real sick and died. We were nine."

"Ouch. Why don't we pray a minute and ask the Lord to illuminate that memory and see what else you need to know?" Getting the nod from Loretta, Abigail prayed, "Lord, please illuminate that memory or the circumstances around it and show Loretta how that affected her friendships."

"I just remember being mad. I didn't understand and I was scared. I remember thinking, 'I'm not going to have friends anymore, they just die.' Oh, great!" she said as she looked at Abigail. "Another stinking vow!"

"Yep. With the Law-of-Unintended-Consequences, you opened yourself up to a lifetime of not having any more friends."

"I did it to myself again." Loretta hung her head and then looked up with a sheepish smile.

"Now don't beat yourself up. We all made vows. I've had to renounce a few myself. Well, more than a few. But, back to your vow, think about how it would

129

also interfere with your relationship with Jesus –
ironically, the very friend who *did* die for you."

"Ugh! God, I renounce that vow I made not to have
friends anymore and I plead the blood of Jesus over
the strongholds and I renounce any oppressing spirits
that have tormented me and Holy Spirit, please come
and fill that broken place and bless me with friends.
Amen." She looked up at Abigail, "Did I cover it?"

"Amen! You sure did. I think I'm working myself
out of a job here." Abigail beamed with delight.
Nothing thrilled her more than mentoring someone,
watching them take ownership of their choices, and
making the changes necessary to live a full and rich
godly life.

"Am I done?" Loretta asked hopefully.

"Let's ask the Lord if there's anything else
contributing to this life-dominating issue. Whenever I
see a life-dominating issue, I've found that there's
usually more than one vow or event that feeds into it."

"All right. Lord, what else is there?" She quieted
herself for a moment and then looked at Abigail with
surprise.

"What?"

"Simon and Garfunkel. A song that I loved, I mean,
I really loved it. I am a rock. I am an island. Need I go
on? It's all about being alone."

"I remember that one," Abigail said. "Yeah, and
something about my books and poetry are all I need
while I'm safe in my room. Alone."

"So why... oh, never mind. I get it. That song is
nothing but a bunch of vows to be a loner." She
laughed and took charge once more. "God, I did it to
myself again. I renounce all the vows that I sang over

and over and over again that are in that song." She continued her prayer that covered any other songs as well as putting off and putting on things in the spiritual realm.

"How are you feeling now?"

"Great! Tired, but great. I think that was it."

"I'm sensing that, too. Do you want to set up another appointment or play it by ear?"

"I think we can just play it by ear. I'll call you if something comes up, but if all those people at church and work call you, I might not be able to get in."

They laughed together, then finished the session, and hugged briefly before Loretta left. Abigail closed the office and went up to Pastor Spalding's office on the chance that he would have a few minutes for her.

Ginny greeted her in her typical effervescent manner and then got down to business. "Let me check, but I think he's free." She ascertained that it was a good time for him and she beckoned Abigail with a wave of her hand.

Pastor Spalding rose up from his chair and said, "Come in and have a seat." He waved to the set of chairs in front of the desk as he came around it. "What's going on?"

They sat down and Abigail began to fill him in. "I told you that Amy is staying with me. After church Lee and I went to her place to get some clothes and stuff, but it had been burned to the ground."

"Are you kidding?" Pastor Spalding should have known that he would almost always hear something out of the ordinary from this woman. "Would that have been that fire in the trailer park east of here? It was on the news."

"That's the one. She's lost everything except her car. Lee and I met her at the emergency room Saturday night and there was a deputy there who made my hair stand on end. Amy said she thought he was a Satanist, but she didn't know him. She just sensed it. Maybe he was just a jerk. Anyway, Levi and another guy were in the parking lot waiting for her to come out. It's a hunch, but I think they probably torched her place when we went invisible on them and left without them seeing us."

"Went invisible?"

"Yeah, we asked God to make us invisible to them so that we could drive away without them noticing. It was comical. They drove right by us and it seemed like they were looking through us but didn't see us."

"No kidding!"

"No kidding. It was so cool and really boosted Amy's faith."

"So how is she doing?"

"Well, she seems to be holding up all right under the circumstances. I bought her a bunch of clothes that she can't wear yet because she's on bedrest for a while. The doctor thinks that the beating got the bleeding going again and that bedrest ought to do it. But she has nowhere to go right now, and she'll probably lose her job at The Pizza Palace."

"Oh, my goodness," he sympathized. "We have a benevolence fund. If she needs anything else, let Ginny know."

"Thanks, I'll tell Amy. The other thing is that we need more prayer for protection. I did mention that I found out who the Satanist neighbor is, didn't I? And that he took a shot at me and blew out my back door but Earl, my neighbor, saw him and shot his rifle out of his hand. Probably got his hand, too."

"Oh, my!" Pastor Spalding was stunned. "No. You didn't mention any of that!"

"Sorry. So much keeps happening. Anyway, with Amy at the house, I'd like more prayer cover."

"I think that it would be a good idea to send out a prayer request to the Ministerial Alliance and include them and their prayer warriors."

"Thanks; that would be good."

They talked a little longer. Abigail filled him in on more details when he asked. He asked if she and Lee had set a date yet. He seemed pleased that she had some happiness in her life. She was happy before, but there was a deeper sense of contentment in her that was not there before. She and Lee seemed well-suited for each other.

Before long, Abigail left his office and bid Ginny good-bye as well. Friday was still her grocery shopping day. She had expanded her list over the last couple of months because she wanted to be more creative when she and Lee ate together. Now she was pleased to add Amy to the mix. Amy was a picky eater, but she was learning to eat a much wider variety of food. Her previous meal selections were mostly limited to the dollar menus at the local fast-food establishments and an occasional bowl of cereal or leftover pizza that her manager let her take home from time to time.

Abigail pulled up to the house, scanning the property for anything amiss. Seeing nothing, she slipped the handles of the plastic bags around her wrists and lugged them up to the house. Abigail thought Amy might be sleeping so she slipped into the house as quietly as she could. She was surprised to see Amy wandering through the kitchen.

"Amy?" Abigail asked with concern. "Are you all right? You should be in bed."

When Amy turned around, it was obvious that the host had switched into another personality who was startled by Abigail's presence. "Don't hurt me," she whimpered and squatted down in the corner.

"Sweetheart, I won't hurt you. I'm Abigail and you're safe here at my house. Who are you?"

The little one balled her fists up and started crying, "I don't know. I don't know."

Abigail did not want to make her feel trapped in the corner so she put the groceries on the table and sat on a chair. "You're okay. You're not in trouble, but we have to get you back to bed, okay? Do you have to go potty first?"

"I already did and it's bleeding again and I can't find my mommy." The child personality wailed her distress.

Abigail figured that Amy must have used the toilet and the sight of the spotting triggered the presence of this little one who must have been sexually abused to the point of bleeding. She just wanted to pick her up and rock her, but that was impossible given that the child was in Amy's adult body. *God, it's so complicated. Help me help her.*

"Would you like some grapes? I just bought some nice grapes."

"I want my mommy."

"She's not here. I don't know where she is, but I'm taking care of you right now. Can we get you back to bed? That will make the bleeding stop."

"No! Mommy has to make it stop. She's the only one who can make it stop."

"How does she do that?" Abigail was more than curious.

"She kisses it and makes it better. She says if I let the man... um, if he makes it bleed... Mommy fixes it."

Abigail was revolted by the images that came to her mind. *Oh, Lord. Her mother, too? I should expect it but I'm always shocked.* "Can I talk to the big Amy that's in there?"

"Hey," Amy straightened out her cramped legs. "What am I doing down here?"

"Apparently some little kid switched in – maybe you used the toilet and she saw the pad and it triggered her."

Amy struggled to get to her feet. Abigail helped her up and together they walked back to the bedroom. "How about if I make us some lunch and then we do a little session afterward to get some healing for that little girl?"

"Yeah, I guess we'd better. I'm not very hungry, though."

"You have to eat something. It's hard work making a baby. How about if I just make a grilled cheese sandwich with some fruit and veges on the side? I'll cut it into butterflies." Abigail hoped the teasing lilt would get a smile out of Amy.

Amy sighed, "All right."

Abigail put the groceries away and made lunch. When they finished eating, Abigail retrieved her office-

135

in-a-bag from her truck and returned to Amy's room. "Ready?"

"As good a time as any."

They opened with prayer and Head Honcho switched in. He had anticipated Abigail's questions and gave his report. "We're not sure where the little girl came from, but we think she's a straggler from Mayor's sector. I don't know where she was hiding, but she's one of the ones who had to deal with the so-called ordinary abuse from her parents. They'd let men use her and, well, you heard what she said about her mom."

"Thanks. I kind of figured something like that. She must be terrified."

"One of my female officers is with her. She goes hysterical if she even sees a guy so we have them in the back room."

"Good thinking. Do you think she'd talk to me again?"

"I'll ask." Head Honcho disappeared for a blink and then reported, "She'll talk to you if she can bring the guard with her."

"Absolutely. Whatever makes her comfortable."

The little girl appeared to be about four or five years old. She looked furtively around the room and quickly averted her eyes when she saw that Abigail was looking directly at her.

"Hello again," Abigail said softly. "Did you bring your new friend with you?"

Nod.

"I think someone hurt you and I want to make sure that never happens again."

The little girl looked doubtfully at Abigail. It was what she wanted all her life but she was always disappointed. Why hope now?

"I know that your mommy and daddy let some people do bad things to you and your mommy tried to make you feel better, but I think that didn't seem right either. Am I right?"

Nod.

"I'd like you to tell me something. When you looked in my eyes, did they look bad like the bad people's eyes?"

She shook her head slightly and ventured a quick look at Abigail before she looked down at her chest again. She was obviously feeling more vulnerable because she was lying down in a bed and in a strange room with a strange lady.

"That's because I'm not a Satanist like those bad people. I belong to the real God and He doesn't like what happened to you either. Do you think it would be all right if I ask Him to get rid of those scuzzy uglies that have been bothering you? Why don't you see what that lady guard says about the real God and the real Jesus?"

Nod.

"Is it okay for me to ask Him to fix you?"

Nod.

Abigail was relieved that it would not take a lot of negotiation to be able to pray for the little girl. She prayed softly but the effect was powerful as strongholds were demolished and demons were removed, programs were dismantled and body memories were healed, emotional pain was salved and the sting of memories was eliminated. "How do you feel now?"

The change in the little girl was remarkable. She smiled at Abigail and said, "I like you. You're not like my mommy."

"Well, thanks. I like you, too. How are you feeling now?"

"Good. I'm tired." Her attention was drawn to the pictures of Abigail's sons on the wall. "Are you their mommy?"

"Yes, I am."

"Did you make them better, too?"

"I never let anyone touch their private parts that way. Not even me. That's not what mommies and daddies are supposed to do."

"You never did?" The little girl was incredulous. It was all she knew and she thought that all moms and dads did the same with their children.

"Never. Well, I think that your job is all done now. Do you want to go back inside where you came from?"

Nod.

Abigail prayed for her integration as well as for complete healing of any other stragglers who may have had the same or similar issues. She liked to pray big and let God sort out the details. When she was finished, Amy was back in control again.

"Glad that was taken care of. Thanks. Oh, and there were a couple of others that came out of hiding and got integrated, too."

"Very cool and you're welcome. It was your appointment day, after all." They shared a laugh and then Abigail said, "Well, listen now, you get some rest and I'll see what kind of trouble I can find outside while the weather is still nice."

Abigail changed her clothes and went outside. She wanted to finish up some details in the newly remodeled tack room. She also wanted to set up the giant tote box for the chicks in the utility room just in case they hatched out earlier than expected. It should be twenty-one days, but when eggs were gathered over several days, there could be uncertainty. Finishing her tasks, she decided that she ought to make the rounds on the cameras just to be sure. She quickly scanned through them and was relieved that there was no unusual activity. After reinstalling the SD cards, she started making supper.

Lee could not wait to get out of town and back into a rural setting. He finished his chores and looked with satisfaction at the progress of the construction. The insulation and drywall were done. Fixtures were installed. Next week the interior doors and casings, window sills and moldings, cabinets and vanities would be installed. The fireplace was waiting for a mantel. Somewhere in that chaos, the painters would prime the walls. Taking one last look around, he closed and locked the front door.

Abigail heard his two soft toots and felt her pulse quicken. "Lee's here," she called out to Amy. "Supper will be ready in about fifteen minutes."

"Okay." A muffled reply floated out of the back bedroom.

Lee left his mud-caked boots on the front porch, entered the open front door, and embraced Abigail. "Mm. Smells good. What's for supper?"

"A kale-spinach quiche and a salad on the side."

"Sounds good. Will Amy go for it?"

"Not sure. I know she'll eat the salad. Maybe she'll try the quiche." Abigail chuckled, shook her head, and added with exaggerated volume, "I think she thinks eating something that doesn't come with fries is worse than going through a session with me."

"I heard that!" Amy joined in the banter as she was heading back to her bedroom. She was clearly feeling much better. "And I'll try that quiche thing. You'll see."

Amy was served her supper in her room. Bedrest was a challenge especially when trying to eat. Lee and Abigail ate in the dining room so that they could watch the last of the sunset soften the evening sky.

"So, how's the construction going?"

"Right on time. I'm thinking that it'll be ready for moving in by the end of May or the beginning of June."

"I'll bet you'll be so glad to get out of town and hang out with your horses and heifers and other critters."

"I can't wait! But, I'm really looking forward to hanging out with you. There." He paused and took her hand in his as he fished a small box out of his pocket. "Abigail Steele, may I put this ring on your finger?"

"Oh, Lee! It's beautiful. Yes, yes."

"And can we set a date?"

Abigail got up and retrieved her calendar from her office-in-a-bag. Together they eliminated some dates as being too soon and some as too far away, some were on holidays and one fell on the anniversary of Lee's previous marriage and June first was Abigail's birthday. They finally narrowed it down to June twenty-three, June thirty, or July seven. They were leaning toward July seven just because it would be easier for more of their long-distance family and friends to make it.

"Let's check with Pastor Spalding to see if there are any conflicts."

"Good idea," Lee agreed. "Now, do you want something small or big? I already did the big, formal wedding thing but I can go either way."

They talked and planned. At one point Abigail went to her office for a notebook and a couple of folders. "You make your list. I'll make a list and we'll keep them in the invitation folder," she said as she labeled one folder. "I guess that will determine how big we go."

"Don't forget about people from the church."

"And our neighbors, Earl and Jan."

"Charlie Fletcher?"

"Lee Norris!"

11

Monday, April 23

"I'm going to pick up the chicks with Lee. We should be back in about an hour or two."

"Okay. I'll just be back here doing nothing. Calmly."

"That's what you're supposed to do. Call Earl and Jan if you need anything."

"I'll be fine."

Abigail swung by Lee's farm and picked him up. They took the back road past Charlie Fletcher's place west toward Pines. Following the directions that she was given, they had no trouble finding the chicken farm.

"Well, here they are. Those cute little fuzzy things will be laying eggs for you by the end of summer," Wanda said proudly. It was obvious that she loved what she was doing. She mentioned that she sold eggs to help cover the cost of the feed and upkeep, but that she gave a bunch to her church's food pantry, too.

"Oh? What church do you attend?" Abigail was curious.

"It's just a little non-denominational church in Pines."

"I think I've met your pastor at the Ministerial Alliance meetings. What's his name?"

"Richard Morris."

"Yes. I've met him. A big guy with a big laugh."

"That's him. Come to think of it, he mentioned that there were some serious things going down in our county and we've been having special prayer meetings. Something about cults? Some counselor has been telling them all about it."

"That would be me. I'm the pastoral counselor that's been talking to them."

"Well, sweetheart, I believe it. I've seen some pretty suspicious things around here from time to time and there are some people that just plain give me the willies!"

They chatted a bit longer about the spiritual condition of the county and then Abigail gave Wanda sixty dollars for the chicks. Wanda had packed them in a cardboard box which Lee held on his lap on the ride home.

Arriving at Abigail's farm, they came in the back door and opened the box. They were greeted by the chirps of twenty vigorous chicks who were only a little stressed by the changes.

"Oh, come on now," Abigail crooned. "You're in your new home." She carefully scooped the scrambling chicks out of the box and gently released them in the large tote box. It did not take them long to begin to explore the larger box, finding crumbles to eat and water to drink.

"They are cute," Lee said. "It won't be long before they'll be ready for the outdoor coop."

"Yes, I suppose just a couple of weeks. I don't know how much pooper scooping I'll be doing, but it'll be worth it to get fresh eggs. I can't wait." She placed the screen over the box and made sure that the heat lamp was positioned correctly. A number of the chicks huddled under the lamp and started to settle down for a nap.

Lee and Abigail ate a quick lunch and then headed back to Lee's farm. They wandered through the house avoiding the construction workers who were installing the flooring and the electricians who were putting the finishing touches on their work. Plumbers were due to come by the end of the next week. It would not be long before the carpet would be installed and the house would be ready for final inspection. Lee could hardly wait to get that certificate of occupancy.

They talked about color schemes for the various rooms and furniture that they would like to get eventually. They agreed that they had enough basic furniture to live comfortably for now with the exception of a bed. His twin would go into the guest room and her full-sized bed had too many memories attached to it so that could go into the other room upstairs.

"Yeah, let's get a nice big cushy bed for these aching old bods."

"I like the way you're thinkin'."

Ariel Miller could not know that she and her mother were being observed, stalked. They were just having a little after school mother-daughter shopping trip at the local department store to pick up some more socks. Cassie could not keep up with the latest most favorite characters that dictated which socks were in and which were definitely out. Dora or Minnie Mouse, Sponge Bob or Hello Kitty? Second graders were already conscious of such critical matters.

"Do you want the anklets or the longer ones?" Cassie was amused at the serious frown on Ariel's face as she made her selections. She jealously guarded the innocence of her child's world especially after the warnings from Jason and Pastor Spalding. She knew that evil lurked around them, but she did not know just how close it could come.

"I think I want the tall ones," Ariel replied exaggerating the lisp that her recently lost front tooth made.

"Those are on the other side." Cassie turned and led the way around the display case.

At that moment, a woman stepped close to Ariel and took her hand. "Come with me and don't say a word."

The stunned little girl was half walked and half dragged along with the authoritarian woman and then began to panic and look for her mother. "Mommy!"

"Don't you talk back to me!" the woman scolded. To the other shoppers who looked her way she said, "They never want to listen, do they?" and gave the kind of smile that many a parent has smiled when a child was disobedient in public. They nodded sympathetically and went about shopping as she hustled the child down the next aisle. It was just another beleaguered mom with a bratty kid.

"Ouch! You're hurting me!" Ariel struggled to get away.

At the same time, Cassie realized that Ariel was not right behind her and heard the distant cry. "Ariel! Ariel, where are you?" Panic seized her as she looked in the immediate area for Ariel. *Oh, Lord, help! Where is my little girl?*

Suddenly, she realized that Ariel might well have been abducted. She dashed toward the front doors of the store yelling, "Someone has kidnapped my little girl! Help!"

The manager heard the commotion and met her in front of the service desk near the outside doors. "Ma'am, did you say someone kidnapped your little girl?"

"Yes, please help me. They might still be in the building."

The quick-thinking manager immediately instructed his assistant to lock all the doors. He hurriedly got on the loud-speaker and made the urgent announcement. "Attention, shoppers. We have a missing little girl. She may have been abducted. We are locking all the doors." He looked questioningly at Cassie and thrust the microphone at her. "How old? What does she look like?"

"She's seven. Long blonde hair. Blue eyes. She's wearing a red jacket and blue jeans," Cassie blurted out, amazed that she remembered any details at all. "She just lost a front tooth. She's almost four feet tall and she weighs about fifty pounds."

The announcement caused a stir in the normally quiet department store. The woman who had taken Ariel was already in the restroom with her. She had quickly injected her with a mild sedative, laid her on the diaper changing table in the handicapped stall, and was in the process of cutting off the child's hair. Hearing the announcement, she abandoned Ariel and furtively wandered back into the layaway department. From there she made it out the employee's entrance before the door was locked. Walking away from the building, she casually strolled to her truck, slipped the wig from under her hood and tossed it behind the seat.

The sheriff had been called and the store remained on lockdown until three deputies arrived. When the situation had been explained, they asked all the shoppers to assemble in the front of the store. One stayed with the crowd and wrote down their names on a report sheet. He asked if anyone had seen anything suspicious. No one was able to recall anything unusual.

The other two officers began a systematic search starting with the dressing rooms and restrooms in the back of the store. That was where the groggy little Ariel was found.

Speaking into the communication device on his collar, the officer let his partners know that he had found the little girl. She appeared to be unharmed so he scooped her up in his arms and walked out to the front of the store with her.

"Ariel! Oh, Ariel!" Cassie ran forward weeping with relief. The officer handed her over to Cassie and that was when they all noticed that half of her shoulder length hair had been cropped to ear length.

Cassie had used her cell phone to call Paul. He left work and was part of the crowd that had begun to gather at the front door of the store. Pounding on the door and yelling to be let in, Paul attracted the attention of the manager and the officers. One was afraid that the window would be broken, the others were edgy enough to arrest him on any pretext.

"That's my husband! That's my husband! Please let him in!"

The manager got the nod from the officer and let the desperate father in. Rushing to Cassie and Ariel, Paul made a quick decision. "We need to get her to a doctor right away."

"We've already called the rescue squad. It should be here any minute."

Paul did not want to wait, but realized that it would be the best way. The crowd parted for the ambulance crew and soon Ariel was on her way to the hospital with her mother by her side. Paul followed in his car. He was angry and scared. How could this happen in broad daylight? Was this the work of the cult? Was this the threat that Jason and Pastor Spalding had warned them about?

Cassie was beside herself with guilt. "I thought she was right behind me. I mean, it wasn't three seconds and she was gone!"

Paul and Cassie were glued to either side of Ariel's gurney in the emergency room. Their sweet little girl was dozing but would startle awake and take her breath in little shudders if her grip on their hands loosened. "We're here, honey, we're here. You're safe now."

The medical staff had been apprised of the circumstances and did not argue with these protective parents who would not leave Ariel's side for a second. They just worked around the parents as they drew blood and checked reflexes. After what seemed like hours, the doctor came in and checked Ariel again.

"She was given a tranquillizer." He looked more carefully at her arms and legs. He took her right arm and pointed to a small puncture wound that was beginning to bruise. "I would guess that this is where it was injected."

"My poor baby! Can we take her home?"

"Yes, she should recover completely from the physical effects within a couple of hours. She's already getting more alert and the effects on the central nervous system will disappear pretty soon. That's why she's having a little trouble with her strength and coordination."

"Thank you, doctor," Cassie breathed her relief.

"She should be okay, but if you notice anything unusual, follow up with her pediatrician."

"We will."

"Let me give you a referral to a pediatric psychologist. She might need some help with the trauma."

They accepted the referral, but determined that they would call Pastor Spalding and Abigail Steele when they got home.

––––––––––––––––

Abigail spent all of Tuesday hovering around the house like a mother hen. There were twenty yellow picking, scratching, chirping fuzz balls and Amy to look after. It was amusing to watch the miniature chickens scratch in the shavings and straw. They danced the ancient dance that their predecessors engaged in without having it modeled. Scratch, scratch, back up a step, peck.

Tomorrow was St. Mark's Eve and Amy was getting restless. The parts of her that were programmed on previous St. Mark's Eve rituals were trying to hide from the internal cult-loyal persecutors. They did not know that Apollyon's level was sealed off for now. They just knew that they had a despicable job to do

149

and then they could hide away until they were needed next year.

Year after year went by, but they could not keep track of what year it was. For them, it was perpetually the same year. They never aged. They remained at whatever age they were programmed to be. The endless hellish life that they knew was dark and dismal. It got worse with each time they were called out to gratify the fiendish desires of the Satanists. They cowered in fetal positions hoping to die.

That was how Abigail found Amy when she checked in with her about lunch. "Amy?" she called softly.

Amy wriggled deeper under the covers.

Perceiving the switch, she said softly, "I'm Abigail and you're safe here in my house." Abigail tried to connect on some level with what she presumed was a terrified child personality. "I'd like to talk to you if that's okay."

The little one had only communicated with outside people at rituals. It was never a good experience. The internal communication with her handlers was not much better. She was confused. The lady sounded nice but she had been tricked before. She was warm and comfortable, it was light and not dark, but it could be another hoax. But maybe it wasn't. What did she have to lose?

"I'm going to talk just a little bit because I want you to think about some things. Okay?"

There was no response so Abigail took it as consent. She went through her usual talk about how the little one was a part of Amy and that Abigail knew that something bad had happened and guessed that it had something to do with St. Mark's Eve. When she mentioned those words, the little one shuddered.

"I want to help you not to have to go with those mean people anymore. But I need for you to be real brave and help me understand some more stuff."

The little one stirred and soon fingers appeared at the edge of the blankets pulling them down enough so that she could peek out, but not enough to make eye contact with Abigail.

"Can you tell me your name? That sometimes helps me understand and then I can help you even better." The child personality decided to take the plunge. "Wraithe," she quavered valiantly.

"That's an interesting name. Do you know why they call you that?" Abigail was racking her brain and praying for insight. Wraith. Ghost. What was St. Mark's Eve historically?

"It's 'cause we see them and tell the bad people who's gonna die."

"What do you mean?"

The little one finally pushed the covers back far enough that she could peek around the room and see Abigail as well. Unfortunately, she could also see the stairwell behind Abigail and that put her into a panic. "The stairs! The stairs! I don't want to see him!" she began to wail and put the covers back over her head.

Abigail sighed. *One step forward, ten steps backward.* "What's the matter with the stairs? There's nothing there. I'm going to close the door. It's okay." *Lord, what is going on?*

Suddenly, Head Honcho switched in and flung back the covers. "How's a body supposed to breathe around here?" he demanded gruffly.

151

"I'm sure glad to see you. Do you have any idea of what's going on with that one?"

"Yes," he heaved and tried to assume a military posture while lying supine on the bed. "She's called Wraithe. It has something to do with being able to see the ghost of someone who is going to die this year."

"Really?" Abigail was intrigued. She knew that there would be a ritual, but did not always know the history of some of the religious festivals and holy days. "Fill me in."

"It goes back to some superstition that if you see the ghost of someone on the stairs of the church, then you will know who will die within the year. Apparently, if you see them early in the day, they'll die early in the year. Late in the day means later in the year."

"Interesting." Abigail's mind raced to connect the dots and figure out some of the implications. "So why is she so afraid to see someone? I mean, apart from being scared of a ghost."

"Last year she picked Mastiff. He died. They didn't care that much, but he was a master. Another one saw Billy. That didn't matter, either. They just shoot the messenger, that's all."

"So, if she sees someone who doesn't want their ghost to be seen on the stairs, and they have enough clout, she's in trouble."

"Precisely."

"So, I would guess that tonight's ritual will be at a church that has stairs."

"Yes."

"That could be just about any church," Abigail mused.

"But more likely a fancy liturgical type church like they had in the olden days in Great Britain."

"Does she have a protector? Are there more than one with this assignment?"

"Yes, they're from Achan's level. Level two. I'll get her leader."

Within moments, an older personality emerged and made brief eye contact with Abigail before scanning her surroundings.

"Do you know who I am?"

"Yeah, I've been listening," she replied warily. "What do you want?"

"Just want to keep you and the others from having to go to the ritual tonight. I know the little one got triggered by the sight of my stairs. Did she see someone's ghost?"

Surprised by the direct exchange, she answered almost as a reflex. "Yeah. She saw some guy. His hand was bandaged and he had long, braided hair and a beard."

"I think I know who that is. He tried to kill me last month."

More surprise registered on her face as she had been trying to figure out if Abigail was friend or foe. *If he was trying to kill her, too...* "What can you do?"

"Were you listening when I was explaining about programming and demons?"

"Yeah."

"Are you interested in getting free of that stuff? We can get your assignment cancelled and you can all get healed and then go back inside where you originally came from. Then they won't be able to access you."

153

Lynda L. Irons

"We'd like that. But first I have to tell you something."

"Sure."

"Another one of the little ones saw someone else." She hesitated and then hastily added, "It was a really old man. He was hunchbacked like really old people get and just all shriveled up."

"Do you know who that might be?"

"Not really. I mean, he was a wrinkled old man wearing a black robe that was too big for him. And whoever he is, well, he's really scary."

"Interesting," Abigail responded. She tucked the information away and turned her attention to praying for them. She asked the Lord to release them and heal them physically, emotionally, mentally, and spiritually. Finally, she prayed for them to be integrated and then Amy was back in executive control again.

"Sure, I'm hungry! I'd love a grilled cheese sandwich," she quipped, acting as if nothing out of the ordinary had occurred since Abigail came in earlier asking about lunch.

"Coming right up," Abigail went along with Amy's humor and made some lunch. Abigail joined Amy in her room and they chatted about the chicks and the weather, Amy's pregnancy and her burned-down trailer.

When they finished, Abigail gathered the plates and napkins and said, "I'll catch you later. I need to make some phone calls and then I'll probably putter around the house."

"I'll be here just calmly reading and napping. Did I mention calmly?"

"I know it's hard, but it'll be worth it."

Abigail did a little research about St. Mark's Eve and the superstitions surrounding it. Then she called Pastor Spalding and told him about the probability that tonight's ritual would be in a church that had stairs leading up to the front doors.

"That could be any church, including ours!"

"Yes, but according to the tradition which was in Britain, I think it would be more likely to be at a more liturgical church – say Lutheran or Episcopal or Presbyterian maybe."

"That would narrow it down some. In our area, we have Mike Griffin's church," he was thinking aloud. "Hm. He has one Satanist there that we know of, that would be a possibility."

"I don't know what the front of the church looks like. We went in the back door."

"Actually, the outside doors are on ground level, but the narthex has stairs leading to the basement off to one side and a really wide set of stairs that lead up to the sanctuary level. I'm thinking about fifteen steps."

"That could be a match. But then, they may have it in some other church in the region, too."

"Well, I think that it would be a good idea for me to call the Ministerial Alliance members and have them and their prayer teams pray about this."

"I was going to suggest that. I think we need to be proactive rather than reactive."

"Amen to that."

After they hung up, Pastor Spalding began calling the pastors. There were ten of them altogether in the last Ministerial Alliance meeting. They all agreed to pray and to have their prayer teams pray as well. This was going to stretch some of them, but many others were open to spiritual warfare.

Mike Griffin asked his prayer team to assemble at the church at nine o'clock that night if they were able. He was not going to take a chance that his church would be desecrated again. He was somewhat worried about the possibility of encountering Satanists, but soothed himself by meditating on some of the Psalms. *The Lord is my light and my salvation. The Lord is my strength and my shield. Whom shall I fear?*

All night long the prayers of the saints rose as sweet-smelling incense. This was not the time for timid prayers. This was the time for spiritual warfare. King David had prayed his share of vicious prayers against his enemies who unjustly caused him harm. These saints warred by repeating God's inspired words back to Him in prayer.

Rev. Griffin paced the front of his church with his Bible open to the Psalms and paraphrased the sixty-fourth chapter. "Hear my voice, Oh God, in my complaint. Preserve our lives from the dread of the enemy. Hide us from the secret counsel of evildoers, from the tumult of those who do iniquity, who have sharpened their tongue like a sword, they aimed bitter speech as their arrow, to shoot from concealment at the blameless. They hold fast to an evil purpose, they devise injustices, saying, 'Who can see them?' God You see them and hear them. Shoot at them and make them stumble so all men can see that You are God."

Another took up the warfare using verses from Isaiah twenty-nine, "Your Word says that the multitude of our enemies shall become like fine dust and the multitude of the ruthless ones will become like the chaff which blows away and it shall happen instantly, suddenly. Oh, Lord, we pray for mercy on those misguided Satanists, but if they will not turn to you, manifest Your Word like it says here in Isaiah, that the Lord of hosts will punish them with thunder and earthquake and loud noise, with whirlwind and tempest and the flame of a consuming fire."

The small group that had gathered at the church continued to pray for just over an hour. A few minutes after ten, Rev. Griffin felt peace and noticed that the others had quieted as well. He thanked those who had joined him and they shrugged into their jackets and made their way out to the parking lot. They hurried to their cars in the driving rain.

All night long demons cursed while their likeminded human agents gathered at St. Mark's, the largest Episcopalian church in the region. Father Frank Littleton had risen quickly in the ranks. His bishop promoted him and he eagerly left the tiny wooden parish church in a rural area of the state and advanced until he arrived at the ornate cathedral-like stone church in the large metropolitan area.

Both he and Dr. Alexander Kammad, a.k.a. Luxor, arrived early for this ritual. No one would have questioned a meeting between the father and one of his leaders. They were equally intent on rising in the ranks of both the kingdom of God and the kingdom of Satan.

Dr. Kammad, a psychiatrist, added creative dimensions to their rituals by virtue of his knowledge of how both the brain and the mind work. His great-grandfather was born in Egypt and immigrated to

America many years ago. The Egyptian mysticism that came down his family lines was another attribute that added to Luxor's prestige and value within the cult.

Prinz would be here tonight. It was rumored that Xerxes would show up as well. Everything must be perfect. Flawless. They could hear the sound of the rising winds, but they did not know that a tornado watch had just been issued for their area. It was somewhat unusual for this time of year, but not unheard of.

Participants arrived at discrete intervals and soon the church was filled with blood-thirsty, power-seeking, demon-driven Satanists. By ten o'clock they were fully engaging in the festivities. In the frenzied orgy, no one seemed to notice the sudden increase in the howl of the winds and the sound of sheets of rain that pelted the steep roof until the tip of the tornado ripped into the structure. Peeling away layers of roofing like they were pages of a magazine, splintering the aged plywood, and launching roof trusses like they were mere toothpicks, the twister completely exposed the sanctuary and all its cowering inhabitants.

Chandeliers, anchored to the rafters, rocked and spun like merry-go-rounds. Debris showered onto the crowd that instantaneously stopped their activities and momentarily froze in terror. Arms lifted at awkward angles to ward off the swirling debris that was hurtled at them, they fell over pews and other people in a desperate attempt to flee to safety. Cries sounded out as jagged pieces of the roof and ceiling found their targets.

One of the wounded lay unconscious under a large sheet of roofing that easily weighed five times more than the man. He was bleeding from a laceration on his chin where it met with the unyielding floor. He was bleeding from a line of puncture wounds that came from the nails that stuck out of the wood and impaled his crushed body. The acrid stench of smoke further motivated the revelers to flee the building.

Sirens sounded in the distance as the rain continued to pour, drenching the carpets and soaking the upholstery. Candles were quenched by wind or rain, but the electrical fire smoldered unseen between the walls.

12

Friday, April 27

"Chirp, chirp, chirp!" Abigail fussed over her growing chicks. They swarmed around their box like a school of fish in an aquarium as they moved away from Abigail. "Good instincts!" She praised them for trying to find shelter from overhead predators. "But, I'm your friend." She lifted the edge of the screen and slowly put her hand into their little world to retrieve the feeder. She was rewarded with the frenzied retreat of the panicked chicks. They headed to the heat lamp. "Okay, I guess you think that's your mama. Just don't peck the hand that feeds you." She continued to carry on a conversation while she refilled the feeder and the water dispenser and replaced them.

"Okay, okay," she shushed them. "I'll leave you alone."

Amy giggled from her vantage point behind her. "I see you're busy counseling your little peepsters."

"Oh, yes, that I am." Abigail joined in the levity before frowning, "Don't you have an appointment with your bed?"

"Hey, I gotta use the bathroom sometimes. Someone keeps feeding me."

"How are you feeling today?"

"Pretty good. I haven't had the queasies for a couple of days, so that helps."

"Good. Well, I'm going to be heading over to my office pretty soon. I've got a couple of appointments scheduled. I'll stop by the store on my way home. You need anything? Got a taste for anything?"

"No, can't think of anything. You've been feeding me real well." Amy hung her head and added awkwardly, "I really appreciate everything you're doing for me."

"You're welcome. You just keep working on that beautiful baby and God is going to make a way for both of you. You'll see."

"I wish I had your faith," Amy muttered under her breath as she continued to the bathroom.

Abigail put a sandwich together for Amy and left it in the refrigerator and then brought her some fruit, granola bars, and a bottle of water. "The sandwich is in the fridge. Call Earl and Jan if you need anything. I'll be back in a couple hours."

"Thanks, but I'll be fine. You worry too much."

Carrie Sue was waiting at the church. They entered and set up the office. Abigail was expecting another client today as well. After chatting about mundane things and getting caught up on her mother's antics, they opened with prayer.

"I'm thinking about my shrink for some reason."

"In what way?"

"His office keeps calling and insisting that I need to be admitted to the hospital for tests and bloodwork. I don't get it."

"That seems a bit unusual, but then, I'm not a psychiatrist. How long have you been seeing him?"

"About as long as I can remember," Carrie Sue said sadly. "My parents insisted that I see him. He put me in the hospital a couple times a year until recently."

"Maybe he's trying to drum up business."

161

"Not likely. He's from the big city and his waiting room is always crowded. Ever heard of him? Doctor Alexander Kammad." Carrie Sue involuntarily shivered at the mention of his name.

"No. Doesn't sound familiar." Abigail noticed the reaction and asked, "So what did you feel just then?"

"I don't know. I just got a creepy feeling and I don't know where that came from."

Abigail sighed and smiled, "I know you don't want to hear this, but it might be that we have tapped into one of your hidden stragglers. We haven't talked about Doctor Alexander Kammad yet." Abigail intentionally repeated the man's full name to see if there was another reaction.

Carrie Sue jolted this time. "I guess we're on to something."

"I guess that's why God had you thinking about your shrink today. Let's pray and ask the Lord to bring out anyone that might know about the doctor."

"Okay. God, You know I'm disappointed that there are still some stragglers, but they're a part of me and I want to help them. Please give them the courage to come out and talk. Amen."

"Amen." Abigail paused for a moment watching Carrie Sue for any tell-tale signs of switching. She did not notice anything and asked, "What are you sensing?"

Carrie Sue kept her eyes closed and reported, "It's dark inside, but I'm getting the feeling that there are a bunch of … I'm not sure how to say it… a bunch of really disturbed parts in here. They're scared… maybe paranoid might be a better word." Carrie Sue's forehead was creased with wrinkles as she focused on the internal world. "It's like they're all in a psych ward, a rubber room. They can't think straight."

"That would make sense if they were subjected to some satanic psychiatrist. I've had other counselees who told me that they were put in the psych ward a couple times a year and ended in some secret place where they were heavily medicated and some of them even had operations."

"Operations?" Carrie Sue said it like it was bringing back memories or maybe it was something that happened to someone else or maybe she read about it or saw it in a movie.

"Yeah, it was weird," Abigail continued. "They had scars in weird places. One of them had a chip implanted in front of her ear and she was told that they could hear everything she heard and they would monitor her. Another one had all her teeth yanked. I mean, when she was young! It seems like every organ that could be removed without killing them was removed."

Suddenly Carrie Sue winced and clasped her hands on top of her head. "No, no, no," she wailed. "Ow."

Body memories or another personality. "What's going on? Is this still you, Carrie Sue?"

Her hands came down and she answered, "It's me, but I just got a sharp pain on the top of my head."

"It's probably a body memory from the ones that the doctor worked on."

"I'd say so. I don't see anyone, but I get the feeling that there's a bunch of them. What do we do about it?"

"Let's pray, assuming there was some kind of surgery and then see what happens."

"Yeah, hurry! My head's killing me."

"Lord, we plead the blood of Jesus the Christ and the balm of Gilead over every part of Carrie Sue that was subjected to any kind of surgical procedure, especially on her head, and ask that You would remove or dissolve or neutralize anything that they implanted or injected or introjected into her, including drugs and anesthesia. We plead Your blood over the words that were spoken over her and ask that You would render them null and void. We also ask that You would demolish all strongholds associated with whatever they said or did. Release from body memories and all emotional pain. And Lord, would you restore anything that was removed or ruined or scrambled in their mind or brain and align it according to the way that You designed for her to function – whole, healed, and delivered from all demonic oppressors that have been assigned to these particular personalities. Fill them with Your Holy Spirit, blessings, truth, and the mind of Christ, amen."

"Whew!" Carrie Sue exclaimed as she sat back up without pain. "Thanks; that took care of a lot!"

"Can you tell how they're doing now?"

"Yeah. They can think straight. Some of them are in strait jackets. Some of them are tied down on beds."

"Let's pray some more. Lord, You said that You have come to set the captives free. We ask that You would free each one of these captives and recompense them for the years that the locusts have eaten, amen."

"Amen!" Carrie Sue happily repeated. "They're pretty happy now."

"Is there anything else we need to pray about, or can they be integrated?"

After Carrie Sue checked, she reported, "It's all good. Pray 'em in!"

They prayed and Carrie Sue reported that she felt them come in. "I feel more clear-headed. There's no telling what they did to me in that hospital. And it just makes me wonder how much of those meds I really need to take."

"What are you on?"

"Anti-depressants, anti-anxiety, and something to help me sleep at night. And something else I can't pronounce and don't know what it's for. I think I'll just quit taking them."

"Whoa! Not a good idea. I agree that you probably don't need them anymore either, but if you go cold-turkey on some of those meds, you can have a pretty severe reaction."

"What should I do? I'm not going back to Dr. Kammad, that's for sure."

"Do you have a family doctor?"

"Nope. But I've been on lots of these meds most of my life. I know how they drop the dose gradually. I think I can do that on my own. I'll cut the pills in half for a week and then quarter them. I'll be all right."

"I'm not a doctor, and certainly not a shrink. Promise me that you'll see a doctor if you have any reactions. Let me give you the name of my doctor. He's a Christian. And my best friend sees his partner for her family."

"I promise." Carrie Sue accepted the referral and they closed their session.

Abigail was curious to see if Pastor Spalding had gotten any feedback from anyone in the Ministerial Alliance. She locked up her office area and went up to the church office. Ginny greeted her and told her that Pastor Spalding was probably eating his lunch. She checked and then motioned for Abigail to enter the Pastor's study.

"Mm," Pastor Spalding chewed and swallowed quickly, "come in and have a seat." He indicated the chair in front of his desk. "I hope you don't mind me eating my lunch. I need to go meet with the Berryman's today."

"Is Max all right?" Abigail assumed it was about Max.

"Yes, yes he is. I think our prayers are being answered. Apparently, he had some kind of experience Tuesday night and he's willing to talk about it. I sure wish you could come with me, but I don't want to push it. I think it's a miracle that he'd talk to me. But then, maybe it's Ted and Barb's idea and he's just going along with it."

"Either way, it's another chance that he can hear truth. I will definitely be praying for you, but I've got Ariel coming in a little bit."

"Oh, that's right. I'll be praying for you, too. What brings you up here today? Is everything going all right?"

"Yeah, pretty good. Amy's pregnancy seems to be stable for now and we'll just figure out her housing and job and other stuff when the time comes. She can just stay with me as long as she needs to."

"Good, good," Pastor Spalding replied. "What can I do for you today?"

"I was wondering if you had gotten any feedback from any of the prayer groups on Tuesday."

"No, but Mike Griffin called to say that his group was powerful and they felt like something broke in the heavenly places. His custodian, Greg, found no evidence of a ritual at their church."

"That's good."

"But, he did say that the – get this: St. Mark's Episcopal Church in the capital got hit by a tornado. Ripped the roof right off."

"No kidding! I hadn't heard about a tornado, I just knew we had a doozy of a spring storm."

"Apparently, there were a number of injuries because when it hit at – get this: just after ten o'clock, there were a bunch of people in there having some kind of special St. Mark's Eve service. At least that's what Father Littleton told the press."

"Very interesting," Abigail nodded her head. "I'll bet that's where the ritual was."

"Mike said that they were praying all kinds of warfare scriptures and then just after ten, they all quieted and felt like they were done. So, they went home."

"Yes!" Abigail pumped her fist victoriously. "I mean, I hate that anyone got hurt, but if it's an unrepentant Satanist, this might be God's way of taking them out of the game."

"True."

"Well, thanks for the info. That makes my day. I can't wait for the next meeting."

"A week from Monday."

They finished their conversation and then Pastor Spalding finished his lunch. Abigail went back to her office to wait for the Miller family while Pastor Spalding drove to the Berryman's residence.

167

Parking in the driveway, walking up to the front door, Pastor Spalding breathed a prayer for favor with Max. The doorbell had not finished its chiming before Barbara swung the door open.

"Come in, Pastor," she said graciously. "Everyone's in the living room. Would you like a cup of coffee?"

"Thank you. I'd love a cup of coffee if it's no bother."

Max was clearly nervous and looked furtively around the room. He avoided making direct eye contact with anyone.

Pastor Spalding paid no attention to Max's discomfort and treated him as if he was his best friend. Walking over to the couch, he extended his arm and shook Max's hand. "Good to see you, son. You look better every time I see you. How are you feeling these days?"

"Uh, thank you, sir," Max glanced at his father. Apparently, he was under strict orders to be amiable. "I'm getting around without the cane. Still need the stupid brace. I can drive again."

Apparently, Ted had provided his son with yet another vehicle. This time, however, it was not a powerful, top-of-the-line muscle truck. It was a white mid-sized truck with a six-cylinder automatic. And this time, it had strings attached. Max would work at the shop and make monthly payments to his father until it was paid off. Quite a step down for Max.

"Wonderful! I'm glad to hear it. That's progress."

"Yeah, progress," Max agreed with an edge of sarcasm as he directed a resentful glance at his father.

"What else is going on?" Pastor Spalding wanted Max to bring the subject up.

Max looked at him and then at his parents. Huffing a deep sigh, he plunged into it. "I was out for a drive Tuesday night. I, I mean," he stopped and looked at his father who nodded for him to go on. "I was going to go to the capital for um, for a meeting that I wasn't sure I really wanted to go to... and... um, well, I just kind of threw up a prayer and told God that if He could take me back that He'd have to do something to stop me from getting there."

"Go on," Pastor Spalding encouraged him. *Oh, Lord, let this be going where I hope it's going!*

"The weather was crazy, you know? And I was almost there and was getting blown all over the road. I don't know if I was scared because it reminded me of the accident or what, but I pulled over and right in front of me, a huge tree fell down over the road."

"Whoa!"

"I mean, if I hadn't pulled over, I would have been under that tree. I think this time I wouldn't have lived to tell about it."

"You might be right. Sounds like the Lord answered your prayer."

"Yeah. I mean, I just sat there shaking like crazy for a while. Then I said, 'Thank You, God' and I got real calm. I mean, like spooky calm, so I turned around and came home."

"Out of curiosity, do you happen to remember what time that was?"

Max thought for a moment and then said, "Yeah, it was about ten o'clock. That's when the meeting was supposed to start but I was running late."

"Interesting."

Lynda L. Irons

Ted was puzzled by the pastor's question. "Why is that interesting?"

"From what I understand, that was about the time that the tornado hit the Episcopal Church and the same time that some of the local prayer meetings about St. Mark's Eve were finishing."

Ted was even more puzzled but he did not pursue it. He just wanted Max to get help.

Max did not say anything so Pastor Spalding pursued the conversation. "Do you believe that God can take you back?"

"Yeah, I think so, but I'm not real sure. I guess that's what's got me so crazy these days. I mean, I think that tree blocking the road was Him saying that He could, but I don't know how."

"Let me see if I can help you with that," Pastor Spalding said as he pulled out his pocket New Testament. Turning to Ephesians two, he started to paraphrase some of the verses. "Max, it says here that we are saved by grace through faith and even that faith isn't of ourselves, it's the free gift of God. It says that it's not of works. In other words, we don't have to be good enough to be saved, we just have to accept the faith that the grace is there for us. In verse ten, it says that we will walk in good works that God prepared beforehand for us to walk in. The good news is that the grace comes first and then good works flow out of that. We get it turned around and think that we have to be good enough, like we have to do good works and to stop smoking and cussing and all that first." He paused and looked at Max to see if he was following.

"Max, I baptized you about... what? Ten or twelve years ago?"

170

"Yeah. I was thirteen or fourteen."

"You said that you got saved at that time. Were you just saying that and getting baptized because your buddies were? Or did you truly confess your sin nature and all your sins and receive that free gift of salvation?"

"I, I really meant it back then," Max said slowly. His brows furrowed and he winced as if he had been kicked in the ribs.

"So, you think that somehow you lost your salvation along the way?"

"Something like that."

"Do you think you would feel better about your situation if you just kind of started over and confessed everything to God?" he asked gently and continued. "You remember I John 1:9 don't you? If we confess our sins, He is faithful and just to forgive us and cleanse us from all unrighteousness. Right?"

"Yeah, I remember."

"All unrighteousness, not just some of it. All unrighteousness. Not just petty things. Big things, too."

Max was clearly uneasy. He looked at his parents and then back to Pastor Spalding.

"Max, dear, would you feel better if your father and I gave you privacy with Pastor Spalding?"

"Uh, yeah," he said, and barely audibly he added, "Sorry."

Ted and Barbara stood and walked out of the living room together leaving Max and Pastor Spalding.

"Where would you like to start?"

171

"I think I need to tell you what I've done." He paused and hung his head before adding, "It's bad. It's really bad."

"I think I have a pretty good idea of what you've gotten mixed up in but I guarantee you that it can all be forgiven. Now there may be some consequences, but forgiveness is a guarantee. Do you want to tell me or do you want to just go straight to the throne of grace and dump it there?"

"I, I'm not sure. I think maybe I need to talk about it some first."

"I'm listening. And Max, I won't think any less of you no matter what you tell me."

Max puffed out his cheeks as he let out a long breath through barely parted lips. "Okay, I might as well tell you everything. Well, at least the big stuff. You and that lady were right about me getting suckered in by Levi when we were in high school. He got me all the booze and sex I wanted. Later he supplied me with marijuana and then pills." He paused and then cleared his throat as he noted the irony, "Humph. Now I get pills from the doctor and I don't even want 'em."

Not wanting to rush Max, but hoping to give him a lead, Pastor Spalding asked directly, "So what did you do that convinced you that God would turn His back on you?"

"At the end ... of the, um, ritual... they said I was going to be honored with a powerful name and, um, if I ... well it came with ..." Max winced again.

"What is it, son?"

"Demons," he blurted out and was rewarded with another painful jab.

"They don't want to lose you, Max. Mrs. Steele knows a lot more about this kind of thing, but I do know that since you belong to Jesus, they are trespassing. You have the right to renounce them."

"I don't know how."

"Would you be willing to meet with Mrs. Steele? She's offered to help you. I'll be there, too."

"Yeah, yeah, I'd like that. If you're sure."

"Let me call her right now and see what her schedule looks like."

Max had his arms wrapped around his belly and sat with his chin on his chest. "Sure."

"Hello? Abigail?"

"Oh, hello Pastor." Abigail rarely got a call on her cell phone but she managed to answer before it went to voice mail.

"Listen, I'm here with Max and he would like to meet with you and me and see if we can get some of this ritual monkey off his back. When are you available?"

"Would Monday morning be okay? Say ten o'clock?"

"Works for me. Let me double check with Max." He relayed the message to Max and got a nod. "It works for Max, too. Any parting words of wisdom?"

"Yes. Is he under attack right now?"

"He's been wincing, but I don't know if it's his injury or demonic pay-backs. Let me put you on speaker." Pushing an icon on his phone, Pastor Spalding announced, "Okay, you're on speaker."

"Max, I'll be direct if that's okay. Are you feeling pain from the demons?"

"Yeah, I think so."

173

Lynda L. Irons

"Okay then, let me pray and have you and Pastor pray in agreement so that you can have an easier weekend."

"Please," he grunted.

"Lord Jesus, Max is Your child by his own confession. We ask that You would cover him from the top of his head to the soles of his feet with the cleansing blood of Jesus the Christ and separate everything of the enemy's kingdom from him right now and set them aside so that they can't agitate in any way. Place Max in the cleft of Your rock and surround him with Your warring angels. Lord, we know that these demons have claimed a so-called legal right to harass him, but we are asking for Your merciful protection so that Max is safe from attack until we can deal with the issues. We pray this in Your name, amen."

"Amen! Lord, I agree and ask that you keep this whole household safe – especially this weekend."

"Amen," Max ventured into a foreign area with less enthusiasm than Pastor Spalding and Abigail, but he had more hope. Or perhaps it was desperation.

Oh, how the demons howled! No! No! No! They could not lose another one to the Great Enemy. Soaring and shrieking, cursing and accusing, they swore vengeance on the whole lot of them. The upper level celestial beings were beginning to notice and that was never good because what they noticed, Satan eventually noticed. They did not need any more painful retribution than what they were already experiencing. They were further exasperated because their inside agents had been bound by that damnable woman.

Abigail hung up and pumped her fist again. "Yes! Thank you, Lord!"

Within a few minutes, the Miller family ventured into the waiting room. "Hello?"

Abigail quickly came around her desk and greeted them with a warm smile and her clipboard. "You found me. Come in. I hope you don't mind filling out this paper first," she said as she handed it to Cassie.

Ariel was standing behind her mother. Clinging. Not wanting to press too quickly, Abigail turned her attention to Jason. "It's good to see you again. How's it been going?"

"Great. I'm even more determined to get to Bible College so I'm working at The Taco Tower and trying to save up some money. Right now, I'm taking some classes on line and I'll do that this summer, too. I've been accepted already and will start full time in the fall."

"Excellent! We definitely need more people in the ministry."

Cassie finished the paperwork and handed the clipboard to Abigail.

"Do you all want to come in? I think we can squeeze in, but you'll have to grab an extra chair."

Once they were settled with Ariel sitting on Cassie's lap, Abigail talked about some counseling principles and what they might expect. She also asked them to be quietly praying and let Ariel speak for herself.

"So, you are Ariel. It looks like you have a family that really loves you."

The little girl looked as if she wanted to climb inside her mother. This was more than a case of shyness and Abigail wondered how the little girl would react to her since it was a woman who had traumatized her. She tried a different tack.

"Do you know my friends Traci and Bryan?" Abigail hoped the connection would open some level of trust. "I think Traci is in your Sunday school class. Their mommy is my best friend."

Ariel nodded.

Good. She might open up. "They used to come to my house and play with my dog and ride my horse sometimes."

Ariel brightened.

"But, you know what? Some bad people gave my dog some poison and he died." It was a risky start, but Abigail believed that the Holy Spirit was directing her to establish some common ground. "I was mad and sad. And I was scared that they were going to hurt my horse, too. So, my friend has my horse and we can still ride him."

Ariel's teeter-tottering emotions rose and fell as she followed Abigail's story.

"The bad people said that they wanted to hurt me, too."

Ariel's face clouded.

"But, you know what?" Abigail asked and then answered. "They keep trying, but Jesus won't let them. Jesus kept me safe even though they hurt me a little bit."

Ariel was following Abigail attentively.

"The bad people wanted to hurt you real bad, too, didn't they?"

Nod.

"But Jesus kept you safe. He used your mommy to get the store closed and He used the sheriff to find you and He used the doctor and nurses to make sure that you were okay."

Nod.

"Ariel, sometimes when bad things happen to us, we still have yukky feelings. Do you still have yukky feelings from what happened?"

Nod.

"Can you tell me what yukky feelings you have when you think about it?"

"I don't want to think about it."

"I know. But I'll tell you a secret about how to not ever have to think about it again."

Ariel straightened a little in her mother's lap. She was interested.

"Jesus was in the store that day with you, but you couldn't see Him with your eyes," Abigail pointed to her own eyes. "And you couldn't hear Him with your ears." Abigail tugged lightly on her ear lobe. "But Jesus said that He's the same yesterday and today and forever so that means that even though that bad thing happened last week, we can ask Jesus to let you sense His presence there and take away the yukky feelings now. Do you think you would like to do that?"

Nod.

"Good. First, we need to figure out what those yukky feelings are. Can you tell me?"

"Scared."

"Can you tell me what you were scared of?"

Ariel's face crumbled and she buried herself deeper into her mother's arms.

"You're doing really well. Can you tell me what you were scared of?"

Silence.

177

"How about if I guess? If I guess right can you give me a thumbs-up?"

Nod.

"Were you scared that you would never see your mommy and daddy and brother again?"

Ariel slipped a fist out and put her thumb up.

"Were you scared that the lady was going to hurt you?"

Another thumbs-up.

Abigail pulled out a sheet of paper that had ten faces on it that ranged from very, very upset to very, very happy. Another row went from very, very angry to very, very happy. Another went from terrified to peaceful. "Can you look at these faces and tell me which one looks the most like how you feel when you think about that day?"

Ariel roused herself with her mother's prompting and looked with curiosity at the faces. She reached over to the paper that was now on the edge of the desk and pointed to the last one in the fear row. Very, very.

"How about if we ask your mommy which one looks like the way she felt that day when she couldn't find you?"

Cassie was not expecting to be included and had focused on Ariel so much that she had shoved her own terror into the background. "Oh, wow. Yes, I think that same one for me. I was really, really scared that I would never see my Ariel again."

Looking at Paul and Jason, Abigail asked the same questions. They all indicated that they had felt intense fear. Paul added, "I'm very, very angry that someone would try to hurt my little girl so I have that one and that one," he said as he put his index finger on the last fear face and the last anger face.

"How about you, Jason?"

"Do you have one for guilt? I'm angry at them and myself."

"Okay, then. Is everyone willing to go back to the memory where those yukky feelings are and give them to Jesus?" Looking at Paul and Jason, she added, "That will mean being willing to forgive that lady and whoever was behind it."

She got yesses and nods from the Miller family. "Good. I'm going to pray a little bit while all of you close your eyes and go to the scariest part of that memory. We're going to ask Jesus to let you see Him with your spiritual eyes or hear Him with your spiritual ears, or sense His presence in some way. Your job is to give Jesus the yukky feeling and let Him give you something in exchange. Okay?"

They were not accustomed to praying in this way, but they each closed their eyes.

"Jesus, You were there that day when that scary lady took Ariel. We plead Your blood over that store and every minute of that day. Would You let Ariel and her family see You with their spiritual eyes or hear You with their spiritual ears or sense Your presence? We ask You to lift the fear from them – You said that we do not have a spirit of fear but of power and love and a sound mind. Please bring them truth that will set them free, amen."

The most difficult part of Abigail's job was to keep silent while the Lord worked. How she longed to have a spiritual periscope that would allow her to see what was going on in the minds of her counselees. Within a

179

few minutes, she could see tears seeping down Cassie's cheeks. Something good was happening.

"Cassie, what are you sensing?"

"I don't know if it's just my imagination or not, but I was looking at myself coming around that display and not finding Ariel. I was so panicked, but this time, Jesus was standing where I had last seen Ariel and He grabbed my hand and said, 'Come with me' and rushed me up to the manager. But while we were running I was looking down the aisles and I saw Him holding Ariel's other hand and going with her, too." She caught a sob. "Thinking back, it was amazing that I had such a quick reaction. Jesus *was* with me."

"Ariel, did you sense Jesus there?"

"Uh huh. He was holding my other hand. The lady was dragging me with this arm," she paused and held up her right arm. "But Jesus was holding this one." She held up her other arm.

"Cool. What else?"

"He was mad when she put the shot in me, and He picked up all my hair when she cut it off and I saw Him crying. Then He shook His finger at the lady like she was naughty."

"Did you give Him your yukky feelings?"

"Yep," she brightened and sat up straight. "I don't feel so scared."

"Are you sure? Think about that lady and about maybe never seeing your family again."

"Jesus said He is always with me even when I don't see Him."

"That's right," Abigail affirmed. She turned to Paul. "How about you?"

"Well the fear is gone, but I'm still angry."

"Me too," Jason chimed in. "But my guilt is gone. I, uh, I kind of blame myself because if I hadn't gotten involved with Max in the first place... well, you know."

"Let's look at some principles of forgiveness and see if that helps." Abigail opened her Bible and brought them through several passages that explained biblical forgiveness. When she was finished, both Paul and Jason forgave the woman and whoever else might have been behind the abduction.

"How is everyone now?" Abigail wanted to make sure that everything was covered.

"Great. Amazing."

Ariel had slid off her mother's lap and was looking at some of the things Abigail had on her bookshelf. "That's the farthest she's been from my side since it happened," Cassie said with tears of gratitude welling up in her eyes. "Thank you!"

13

Monday, April 30

It had rained over the weekend so Lee and Abigail used the time to go over their wedding plans. Dreaming and planning, they walked through the new house again on Saturday. Lee anticipated being able to move in by the end of May and had given his landlord his thirty-day notice.

"What if the work isn't done by then? What if the inspector can't get the final inspection done in time? How long does it take for the certificate of occupancy to be issued anyway?"

"I'm not worried. I can always store my stuff in the house and live in the barn," Lee laughed.

"Seriously?"

"No. Grandpa said I can crash there as long as I need to. And Bryan insists that I come to their place again."

"Well, aren't you popular?"

"I really want to move in with you. Here. I can't wait for July! Seven, seven, seven. I like it."

"Me too. God's number."

On Sunday Paul and Cassie had made it a point to find Abigail after church to thank her again and give her an update on Ariel. Ariel quit her clinginess and slept in her own bed, she went to Sunday school without a problem and she was ready to go back to school. Of course, practically everyone in town knew about the abduction so Ariel got a lot of attention at church.

Max was at church too. He didn't sit in the balcony this week and used his brace as an excuse not to go up the stairs but rather to sit with his parents. That did not go without notice by most of the congregation. Max was a bit uncomfortable, but he managed to hide it under his thinning veneer of cockiness. He was surprised at how well he was able to follow the sermon. *Something has changed.* He was not entirely sure, but he was okay with it. He saw Abigail sitting on the other side of the church and felt a lurch in the pit of his stomach. *Tomorrow! Hoo boy. What have I gotten myself into?*

Monday promised to be a sunny spring day. Sunny daffodil blooms were beginning to open. The air was fragrant and new grasses and foliage assured her that the fire-scarred woods would be restored. Abigail checked on her chicks and set Amy up for breakfast and lunch in case her session with Max and Pastor Spalding took a long time just before she headed out to her truck.

She and Pastor Spalding met early for a few minutes to discuss the upcoming session with Max.

"What do you want me to do?" Pastor Spalding asked. He was clearly out of his comfort zone.

"Pray without ceasing. And make sure that you 'watch and pray' so you can pick up on body language," she added with a grin. "You might want to write some stuff down. We can compare notes later and you might have some questions."

"Sounds like a plan."

Soon they heard the sound of the outer door opening and closing and then Max shuffled into the outer office in front of his mother. The weakness in that left leg altered his gait. He was clearly agitated and not very happy about being here. Barbara had a determined look on her face. Abigail could only imagine the battle that went on earlier that morning.

"Hey, good timing," Abigail said cheerily. "Everyone's here. Max, could you fill this form out for me? I just need a little basic info."

He grudgingly took the clipboard and gingerly flopped into a chair.

"I have some errands to run," Barbara announced, "so I'll be back in an hour or so. If you need me before then, Max can call me. Alright?" Without waiting for an answer, she turned and left the room.

Max scribbled his name at the bottom of the form and brought it to Abigail.

"Let's go into the office. The chairs are more comfortable there."

Pastor Spalding sensed that Max was ready to bolt for the door. He walked over to him and shook his hand. "Max, you're doing the right thing. I'm so glad you're here. We'll get you through this."

"I sure hope so." He hooked his cane over the arm rest and settled into his chair. "Like I said, I'm not sure even God can get me out of this mess."

"I'd like to open with prayer and then we'll start sorting out that mess, okay?"

Max nodded his assent and respectfully bowed his head and folded his hands as Abigail prayed. Pastor Spalding awkwardly kept his eyes trained on Max.

"Lord, we come before Your throne of grace and ask that Your presence would be manifested here. We plead the blood of Jesus over this place, this time, and each of us – body, soul, and spirit. We ask that You would restrain any and all demonic forces and not allow them to agitate in any way, shape, or form. You are Truth and we also ask that You would compel any demonic entity that might show up to speak truth and only truth. Come Holy Spirit. Give us wisdom and discernment as we follow Your lead. Start us where we need to start – whatever thought, word, issue, emotion, or physical sensation that we need to follow Your lead to get to the root of Max's issues. Thank You, amen."

"Amen."

"Max, what are you sensing? What came to your mind? Even if you think it has nothing to do with anything."

"I'm thinking about when I first met Levi Blevins in high school. We're the same age, but he was a couple of years ahead of me." Max looked down and seemed preoccupied with his hands. "I, uh, I got held back a couple of times."

"Why was that?" It was obvious that Max was intelligent so it surprised her to hear that he was held back.

"I started school a year late because I had leukemia when I was about four or five. I guess they wanted to make sure I was strong enough. My immune system. They were always overprotective. They wouldn't let me go play with other kids or do anything that might be too hard. You know, like sports and four-wheelers. Scouts. They said I was too small."

"I suppose I would be a bit protective, too. They must have been scared."

"Yeah." He said it with a tinge of resentment that did not escape Abigail's notice.

185

"So, how did you react to their over-protection? What did you say to yourself?"

"I was mad," he said hotly and briefly looked her in the eye. "I wanted to show them that I had power. I'd show everyone that I wasn't just some scrawny little kid that they could pick on."

"So, let's get back to Levi. How did that relationship start?"

"He just sat down next to me at lunch one day when I was a freshman and started talking to me. He didn't talk down to me like most of the other kids. He's not a real big guy, either, and he told me that no one picked on him. He told me that he had some kind of power and if I was interested, we could talk about it more later."

"That would be appealing."

"He kept talking to me at lunch and after a couple of months he asked if I wanted to go to a party. Said there'd be plenty of booze and girls to go around. I snuck out of the house and he picked me up in his Mustang."

"Pretty heady stuff. Go on."

"Like I said to Pastor, later he supplied me with drugs. That's when he started pressuring me. He said I owed him some favors for all the parties. I didn't care."

"You were accepted."

"Yeah. He treated me with respect. Not like I was some sickly kid who couldn't do anything."

"Tell me about the favors."

Max hung his head but he was committed to coming clean – at least mostly. "He asked me to rip off my father's business. It started out little like with oil or parts. Tools. Later on, it was tires. I didn't care. I was mad at my dad. He didn't pay any attention to me. I figured it was going to be my dealership someday, so technically I wasn't stealing."

"Let's talk about the vow you made earlier."

"Vow?"

"Yeah, uh," Abigail looked back in her notes. "You said something like, 'I'll show you that I have power.' That's a vow. You bound your soul with an oath and put up a fence. Vows are self-protective. We all make them." She paused to make sure that he was following. "You locked yourself into doing whatever it takes to do that. Even though you meant it in kind of a narrow sense, the legalistic demons used it for their advantage. When we make that kind of vow, a stronghold is established in the spiritual realm and that's where the enemy hangs out. It's like your demons attract Levi's demons and they get the two of you together for the demons' best interests."

Max's eyebrows went up as he realized the implications. He did not like the idea, but he was beginning to realize that he had been used. By Levi. By the demons. "What can I do about it?"

"You can renounce the vow. You announced it a long time ago when you were a minor. You can renounce it now as an adult. You just say something like, 'God, I made that vow when I was a kid and I renounce it now' and then I'll pray in agreement with you."

"Uh, sure." Max was unaccustomed talking to people like Abigail and Pastor Spalding and praying out loud was really stretching him. "Um, God, I made a dumb vow when I was a kid and I'd like to renounce it right now. Amen."

"Lord, I pray in agreement and ask that You would go back through Max's history and render those words null and void for every time he said or thought or acted on them. Demolish the strongholds and release Max from every tormenting spirit attached to this issue. Please send them to a place where they will never afflict him or anyone else again. Fill with Your Holy Spirit and blessings and peace, amen." She looked expectantly at Max.

"I think something just happened. I can breathe a little easier."

"Good! Just wait until we get the rest of the stuff taken care of. You'll really breathe easy."

"What now?"

"Do you want to go after the big one? The thing you did that got you trapped?"

Max shifted uncomfortably in his chair and looked at Pastor Spalding who gave him an encouraging nod. "Uh, sure."

"Let's ask the Lord to start us where we need to start. I'll pray and then you let me know what comes up." He nodded so she prayed and then looked expectantly at him.

"I'm remembering that first, um, that first ritual."

"How old were you?"

"I was a Soph. I would have been sixteen. Almost seventeen."

"Tell me about it." It was like pulling teeth with some people, but Abigail tried to work at a pace that was comfortable for them. Max might bolt and run if she pressed too hard.

"I snuck out of the house. It was a week night. Some kind of Halloween party. I thought it was going to be lame, but Levi picked me up and drove me out to the woods way out somewhere. He gave me a drink on the way and everything went a bit hazy."

"He probably spiked it."

"That would make sense because it really hit me hard. I felt woozy and things seemed kind of surrealistic. There were a bunch of people there wearing hooded robes and I just remember thinking that it was really creepy. But it was like I couldn't make myself do anything. Besides, I didn't even know where I was." Max continued to elaborate on more of the details that led up to the sacrifice of the young child and his role in it.

"Max," Abigail said tenderly, "they manipulated you. That child was going to be sacrificed that night regardless of whether or not you were there. Do you remember actually using the killing dagger?"

"No, not really. I just remember standing over the little boy with the knife in my hand. Blood was dripping from the tip and I can't get that picture out of my head."

"It's highly likely that they staged that same scene for more than one person. I've heard that from others I've worked with. Do you remember what they said to you?"

Staring at a spot on the floor, Max spoke softly. He was clearly uncomfortable about telling his story. "I, I don't remember exactly. Just something like I did it and now I was one of them. And that if I ever said anything, they'd kill me or tell the demons they gave me to do it. They said that now I would have all the

189

Lynda L. Irons

power I wanted. And, uh, and they gave me a name. A power name."

"What name did they give you?"

Max heaved a big sigh and said, "Mot."

"I think that's the name of some ancient god."

"Yeah, the god of death."

"Is that one of the ones that we asked God to bind?"

"I'm pretty sure. I'm feeling pressure, but not like before."

"Let's pray about that ritual and everything that you did or believed that you did - either way it has the same effect on you. How about if I pray first and then you pray in agreement? It's important for you to confess and renounce. Then I'll pray some more as the Spirit leads."

"Uh, sure." Max glanced at Pastor Spalding who gave an encouraging nod and smile.

"Holy Father, Judge and God of all, we would like to come before Your council and open a case on behalf of Max as the plaintiff with Jesus Christ as his advocate. We'd ask that You keep this case open until all issues are resolved. Would You begin to call forth every defendant in the matter of Max having been manipulated into the cult and whatever else happened as a result of it? We ask that as Max confesses anything that he hasn't already confessed that You would cleanse him of all unrighteousness and release him from any and all strongholds that are associated with whatever he spoke or was forced to speak or whatever was spoken to or over him - spiels, hexes, chants, curses, programming, etc. Render them null and void. We ask that You would sever any and all direct and indirect unholy unions, soul ties, and/or

190

flesh links associated with the sexual activities. We ask that you would neutralize any drugs that he ingested and demolish strongholds associated with them as well. Send the reproaches where they belong. We ask that You would send all the demons associated with Max including their entire hierarchies up to the ones that answer to Satan himself to a place where they will never afflict Max or anyone else ever again. Heal and seal these broken places and fill with Your Holy Spirit, Your truth and goodness, and the fruit of the Spirit, amen."

Max took a deep breath and prayed, "God, I'm sorry for everything I did. I'm sorry that I got suckered into it and kept doing it. I'm sorry for all the stuff I did to this lady and how I hurt my family. Please forgive me. I don't want to be a part of that cult anymore. I don't care if they kill me if You can take me back I want to start over and do things right. I don't want that cult name anymore and I, I re..." Max choked and coughed.

"I renounce it in the name of Jesus," Abigail prompted.

"I renounce it in the name of Jesus," Max repeated and then looked at Abigail. "Anything else?"

"What are you feeling?"

"Peaceful. Calm."

"Do you sense the presence of any of those demons anymore?"

Max shifted his eyes back and forth a couple of times and then looked up in wonder, "No, I think they're gone. I don't think he can touch me now, but I have a feeling that the death demon is not done." He sagged in his chair exhausted.

Interesting. Abigail decided not to pursue that for now. "Is there anything else uncomfortable in that memory?"

"Yeah, I just can't get the picture out of my head... the blood and all."

"One more prayer," Abigail announced. "Lord, would You now cover Max from the top of his head to the soles of his feet with Your healing balm? Give him 'divine forgetfulness' for those images and take the sting out of the memory. Release him from all body memories – what he saw, heard, smelled, tasted, touched, or felt. Release him from the emotional pain as well. In Jesus' name, amen."

"Amen." Max was catching on. "It's like I look at the memory, but it's blurry or faded. Not graphic like it was."

"Very good." Abigail smiled. "Question: do you think God is willing to take you back?"

Looking directly at Abigail, Max gave a half smile, "Yeah. I think He just did."

"You did great, Max. I know it was hard. I'm proud of you. What you did today shows me that you have a lot of power. Strength of character and God's power, too; not the counterfeit power."

"Max, I'm just sitting here totally blown away!" Pastor Spalding chimed in. He could hardly contain his enthusiasm. "I know you still have a way to go, but you sure took a big step today! I'm so proud of you, too."

They heard the waiting room door open and Abigail saw that it was Barbara returning from her errands. "It's your mom. Do you think you've had enough for today?"

"Oh, yeah!" Max stood up. A surprised look came over his face and he started to twist his torso and then bent from side to side.

"Are you okay, son?" Pastor Spalding was concerned.

"My back! My ribs!" he touched the spot where his sternum had been fractured. "It feels normal. I don't feel the bumps on the bones right here," he said with wonder as he touched his sternum.

"Hallelujah! God healed you!"

The realization registered and an exultant Max burst out of the room and startled Barbara. She expected that he would angrily demand to leave and berate her for leaving him there so long. "Mom! God just healed me. It's like I had a belt cinched around my chest and it's gone. I can breathe! I can move!" He started gyrating to demonstrate the healing.

Abigail and Pastor Spalding followed him into the waiting area. He was still limping, but he didn't seem to notice. His hands were in the air celebrating the freedom. Once the shock of what she saw and heard wore off, she hugged him and wept for joy.

"I've never seen anything like it," Pastor Spalding was muttering to himself.

Abigail just grinned. This is why she did what she did. This was worth broken brake lines and fires, poisonings and break-ins, threats and bruises. *Thank You, Lord.*

The howls increased in intensity. Watching Mot and his henchmen being escorted to a place of captivity, they plotted revenge. They called her Demon-slayer

Lynda L. Irons

because they never saw their comrades after an encounter with that woman, but a better name would be Warrior-of-God. The casualties of her skirmishes seemed to be taken prisoners of war.

They would mete out the reproaches. Gladly. A curse without a cause cannot alight, but a curse with cause certainly would. These demons were free to operate within the righteous judgment of the Great Enemy. If He allowed it, they would do what they did best. Revenge. Retribution. Reproaches returned upon the heads of the ones who sent them.

Having been accustomed to robust health and supernatural stamina and strength, Prinz had never experienced anything like he had in the last three days. His unconscious body was discovered by the fire fighters and he was rushed to the hospital. He groaned today as he tried to roll onto his side. His head hurt and there were various contusions and cuts, punctures and bruises all over his body. Dr. Bacchus had been attending to his injuries since they pulled him out from under the rubble of St. Mark's Episcopal Church on the night of the freak tornado.

Dr. Bacchus discharged him yesterday and today he was recovering in his own home. Pulling himself to a sitting position on the side of his bed, Prinz donned his robe and gingerly made his way down to his private inner sanctum. It was almost as if his powers had leaked out of his punctured body much like air left a ruptured tire. He was unaccustomed to feeling stiffness and pain. He lit the candles that were precisely positioned on the Baphomet. Bowing to his lord, he began familiar incantations. His invocations summoned demonic entities.

They gladly came. Another agreement had been broken and now was being reversed, compounding his disgraceful demise. A decade ago, Prinz bargained for Max with these fiendish beings. Max received his demons which both empowered him and tormented him. Prinz received demons as a reward. But with Max's renunciations, the deal was off. Max was released from his tormentors and Prinz was relieved of his empowering demons. Prinz was going down!

Slowly and painfully.

Pastor Spalding and Abigail went up to his office to debrief. Ginny easily picked up on their elation. "It must have gone well," she said with a light laugh.

"Oh, I wish you were a fly on the wall." Pastor Spalding was still marveling at the transformation in Max. Not only had he witnessed the recommitment to Christ, he saw the miraculous healing. "But Max is going to have to tell his story."

After they settled into his office, Pastor Spalding pulled out his notes and jabbed at one of the lines. "What do you think he meant when he said that the death demon wasn't done?"

"I'm not sure. I just had a feeling that we didn't need to pursue that today."

"At least Mot can't go after Max. Right?"

"Death. I wonder if it's Mot that's not done or if it's death that's not done. You know, like it says death is the last... humph! Oh, I hate it when I can't remember the verse… it's somewhere at the end of first or second Corinthians."

"I know that one. I use it in funerals all the time." Pastor Spalding chuckled at her touch of annoyance and reached for his Bible. "1 Corinthians 15:26. *'The last enemy that will be abolished is death.'*"

"I wonder if the death demons think they can hang around until the end," Abigail mused. "Well, I guess it doesn't matter because Max renounced it and I believe that Mot is gone, but maybe some other death demon might try something. It's not like there's just one of them."

"When Christ returns, He'll abolish death. We'll live in eternity rather than time. Until then, people will still die."

Abigail was pleased with the session and was beginning to think that it was possible to turn the Titanic, to shift the tide of evil in their region. Jesus called His disciples to be fishers of men. It was a team effort. They didn't go out in a one-man dinghy and fish with poles. They went out in larger boats and fished with nets. It would take a team of committed disciples to bring about transformation. The Ministerial Alliance was a good start. The Church of Jesus Christ consisted of all believers of all denominations. "Oh, Lord I pray for unity in a bond of peace. Let us rally around our common beliefs and not hassle about the rest. Lord, bring us more like-minded, like-spirited believers. I know there are more of us than there are of them. Transform those who have been committed to Satanism. Stir up those who are lukewarm and sitting on a fence. Light a fire under us and cause Your name to be glorified. Expose the corruption in our politicians." Abigail prayed passionately all the way home.

It was Beltane Eve. Abigail was aware that it was an important Witches Sabbat. She was not sure how much witchcraft was prevalent in her area, but she knew that many who took part in one form of occult practice often participated in other ones. *Tomorrow is May Day and then comes the full moon. I guess we'll find out if Amy reacts.* Abigail half mused, half prayed.

Rolling up her driveway, Abigail breathed a contented sigh. She loved being home especially in the warm weather. She began a mental list of all the outdoor chores that needed her attention. But first, she needed to call Cindy.

"Hello, lady! What's up?"

"Hey. I have a question for you. I happened to find out that Lee's birthday is on the eleventh. I was wondering if you'd heard any rumors in the family about a party or anything."

"No. No, I haven't. You got something in mind?"

"Not really. I just think something should be done about it," Abigail said conspiratorially.

"Yeah, let's put our heads together and come up with something. He's been alone so long, I doubt he even remembers when his birthday is, let alone having a party. I'll talk to Gary and see what he thinks."

"Good idea."

After hanging up from Cindy, Abigail called her father. They talked about the weather and plans for the spring, the new venture with the chickens and that she had a house guest. Abigail finally took the plunge and told him about Lee.

"Dad, I met a guy. Actually, he's Gary McCord's cousin. You remember Cindy and Gary, don't you?"

"Yes, you introduced me to them at your church when I visited you."

"That's right. Anyway, Lee and I have, well, he's asked me to marry him and we're engaged and I'd like to drive up to visit you and introduce you to him. Memorial weekend? If that works for you."

"Well, that is big news! Yes, I'd love to meet him. And I think Memorial weekend would work just fine. You know your brothers usually have a barbeque over here. Do you think he could handle meeting everyone?"

"I'm sure he can handle anyone, after all, Gary is his cousin."

"Well, you know your brothers. If they don't approve of him, they could barbeque him," he teased. It was good to hear her father laugh. They finished making plans and after she hung up, Abigail checked on Amy.

"Doing great. I called my doctor this morning and she said I could try a little more walking and a little more sitting up and see if I'm still okay."

"Great! I was about to change my clothes and see if I can clean up the flower beds and whatever else I can get into. It's beautiful outside."

"I poked my head out the back door a little earlier. It's nice. I love spring!"

"I'll bring out a couple of the lawn chairs and you can sit out there and soak up some sun. I'm going to drag out the grill, too. I think we're going to put Lee to work tonight cooking our burgers. What do you think?"

"I'd love to sit outside for a little while, thanks. And burgers on the grill sound great! I wish I could help."

"Pretty soon. Hang in there."

Abigail happily worked in the yard and gardens, the orchard and vineyard while Amy watched contentedly from her chair on the back deck. Inside her womb, the baby was waving and kicking stubby arms and legs completely oblivious to the currents of turmoil that swirled around it. Just over an inch and a half long, the baby was making its presence known. Amy absentmindedly sat with her hand on her lower abdomen which was beginning to swell ever so slightly.

14

Friday, May 4

"I'm feeling great since last session. I mean, nothing bothering me, no nightmares. I'm beginning to think that I'm pretty much healed of all the SRA stuff."

"That's fantastic! What are we doing here?"

"I don't know. That's what I was going to ask you."

"Let's ask the Lord."

After they prayed, Carrie Sue said, "I think it has something to do with Mom."

"Like what?"

"Like, what do I do about her? She's still obviously controlled by the cult and that Dorkas character hates my guts. I don't know if I should stay away from her completely or try to get her out of it or what."

"Does she call or come over as much?"

"Yeah, but it's kind of weird. I mean, we can't relate or even hold a normal conversation like a mother and daughter should, or even like two women should. It's just weird. Awkward. She's my mom, but she's not."

"So, is the problem that you don't know *how* to relate to her or is it that you keep hoping that she'll be motherly?"

"Maybe that's it. I mean, I'm seeing how mothers and daughters should relate and I never got that."

"Perhaps you just have to accept reality. This is your mother and this is how she is. This is your mother and, until God changes her, this is how she is."

"Yeah. You keep saying that. I guess I'm always disappointed that she never believes me about the abuse. She's either that mean Dorkas or Martyr Mom most of the time. Neither one is what I need."

"I'm sorry." Abigail truly was sad. "I'm sorry that you never had a mommy and probably never will. And that's a tough piece of reality to have to chew and swallow."

"So how do I do that?"

"I think that's something that you need to grieve. It's a loss. It's the absence of good. It's something that should have been but never was. You have to be able to say that she never wanted or loved me; she only used me and still tries to."

"It was a whole lot easier to go after demons," Carrie Sue said with a mirthless half smile. "Okay, let's pray."

They spent time in prayer about Carrie Sue's grief after which they both reached for the tissues.

"Oh, guess what!" Carrie Sue brightened and changed the subject.

"What?"

"I got the job! But I don't know if I'm excited or scared."

"Congratulations! You'll do a great job. When do you start?"

"Monday. She wants me to work from ten 'til noon for the first couple of weeks for training and orientation and then when we're both comfortable, she wants me to start working a couple of full days."

"You'll do great. You're a whiz with computers so the cash register will be a breeze."

"I'm just not so sure about interacting with people."

"Just look them in the eye and smile. You don't have to entertain them, you just have to show them where to find what they're looking for.

"Yeah, I guess you're right. It shouldn't be a big deal, but I'm still a little nervous."

"That's normal," Abigail said light-heartedly with a sing-song tone. They set up an appointment for two weeks out because Carrie Sue was doing well enough that she would not need weekly sessions. Abigail tried to work herself out of a job and was delighted when a former counselee became a friend.

Since their session was shorter than usual, Abigail used the time to do her grocery shopping. Storing the perishables in the church kitchen and finishing her lunch, Abigail waited in her office for Max and Pastor Spalding to come for Max's appointment.

Max arrived shortly after Pastor Spalding did and they sat down with much less awkwardness than their previous meeting on Monday. Max looked better, healthier. He still walked with a limp and was still wearing the brace, but he reported that his chest and back and ribs felt great.

"I wonder what an X-ray would look like," he said.

"I wouldn't be surprised if God took all the metal out to boot!" Pastor Spalding's optimistic spirit soared like few others.

Max just looked at him as if he were from another planet. It was ironic since Max had seen some feats of wizardry that defied imagination. Because of the altered state of mind he was in at those times, he assumed it was something he made up while in a trance state. That served the cult well.

"How was your week, Max?" Abigail began.

"Well, I felt good for a couple of days, but Wednesday and Thursday were a bit rough."

"Let's open with prayer and then get into it." Abigail led the prayer and made it a point to ask God to cover the place, the time, and each of them with the blood of Jesus Christ. She asked Him to restrain any demon from interfering in any way and that any defiant ones would be escorted away.

Max kept his head dropped for a moment after she was finished, took a deep breath and then looked Pastor Spalding in the eye. "I took too many pain pills. I just wanted to get high again. I just kept hearing, 'Go ahead, it won't hurt you. Take the pills. Take the pills.' So, I did."

"Where do you think those thoughts or words came from?" Abigail pursued. As she waited for his response, she mentally thought about the full moon that occurred about the time Max was having this trouble.

"I don't know. I mean, it sounded like my own voice, and like, somehow it was me but it wasn't me. I don't know how to explain it." He was confounded and genuinely wanted to figure it out. He was afraid that he was crazy. *Crazy people hear voices, right?* Max did not want to voice his fears, but his desperation and the obvious love of these two people compelled him to pursue it anyway.

"The voices and thoughts can come from one of three places that I know of," Abigail began. "It can be from you, or the Holy Spirit, or a demon. And we know it wasn't the Holy Spirit. That leaves you or a demon or maybe a part of you that's demonized."

Max just nodded as he processed what she was saying. He was not sure which of the three options was the least disconcerting.

"Tell me what your thoughts are like. What does it sound like inside your head when you're thinking? Like when those thoughts about taking the pills came."

"It sounded like I was, um, oh this sounds crazy," Max hesitated. "It sounded like I was having an argument with myself."

"Okay, it's my turn to sound a little crazy. Look me in the eye, if you would, while I ask you this." She waited a moment for the eye contact and then continued, "Is there anyone in there who can tell us about 'take the pills' and then using them?"

Almost instantly Max's countenance darkened and his voice sounded defiant, "I do. What of it?"

"Who are you?"

"I'm Max"

"You look like him, but you sound like you're younger, like maybe sixteen or seventeen."

"Bingo! Give that lady a big prize."

"Thanks." Abigail was not fazed by the dripping sarcasm. "Can I assume that you're the part of Max that does the drugs?"

"That's me! Max-to-the-max."

"And Max-to-the-max would mean that you're fueled by that spirit of pharmakia," Abigail pressed as she discerned the demon.

Max's body was jolted as if he was kicked in the side. His eyes dulled and darkened. That demonic entity had been invited into Max's life with the use of hard drugs and likely with an intentional assignment by the cult as well, because of the concoctions that Max ingested either willingly or through trickery.

"In the name of Jesus the Christ, you spirit of pharmakia are not in your assigned place. Holy Spirit, we ask that You would fill that place with Your presence in Your child so that it cannot return there."

Panic was etched on Max's face as the demon contorted his features.

"You have two choices: You can either face Satan to explain to him why you have failed to keep your assignment or you can cut your losses and go wherever the true Lord Jesus Christ sends you."

A much less cocky Max-to-the-max looked at her with astonishment. "How'd you do that?"

"Do what?"

"Get rid of him."

"Where do you think he went?"

"I don't know exactly, I just heard him scream, 'No, not Satan!' and then he took off."

"So, how do you feel now that he's gone?"

"I don't know," he said slowly. "I've never really been without him. I, I guess I don't feel so, so empty maybe. I don't know how to describe it. Desperate? Angry? Like I'm looking for an edge?"

Abigail let him ponder the changes that the absence of the demon and the presence of the Holy Spirit brought before she continued. "So, you came with a job and a demon that had an agenda. Can I assume that your job was to keep Max high?"

"High and dry."

"So why did you want Max to take the pills the other night?"

"If he's high, he does what he's supposed to do. He does what he's supposed to; we don't get punished."

"Makes sense. What do you want to do now? Do you still want to take the pills?"

"Not really. I mean, that demon is gone, so I'm not getting my, uh, my butt kicked. I just feel off balance. Like I'm drugged still."

"Would you like for me to ask God to take care of that?"

"Uh, sure."

"Okay then. Lord, we ask You to go back through Max-to-the-max's history and neutralize all the effects of every drug that he ever ingested or that was injected into him." Abigail was suddenly jolted by another thought that she believed came from the Holy Spirit. "Lord, we want to include any drug that Max was given as a child. We ask that You would do that same kind of healing in Max or any other part of him that may have been affected by any kind of drugs or mind-altering substance or even hypnosis and programming. We pray this in Jesus' name, amen."

"That's better," he reported. "Whew! I'm tired." He thought for a moment and then added, "I think you're right. It started when I had the leukemia. All the chemo and pain meds."

"Interesting. It sounds like maybe that demon took advantage of the circumstances," Abigail agreed and then moved on. "Do you think you're ready to be integrated?"

"What's that?"

"Oh, sorry. That's when we ask God to reverse the dissociation and you get to go back inside where you came from."

"Yeah. Sounds good. I'm tired."

Abigail prayed for his integration and then Max reappeared.

"That was weird," he said. "I heard the whole thing and it was like I was here but I wasn't."

"That's dissociation. Max-to-the-max took care of that assignment. Apparently, you weren't co-conscious with him whenever he came out before or during the rituals."

"Never."

"That would be why you have blank places in your memory. I would guess that his job was to get you high and out-of-it enough to be accessed and manipulated by the cult."

"Yeah," he hung his head as he tried to process this information. He felt weak. Used. Out of control. And that was exactly the opposite of what drew him to Levi and the cult in the first place.

"Just remember that there are no bad parts, just parts with bad jobs," Abigail said compassionately. "The good news is that he's integrated and you are much less vulnerable."

"What now?"

"Are you up for more?"

"Nah. I'm kind of tired and I want to think about this stuff for a bit if you don't mind."

"No problem. I think you're doing great. Hang in there and we'll get through it."

"Max," Pastor Spalding injected, "you know that you can call me any time. I'm in your corner and I'm proud of you."

Lynda L. Irons

"Thank you, sir," a much humbler Max replied. "I do have one question, though. Why do you suppose that my chest got healed but my leg didn't?"

"I've been wondering that myself," Abigail said thoughtfully. "I really don't have a good answer. What do you think, Pastor?"

"Maybe a better question would be 'why did your chest get healed at all?'"

"Yeah. I guess I'll take what I can get."

After closing with a prayer of blessing, Max left, leaving Abigail and Pastor Spalding to talk about the session. Pastor Spalding was learning much about Satanism and dissociation, spiritual warfare and grace.

Abigail gathered her groceries and hurried home. She wanted to have a session with Amy before supper if Amy was feeling well enough.

"Hey, Abigail, I'm awake."

"Good. You up for a session?"

"Yeah. Let's do it," she replied with genuine enthusiasm.

They opened with prayer and by the time they were finished, Head Honcho was in executive control.

"How are things going inside? It's been awhile."

"The rumblings from Apollyon's level are still pretty intense, but they seem to be contained. Fuchsya is more active. Frustrated. Probably because there's a steady stream of defectors coming up through the central hub into Nicholai's level. Most of them are getting healed and integrated. A couple are sticking around to help out. Some have gone back to their levels to – what's that word you use? Evangelize?"

"That's amazing! No wonder Fuchsya's so upset. She's probably feeling the heat from her demons."

"So, the genius counselor thinks she has this all analyzed?" Fuchsya displaced Head Honcho.

"Well, I'm sure I'm missing a few pieces. I'd be glad to hear your take on it," Abigail said amiably.

"I'll have you know that I'm not taking any heat from my demons."

"That would be a first."

"We're on the same side. I help them; they help me."

"Unless you fail in your assignment and they become displeased because they're taking the heat from their superiors."

"I'm not failing!" she said vehemently.

"Good. Why are you more 'active' as Head Honcho said?"

"I'm always active. He's just paying more attention, that's all."

"I have a question for you, if you don't mind."

"Go ahead." She tossed her head in a cocky movement and allowed a condescending sneer to form.

"If you're the top leader over all sectors, that would mean that you represent all sectors and therefore you're over all the parts."

"Yeah."

"So why do you appear to be purely demon and cult-loyal? Why don't you represent and protect the ones that are in the kingdom of Light? Hang in there with me," Abigail added hastily to keep Fuchsya from interrupting her train of thought. "If your greatest quest as a Satanist is to rise as high as you can in Satan's kingdom as well as in God's kingdom, then wouldn't it be in your best interest to support all of them? I mean, it seems like the cult-loyal ones are the ones who get supported and promoted the most and the Christian ones are suppressed and therefore, you'd be failing to rise in God's kingdom and by extension, failing to rise in Satan's."

"They," Fuchsya emphasized heatedly, "are messing up the rise."

"What do you mean?"

"They have defected. They were tricked into believing all your lies so they're not doing their job."

"Okay. So, you're saying that they were supposed to infiltrate God's kingdom and act like Christians and rise in that kingdom, but not really be Christians."

"Yes. No. They're supposed to be Christians."

"Genuine Christians who follow the true Jesus the Christ?"

"Yes."

"So – help me understand – how is someone supposed to become a genuine Christian and rise in God's kingdom and yet still serve Satan? Wouldn't that negate their Christianity?"

"I don't understand your problem."

"Well, let's turn it around. What if being successful in God's kingdom meant rising in Satan's as well. Let's say I join your cult and go to your rituals and participate in all the activities as a genuine Christian and seek promotion and pass all the tests and become a master level Satanist."

"Well, you couldn't do that."

"Why not?"

"Because you wouldn't really be a Satanist. Your Christianity would negate your status as a Satanist."

"So then, what you're saying is that someone can't be a Christian and a Satanist. It's one or the other. Someone can only be a pseudo-Christian and a Satanist or a pseudo-Satanist and a Christian. And by being a pseudo-Christian, you're not really being a Christian at all and so you really can't rise in the kingdom of God and therefore you will never be able to satisfy Satan."

"Lady, you're trying to trick me."

"I'm really just trying to understand."

Fuchsya crossed her arms and grunted in frustration. She was thinking. She did not like what she was thinking.

"Fuchsya," Abigail said softly, "I hate to say it, but they've set all of you up for failure. You can't win. Ever. You'll never be able to rise to a position of any real power. Satan is just pedaling a counterfeit. Your only hope is to defect and have genuine power that only comes from God."

"Never!" With that, Fuchsya fled to her secret place deep inside.

Head Honcho resumed control and wryly commented, "You got her thinking about stuff she doesn't want to think about."

"I can't imagine what it's like to invest all my time and energy into something only to find out that it's all a sham."

"I can."

"Yeah, I guess you can. I wonder if she'd be more willing to listen to you now."

"Maybe. I'll certainly give it a try, but she's disappeared for now."

Amy reappeared and looked tired. She decided to take a nap while Abigail attended to her dinner plans.

Deciding that she had enough time, she changed her clothes, donned her boots, and rode the four-wheeler to Lee's farm. She had Earl and Jan's permission, which was actually more like an order, to use their access road and cut down their driveway so that she would avoid any potential encounters with Charlie Fletcher on the direct trail.

Lee heard her coming and stepped out onto the front porch of the nearly completed house with a broad smile on his face. They embraced and then went arm in arm into the house where Lee pointed out all of the most recent changes. There were still some things that needed to be done, but the whole project had been masterfully orchestrated by the contractor. They had prayed for favor and certainly obtained it.

15

Sunday, May 6

Amy was still mostly confined to bed. She continued to have trouble with spotting and sometimes cramping if she was too active. She stayed home alone while Abigail and Lee went to church together.

"Amy, Lee and I are going to have lunch with Gary and Cindy so I put a sandwich together for you and it's in the fridge next to that big bowl of salad." Abigail wanted to make sure that Amy spent as little time as possible on her feet. "Make sure you eat and stay hydrated, too."

"I will, I will." Amy was still uncomfortable with all the attention. "Thanks. I really mean it."

"You have to take care of that mighty man or woman of God in there! Grab whatever you want. There's yogurt and granola bars and fruit. And pickles and ice cream."

"Yes, Mom," Amy teased back. "I'll be good; I promise."

They both heard Lee's toot-toot and said their goodbyes. Lee was at the front door by the time Abigail walked through the kitchen and living room. Grabbing her light jacket, she was careful to lock the door behind her.

Lee gave her a quick kiss and then extended his elbow. Abigail took his arm and they walked to his truck together. They were becoming more comfortable as a couple. Their conversations ranged from the practical and logistic issues of the construction and farm management to the light-hearted humor that they shared as well as deep spiritual matters. Life had been too serious for too long for both of them.

Carrie Sue was already sitting next to Cindy by the time they got there. She was much relieved to know that Sheriff Bynum was no longer attending this church. The ladies quietly greeted one another with hugs and pats. Gary, on the far side of Cindy, nodded to Lee who reciprocated. It appeared to be much less complicated for men than for women to relate to each other.

The music died down as Pastor Spalding moved to the podium, placed his Bible on it, and then smiled broadly at the congregation. "Good morning! I was glad when they said unto me *'let us go up to the house of the Lord.'* Aren't you glad to be here today?"

He got a hearty response from the congregation. "The weather is getting warm. Wouldn't this be a great day for fishing?" He caught puzzled looks from some of the people and smiled before he continued. "Today, we're going fishing with the disciples. We're going to look at Luke five and John twenty-one and focus on Simon Peter."

He opened with prayer and then directed them to the book of Luke. "Now this passage describes a fishing expedition that happened near the beginning of Jesus' ministry. He had just healed Simon's mother-in-law prior to this story." Pastor Spalding read the passage and began to elaborate on some of the verses.

"So here we have a career fisherman who came up empty after working hard all night. He and his partners were washing their nets and getting ready for the next night's work when Jesus got into Simon's boat so He could teach the crowd from a little distance. I could just imagine Simon Peter thinking, 'Dude, I just worked all night, I'm tired, I need to get some shut-eye, and You want me to be Your floating pulpit?' Can anyone relate?"

Pastor Spalding paused for the murmured responses before continuing. "And to top this off, when Jesus was finished speaking, He told Simon to go back out to the deep water and put his freshly cleaned nets back down for a catch. I don't know about you, but I'd be thinking something like, 'Hey, I'm the professional fisherman here and anyone who has any brains knows that you fish at night, not during the day when the fish go too deep to catch.' But he didn't say that. Instead, he did it. And you know the rest of the story: they had to call their partners with the other boat to help them haul all the fish to shore because their nets were so full that they were breaking. Look at Simon's response. *'Depart from me, for I am a sinful man, O Lord!'"*

Pastor Spalding then directed them to the book of John to compare and contrast the fishing stories. "This one happens after Jesus' death and resurrection. It happened after Peter betrayed Jesus. He tells his buddies that he was going fishing. I wonder if he was thinking that he had disqualified himself as a disciple and so he was just going to go back to his old job; something that was familiar; something that he was good at. Sort of. Can anyone relate?"

He saw some thoughtful expressions and some nods. He continued to discuss more of the details in the passage and then concluded his message. "Now look at Simon Peter's response. This time he couldn't get to shore fast enough. I'll bet he wished he could have walked on water that day!"

A gentle wave of chuckles rippled across the auditorium. "Both times he and his fishing buddies came up empty. Both times, obeying Jesus' illogical commands, they came up full. The first time the nets broke. The second time, they didn't. The first time Simon was so awed that he wanted Jesus to depart from him because he recognized that he was a sinful man. This last time, Simon was so awed that he didn't want Jesus to get away from him."

Winding down, Pastor Spalding said, "Folks, apart from some principles that you might relate to with Simon Peter's responses, let's look at one final thought. When Jesus calls us to be fishers of men, He was not talking about fishing like we Americans generally do. We stand far apart from our fishing buddies so that we don't get our lines tangled and maybe so we can protect our own special fishing hole. We need to be fishers of men like they fished back then. They were teams, they were partners, and they used nets. If we want to have an impact on our communities, we need to be a part of a network of fishers of men."

Abigail lightly poked Lee and whispered, "I was just thinking about that this week!"

"Good confirmation," he whispered back.

Pastor Spalding saw more thoughtful nods. "Here's what I would like you to pray about. Our community needs to be redeemed. The only way that we can do it is as a part of a team that consists of the entire Church universal. We can't be fishing with our Baptist poles way down shore from the guy with his Methodist pole or the guy with his Presbyterian pole. We will have to unite as the Body of Christ holding onto the same net, rallying around those things that bind us together and let go of those hobby horses that divide us."

Pastor Spalding was intentionally stretching his congregation. It was stretching him. "Folks, as a member of the Ministerial Alliance in our area, I am having a wonderful time getting to know my brothers in Christ who are leaders from various denominations. We are planning on having community-wide prayer meetings and ministry out-reaches. Please pray about your involvement. We need everybody to grab hold of the nets."

He concluded his sermon and invited people to pray with members of the prayer teams. The McCords, Carrie Sue, and Lee and Abigail made their way out of the auditorium with the majority of the congregation. Abigail overheard some snippets of conversations about the sermon. Some were embracing the call to unity with other denominations and others were wary of it.

"Carrie Sue, you're welcome to join us," Cindy invited. "A bunch of us are getting together at our house for lunch. I'm sorry I didn't think to ask you earlier."

"Oh, well," Carrie Sue hesitated.

"Come on," Abigail encouraged. "You're part of the gang."

"Bryan and Traci love when you play with them," Gary added. The last time she was there, Carrie Sue had drifted off to join the kids and had switched into a child personality. No one noticed the switch. She just looked like an adult who really knew how to relate to children.

217

Lynda L. Irons

"Okay, count me in. Thanks."

They split up to get to their vehicles and eventually met up at the McCord's home. After getting the food out of the oven and onto the table, they gathered for a meal. Amiable chatter was interrupted by requests to have condiments or platters passed around for seconds.

"So, Lee," Gary asked, "how are your cows doing? How soon can they be bred?"

"Are you going to make bread out of your cows?" Bryan asked incredulously. He was even more perplexed when the adults erupted in laughter.

"No, son," Lee answered with as serious a face as he could manage. "Your daddy wants to know how soon my cows can be mommy cows." Looking at Gary with a gleeful you're-in-trouble grin, he continued, "Your daddy will explain it to you later."

"Okay."

The adults were grateful that Bryan did not pursue the subject.

"Well, they're just over seven months old and just over five hundred pounds, I'd guess. They need to get up to about eight hundred pounds since this will be the first time they'll be mommy cows." He winked at Bryan. "I'm guessing that with the pastures coming in, they'll be ready by fall. We should have calves by next summer."

They continued to discuss the cows and moved on to Abigail's chickens and Gary's work. When Lee excused himself to use the bathroom, Cindy leaned over the table and whispered conspiratorially, "Hey, it's Lee's birthday on Friday. What are we going to do?"

"Can we do something over here?" Abigail asked. "He comes over to my house so often that I won't be able to surprise him with anything."

"Let's do it here," Gary chimed in. "We can just grill some steaks with all the fixings."

They continued to make plans to invite friends and family which included Carrie Sue. They also decided that they would see if Lee's daughter, Lisa, could make a quick trip out for the occasion. It was all settled by the time Lee rejoined the group.

Max slid into his chair at the kitchen table. He was beginning to reconnect with his parents by eating with them and occasionally watching a television program with them. He was becoming less sullen and more communicative. Ted and Barbara were seeing glimpses of the son that they thought that they had lost forever.

"So, Max, what are your plans this week?" Ted asked. "I mean, besides your therapy."

"I'm not sure. I have that meeting with Pastor and Mrs. Steele on Friday. I was thinking that if you'll have me back, I'd like to work for you again. I mean, really work this time."

"I've been hoping that you would come back. I'd be glad to have you for any hours you can be there. Just take your time and build your stamina."

"Can I start with Tuesdays, Thursdays, and Saturdays? I have P.T. on Monday, Wednesday, and Friday still." Max hesitated and scrutinized his plate as if the words he was trying to formulate might be written there. Finally, he looked his father in the eye and said, "Dad, I, I stole a lot of stuff from you and I want to pay you back."

"I know you did, son." Ted was torn between wanting to pardon his prodigal and needing to let him make restitution. "I'll tell you what. You figure out your best estimate of what you think you owe the company and keep track of your hours and how much you would have been paid. When your debt is paid, just let me know and I'll put you back on the payroll."

"I'll work on it tonight." Max looked his father in the eye and extended his hand. As his father shook his hand, he said humbly, "Thanks, Dad."

Hope welled in her heart as tears welled up in her eyes. Barbara observed the amazing exchange between her son and her husband. Her heart ached for her damaged son as she watched Max limp down the hallway toward his room. Her heart warmed as she looked at Ted and the tears that flowed down his cheeks.

They thanked God for doing whatever it took to straighten Max out. They knew that there would be ups and downs, but Max had turned another corner in his journey to turn completely around. They could only hope and pray that it was as genuine as it seemed.

Various members of the Ministerial Alliance were making their way to Kingston. Rev. Benjamin Morgan was already at his United Methodist Church. Benji, as he was known by his close friends and family, was an out-going young man. His sympathetic blue eyes opened many bolted heart doors.

He had a wonderful committee of ladies in his congregation who gladly made and served luncheons for every occasion. Today was no exception. He told the ladies to plan on a minimum of a dozen people but be prepared for another dozen. He was an optimist. And he was right. They had just about doubled their number since their last meeting.

Several of the pastors had brought their key intercessors along. Abigail asked Cindy McCord to come as well. She was also pleased to see Wanda, her chicken lady from Richard Morris' church in Pines, come through the doorway. She introduced Cindy to Wanda and the three of them found seats at one of the tables and immediately started talking as if they had known each other for years.

Paula Archer also came at the request of her minister, George Bordman, of the Hawville Presbyterian Church. She excused herself from her duties at her Iron Skillet Restaurant to be here. Joining Abigail at her table, she joined the chatter.

By noon everyone had expectantly settled into their places around the tables. Their taste buds were anticipating a flavorful meal and their souls and spirits were expecting spiritual refreshment. Rev. Morgan opened with prayer and once the meal had been served, conversations flowed.

Before long Pastor Morgan got everyone's attention and then introduced Pastor Spalding to those who had not yet met him.

"Thank you," Pastor Spalding began, "I am delighted to see such a good turn-out. Let me just briefly get you newcomers caught up on the Ministerial Alliance and what our purpose is here. A couple of us pastors have been meeting for quite some time now, but more recently we realized that we had more to do than just socialize interdenominationally. I'll get right to the point. A couple of us have become aware that there is a strong satanic cult presence in our area. We also realized that some of us have Satanists in our congregations."

He paused as he heard a couple of the new people suck in their breaths. "As we discussed last time, these people are not our enemies, Satan is. And he's been defeated. What we also realized is that this community-wide issue is too big for any one of us. Now, I'm not going to preach yesterday's sermon all over again, but I want to encourage all of us with the truth that we need to be fishers of men manning the nets. We have come to believe that Christ is calling all of us and our fellow-believers in each church and denomination represented here to grab hold and help haul in the catch. We can't do it like we have been, that is, with me holding my Baptist fishing pole and you," he nodded to Benji and Paul, "holding your Methodist fishing poles and all the rest of you holding your own brand. You get the idea."

"What are we going to do?" Rev. George Bordman asked. "I mean, practically speaking, how do we do this? What does it look like?"

"That's something that we've been praying about and mulling over for a while now. I'd like to throw that question over to Abigail Steele," he smiled and extended his palm toward Abigail. "She is a remarkable counselor who has years of experience ministering to Satanic Ritual Abuse survivors. Abigail?"

Abigail was prepared for this but she was always startled when the moment came. She gulped and then stood so everyone could see her. "Thank you, Pastor Spalding. I think we can build on the fishing analogy to answer that question. When Peter and his partner needed help, they called for their other partners who were in another boat. Let's say that each church represented here is a boat with a team of fishermen. We can and must navigate our own boats following the lead of the captain of the boat, and when the time comes for one team to help another team, the captains will ideally communicate with each other and with their respective crews."

"That'll preach!" Dennis Walsh encouraged her and drew some chuckles.

"So," Pastor Don Wilmore added, "last time when I found out that my boat had been invaded by Sheriff Bynum the Satanist, Pastor Spalding's boat came along side to give me direction so we didn't sink."

Robert Warrens chimed in. "And now I know for sure about that lady that comes to my church and better understand what I'm up against."

Some of the newcomers were sobered by the conversation. Cindy just smiled. She was proud of her friend and pleased to be included in this gathering. She was an intercessor and when her spiritual gifts and calling intersected with situations like this, she was energized. She was a boot-wearing, sword-wielding, armor-bearing warrior disguised as a homemaker.

"How are we going to practically do this?" Asked Clara Bardwell, pastor of the little non-denominational church that teetered on the edge of the county. "I can't say that I've got anyone in my church like that, but I do know that my little congregation can't do much alone."

"Last time we talked about joining together interdenominationally for community and county events," Pastor Spalding said. "Why don't we take some time right now to pray and discuss how we might do this? We have four tables. Let's each discuss and pray for about fifteen minutes or so and then share what comes up."

There was shuffling of chairs as various men and women settled into the assignment. Calendars and notebooks came out and soon there was the hum of whispered prayers and quiet discussion at each of the tables.

When the time was up, Pastor Spalding directed his question to the table on his right. "What have you come up with?"

Pastor Walsh answered for the table. "We started thinking about the Memorial Day parade in Springfield. We thought that since the parade route goes past a couple of our churches, we could use that opportunity to gather and pray."

George Bordman, the Presbyterian minister, spoke for the next table. "We thought about Memorial Day, too. We're not sure what to do with it, though."

Pastor Spalding looked at the third and fourth tables and they, too, indicated that they were thinking about Memorial Day. "Okay, I think we have a consensus that we need to do something interdenominationally on Memorial Day. But what?" He got a chuckle out of the group. "Any ideas?"

Cindy raised her hand a little timidly and was recognized by Pastor Spalding. "I think we have to ask what our goal is. We want the community and members of our churches to see the unity we are building, but what do we want the spiritual forces of darkness to see?"

When she said that, there was a collective recognition that they needed the dual focus with an emphasis on the message to the spiritual realm. "Of course! Thank you for that, Cindy."

"Well, then I wonder if we need to do something public at this point, or something private like we're doing right now," Robert Warrens, the bi-vocational pastor of the little store front church in Bluebrook, stated.

"I think we need to be out there somehow," Rev. Mike Griffin stated firmly. "It would be a bolder step. If we include the community, it would have an even greater impact."

"Okay, what shall we do? Let's take a couple of minutes and pray in small groups again and see what the Lord shows us."

Once again fervent prayers went up and spiritual ears were tuned in to hear the Holy Spirit's still, small voice. At the invitation of Pastor Spalding, the spokesmen for each table spoke up.

They independently came to the consensus that they needed to do something that the community could see and participate in.

"We know that the parade route will be the same as it always is and that it goes past my church and past Pastor Spalding's church," Rev. Mike Griffin of the Presbyterian Church said. "I'm offering mine and I'm sure Pastor Spalding is open to using his." He looked at him for confirmation.

Lynda L. Irons

"Okay, we have who, when, where, and why. We need the what."

Cindy had an impression that she believed came from the Holy Spirit. "What if we were to divide the time – nine to noon – into six thirty-minute blocks? Each half hour could be devoted to a targeted community issue with prayer and maybe some appropriate music to go with it. I'm sure we can come up with six issues. Unemployment, sickness, emotional issues…"

"The youth and our schools," Wanda added.

"Political corruption," Clara Bardwell joined in.

"Families."

"Homelessness."

"Spiritual atmosphere."

"I think we're rolling, folks." Pastor Spalding beamed.

They kept talking and throwing out ideas. Excitement and unity built among them. They chose six volunteer ministers to take each of the thirty-minute time slots. They were free to pray, read pertinent Scriptures, bring in a worship team or an entire choir if they chose to do so. They created a sub-committee to decorate the church, make a sign, and craft a flyer that could be distributed. Someone else volunteered to purchase advertising in the local paper to invite the public to join them for all or some of the activity. Those not speaking would be available for prayer and ministry, distribution of Bibles and pamphlets. Of course, there would be baked goods and drinks to give away as well.

How they howled! This could not be happening! Urdang and his evil minions were stirred up in the heavenly places. Dodging the incense, the prayers, the sacrifices of praise, they whirled and cursed. Those walking, talking, breathing sacks of dirt! How could that Original Breath inflate and sustain His image-bearers generation after generation? And when they breathed back His words to Him! Oh, the power. How infuriating that they could not thwart the answer any more than the Prince of Persia and the Prince of Greece could impede the angelic messenger to Daniel, the man of high esteem.

Internally filled with violence, he shrieked, "We must take them down. Compromise their integrity. Diminish their esteem. Trip them up. Find their weak spots." Urdang growled and ordered his depraved corrupters to debase the dust puppets that fell under their domain. His voracious appetite for bloodshed and violence was never soothed.

His underlings delighted to do his will. Rising like vultures, eyeing their selected prey, plummeting through the atmosphere, the fiends attacked and taunted their quarries. They plagued and oppressed, tormented and deceived wherever anyone carelessly opened a door.

The teenaged boy with the occult card game hidden in his glove box was clipped in the parking lot by a hit and run driver. The normally upstanding elder feasted his eyes on the scantily clad young lady as he white-knuckled his Christianity. A number of married couples bickered over trivial matters. Teenagers escalated their rebelliousness. More than one small child pocketed a toy or piece of candy at the store.

227

Items were fudged on tax returns. A young woman overdosed on her mother's pain medications. A young man beat his girlfriend. Seeds of unrest and conflict, prejudice and strife, division and jealousy were sown, cultivated, and harvested all over the area.

Lisa Norris was excited about the prospect of flying in for her father's birthday party. She was torn because Sunday was Mother's Day and she would have to miss a visit with her mother. Of course, Mother pouted when she heard of her plans. Lisa had lived with her mother after her parents' divorce and she heard so many negative things about her father. Only recently did she begin to think that perhaps her father withdrew from the marriage because her mother could be very demanding. Selfish and self-centered might be a more honest evaluation. After their visit in February, she saw him through her mostly adult eyes. She decided that she wanted to connect with her father and find out if he was the ogre that her mother had made him out to be. Every daughter yearned for her daddy and Lisa was no exception.

Days flew by that week. Abigail divided her energies between caring for her rapidly growing chicks and Amy who was still mostly bed-ridden. They had gone for another ultrasound and some lab work. The doctor discovered a progesterone deficiency and prescribed the medication she needed. Amy had lost her job and her insurance as a result. She felt humiliated to have to apply for public assistance.

228

Abigail had a much smaller problem. She hated shopping for herself and loathed buying things for other people. She was afraid that the present would be disappointing. *I just have to get over it and find something cool for Lee.* She and Amy tossed ideas around and finally she decided that she would go to the big city and buy him a gift certificate and anything that caught her eye from the Outdoors Warehouse.

"I'll be going close to your old place. How about if I check your mailbox just in case something missed the forwarding order?"

"Thanks; that would be nice. I should be getting my tax refunds pretty soon. I hope they're going to come here. Soon."

"It'll work out. You need anything?"

"Yeah, a house, a job, furniture, clothes." She tried to make light of the situation.

"I'll see what I can find."

"I just wish I could get out and take care of stuff. I probably should close my checking account over there and open one around here."

"Stop," Abigail said with a friendly command. She got a deep sigh as a response. "Rest. I'll be back when I'm back."

Abigail headed down the driveway and drove uneventfully to her destination. After browsing for a short time, she was more convinced that a gift card would be the best idea. She purchased one and headed towards home. Making a turn off the main highway, she found Amy's mobile home park and stopped in front of Amy's lot. It still had not been cleaned up and the odor of the charred mess was still quite strong when the breeze shifted.

Lynda L. Irons

Opening the mailbox, she found flyers and newspapers, bills and advertisements. Frowning at the inefficiency of the postal service, she emptied the box, wrote a note on a piece of paper requesting the local carrier to check the forwarding order, and put the flag up. She would check again in a few weeks just to be sure that some important piece of mail did not get lost or stolen.

Levi was stirred up by his entourage of demons. Getting into his sleek sports car, he was directed down the roads until he was close to the mobile home park. He did not want to think about his encounter there when Amy beat him off. It still baffled him but he put it out of his mind as he caught sight of Abigail Steele's pickup truck when she swung onto the highway in the opening ahead of him. *Ah, time to have some fun.* He abruptly depressed the accelerator pedal. The peppy eight-cylinder engine responded and he was quickly on her tail.

Abigail noticed the car as it came close to her bumper. Glancing at the speedometer, noting that she was doing fifty, she accelerated slightly hoping that the man would back off. He didn't. *Lord, is that one of the cult guys? Was he watching for me and I missed him? Help!* She prayed and thought about what to do next. The long stretch of highway had few houses and no stores. She decided that if there was going to be a collision, she would rather that it was at a lower speed. She rode her brakes and slowed to thirty hoping that he would give up and pass her. He didn't. She slowed even more.

"No weapon formed against me will prosper! I declare it. Lord, would You please send Your warring

230

angels to protect me? Thwart the plans of the enemy!"
Abigail prayed and declared Scriptures as she
continued to drive with Levi inches from her bumper.
She did not dare stop. After several harrowing miles
of driving well under the speed limit, Abigail began to
feel as if she were at the head of a parade. Impatient
drivers were honking their horns and those who
managed to pass glared at her for holding up the
traffic.

The convenience store was a welcome sight.
Turning on her signal, Abigail eased into the parking
lot and stopped her car right in front of the doors in
the fire lane. Levi was right behind her and getting out
of his car. "God, do I pull out Walther?"

Put down your sword, Peter. Abigail heard the still
small Voice and kept the Walther in its holster.

Abigail got out of her car and stood facing Levi.
"What do you want?" she demanded loudly causing
patrons at the gas pumps to look their way. In a bold
move, she walked around him to the back of his car
and looked at the license plate. "B-L-A-Z-E. Well,
Blaze, or whoever you are, I'm going to report you."

Not expecting her assertiveness, Levi swore at her
and then pointed his finger at her face, "You're going
down! We know where you live and you're going
down!" Backing off, he hastily got into his car and
roared back down the highway.

"Are you all right, ma'am? I heard what that punk
said," an elderly gentleman sympathized. "This
generation!" Without waiting for her answer, he
walked to his car shaking his head.

Abigail did not realize how shaken she was until
she resumed her trip. She began to tremble slightly

231

and then the tears came. *Stupid tears!* By the time she topped the final hill on her road, she was much better. She thought. Impulsively, she turned into Lee's driveway. She needed to be completely calm before Amy saw her and besides, she needed a hug.

Lee could tell that something was wrong as he walked up to Abigail. She flung herself into his arms and quaked again. "What's wrong? What happened?"

Taking a deep breath, Abigail finally composed herself long enough to recount her harrowing trip. She omitted the part about getting him a gift card and told him about picking up Amy's mail and being tailed by some guy that she assumed was from the cult based on his threat.

Lee burned inside. His instinctive protectiveness flared. He wanted to find the man and throttle him. Or worse. He wanted to call down fire and brimstone. On Blaze.

"Come on," he guided her with his arm around her waist. "Let's see what Buster and the girls are doing."

Seeing Buster brought mixed emotions for Abigail. Buster sensed her distress and after finishing his showoff galloping and rearing up, he settled into a prance that brought him up to the fence. Nuzzling her pockets and hands for a treat, Abigail laughed and was comforted by his familiar warm breath. However, she was also reminded of just why he was here instead of in her field. And that thought brought her back to her present reality.

"He said he knows where I live. Makes me wonder if he's one of the guys that started the woods on fire or came into the house or up the driveway or followed me before." Abigail was more worried about Amy than she was for herself.

"No weapon!" Lee reminded her.

"No weapon!" Abigail agreed.

"But we still need to pray," he said and then launched into a simple prayer asking God to cover their properties and protect everyone on it.

16

Thursday, May 10

The hormone supplements seemed to be making a difference and Amy was able to be up more and more. Color was returning to her face as she spent time basking in the sunshine when it was warm enough. The unseen battle that waged internally was another story. Abigail sensed it and Amy agreed to a ministry session that morning.

"Let's open with prayer." Abigail started their session as usual with prayer and the standard question asking Amy to let her know what she was thinking or feeling.

"Just recently I've started feeling like there's something going on with the baby. I can't explain it. It's not medical, it's just..." Amy blushed, grunted in frustration, and put her head down. "Well, I find myself feeling like I'm repulsed by the baby and I just want it out of me." Amy was torn. Embarrassed. Scared.

"Let's keep going and we'll see where this is coming from." Abigail prayed again and waited.

Head Honcho reported in. "There's been a lot of movement in here lately. It seems like a lot them are trying to escape from every level. Except for six, that is."

"What's going on?" Abigail was mystified. This seemed like an entirely different issue, but if she had learned anything over the years, she learned that eventually an apparent rabbit trail would lead to the right destination.

"They keep saying something about needing refuge. They're looking for a city. I don't know if they're talking about Mayor's old turf or what. That was more like a town than a city though. They don't seem to want to go to Nicholai's level for some reason. I don't get it."

"Let's pray and see if anyone can help us out."

Amy's body shifted nervously in the chair as the internal deliberations took place. Before long, a personality emerged. It almost seemed like he was shoved out against his will. Looking warily around the room and finally at Abigail, he seemed to settle down.

"Hi. I'm Abigail. Are you comfortable with telling me who you are?"

"Hebron."

"That's an interesting name. A Bible name."

"I don't know. That's just my name."

"Can you tell me about your job?"

"I'm supposed to hide the others. Keep them safe."

"I know it's kind of a stupid question, but can you tell me exactly what or who you're keeping them safe from?"

"Uh," he hesitated and looked nervously around the ceiling of Abigail's living room.

"Are you being threatened by demons?"

Nod.

"Sorry about that. They have no business trespassing here." She did not stop to explain but launched into a prayer. "Holy Father, Your Word says that every place that we put the soles of our feet belong to us. This is my place in the natural and in the spiritual. I ask that You would command that these intruders be sent to a place where they can never afflict anyone ever again; along with their entire hierarchies including the ones that answer to Satan himself. Amen."

"Thanks," Hebron exhaled. "Me and five other guys are supposed to keep the others safe from Blood Avenger."

"Blood Avenger!" Abigail began to connect the dots in her mind. *Now I know why I was reading the book of Joshua last week!* Abigail thumbed back to Joshua twenty and quickly reviewed a very mysterious passage.

"He's on the loose. He's from Judas' level. Level five, you know. I don't know what set him off, but he's going after all of our people."

"Interesting." Abigail mulled over the myriad of thoughts that connected the biblical account with what was going on inside Amy's system. She recalled that Judas' level had a lot of persecutors whose jobs were to punish any so-called traitors. "Can you tell me what the common denominator is with all of your people? And are your people similar to the ones the other five guys keep?"

"Well, I hadn't really thought about it, but it seems like – at least in my group – they all had to... um, they all had to do something they didn't want to do. Sometimes there were accidents."

"Diplomatically put." Abigail gave him a gentle smile. "May I assume that they were made to do some dirty work for the Satanists? And that assignment resulted in someone's death?"

236

Hebron recoiled as if he had freshly gazed on some atrocity. "Yeah."

"So how do you and the other five fit in? By the way, are they listening in?"

"Yeah, they're here. Well, except for the one from Apollyon's level. He's trapped down there."

"I don't suppose their names are, uh, let me see." Abigail looked down at her Bible. "Kedesh, Shechem, Bezer, Ramoth, and Golan?"

"How'd you know?" Hebron was dumbfounded and a little shaken by her knowledge.

"It seems that the Satanists like to twist Scripture. I got those names from the chapter that describes setting up cities of refuge for people who accidently or unintentionally kill someone else."

"Yes! Yes! That's it!" He emphasized his words by jabbing his index finger in the air. "All of the ones in our shelters accidently killed someone. It was always some fluky thing. They were told that they would be safe until the high priest dies if they stayed hidden with us."

"Who's the high priest? Is there someone inside with that name? That assignment?"

"No. No one that we know of."

"Interesting." Abigail was praying silently and asking for wisdom. "Let me tell you what the Bible says about cities of refuge and the blood avenger and maybe we can make sense out of this. If we know what the real thing is, we'll know what they're counterfeiting."

"Okay."

Abigail paraphrased the biblical account, "Moses had Joshua set up cities of refuge for people that

237

unintentionally killed someone. Manslaughter. The avenger of blood could not kill them if they stayed in the city of refuge and they could only return home once the high priest died. Perhaps the high priest's death symbolized atonement or maybe it marked the end of a legal limitation on his sentence. It certainly was a type of what Christ did when He died and our sins were forgiven and fully paid."

"But Blood Avenger is trying to *kill* our people. He says the high priest is dead and they're fair game now."

"That would certainly be the opposite of the biblical principle. I wonder if the high priest is someone associated with the cult."

"That would be Prinz," Hebron spontaneously blurted out surprising both of them.

Immediately Amy switched in, placed both hands on her belly, and moaned with pain.

"What's going on?" Abigail was alarmed and hoping that she was not going into labor. It was chancy to distress a woman with a high-risk pregnancy, but *not* to process issues could prove to be more perilous in the long run.

"I don't know. It feels like the baby is trying to kill me," she gasped.

The baby was only inches long and merely ounces in weight so this did not make any sense in the natural. That understanding reassured Abigail that they were dealing with a spiritual matter. *Holy Spirit, help! Wisdom! Knowledge! Discernment!* "Let's pray."

Amy surprised her by taking the lead. "God, I need some help here. What's wrong with my baby? What's wrong with me?" She put her face into her open hands and began to weep.

"Oh, Father, bless Your child – Your children, Amy and the baby, with peace that passes understanding. We plead the blood of Jesus the Christ of Nazareth over Amy and her child from the tops of their heads to the soles of their feet. We ask You to separate everything that's of the enemy's kingdom from them: programming, curses, assignments, strongholds, and demons. Fill with Your Holy Spirit. Illuminate this issue and give us clarity of thought." Abigail quieted and continued to pray silently.

"Are you sensing anything?"

"It's a little better," Amy said and then looked at her with a puzzled expression. "I'm seeing an old photograph that used to be on my folk's mantle. It was a picture of Dad when he was a little boy. There were a bunch of uncles and aunts and grandparents in the picture, too. Humph. They all looked mad, but I guess that's how they took pictures back then. Why would I think about that?"

"I think God is trying to tell us that we're dealing with a generational issue here. Familial spirits and generational curses maybe. Let's keep praying." Abigail was relying on her experience. God often indicated that generational junk, as she called it, needed to be addressed when someone described a multi-generational family picture or when something reminded them of one of their parents.

"Sure."

"Thank you, Lord. What else do You want us to know? Light of the world, we ask for Your illumination."

"Yuk. Now I'm seeing Prinz." When she spoke his name, she put her hands protectively on her belly.

"There's some connection between that guy and your baby," Abigail observed. She was careful not to mention the name as it was apparent that it triggered something with the baby. Or at least something going on in Amy's womb. "Lord, we plead Your blood over that name and ask for more illumination. What are we dealing with here?"

"Oh, God, no," Amy's shoulders sagged. "No, not him!"

"He's the father," Abigail stated flatly as she connected the dots. "That would make so much sense."

"They're all slime bags, but..." Amy could not find the words to express her horror.

"Well," Abigail said dryly, "won't he be upset when he finds out that his kid isn't going to be a Satanist?"

That broke the tension a little and Amy giggled mischievously. Having another thought, she looked at Abigail with a serious expression and she asked, "Do you think that's true? I mean, the thought just came to me and I don't know if I made it up or not."

"Well, it either came from Satan, yourself, or God. I doubt it was Satan or one of his demons. If you weren't thinking about that before, it probably wasn't you. That leaves God. And if it's any comfort, it sits right with me."

"Makes sense."

"Don't forget what Hebron said about the high priest being dead. It makes me wonder if that guy died. Remember that one named Wraithe? She said something about an old guy dying."

"It could be Prinz. But how would Hebron get that info?"

"Don't know for sure. I have a hunch, but let's see if we can touch base with him and find out." Abigail was being careful not to inject her ideas into the conversation. Sometimes she ran into parts that wanted to please her and would use any hint of a suggestion to say what they thought she wanted to hear.

Hebron resurfaced. "Hi."

"Have you been listening?"

"Yep."

"Can you verify anything or help us understand the high priest thing?"

"All I know is that he is definitely the high priest of our region."

"Is he dead?"

"I'm thinking that he must be or Blood Avenger wouldn't be on the loose."

"Okay. Why don't we assume that he's dead? That would explain the Blood Avenger thing and that would explain why Amy's baby – assuming that he's the biological father – is suddenly having problems. So, we have two big issues to deal with: familial spirits moving down to the next generation and programming associated with his death kicking in Blood Avenger's assignment."

"What do we do?"

"If you and your guys could hang around while I pray with Amy, I think we need to take care of the generational junk first. Then we can address the Blood Avenger."

Hebron switched out and Amy switched back in again. "Wow! That makes so much sense. Can you pray first? I'm not sure I can do a good job on this one."

"No problem. Holy Father, we come before Your throne of grace in the name of Jesus the Christ. We lift up this child that is being formed in Amy's womb. We ask that You would go back through the generational lines on the baby's father's side and on Amy's side as far back as You need to and cleanse from every stronghold associated with sins committed by or against any family member. We confess the sins of the previous generations like Ezra, Nehemiah, and Daniel did. They said that they were slaves to kings because their fathers had committed iniquity and they had sinned just like them."

She prayed in some detail about verbal assaults and sexual sins, occult issues and addictions, trauma and crimes, physical and emotional wounds, mental and social issues, ethnic and national sins, geographical and territorial spirits. She prayed against the strongholds and demons associated with these things and asked the Lord to heal and seal any brokenness and fill with the Holy Spirit and all the goodness that countered the evil. Put off and put on.

"Lord, I agree. Clean up my family lines and the family lines of my baby on its father's side, because whoever it is, he's a Satanist. Amen."

"How are you feeling?"

"Whew! Much lighter. Like a weight came off my shoulders." Amy slumped in her chair exhausted from the session, but managed a weak smile. "And I don't feel like I want to get him out of me."

"Wonderful!" Abigail was pleased that this part of the Prinz equation was settled. "Now I think I need to talk to Hebron again and see what we can do about Blood Avenger."

"Screw him!" Blood Avenger snarled. "You want to talk, lady? Talk! I got things to do."

"Thanks for coming out," Abigail said pleasantly. "I'll get right to the point. Do I understand that your programming kicked in because Prinz just died?"

"I ain't programmed."

"You all are, but let's not argue about that right now," Abigail again answered as agreeably as possible. "So, your job, as I understand it, is to round up all the man-slaughterers and kill them because the high priest is dead now and you're free to kill them."

"Something like that."

"And Hebron and his counterparts can't hide them anymore."

"You got that right."

"I suppose you have a posse of some kind to help you."

"Yep. You're pretty sharp for a woman."

"Thanks. This ain't my first load of pumpkins," she said with a smile as if it were a genuine compliment from a close friend.

He was not amused and just glared at her.

"So, if you kill someone who killed someone by accident, then that makes you a murderer and you should be killed by an avenger of blood. Who's going to kill you and your guys now?"

He had to think about that for a moment. He did not have a ready retort. "That's not how it works."

Lynda L. Irons

"Oh, but I think you may be deceived here, my friend. Think about it. They used the ones you're trying to kill off to do their dirty work. That set them up to be killed off by you. Now you kill them and you become the next target."

He still did not have an answer for her. He was completely off-balance and that was disconcerting since he was accustomed to being the pursuer. He had not considered that he might be pursued as well.

"Think about what they do. Not just inside Amy but with all the other victims. You know, the way they set things up and programmed everyone but you." Abigail was hammering her point about programming but continued before he could protest again. "Kill. Steal. Destroy. Think about what happens to those inside and out. It's just a matter of time. When you finish your assignment, you're toast. You won't be useful to them anymore."

"You're wrong!" Blood Avenger protested vehemently, but he had no rational argument to support his assertion.

"If you say so," Abigail said lightly with a small shrug of her shoulders.

"It's my job. It's always been my job. It'll always be my job."

"Right. Like the man-slaughterers will always have their job. Oh, wait," Abigail said slightly sarcastically, "I forgot. Their jobs end when you kill them off."

"Lady! I should kill you right now!"

"I'm trying to save your tukkus. Think about it. Think about Prinz being dead. Why do you think he died? All the stinking demons that empowered his ancient carcass are being removed. He has lost his power. Is that what you want? Ask yourself if you want his kind of power or the kind of power that overpowered his power."

"You don't know what you're talking about," he said with less conviction.

"About power or about him being dead?"

"Power."

"Would you like to check it out?"

"You can't prove anything to me."

"What if I got rid of your demons through the power of the Holy Spirit of the true JHWH God?"

"No."

"Because you're afraid that I might be right? Because if I'm right that means that you've been climbing the wrong ladder all your life?"

She got no answer. Blood Avenger was clenching and unclenching his fists. Abigail was sure that his demons were getting very edgy. This was a common response when they sensed that they were about to be evicted.

"Look," Abigail said gently. "What have you got to lose? Trade in the counterfeit for the genuine article."

"I can't do that," he winced as he said it.

"They're tormenting you, aren't they?"

"I can handle it. I deserve it because I'm not doing my job."

"You can't do what they want you to do if my God won't permit it," Abigail replied evenly. "They want you to leap over here and kill me with that poker," she kept eye contact with him as she nodded toward the rack of fireplace tools.

"How did you know that?" He was shaken by the word of knowledge.

"The Holy Spirit of my God told me."

"Humph!" His bravado was fading but he was still desperately trying to justify and maintain his position. He had only known one thing. He had been prepared for only one thing. His time had arrived and now he was stymied.

"Would you let me help you figure a way through this mess?"

"Why would you want to do that? I'm a killer and I wouldn't mind killing you while I'm at it."

"Because you're a part of Amy and I happen to love her."

"I ain't got nothing to do with her."

"I know that you've been programmed to believe that, but you are a part of her."

"You and your programming!" He acted as if he wanted to get out of the chair, but it was as if he was glued to the seat. "I ought to kill you right now!"

"Me thinks you protest too much." Abigail took a stab at quoting a Shakespearean character.

"What's that supposed to mean?"

"It means that if there was nothing to the programming you wouldn't react so much. Why don't you let me prove it one way or the other?"

"What? The programming or that I'm a part of Amy?"

"Either one or both."

"You'll trick me."

"Nope. That's their job."

"Lady! Fine! Take your best shot, but I'm warning you: I'll kill you if you pull anything."

"I'm going to ask my God to remove the lie of multiplicity and let you realize the truth of the dissociation. Okay?"

"Fine!" he snarled. "Prove your stupid point."

"Holy God, would You please break the lie of multiplicity and bring Blood Avenger truth about the dissociation and his place in Amy?" She was careful to keep the prayer short and to the point with very little "prayerishness" to minimize things that would antagonize this hostile part.

After a few moments, he said, "Okay, so I'm a part of Amy. Nothing's changed."

"Nothing's changed except that you now know that somebody kept that information from you. Now you've got to ask yourself what else they've kept from you. How else have they deceived you?"

"They didn't," he said with less conviction.

"On the off chance that they did sneak in some programming, wouldn't you want to know?"

"No. Yes. I mean, no, they didn't."

"You're willing to stake your life on it?"

"Yes. No. Oh, lady! You're confusing me." He was clearly frustrated and becoming more desperate as the demons that were assigned to him were becoming more agitated. They knew that their time with Blood Avenger was short.

"Look, if you're right and I'm wrong, you have nothing to lose. I'll stop bugging you and you can go on your merry way and you've only wasted a couple more minutes."

"Fine. Do what you gotta do."

"You sure? I don't want to be like your Satanist buddies and force something on you." Abigail was convinced that since her last prayer, Blood Avenger was beginning to see more truth than he had let on. She was also sure that he wanted deliverance but was being intimidated by the demons. This was her way of allowing him to maintain some dignity while giving him a way out without increased retribution.

"Just do it."

Keeping her eyes focused on him, she prayed, "Holy God, we are asking that You would remove all programming along with whatever situation installed it and whatever words were spoken. Demolish the strongholds and send any oppressing spirits associated with the programming to a place where they'll never afflict anyone again. Fill with Your Holy Spirit and all the goodness and truth that he can receive right now. Amen."

He shifted in the chair to a more relaxed position. He almost did not seem like the same personality because of the dramatic change.

"Are you still Blood Avenger?"

"Yeah. I don't like that name. You were right. Why couldn't I see it?"

"Programming and demons. It's almost impossible to take care of it without help. Are you interested in getting more healing?"

He was weary and willing. Abigail prayed with him and it was not long before he was healed, delivered, and integrated. The demons assigned to him as well as demons that empowered his tormentors were gone. Amy resurfaced and was exhausted and very much relieved. Her internal world was much calmer. After ending their session, Amy took a nap and Abigail worked on some outdoor projects.

It was an ugly end. They found Prinz' tortured body in his inner sanctum. The candles had long ago burned themselves out. His face was rutted and cracked like drought-stricken earth. His skin had shrunken down to a fragile, wrinkled shroud that covered his shriveled corpse. His remains resembled something that might have been discovered in a sarcophagus. How appropriate for his ancient body.

It was an unexpected end. The expression that was forever frozen on his face was a cross between horror and shock. He learned too late that he was wrong, that Satan was wrong. He lost his quest for power and his accursed spirit was heading for the lake of fire that had originally been prepared for the devil and his angels who gleefully escorted him on his journey into the nether world.

It was an unending end. He had planned on living for many centuries, but the days that had been ordained for him were over. It was time for eternity. The celestial beings that had empowered him had either been legally evicted or else they abandoned him like rats deserting a sinking ship. He had fulfilled the number of his transgressions and become an abhorrence and thus was condemned to that hell where the worm does not die and the fire is not quenched.

Jesus wept as He blotted another name out of the Book of Life.

17

Friday, May 11

Lee recognized Lisa's number and happily answered his phone.

"Hey, Dad. Happy birthday," she said cheerily.

"Hello, sweet! What a nice way to start my day!"

"Are you going to do anything special to celebrate?"

"No, not really. Gary and Cindy asked Abigail and I to come over tonight. We're going to grill some steaks and just have a quiet evening."

"That sounds nice. I sure wish I could be there," she said knowing that she would be there. She had flown in the day before and was staying with Grandpa and Grandma McVeigh who were delighted to see their great-granddaughter. It had been so long.

"Me too, sweet. I miss you. Do you think you'll be able to make it out here pretty soon? I really want you to meet Abigail before the wedding. You *are* going to be able to make our wedding, aren't you?"

"I wouldn't miss it, Dad. And, yes, I'm working real hard on getting out your way. I'll let you know when I get a break in school. You know how it is. I can't wait to see your new place. It sounds great."

They continued to chat for a few more minutes. Lisa was very good at being evasive and more than once she wanted to blurt out the truth so she would not have to wait until the evening to see him. She was going to join them for dinner and the rest of the clan would descend on the McCord residence for dessert.

Meanwhile, Abigail was heading to church to meet with Max Berryman and Pastor Spalding. Abigail and Pastor Spalding did not have to wait long before Max showed up. He drove himself this time.

"How's it going?" Pastor Spalding shook Max's hand before they sat down.

"Pretty good, sir," Max said. "I'm trying to make things right."

"Oh?"

"Yeah, I, uh, well, I came clean with my dad about all the stuff I stole from his business."

"How did he take that?"

"Actually, pretty good. He said that he knew about it all along. He's willing to let me work it off." Max hung his head momentarily. "It'll take me awhile, but I'm going to make full restitution."

"I'm proud of you, son. I'm sure your father is, too."

"Thanks."

"How has it been internally this week?" Abigail asked.

"A bit quieter. I mean, I wasn't being harassed with thoughts like last week."

"That's good. It's a calmer week as far as the rituals go; so maybe that had something to do with it. Why don't we open with prayer and see where the Lord leads us this week?" Abigail suggested and then launched into her opening prayer. When she was finished she asked Max what he was thinking.

"I don't know. For some reason I'm thinking about the leukemia and the hospital. I don't really remember much. I guess I pretty much blocked out all that hospital stuff."

251

"Let's go with it. Lord, would You illuminate this and make it clear to Max what You want him to see or understand about the leukemia?"

"It's like I'm in the hospital room watching them strap him down. He has I.V.'s in his arms and they're giving him chemo. He's just screaming and begging his mom and dad to make them stop." Max unconsciously folded his arms in such a way that he could grasp the inside of the elbow of the opposite arm with each hand.

"Did you happen to notice that you referred to the little boy in the bed as 'him' instead of 'me' when you told us this memory?"

"I did?"

"Yes. You said that *you* were looking at them strap *him* down."

"Oh." Max did not catch the significance and asked, "What does that mean?"

"I think it's a clue to why Max-to-the-max and maybe some other parts of you exist. That may have been where Max-to-the-max got his start and why you hear those conversations inside your head sometimes. And maybe why you have some gaps in your memory. It describes a traumatic dissociative event. You separated yourself from the leukemia memories because they were so horrible and that little Max that you saw in the hospital bed holds all those memories. I think the Lord is showing us where your dissociation got started."

"Dissociation?"

"You probably had a traumatic dissociation. When you couldn't process the overwhelming trauma as a little guy, your brain and mind split off a part of you that handles the leukemia memories."

Max tilted his head with a questioning look but said nothing. This was a totally new concept and although he had an inkling, he did not have the vocabulary to ask a sensible question.

"Let me see if I can explain it. You know how you can be driving along and after you've gone through an intersection you suddenly look in the rear-view mirror and think, 'Oh, no! Was that light red or green?'"

"Yeah, I've done that."

"Me, too," Pastor Spalding chimed in.

"It's common. When we do mundane things, the brain dissociates on a normal level. We can focus on other thoughts or conversations, listen to the radio or look at the scenery. We do that when we mow the lawn, do housework, or any number of boring, ordinary tasks. Your brain says, 'ho-hum' and kind of dismisses the memory and you don't remember it. But if something special happens, like maybe you're mowing the lawn and you run over a snake, your brain says, 'this is interesting' and you remember mowing the lawn that day. Now, if we take the brain's God-given capacity to dissociate and put you into a traumatic situation, like the physical and emotional pain of being strapped down in a hospital bed to get chemo, your brain says, 'Overload! Overload! I'm misfiling this info. I don't want it stored on the cognitive side of my brain.'" Abigail tapped the left side of her head with the tips of her fingers.

Max nodded as he followed her explanation.

"But memory isn't just the pictures we see, like the memory picture of you in the hospital bed. A complete memory will have the emotional component as well as the body memories – what you see, hear, smell, taste, touch, or feel physically."

"Okay."

Abigail chuckled, "You didn't think you were going to get an anatomy and physiology lesson today, did you?"

Max gave her a half smile.

"Hang in there with me. Let me take a guess: you hate needles and shots."

"With a passion! I can't stand it. I avoid doctors and dentists." Again, Max clutched the insides of his elbows. "How did you know?"

"Look at what your body is doing," Abigail said and imitated the way he held his arms.

Max looked down with surprise. He did not realize his automatic response.

"The brain works by association. Let me give you an example. I worked with a lady one time who couldn't stand the color yellow. Hated it. We prayed and asked God why she hated yellow and He took her to a memory of when she was about two years old. Her family was at a lake and they were heading home for the day. Her mother was carrying her little brother and her father picked her up. But as he did, he smooshed her face into his crotch. It was amazing! She had body memories and described tasting the fishy lake water and feeling like she couldn't breathe. Those were body memories. And, guess what color her father's swim trunks were."

"Yellow?"

"Yep. So, as a little kid, she misfiled that memory. Instead of hating her father or what he did, it was safer to hate yellow. And she now understands why she hates swimming in lakes. Swimming pools are fine, but she won't go into a lake."

"That makes sense," Max mused softly as he absentmindedly rubbed his arms.

"So, I would guess that you're having a bit of a body memory now from the IVs that Little Max had."

"What do we do about it?"

Looking Max in the eyes again, Abigail said, "Is there a little Max in there who can tell us about being in the hospital?"

Max's eyes widened and he reported, "I hear a little voice saying yes."

"Little Max, would you like Jesus to come and make you feel better?"

Max was the mediator between Little Max and Abigail. That was also common with some of the dissociative people with whom Abigail worked. "He's nodding his head and sucking his thumb. Huh! Mom used to get on my case for sucking my thumb when I was four or five."

"It was probably him feeling upset or scared."

"Yeah. She'd yell at me and tell me I couldn't go to school if I sucked my thumb."

"I'm going to ask Jesus to show you where He was in the hospital room. Little Max, I know that you didn't know Him then, but He knew you and He was there. I'm going to pray and then you tell me what you see or hear or sense, okay?"

"He nodded his head."

"Are you looking in that room, too?"

"Yeah."

"Good. Let's pray," she said and waited for Max to close his eyes and focus on the hospital scene. "Lord Jesus, You were there that day, would You please let Max and Little Max see You with their spiritual eyes or hear You with their spiritual ears or sense Your presence? Would You please take away the fear and confusion and heal the pain and the body memories?" She glanced at Pastor Spalding who was watching Max intently.

After a few moments Max opened his eyes and breathed a sigh of relief. "You're not going to believe this," he began, "well, maybe you will." He looked at Abigail and then at Pastor Spalding's expectant face. "I saw Jesus kneeling at the head of the bed. He was stroking his hair, and He was crying, too. He kept saying, 'You'll be all right. I'm with you.' And then he, uh, I, calmed down and fell asleep."

"Cool. How does that memory feel now?"

"Peaceful."

"Let's see if it's time for Little Max to integrate with you."

"Sure."

"Lord, we ask that all the issues with Little Max are resolved – all body memories and emotional pain, all strongholds and demonic oppressors and any other brokenness is healed – and that You would join Little Max with Max. Reknit him back into his rightful place unless we need to address anything else, amen."

Max sat with his head bowed for a few moments. Smiling a crooked half smile, he said, "I saw myself go down into the bed and, um, like we just merged together and then I saw the adult me laying there sleeping without IVs or anything. Actually, it kind of morphed into my bed at home with Jesus still kneeling there."

"I think you're integrated. How do you feel?"

"Like I'm a little fuller. And I remember the leukemia years. I was mad at Mom and Dad for letting them do that to me. I didn't understand. No wonder I resented them."

"Is there anything that you need to forgive?"

Max inhaled and slowly let out his breath as he glanced at Pastor Spalding. "Yeah. I'm not good at this forgiveness thing but my parents forgave me so much on Sunday."

Abigail gave Pastor Spalding a nod. He took the lead and coached Max through a prayer of forgiveness and then they closed for the day. After making another appointment for next Friday, he limped out to his truck and headed for his father's shop. Pastor Spalding and Abigail debriefed for several minutes. He asked for clarification on a couple of points and thanked her again for mentoring him about things that he never learned in seminary.

Lisa was so excited. It was great visiting with her grandparents and cousins, but she really wanted to see her dad. She was a bit nervous about meeting Abigail and took extra care with her nails and selecting an outfit for the party. Cindy had picked her up earlier and she was standing back from the window watching for her father and Abigail.

Lee was just excited to have a steak for dinner. Abigail fed him well, but there was something about firing up the grill and having a steak grilled to perfection. Cousin Gary was a grill master. Picking up Abigail, they headed over to the McCord's house.

"Cousin Lee!" Bryan barely let him out of his truck before assaulting him with questions. "When can I come and see your cows? Can I ride your tractor again?" He jumped up and down as he peppered Lee with questions while Lee walked around the front of the truck to open Abigail's door.

"Well, you let me talk to your daddy about that and we'll see what we can do."

"And I'm not supposed to tell you about your surprise."

"Okay, buddy, you keep it a secret. Is it a good surprise?"

"Yeah," he said quietly and stole a glance at the front of the house.

Lee followed his gaze and saw Lisa run out the front door.

"Lisa! You're here?" He was dumbfounded and strode quickly to meet her. "Oh, sweet! It's so good to see you, you little stinker. You made it sound like you were still at school when we talked this morning."

Giggling, she hugged him around the neck and planted a kiss on his cheek, bringing back fond memories for Lee. He blinked rapidly to keep any telltale tears from tumbling down his cheeks. He composed himself and then turned toward Abigail who stood a few feet away with Traci and Cindy. "Abigail, come here and meet my daughter, Lisa. Lisa, this is Abigail Steele."

The two women approached each other smiling.

Abigail shrugged her shoulders, smiled, and asked, "Do you do hugs?"

"Sure do!" Lisa replied and opened her arms for a quick hug.

"Hey, you guys," Cindy interrupted. "Gary will be here in about a half hour. Why don't you come in and get some refreshments and visit? We should be able to eat in about an hour."

They drifted into the family room and it was not long before Gary came home. "Let me shower some of this grime off and I'll be right with you. Happy birthday, old man," he yelled over his shoulder as he went down the hallway. "How old are you anyway? Hit the big Five-O yet?"

"Almost. I'm just forty-eight."

"Wow!" Traci said. "I'm eight this year."

Lee just smiled.

Bryan and Traci were excited about the birthday party. They had helped Cindy decorate the house with balloons and other festive touches. Traci helped make the cake and Bryan picked out the ice cream. He was disappointed that his mother would not let him choose the bubble-gum kind.

Gary did a masterful job of getting everyone's steak done the way they wanted. Cindy had made some double baked potatoes and served salad and vegetables as well. They were just finishing their meal when the sound of many car doors was heard.

"All right, you guys," Lee looked around suspiciously, "what's going on?"

"More surprises!" Bryan piped up.

"Go open the front door," Gary said.

Bryan sped over to the front door, yanked it open, and yelled, "It's Grampa and Gramma!"

Lynda L. Irons

Traci was right behind him, "Shannon!" Her
favorite cousin was here along with her parents and
several relatives that Traci vaguely remembered from
other family gatherings.

This was another four-generation family gathering.
Lee was overwhelmed by all the attention. He was
tickled that someone had thought enough about him to
throw a steak dinner for him, but all this on top of it
was very touching. It had been a long time since he
had been celebrated. Cake and ice cream, coffee and
punch, cookies and candy, fruit and nuts added to the
festive atmosphere.

Gary tossed a package to Lee. "Here, open this."

Lee looked suspiciously at his cousin. "It won't
blow up or anything, will it?"

"Nah. You're good."

Tearing the paper, opening the box, Lee pulled out a
cap. The back of it said, "DIDN'T." He turned it
around and read the front of it: "WOULDA, COULDA,
SHOULDA."

"Funny," he said as he put it on his head. "I'll
treasure this."

18

Saturday, May 12

Lee was up early on Saturday morning. He drove over to his grandparent's house and visited with them while Lisa got ready for her day with her father and Abigail. Grandma McVeigh did not need to coax Lee very much to accept a plate of blueberry pancakes and a couple of eggs.

"We'll have to get out to your place one of these days," Grandpa McVeigh said.

"I'll tell you what," Lee answered. "You come over any time you want and I'll give you the nickel tour. They're getting real close to finishing. I might not have to prevail on your hospitality, after all."

"Well, you just let us know. We have plenty of room in this old house. We just rattle around in it and don't use half this space anymore. It's kind of like a museum."

Lisa bounced lightly into the room, "Good morning, everyone! Hi Dad." She planted a kiss on his cheek before she sat down at the table.

"Hey, kiddo. I still can't get over you being here."

"Me either. It's so good to see everyone again. It's been way too long. I feel bad that I haven't kept in touch."

"Well," Grandma said, "you must be getting older and wiser. That's when you realize that family is important. We're glad you're here and you just know that you are welcome here any time."

"Thanks, Gram."

"So, how many pancakes for you?"

"None."

"Eggs?"

"That would be perfect. I can cook them. You rest."

"Oh, no, young lady. You're a guest. I'm cooking. Two?"

"Yes, please."

Once breakfast was finished, Lisa and Lee went to his truck. He drove out to Route 1950, took the short cut to Kingston Road, and caught York Creek Road from the south. He called Abigail to let her know that they would be at his place within ten minutes.

"Amy, I'll be at Lee's. Not sure what we're going to do but will probably end up here for lunch and maybe supper. Lisa will be with us. Are you okay with meeting her?" Abigail knew how shy Amy was.

"Yeah, no problem."

"You need anything before I go?"

"I'm good. I'll probably just take a calm nap or sit calmly on the front porch. Or, maybe I'll sit calmly on the back deck." She emphasized how calm her day would be with her tongue firmly planted in her cheek.

"Later." Abigail shook her head and smiled at Amy as she headed out the door. She decided that she would walk to Lee's place today. The sun was warming up the air. The springtime scents were sweet. The trail between their places was dry since it had not rained recently. Watching warily for any signs of Charlie Fletcher, she walked as quietly as she could in her boots. It was not quite quiet enough.

Just ahead of her she heard crashing through the stand of woods. Her heart pumped and she froze and dropped to a half squat trying to visualize the source.

Catching a glimpse of three white tails, Abigail resumed breathing and stood tall again. "Thank You, Lord," she sighed. It was just a doe and her two fawns. "Hey," she called out to the retreating deer, "I'd love to have you over for dinner!"

Lee and Lisa were on the front porch of the house waiting for her. Together they went inside and looked at the progress of the workmen. "I love the new smell," Lisa said as she breathed in deeply.

"I do too," Lee agreed, "but there's something homey about an old farmhouse, too. Maybe it's nostalgia, but I love to be in Grandpa and Grandma's house."

"Well, now we have the best of both worlds," she said brightly.

When they got upstairs, Lee said, "And here's the guest room. You are welcome to stay here any time." He looked at Abigail who smiled and nodded.

They continued to wander through the rooms and eventually came out on the back porch. Lee pointed out the well house and the pond, the cow pastures and the horse pasture. Of course, it was on the other side of a stand of trees so they could not see the horses.

"Oh, Daddy, can we go see the horses? I haven't seen them in forever!"

"Sure, let's go. In fact, if you want to, we can go for a ride today."

"Really! I'd love to!"

Lee laughed as she resembled a teenager more than a sophisticated college co-ed. "Let's grab some halters and bring them up to the barn. Who do you want to ride?"

Lynda L. Irons

"Oh, I don't know. Who did you bring? I forgot. Misty?"

"Yep, she's here. I brought Lady, Sassy, and Sparkles, too."

"Sparkles. I want Sparkles. I love her blue eyes!" They walked down the path that had turned into a lane with all the traffic to the horses with their halters and leads. The horses whinnied and tossed their heads as they came up to the gate. After lavishing attention on all the horses, Sparkles, Lady, and Buster were finally walking behind Lisa, Lee, and Abigail respectively. After grooming them and shaking out blankets, saddling and mounting them, the trio headed back down the trail to Abigail's house to pick up bottled water and snacks.

Abigail paused at the mailbox and retrieved the mail. *Amy will be happy. Her federal tax refund came in.* Lee and Lisa waited in the back yard while Abigail dropped off the mail and picked up the water and granola bars.

"I'm outta here! Call Earl and Jan if you need anything," she said as she left.

Striding over to Buster, she put the refreshments in her saddlebags and remounted Buster. "Let's head down through the pasture. I want to pick up the SD card and then I'll show you my back yard," she said mostly to Lisa as she made a broad gesture with her arm.

Lisa did not ask any questions, but it was apparent that she was curious about the security camera. Soon all questions were left behind as they began to lope across the field to the line of woods on the far side.

Slowing for the trail entrance, Abigail asked, "Are you up for a long, short, or medium ride?"

"Let's go medium. I have a long plane ride back and I don't want to be too sore."

Squirrels scurried in the leaves looking for buried treasures. Birds called to each other. The sound of frogs was heard in the distance. Box turtles cowered. Green shoots pushed through crusty leaves. Bright yellow flowers faced the sun. Spring! They did not talk much as they drank in the sights and smells. The horses were enjoying the change of pace as well, with ears canted forward and nostrils flared.

Abigail led them down the trail upon which she had found the container of rat poison and the symbol for a traitor. She felt confident about taking this trail with Lee along for the ride. Besides, Charlie Fletcher probably would not be riding out here today and Max appeared to be on their side. When their trail intersected with another trail, Abigail halted Buster.

"This is as far as I've come on this trail. I'm pretty sure that if we go to the right it'll connect us with the trail that comes out near your driveway. I'm not sure what's to the left, but that's where I saw Charlie Fletcher's big horse tracks. You want to explore a little or head back?"

"How's your bottom?" Lee laughed as he deferred to Lisa.

"I'm up for exploration. This is beautiful and I feel like I could ride all day."

"Okay, then, let's go," Abigail said.

"Wait," Lee said. "Let me take lead for a while and you take the rear."

"Works."

Lee was on high alert and scanned the woods with all his senses. He paid attention to the slightest nuances of Lady's body language as well. She would pick up scents and sounds far before he would. About a mile down the trail Lee halted Lady. He saw the outline of a shack ahead.

"What do you think?" he asked.

"I wonder if that's the place Jason was talking about," Abigail answered.

"What place?"

"Some place that Max took him and Nathan to show them a skull. That's what I wanted to check out on one of my rides." She did not mention any details about the rat poison and the traitor sign.

Lisa looked from Abigail to her father and back again as she tried to follow their conversation.

"Let's check it out," he said.

"Yeah, I'd like to. It'd be nice to get confirmation about stuff I hear."

They cautiously rode into the clearing. Lee checked the perimeter carefully for signs of recent visitors but nothing was evident.

"Let's take a break and grab a snack," Lee suggested.

They dropped the reins confident that the horses would not wander while they took their break. Ambling around the clearing, Lee came to the little shack. Peering through the cracks in the warped old boards, Lee did not see anything alarming. Abigail meandered around the perimeter and wondered if there might be evidence of Jason's story about Max digging up a skull. She saw some disturbed ground and called Lee over.

"What do you think?"

"Looks like someone dug a hole here."

"I'll bet this is where Max dug up that skull."

"Easy enough to find out," Lee said. He used the heel of his boot to kick the soft dirt away.

"What are you looking for?" Lisa finally voiced her curiosity.

"Oh, I have a client that said he came out here and the guy he was with showed him a skull."

"What kind of clients do you have?"

"Most of them are just ordinary people with ordinary issues. A couple of them are ritual abuse survivors." Abigail did not want to alarm Lisa so she did not elaborate. Lisa would ask questions and she would answer them in due time.

"Oh."

After some minutes, Lee's heel contacted something hard. Dropping to one knee, he swept the dirt away with his gloved hands and uncovered a small human skull that was missing the lower jaw. "That definitely looks like a human skull," he confirmed.

"Looks like a child by the size of it just like Jason said."

"Don't you have to call the police or something?" Lisa asked with alarm.

"Not around here," Abigail said. "Unfortunately, there's, uh, corruption in the sheriff's department."

"Well, what are you going to do?" Lisa looked from Abigail to her father.

"Did you bring your cell phone by any chance?" Abigail asked Lee.

"Sure did." He reached into his pocket and took it out. Powering it up, he tapped the face of it a couple of times and took pictures of the skull. He stepped into the woods and found an angle that would show the skull with the shack in the background.

"Let's cover that back up and head back," Abigail suggested.

Their contemplative silence on the way back was different than the contented silence that they had enjoyed on their way out. Buster knew that they were heading home so he quickened his pace. Within a few miles they entered the pine stand and soon were on the lane that led out to York Creek Road. They were able to gallop for a short way but slowed down as they neared the road. Crossing it and walking carefully on the shoulder, they were soon dismounting at the barn.

"I'm starving!" Abigail declared as she finished grooming Buster.

"Me too!" Lee said heartily.

"I sure worked up an appetite," Lisa concurred.

Without verbalizing it, they had tacitly agreed to put the disturbing find behind them for now.

"I've got plenty up at the house for lunch."

"Sounds good."

They led the horses back down to their pasture where both Lady and Buster dropped and rolled, perhaps to eradicate the residual feelings of saddles and blankets from their backs. Soon they were up and shaking like giant dogs. Blowing through their nostrils, they wandered off, grazing as they went.

Arriving at Abigail's house, they scrambled out of Lee's truck and went in the back door. Amy was sunning on the deck.

"Hey there," she greeted them. "Did you have a good ride?"

"Sure did. It's always interesting," Abigail said. "Amy, this is Lee's daughter, Lisa. Lisa, Amy."

They chatted for a few minutes and then headed inside were Amy declined their invitation to join them for lunch. Kicking boots off in the utility room, they checked on the chicks who had huddled under their light with all the sudden activity. But stomachs rumbled and they were soon settled around the kitchen table. Hummus and blue corn chips, "angeled eggs" and tuna salad sandwiches, home canned applesauce and pickles satisfied their appetites.

Abigail sensed Lisa's restrained curiosity. She also wanted to be sensitive about her need to visit with her father. "Lisa, I know that you must have a gazillion questions about me and my life. I'm an open book. You're free to ask me anything you want." She added mischievously with a wink and a smile, "and if I don't know the answer, I can make up facts."

Lisa smiled at the crack but was silent for a few moments before she said, "I guess I wasn't expecting to find a human skull on our ride. And if the sheriff is corrupt, it makes me wonder how safe it is to live around here. I mean, Dad told me a couple of things." Her voice trailed off as she searched for the right questions.

Lee put his calloused hand on Lisa's delicate hand and gave her a comforting smile. "Sweet, I had and actually still have questions about this area, too. But this is where your great grandparents live, your cousins and other relatives, too. It's a good place to live in spite of some bad characters. Corruption is everywhere."

"Yeah, I know, but dead kids?"

"You're right, Lisa," Abigail injected, "there is a certain amount of risk for someone like me who works with satanic ritual abuse survivors." She paused and studied Lisa's face. "We have to focus on our calling as believers. This is my calling and I believe that God has and will protect me. He says that no weapon formed against us will prosper. That doesn't mean that they don't get a shot in from time to time, but they won't prosper."

"Just what *do* you do?" Lisa asked.

"I work with the survivors of ritual abuse. The cult doesn't like it. I help them get deprogrammed. They all have multiple personalities and I help them get healed and integrated. There's a lot of spiritual warfare involved. And I work with all kinds of ordinary people with normal issues, too. You know that ticks off Satan and his buddies so I'm on his radar maybe a little more than the average Christian."

"The cult." It was obvious that Lisa was about as uninformed about these matters as her dad had been.

"The local cult is part of a world-wide network of Satanists. The illuminati, witchcraft, Hoo doo, Voo doo, macumba, kabbala, Rosicrucians. They're all part of the new world order. In one way or another they carry out the Luciferian agenda to overthrow Christ and His rule. There are international, national, regional, and local masters all over the globe." Abigail paused to let some of this sink in. "We just happen to know who some of the players are around here."

"I guess it makes a weird kind of sense. I just never thought about stuff like this before."

"I'm glad that you never had to. Your father," Abigail nodded at Lee with a soft smile, "got initiated when he met me."

"You could say that again," Lee agreed.

"And I keep asking him if he's sure he wants to sign up for this."

"And I keep telling her that I do."

"You can't say that I didn't warn you."

"You've warned me and I'm not going anywhere." Lee clasped her hand with his free hand and exclaimed, "No weapon!"

"No weapon!" Abigail responded.

"You two!" Lisa laughed. She was delighted to see the sparkle had returned to her father's eyes again.

"Listen, I know you two only have a few hours to spend together. Why don't you scoot and have some good father-daughter time? I have a few chores and errands to do, too. Will I be able to see you at church tomorrow? What time is your flight?"

"I'd love to go to church with everyone, but I have a late morning flight. I do want to spend a little time with Mom when I get back there. She'll pick me up."

"Then let me say good-bye now. I am looking forward to seeing you in July and hope you can make it back before then, too. Somebody has to break in the guest room."

"Thanks," Lisa said with genuine warmth in her voice. "Abigail, I'm really glad Dad found you."

"Me too. Thank God for second chances."

"Amen!" Lee echoed. "I was fast enough to catch her."

"Actually," Abigail winked at Lisa, "I slowed down enough to let him catch me."

271

They laughed and hugged and then Lisa and her father headed to the utility room to don their boots. They got into Lee's truck and were soon off to his farm to explore more of the property. Abigail very much wanted to be with them, but she knew that this was an important time for Lee and Lisa. She would have plenty of time in the future.

Abigail rapped lightly on the door frame. "Hey, Amy, how are you doing?"

"I'm good, just bored out of my gourd. I can't wait to be able to do more."

"I need to run to town. Can you think of anything you need? Or want?"

"No, not really."

"Okay, then. I'll be back when I'm back. Let's do supper together, okay? If you're up to it, we can work on your stuff."

"Sure."

Abigail headed to her room to get her wallet, picked up her keys on the way out the front door, and got into her truck. "Lord, I'm not good at shopping, please direct me. What store should I go to?" She had a secret mission that she needed to complete today. *Oh, why didn't I call Cindy and have her help me?* Abigail berated herself.

She intended to go to Springfield, but as she was approaching the town square, she had a sudden thought. Going around the courthouse on the sets of one-way streets, she found a parking spot right in front of the thrift store. She was delighted to see Carrie Sue helping a customer.

As soon as she was free, Carrie Sue walked over to Abigail with a big smile. "What brings you here?"

"Well, I need a little help. I need to get some maternity clothes."

Carrie Sue could not help herself. Stepping back, looking at Abigail's belly with raised eye brows, shaking her head, she said with mock seriousness, "Abigail, Abigail," as if she were disappointed with her own child.

"It's not for me," Abigail protested with a laugh. "You see any wise men in the parking lot? No! It's for the lady that's staying with me."

Carrie Sue enjoyed a giggle and then replied with mock seriousness. "If you would follow me, ma'am, I'll show you our maternity section. It just so happens that we recently received a shipment of clothing from a store that was going out of business. Some of the items still have price tags on them."

"Really? That's great!" Together the two of them sifted through the clothes, screeching metal hangers on metal racks. Amy was slightly shorter than Abigail, but she was a little stockier so they thought they found the right size by holding them up to her shoulders. They were able to mix and match three tops with some shorts and a pair of pants with the expandable waistlines.

Abigail bought the bag full of clothes for cents on the dollar. Driving home, she praised God for answering her prayer for guidance. She would give them to Amy tomorrow morning.

19

Sunday, May 13, Mother's Day

Mother's Day was still difficult for Abigail, but with each passing year the sting of death continued to fade. She missed her boys. They would have been twenty, eighteen, and sixteen. If only.

She moved on with her thoughts and smiled as she remembered the handmade cards and the stemless dandelions they would pluck from the yard. She remembered how Darryl honored her for being the mother of their sons. It helped to be able to focus on Amy this year. It helped to have Lee in her life.

"Good morning, Momma!" Abigail greeted Amy when she emerged from her bedroom. Even though Amy was just starting her second trimester she was still a mother in Abigail's book.

Apparently, Amy had not thought about celebrating Mother's Day as a pregnant woman by the expression on her face. "Well, thank you! Happy Mother's Day to you, too." Amy was not exactly sure of all the details of Abigail's story, but she knew that Abigail had lost her family in an accident. "Are you okay with it? I mean, I know your boys are gone and all."

"Thanks for asking. I'm okay. I miss them on days like this, but I'm okay. It helps me to have you around to celebrate it again." Reaching behind her, she produced a large gift bag and handed it to Amy. "I got you some stuff."

Amy's jaw dropped. She was not expecting this kindness. "Aw, man. You shouldn't have. You've done so much for me already." Her eyes were beginning to mist.

"Hey, don't be too impressed. I got the stuff at the thrift store and they just *happened* to have a shipment of brand new stuff from a store that went out of business. I got it all for just a few bucks. That was a God thing."

"Okay, I feel better about it," Amy conceded. She began to pull the items out of the bag and hold them up against her chest. "These are perfect. Wow. All dressed up and no place to go."

"You'll be out and about again. Soon. In fact, I'll bet that after your next doctor's appointment she'll lift all restrictions."

"I sure hope so. I love your place, but I'm getting cabin fever. The best thing I did all week was get in my car and let it run for a few minutes. Maybe I can drive to the doctor myself."

"I don't think that'd be a good idea."

"What's the difference between sitting in the passenger's seat or the driver's seat?"

"You know it's a bit more stressful. Do you really want to risk it?"

"No," Amy said sullenly. "All right, I'll wait until I get the go-ahead."

"Good choice. Well, I need to get ready for church. I'll take care of the peepsters when I get back. I'll be glad when I can move them out to the coop. Maybe another week or so."

Amy returned to her room and put the new clothes in her closet next to the other clothing that Abigail had purchased for her after her trailer burned all her worldly possessions. *Well, it's a start.* She sighed and returned to her bed to rest and think about her life.

Abigail got ready for church and mentally braced herself for a Mother's Day Sunday. She was glad that she would be sitting by Cindy and wondered if Carrie Sue would be up for it. With all the babies that were torn from her womb, this could be a very difficult day. Abigail began to pray for Carrie Sue and for all the other mothers who had lost their children.

Arriving at the church, Abigail chatted briefly with some of her acquaintances as she headed to her usual pew. The McCords were running late today and the bench was empty. Lee was driving Lisa to the airport so it felt doubly empty until Cindy and Gary arrived.

"Happy Mother's Day," she said to Cindy.

"You, too," Cindy responded squeezing Abigail's hand. "You okay?"

"Yes. This year is better. I think it helps to have Amy around. I should have called you yesterday."

"Oh?"

"Yeah, you know me and shopping. I wanted to get some maternity clothes for Amy. She's starting to show a bit. Besides she needs some summer clothes."

"That would have been fun," Cindy sounded a little disappointed. "What did you do?"

She told Cindy about her great find at the thrift store and how she had seen Carrie Sue there. Before they could get much further in the conversation the musicians were starting their first song. Forty minutes later Pastor Spalding stepped up to the podium. Carrie Sue slid in late.

"Happy Mother's Day to all the wonderful mothers out there! I don't want to diminish the celebration in any way, but I know that there are some of you who have lost children and this can be one of the most difficult days of the year. And I know that there are others who have lost mothers recently which makes it difficult in another way. Please know that we bless you and want to acknowledge how challenging it can be to keep a smile on your face when your heart is still feeling grieved."

He had them turn to Philippians four and he read verses four through nine. "Folks, the Lord laid it on my heart to talk to you about fear and anxiety today. We're living in some stressful times. Just recently, there have been accidents and deaths in the community, I've gotten calls from distraught parents and learned about financial challenges and health issues from others. Fear comes knocking on everyone's door at one time or another and we need to know how to answer it."

He went on to talk about how traumas, circumstances, and perhaps generational modeling causes fear to invade. He spoke of the different emotional, attitudinal, and behavioral responses that are typically seen like OCD, perfectionism, addictions, and more; as well as the off-the-charts forms of fear like paranoia and phobias.

Since he was getting more familiar with spiritual warfare, he boldly stated, "Folks, when fear drives us to sin, or when the event that caused the fear occurs, there's a stronghold created in the spiritual realm. That's where the enemy hangs out and draws us into more distressing circumstances and encounters with scary people."

The old-timers were not accustomed to hearing ideas like this. Especially not on Mother's Day. But

Pastor Spalding had a way of disarming their skepticism and traditionalism.

He went through the Philippians passage and then began his concluding remarks. "The Bible exhorts us to put off the old and put on the new. I'm like the apostle Paul. I want you to stand firm like it says in verse one. Let's see what Paul's solution is. I'm going to give you seven quick points: One. Choose to pray, praise and thank God. Rejoice always. Two. Know that God is in charge of guarding your souls. He shall guard your hearts and minds. Three. Focus on truth, not deceptions. Four. Dwell on excellent, honorable, pure, and lovely things. Five. Watch a mature mentor who models fearlessness. Six. Practice what you hear and see in the mature believer. Seven. The result is that the God of peace will be with you."

He was pleased to see some of the people taking notes and others underlining phrases in their Bibles. As usual, he invited people to come for prayer.

"Did you give your friend the clothes yet?" Carrie Sue asked.

"Yes! She seemed really pleased. And thank you so much for helping me. It really made it easier."

They chatted about Carrie Sue's job and then Abigail asked her if she was doing all right with Mother's Day.

"I'm really all right. I think the worst part is having to deal with my mother. I have to go there for lunch today."

"Sorry."

"I'll be fine as long as Dorkas doesn't show up. How are you doing with Mother's Day?" Carrie Sue knew that Abigail had lost her family and was concerned for her as well.

"I'm really all right."

The crowd kept moving steadily towards the exits. Soon Abigail was breathing warm spring air. She gave Carrie Sue a quick hug after they affirmed their meeting on Friday. Driving home, Abigail was restless. It took her a short while to realize that it was because she would not be able to take her Mother's Day ride on Buster this year. She would turn her attention to making a good dinner. Lee would be back from dropping Lisa off at the airport and would join her and Amy later.

Dorkas was in a foul mood. Of course, hostility was her programmed job. She was a very cult-loyal, demon-loyal part of Susan Wagner. She did not care one way or another about any of the off-spring that came from Susan's womb. Dorkas was not a mother. She had no maternal instincts. A child was simply a potential sacrifice. A child was merely someone to torment for personal gain. Her treatment of Carrie Sue, Billy, and Danny gained her some power. She had no conscience as she partook in the torture and sexual abuse of each one of them.

Lately, she noticed her own weakness. She noticed that many of her celestial companions were missing and others were becoming hostile toward her. They acted as if she had something to do with it. She knew it was because of Carrie Sue. She let out a string of curses and intended to show up when Carrie Sue did.

That sniveling excuse of a woman, Susan, would get out of her way today. She would have her say.

Carrie Sue dreaded this visit, but if she did not show up, her mother or at least some part of her mother would cry. Another mother would berate her. Another one would be openly hostile. *Well, Lord, I'm asking You for protection. Please keep that hostile one away. Please let me minister to my mom. Or at least some part of her. Do I even have a mom?* Carrie Sue prayed fervently as she drove to her mother's house.

Susan was sitting on the front porch waiting for Carrie Sue. "I've been waiting for you. What took you so long?"

Groaning inwardly but putting on the best smile she could muster, Carrie Sue answered, "Sorry, Mom. Church went a little long today. Happy Mother's Day."

"Well, I don't know how happy it can be with both my boys gone and my only daughter paying no attention to me half the time."

"Mom, I'm sorry about your sons. I really am. I have a job now, you know."

"That's no excuse."

"Okay, how about the truth?" Carrie Sue was just sick and tired enough and just bold enough to quit allowing her mother to harass her with false accusations. "If I talked to you the way you talked to me, you wouldn't want to be around me." Carrie Sue continued with as respectful tone as she could muster, "The truth is that I dread coming here. I never know which one of your personalities will show up. You either go martyr on me or cuss me out or something in between; and it's just not pleasant."

"Oh! Well!" Susan sputtered.

That was Dorkas' cue. She came in with a vengeance cursing a blue streak. "I should have killed you when I had the chance!"

Carrie Sue held her hand up and stood at the same time. "I don't know who you are, but I want to talk to my mother. Back off in the name of Jesus Christ of Nazareth!"

Dorkas was flustered. She was not ready for the rebuff. Hastily retreating, she wondered what happened. *How could that insipid whelp talk to her like that?*

The other personality switched back in and did not miss a beat. In fact, she had no idea that Dorkas had switched in for a few moments. "Oh, Carrie Sue, how can you say that?"

"Mom! That mean part of you just switched in a minute ago and reamed me a new one. Don't you get it? You have multiple personalities."

"I most certainly do not! Your asinine counselor brainwashed you."

"Mom, think about your life. How much time is unaccounted for?"

"Everyone forgets what happens in their day."

"No, Mom. That's not normal. Think about all the stuff that shows up around here and you don't know where it came from. Think about times when you found yourself someplace strange and people were calling you something besides Susan. Think about the conversations going on in your head. That's not normal. That's dissociation."

"She's got you talking psycho-babble now."

"Mom. I know all of this because I was like that. I had thousands of different personalities of different ages. And they reacted to all the different personalities that you still have. I don't do that anymore because I'm whole."

"Says you." Susan retorted with less conviction. Some of what Carrie Sue said made sense. "I don't want to talk about it."

"That's fine, Mom. But if you ever want to talk about it, I'm listening. And I need for you to listen to me, too. I have a job and I have a church that I attend. We are going to have to work our visits around my schedule."

Susan wordlessly got up and drifted into her house, closing the door behind her as if no one was on the porch. Carrie Sue's shoulders slumped and she breathed a sigh that was a mixture of exhaustion and relief, hope and despair. Turning around, she got back into her car and went to her apartment. *Yeah, happy Mother's Day. I don't have a mother and they took my motherhood away. God, this is tough.*

Cassie was having the best Mother's Day in a long time. Ariel was safe and seemed to be fully recovered from the kidnapping ordeal. Jason was a joy. He had turned into an ambitious, focused young man. She was happy.

"Dad, Mom; I need some advice," Jason interrupted her pleasant thoughts.

"Oh?"

"Yeah," he said with a troubled expression on his usually jovial face. "There's this girl that works with me at The Taco Tower. Her boyfriend beat her up last week."

"Oh, my!" Cassie exclaimed. She was alarmed by the ring of terror that seemed to be surrounding her family. Pastor Spalding was right on target with his sermon that morning.

"She wants to get away from him, but he says that if she does, he'll kill her."

"Why doesn't she go to the sheriff?" Paul asked.

"I told her that she should, but she said that it would just make things worse. She said that he gets that way when she makes him mad so it's her own fault."

"No man has any right to hit any woman for any reason," Paul asserted.

"What do I tell her? I want to help, but she says that if he stops in and sees her talking to me he'll think she's flirting and she'll be in more trouble."

"Have you seen him?" Cassie asked.

"Yeah. He comes in all the time. It's like he's just watching her to make sure she's not cheating on him or something."

"Who is he?" Paul asked.

"I don't know his name. I just know that he's big and mean and full of tats. He looks evil. Like Max used to look before he changed."

"Well, you just stay away from him. Maybe you can give her some encouragement secretly. Do you think she'd see Mrs. Steele for counseling?"

"Not likely. She's afraid to do anything without her boyfriend's permission. I think they have a kid together, too."

Lynda L. Irons

"Oh dear, that really complicates things. We will certainly be praying."

They continued to talk about the situation until they noticed that Ariel was getting a little upset. Paul stood up and gathered the plates. Jason helped him. Cassie was getting ready to help them when Jason put his hands gently but firmly on her shoulders. "Nope! It's Mother's Day. You sit down and wait for your dessert."

Ariel began to giggle in anticipation. She and Jason had gone out and purchased an ice cream cake that was hidden in the basement freezer. Paul set out dessert plates while Jason went down to retrieve the cake.

20

Thursday, May 17, Ascension Day

Urdang stirred up his troops. "Put the pressure on! Nothing but chaos! A reign of terror!" He barked his orders to malevolent beings whose greatest delight came from inflicting their abhorrent torment on the children of wrath. They wanted to make sure that any misery inflicted on them would drive them further from the Highest One. They provoked each other to hatred and evil deeds.

Craig Jackson was already an angry young man. With uncombed hair looking like a dirty halo around his unshaven face, he sat on the couch stewing about his girlfriend. His father was a wife-beater but when he started to beat Craig, his mother finally got up the nerve to divorce him. Unfortunately, she was attracted to a series of men who were not much better. Craig learned to despise the weaker sex. It was all he knew and he kept the legacy alive.

Jeshbel swooped down on the young man. Demonically fueled gusts of thoughts began to escalate the rage like a breeze stirring up hot coals. *She's been talking to those guys at work. She flirts with them. She's going to leave you like your mother left your father. She disrespects you.* Craig roared his fury with a loud voice. "I'll show her! If I can't have her, no one can!" He was so crazed with wrath that he did not, indeed, could not consider the consequences of his actions.

Dashing out to his truck, reaching under the seat for the stolen gun, slipping it into his waistband, Craig roared over to The Taco Tower. The squeal of tires as he entered the parking lot caught the attention of some of the patrons. The screeching of his tires as he shuddered to a stop just outside of the entrance caught the attention of more patrons and employees.

Gabrielle was always hyper-vigilant. She never knew when he would show up. She saw him coming, knew that he was in a violent rage, and dropped the order she was bringing to the front counter. "Oh, no! I've got to hide! Tell him I'm not here!" With that she fled to the back of the store, opened the maintenance closet, and flattened herself against the wall after closing the door behind her.

Craig yanked the heavy glass door open causing it to clatter loudly against the wall and getting the attention of everyone in the place. He looked wildly around the dining area when he did not see Gabrielle behind the counter in her usual place. Storming up to the counter, he planted one hand on it and vaulted over it so quickly that the stunned employees were frozen in their tracks.

"Where is she?" he demanded as he rushed towards the back. Jeshbel knew. Jeshbel guided his steps. "I know you're in there!" He jerked the door open with one hand and pulled his gun out with the other. "You lying, cheating whore!"

Gabrielle faced him, put her hands out in front of her as if to catch the bullets, and pleaded with him, "No, Craig! Please." Those were her last words as he emptied the gun into her. Her last thoughts were for her baby. The crack and boom of the large caliber weapon echoed throughout the building. People dropped to the floor or froze in place as she collapsed in a bloody heap half in and half out of the closet.

Craig dashed back to the front of the store, pointing the gun in the faces of anyone in his path. Knocking one of the workers to the floor, he hurdled over the counter again. He bolted past stunned customers and sped off in his truck.

"Call 911!"

"Already did. They're on the way!"

"Oh, Jesus! Oh, Jesus! Oh, Jesus!"

"Someone help her!"

Jason picked himself off the floor, assured himself that the madman was gone, and headed back to Gabrielle's inert body. It lay in a pool of her own blood. "Oh, Jesus! Help me." He pulled her the rest of the way out of the closet and despite the ever-widening pools of blood, he began the sequence for starting CPR.

"Help me!" he gasped between desperate breaths. *We've got to save her.* He continued to send futile puffs of breath into lungs that were riddled with holes. In the dead silence of the room, the circle of co-workers could hear the raspy whistle of air bubbles escape in a frothy mix of blood and air.

Law enforcement and paramedics, fire trucks and curiosity seekers descended on The Taco Tower as calls went out from shocked witnesses. One of the paramedics assessed Gabrielle's condition while another one gently pulled the blood-soaked Jason away.

"We've got her, son."

They quickly put her on their gurney and whisked her to the ambulance. Sheriffs began to get witness

Lynda L. Irons

accounts. An alert bulletin went out with a description of Craig Jackson and his truck. The manager found her personnel file and gave them her parent's name and address.

Leaning up against the wall, adrenaline dissipating, Jason slid to the floor and sat with arms folded over his knees. He began to tremble and finally great sobs racked his body. The metallic taste of blood sickened him as the horrendous sights and sounds of the last hour replayed in his mind.

His manager, Todd Bell, squatted next to him and put a hand on his shoulder. "Jason, buddy, you did everything you could. Come on, let's get you cleaned up. You want something to drink? Can I call your parents?"

Jason rubbed his eyes and looked around at the aftermath in the room. He started to pull himself together again and accepted Todd's hand as he got off the floor. "No, no," he said, "I'll be all right." Looking at his bloodied hands, he said, "I better wash this off."

"You got some on your face, too," Todd said. He was worried about Jason and the rest of the young people that were milling around as they waited for the deputies to take their statements and dismiss them.

Yellow tape cordoned off the parking lot. Markers were placed in the lobby and kitchen areas. Someone was taking prints off the counter. It was a crime scene that was so out of place in this small town. News crews and reporters from the larger metropolitan areas arrived in Springfield to capture a headline.

After Sheriff Bynum and the last of his deputies finished collecting evidence, and the building was finally emptied, Todd was alone in the aftermath of the

288

carnage. He sat in his office, elbows on knees and forehead on hands. Staring at the floor, he mouthed wordless prayers, groanings too deep for words. The buzz of his cell phone startled him out of his stupor.

"Honey, are you all right? I heard about the shooting. What happened?" Teri Bell was nearly hysterical not knowing if her husband was hurt or not.

"I'm fine, I'm fine," he assured her. "That maniac boyfriend of Gabrielle came in here and shot her. He just went berserk!" he paused and added somberly, "I don't think she made it. Thank God no one else was hurt."

"Oh, Todd, that's horrible! When are you coming home? I was so worried!"

"I've got to call my regional manager and see what he wants me to do. I'll be home as soon as I can. I'm all right. I'm worried about these kids. Some of them are really shaken up."

"Let's call Pastor Wilmore when you get home. Maybe he can help."

"Good idea."

Todd finished the call with his wife and made the other necessary call to his manager. Making one last round to make sure all the doors were locked, he drove home in a surrealistic haze. He was starting to succumb to the shock of witnessing a murder.

———————————

Craig's rage blackout slowly grayed and he found himself sitting in his living room once again. It was not long before he heard a voice blasting through a bull horn demanding that he come out of the house. Confused and dazed, he ambled to the front door and stepped out onto the porch. He was immediately taken down and hand-cuffed.

Don Wilmore answered the call from Todd. "Yes, yes, I heard about it. What a tragedy."

"Pastor, my crew is all shaken up. I've got to help them somehow, but I don't even know where to begin."

"I'll tell you what," Pastor Wilmore replied, "I'll call Pastor Spalding. He's got a terrific counselor in his church. We'll put our heads together and see what we can do."

"That would be great. I mean, a bunch of them aren't Christians, but I think they'd be open to it."

"What kind of time frame are we looking at?"

"Wow, I hadn't thought about that much. Let me see, um, sorry, I'm not thinking too clearly right now."

"No need to apologize. You've been through a shocking experience yourself. Take your time."

"Okay." Todd took a deep breath. "My regional manager says that he's going to send a clean-up crew in tomorrow. He says that we should stay closed for a few days and open up again on Wednesday or Thursday next week. Maybe Friday. He's a terrific man. He says that anything that I need, he'll try to get it to me. He's even going to pay everyone that's on the schedule anyway."

"Wonderful. Let me call Pastor Spalding and I'll get back with you as soon as I know something."

They said their good-byes so Don Wilmore could call Daniel Spalding. Hitting his speed dial, they were soon connected.

"Don, what's up?"

"You must have heard about the shooting at The Taco Tower by now."

"Yes, I have. One of my young men works there. He was the one that tried to do CPR on the girl."

"God bless him. He must be traumatized."

"Yes. He's pretty shaken up. I referred him to Abigail Steele. They're probably going to meet tomorrow."

"Well, that's why I'm calling. Todd Bell, the manager, goes to my church. He called me and asked if I could help. I told him that I'd contact you and see if maybe your counselor had some ideas about helping his crew."

"Good idea. I'll give her a call. When do you think we'd be able to set something up?"

"He said they have an outside clean-up crew coming in tomorrow but that they're staying closed for about a week. I think we need to do something before they open back up."

"I'll call her right now and get back to you."

Abigail had just hung up from a call with Jason and had set up an appointment for the morning. "Pastor, I was just about to call you. I'm going to meet with Jason Miller in the morning and wondered if you were available to sit in."

"Yes I am. What time?"

"Ten."

"Ten? What about Max?"

"Oh, that's the other thing I needed to tell you. He has an appointment with the neurosurgeon out of town. He rescheduled for next Friday."

291

Lynda L. Irons

"Okay, I'll be there. Listen," he continued, "I just got a call from Pastor Wilmore. He's the manager's pastor and he got a call from the young man asking for help. He wanted me to call you and see if you had any ideas."

"Oh, wow," Abigail was hit with the magnitude of the problem. Jason was severely traumatized, but how many others were as well? "Okay, let me think a minute. What time frame are we talking about?"

"He said that the manager said that a clean-up crew would be there tomorrow and that they'll re-open at the end of the week. He wasn't exactly sure."

"Okay, that's good. I'll tell you what I'm thinking. Let's call a meeting of the Ministerial Alliance and let's put together a team. I'll have to brush up on the CISM debriefing from my chaplain training."

"You're a trained chaplain?"

"I took the training, but I didn't get officially certified. It was a couple of years ago. Anyway, do you think we could tentatively meet on Monday morning maybe at our church? It won't take long to tell them what I need to tell them, but I think we need to saturate this with prayer. Then we can go down to The Taco Tower and meet with the employees there."

"That sounds good. I'll make the calls. What do you think? Ten o'clock Monday morning for the team and noon at The Taco Tower?"

"Sounds good. I'll plan on it unless I hear otherwise."

Calls went out to Todd who called employees. Calls went out to the Ministerial Alliance. The Christian community was mobilizing. Prayer chains were activated. People thought about the brevity and

292

uncertainty of life. The community was shaken. They knew Todd and Teri. They were related to or friends with the employees. They had eaten at The Taco Tower. This violence was hitting too close to home.

Friday morning came too soon. Abigail was up several times during the night thinking and praying. She had spent the evening brushing up on her CISM training. Critical Incident Stress Management. She wrote out a cheat sheet for herself because every point was essential for the best possible outcome for those who had endured this trauma.

Jason was waiting for her when she pulled up to the church a few minutes before ten. Pastor Spalding met them in her office area shortly after she and Jason walked in.

"Good morning. How're you doing, son?" he addressed Jason extending his hand for a handshake, but spontaneously pulled him into a fatherly hug complete with three slaps on the shoulder with his left hand.

After separating, Jason sighed deeply, "Hangin' in there."

"That must have been quite an ordeal," Abigail sympathized. "Let's get started."

The men took their seats and Abigail prayed, "Abba Father, we come before Your throne of grace today with Jason. He has come to obtain mercy and grace in this time of need. We welcome Your Holy Spirit, Your Comforter to minister to him. We ask that You would stir in Jason's mind right now and take us to the place where we need to start today – the thought, word,

293

issue, emotion, or even a sensation in his body. Amen." She quieted and looked expectantly at Jason.

"I've just been sick to my stomach. I can't get the taste of her blood out of my mouth. I can't eat. I keep drinking water and soda. I even tried brushing my tongue with toothpaste and I can't get rid of it." He was clearly distressed and by the look on his face, one would have thought that he had a mouthful of blood at that moment.

"You're having body memories," Abigail informed him gently.

"What's that?"

"Let me try to explain it like this: we usually think of our memories as the visual picture of the event. But memory also consists of sensory and emotional input. Have you ever wondered why you thought of something that seemed to be out of the blue or suddenly had the urge to do something?"

Jason thought a moment and then said, "Yeah. You mean like when I walked out this morning and it's warm and the air smells a certain way and I just want to shoot hoops?"

"Yes. Brains work by association. Likely you played basketball in the spring and when you get a similar sensory input every spring, your brain goes to your basketball playing department."

"Okay. That makes sense. But what does that have to do with me not being able to get the taste of her blood out of my mouth?"

"I'm not a neurophysiology expert, and I probably don't have this exactly right, but from what I understand and what I've observed in folks who've been traumatized, it's like the brain freezes up so that you can't go through the normal neurological channels to process the trauma. Bottom line: you're stuck in the sensory part of the memory."

"Yeah. But I can't stop thinking about it either. Wondering what more I could have done... I keep seeing the fear in her eyes when Craig came in."

"Let's start by asking the Lord to take the sting out of the memory and to heal your body memories. Can you focus on the part of the memory where you tasted the blood right now? I'll pray and you just look around in that memory for the Lord."

"Sure." He bowed his head as Abigail took the lead.

"Lord, as Jason is focusing on that part of the memory, we ask that You would manifest Your presence in that memory. Let him see You with his spiritual eyes or hear You with his spiritual ears or sense Your presence. We ask that You would release him from the sting of the memory and from the body memories, especially the taste of blood. What is the truth that he needs to set him free?" Abigail studied Jason's face and continued to pray silently for the young man. Pastor Spalding was doing the same.

Jason sat quietly for several minutes with his eyes closed. Soon his eye lids fluttered and he looked up with a smile. "You're not going to believe what I just saw!"

"Oh, I think we will." Abigail had no idea, but from her experience, she knew it would be good. She smiled at Jason and took a quick look at the beaming pastor.

"Okay, so I saw myself sitting there after it was all over. I remember my manager tapped me on the shoulder and helped me up. He asked if he could get

295

me a drink of water or soda. But this time, it was Jesus tapping me on the shoulder and I just found myself standing up, like, with no effort. Jesus was wearing a really, really white robe. You know how snow can look so white that it has kind of a blue tinge to it?"

"Uh, huh."

"Well, He was standing in a river that was, like, coming down from a mountain. And I don't know how I know this, but it was coming from His throne. Like the river of life maybe? Anyway, He reached out His hand and a really ornate crystal glass was in it. It was filled with water that somehow came up through the water that He was standing in and through His arm and filled the glass." He paused to see if they thought he was crazy.

"He moved close to me and extended His hand to me. I just knew He was offering me a drink. When I consented, He moved closer and when I looked inside of it I was kind of shocked to see this beautiful, iridescent red between His palm and the bottom of the glass. I just knew it was His blood. But it wasn't in the glass. I drank it in without moving and it was like I wanted more but just one sip was enough."

"That is amazing," Abigail responded. She felt what she called Holy Ghost bumps as Jason was relating what he saw in the spirit. "So how is your mouth? Do you still taste blood?"

"No! Oh, wow! It's gone. Oh, man! It's all gone! How?" Jason was laughing and weeping at the same time as he tried to comprehend the healing he had just experienced.

Pastor Spalding erupted, "Praise the Lord!

"Could I just imagine this? I mean, just make it up?" Jason was still trying to figure it out logically.

"Well, all I can say is that if you did, you have a great imagination and a great power of self-help." Abigail laughed and then added, "God is pretty consistent in using our natural faculties to bring a spiritual truth. Consider it a parable that brought you truth." She paused and asked, "By the way, what is the truth about that day?"

Jason hung his head briefly and then said, "Okay, when I was sitting there, I have to admit that I was kinda mad at God. I mean, I was *begging* for help. I was begging for Him to save her. Now I know that He was there. And I don't know exactly how I know this, but it seems like He wants to be in the middle of things like this when people make crappy choices."

Pastor Spalding injected, "Maybe like how He showed up in the furnace with the three Hebrew boys? Or in the lions' den with Daniel and shut their mouths?"

"Exactly!"

They continued to discuss a few more painful points and then closed the session. As usual, Abigail answered Pastor Spalding's questions. He was really beginning to catch on.

"What's the word about debriefing The Taco Tower employees?" Abigail asked.

"Thanks for reminding me," Pastor Spalding replied. "I found out that the young lady's funeral is going to be Wednesday. Don said that Todd thought that it would be better to do it as soon as possible. He agreed that Monday would be perfect so we made the calls."

"Wonderful. I'll be ready."

By the time Abigail returned to her office from a short break, Carrie Sue was waiting for her.

"Hey there. How are you doing?"

"Great. I really like my job and my boss keeps telling me that I'm doing a great job. It's so weird to get compliments. I keep waiting for the yeah-but-you-screwed-up-here part, but it doesn't come."

"Hey, hey! Welcome to normal." Abigail grinned. "So how was your Mother's Day? I know you said that you had to visit your mom."

"Well, it was a mixed bag. I wish you could have seen the look on the mean one's face when I told her to get lost in the name of Jesus and let me talk to my mom again."

"That would have been worth the price of a ticket."

"That part felt good. I mean, that she can't bully me anymore. But when I left, I was just sad. I am really realizing that I don't have a mother. Not a nurturing one, that is. And I'm not a mom either. So that was the sad part.

"I'm sorry."

"It's not your fault. Besides, your mom is gone and so are your boys. I'm sorry for you."

"I guess we can throw a pity party and maybe have it catered," Abigail quipped mischievously. She succeeded in getting a smile out of Carrie Sue. "But seriously, tell me about the sadness. Is it like it was before when you had personalities who carried those assignments?"

"It's kind of like I had to experience this for myself so that I can own it. Like I'm living my own life. Does that make sense?"

"Absolutely. That's part of taking back your life. Each time you go through what would be a new experience for you, you own it. You're getting comfortable in your own skin."

"Yeah. Like when I drove for the first time after full integration. *I* drove."

"Exactly." They continued with their session and then Abigail said, "I need help with something."

"Sure."

"Lee and I are going to visit my father and some of my family over Memorial weekend and I have a lady living with me that's still on partial bedrest. I should have asked this sooner, but if it's okay with her, would you consider staying with her at my place?"

"Sure. That should be no problem."

"My neighbors will come over during the day if she needs anything, but I just don't want her alone at night. Oh. One more thing. There's the chickens. I might have them down in the coop by then and they'll need to be let out and put back in every day."

"I'd love to. Who's going to take care of Lee's animals?"

"Probably Gary and Bryan."

They laughed at the image of Bryan and Gary on the farm. They made an appointment for three weeks away but would meet sooner if Carrie Sue ran into any problems.

––––––––––––––

Abigail talked to Amy that night after supper and after Lee had gone for the night.

"Is she the lady I ran into at your office a couple months ago?"

"Yes. She's the one. I remember that the two of you looked at each other kind of funny and I wondered if you might have known each other."

"She looked familiar or maybe something about her just felt familiar."

"It would make sense. She's given me permission to let you know that she's a survivor, too. I've been working with her for a couple of years and she's down the healing curve a little further than you. She and I both thought that you should meet before then so that it's a mutually agreeable thing."

"I think it would be all right. I want to meet her, too. I never talked to someone like me before. I mean, someone who's trying to escape."

"How about if I invite her over for lunch after church on Sunday?"

"Oh, let me check with my social secretary and see if I have an opening." Amy resorted to humor when she was nervous.

21

Monday, May 21

All ten pastors from the last Ministerial Alliance meeting were present. They had put out invitations to other pastors that they knew and some that they did not know. Many of their prayer warriors were there as well. Todd Bell and his regional manager also attended this meeting.

At precisely ten o'clock, Pastor Spalding walked up to the podium that he had placed down on the sanctuary floor. "Folks, it's ten o'clock. If you'd gather up here near the front we can get started."

Abigail sat on the front row next to Cindy McCord and reviewed her notes one last time. Feeling a combination of nervousness and excitement, she prayed that everything she said would communicate well.

"Ladies and gentlemen, welcome. I'll get right to the point and introduce you to Abigail Steele. She's a counselor here at our church. I've had the privilege of co-laboring with her with some folks who have some mighty complex issues. Believe me when I say that God has given her a special anointing for her calling. She's also a trained chaplain – which I just found out. Please welcome Abigail Steele." He extended his arm towards Abigail.

"You go, girl." Cindy patted Abigail encouragingly.

Placing her notes on the podium, Abigail quietly looked at the gathering. "Thank you. I just want to clarify that I've had chaplain training and have done a lot of one-on-one and small group counseling. This will be my first critical incident stress debriefing. CISM. It'll be much different than the simulations we did in chaplain training. But I am confident that God is going to do a work today that will glorify Him. I know what to do, I just may not be smooth," she said with a smile.

"I want to go over the seven steps of CISM with you so that those who will be on the CISM team are tracking with me and those of you who will be interceding can also pray more intentionally." She saw thoughtful nods and then proceeded.

"Step one is introduction. We want to be sure that whoever is in the room is acceptable to the employees. For example, and this would be a worst-case scenario, if one of them has a problem with clergy members, for example, then all clergy must go. Now that probably won't happen, but you get the gist. Also, no notetaking. This is to be absolutely confidential. It's their stories, they are the only ones who have the right to tell it. And we also must honor their choice *not* to speak at all."

"Should we try to get them to talk?" Richard Morris asked.

"Not in the introduction step. They will have opportunities along the way and may choose to join in at some point once they feel safe or think that the discussion is relevant to them. Good question. Let's move to step two. This is the fact step. The 'what happened' step. Each of them tells what they know or saw in their own words and from their own perspective."

"Oh, like when there's a wreck and everyone tells it differently," George Bordman commented.

"Exactly. Step three is the thought step. It's the what-were-you-thinking-at-the-time step. Step four is the reaction step. It's like the-bomb-is-in-the-box-and-we-want-a-controlled-explosion step. This is where emotions will start to surface. And it could sound and look ugly or even violent. They may want to kill the murderer."

"What if they say that?" Don Wilmore asked.

"We just nod and affirm those very strong feelings. Emotions are not sins. Acting on them might be."

"That'll preach."

"Step five is about symptoms they're experiencing. We'll hear about nausea, nightmares, sleeplessness, inappropriate laughing, anxiety or panic. But it's important for the others to realize that this is 'normal' for this abnormal situation and that they are not alone. They're not nuts."

"Oh, that's good." Clara Bardwell nodded.

Step six is where I'll do some teaching to help them understand what is or has or might happen in their minds and bodies. And finally, in step seven we look at re-entry back into life. I'll ask them if they can think of even one good thing that has come from this incident."

"Any questions?"

"What are we supposed to do while you're going through the steps with them?" Paul Overton asked.

"Excellent question. Todd, I'm going to assume that we'll be in your dining area for this meeting."

"Yeah, that will work."

"Can we arrange for an inner circle for the participants to sit?"

"Yes."

"Good. Then what I would suggest is that the team sits back a little bit so that you can hear their answers but they won't feel like we're breathing down their necks."

"We can do that," Todd affirmed.

"Once we're finished with giving each of them a chance to speak in each of the steps, we're going to spread out in the lobby and each team member will have an opportunity to meet with one of them. This is where you can ask them if there's anything else they want to say but might have been too embarrassed or shy to mention it in the group meeting. This is where you can ask them if they would like you to pray with them. Ask if they have supportive people to help them."

"Can we invite them to our church?" Robert Warrens asked.

"If it seems appropriate, I don't see why not. Now, I need to emphasize a couple of things. Do not! I repeat, do not say, 'I know how you feel' unless you actually experienced exactly what they did. Don't say, 'I can only imagine' because that's irrelevant. This is about them and not us. And don't censor their thoughts, perspectives, or feelings. Some of them might use rough language. Don't go pastoral on them so try not to flinch." Abigail smiled briefly at Pastor Spalding. "Also, be very careful about touches or hugs. It can be misconstrued or distracting, and it can squelch them. Do *not* hand anyone a tissue if they cry, either. That's another subtle message that tells them to get it together."

A chuckle rippled through the grim group.

"Todd, can you tell me how many employees will be there?"

"Let me think a minute," he said. "There were eight working that day but I've invited the five who weren't working to come, too. I hope that was okay."

"Does the eight include you?"

"Oh, no. There could be fourteen there, then."

"Good. We don't want to overwhelm them by bringing a crowd in so in our prayer time let one of the prayer points be about who should be on the debriefing team. I'd like at least fifteen of us to be there inside. Todd, how many are guys and how many are gals? I want to make sure that the girls have a lady to talk with if they're uncomfortable talking one-on-one with a man."

"Nine guys and four ladies," Todd said. "Most of them are teens and early twenties, but we have one older lady. She's really broken up because she treated Gabrielle and all the others like they were her kids."

"Okay. Let me turn this back over to Pastor Spalding for the prayer time." Abigail noted that she took about thirty minutes. That left one hour to pray and get the team over to The Taco Tower.

"Thank you, Abigail. That was very informative. I don't know about the rest of you, but I wouldn't have even known where to start. Why don't we get into groups of four or five? Don't forget to pray specifically about being on the team." He pulled his cuff up with his right index finger and glanced at his watch. "Let's pray until eleven-thirty and then we'll put the team together and head over there."

It did not take long for these earnest and concerned clergy and laity to get down to the business of prayer. They prayed for the employees and the managers, the team members and the prayer supporters, the families and community that were directly and indirectly affected by this tragedy. Some of them surrounded Todd and his manager and prayed for them.

"Okay," Pastor Spalding announced, "let's regroup and see who's going in. I think it would be great if the rest of you could be outside in the parking lot praying. That way if we need extras we can grab you."

"Good idea, Daniel," Dennis Walsh said. "With all the cars in the parking lot other people might come in thinking it's open again. Or they might need prayer."

"Excellent! Okay, what is the consensus? Don't be shy. If you think you're supposed to be on the team, just get up right now and come up here."

All ten of the pastors came forward. Clara Bardwell was the only female. Cindy McCord stood up and walked forward and two other women came up as well."

Abigail did a quick head count. Nine men and three women. "Can we get one more guy and one more lady?" she asked.

Immediately two people stood and joined the group.

"Okay," she said feeling a little self-conscious as she facilitated a room full of spiritual leaders, "is everyone clear on the plan? And I need to warn you that this could take a couple of hours."

There were no questions so they began to head out to the parking lot. Abigail felt like she was leading a parade with twenty-some cars driving the short distance from the church to The Taco Tower right behind her. In the fifteen minutes before the noon meeting they set up the lobby area.

Todd stood outside the door and watched for his employees. He told them that it was a mandatory meeting for which they would be paid. When Jason came in he waved at Cindy and Abigail and then went over to stand by Pastor Spalding. It was good to see a smile on his face again.

Abigail had prepared Todd about his dual role in the meeting. He was both manager and participant. She asked him to be a role model especially for the first step or two.

"Okay, everyone," Todd said to his employees, "I know this seems strange, but we've been through an extraordinary incident. This gentleman," Todd said indicating his manager, "is our regional manager, Mr. Charles White. He's here to offer his support and help us get back on our feet again. As part of that support, we've invited some people here to help us process what happened." He made a broad sweep with his hand and said, "These people are from all different churches in our community. And this lady," he indicated Abigail, "is a trained professional who is going to facilitate our time together. Abigail Steele."

"This is the lady I told you guys about," Jason injected with enthusiasm. "She really helped me."

"Thank you," Abigail said as she sat in a chair next to Todd with the employees in the inner circle. "Let me explain a few things and then we can get started.

307

First of all, this is about each one of you. It's not about the rest of us. I want to emphasize that this will be confidential. You are free to talk or to pass. You do whatever you are the most comfortable with. All right?" She paused and looked around the circle.

Some were fidgeting nervously, some were attentive, one looked bored, others sat with arms folded in defensive postures.

"We're going to cover a lot of different things. The main thing is that I want you to be comfortable. So, the first thing I need to ask is this: Is everyone who is in this room acceptable? Is anyone uncomfortable with anyone else that is here for any reason?" She got no response. "This is really important because if there's any problem, you won't feel comfortable talking." She waited a moment while the employees looked around and either shrugged their shoulders or shook their heads. *Thank You, Lord.*

"We're basically going to systematically cover facts, thoughts, and emotions. And you'll learn a few things about handling the stress of going through what you went through. All of you will think or feel the same about a lot of things, but it's still going to be different in many ways for each of you. So, no one is right and no one is wrong. It just is. Okay?" She could see that they were paying attention and some looked hopeful.

"Let's start with the facts. Pretend you are a reporter and you're just reporting the facts as you know them from your perspective. Mr. Bell, would you be willing to start us off with what you know from your perspective? What did you see or hear?"

Todd cleared his throat. He was feeling the weight of the trauma. "I was in my office and I heard someone yelling, 'Where is she?' or something like that. I got up to see what was going on and I saw him just as he jerked the closet door open." Todd got very quiet and stroked his chin. He was not successful in controlling the quivers as he finished, "I saw the look on her face while he shot her over and over and over." He ended with a single sob and wiped his nose on the back of his sleeve.

Abigail noticed that most of the employees were fighting back tears of their own. This was good. She looked at Jason sitting next to Todd and asked, "Jason, can you tell us what you saw or heard?" This would have been the most difficult one in the group if she and Pastor Spalding had not been able to meet with him earlier.

"Sure. I was up at the counter. I heard him screech to a halt out there so I watched him come in here. He was so angry! The look in his eye! I was standing in front of Gabrielle and heard her tell us to tell him that she wasn't here. She dropped the food and ran. I heard him ask where Gabrielle was. He jumped over the counter and knocked me down so I just stayed there until he ran back out again. I heard the shots and went over to her. I, I," Jason broke down and the girl next to him put a hand on his shoulder. "I tried to do CPR, but she just kept bleeding and bleeding. There was so much blood." His voice trailed off.

The next girl was already weeping. "I was out in the lobby. I just saw Craig coming and I knew he was really mad. I was worried about Gab when I saw her run. I saw him jump the counter and then I heard the shots. Six shots. I just froze until he left and then I don't remember much."

The next young man was not on duty that day. "I wasn't here so I didn't see or hear anything."

"Okay, you can't report directly on this point, but we'll want to hear your perspective when we get to some of the other points," Abigail said.

One by one they went around the circle and reported the facts as they saw and heard them from their perspective. The next round was about their thoughts.

"What were you thinking at the time? Who wants to start?"

"At first I thought someone's car was backfiring, but when it kept going, I realized it was gunshots."

"I thought it was a hold-up."

"I thought he was going to shoot me, too."

On and on, they took turns.

"You guys are doing great," Abigail encouraged them. "Now it might get a little tougher. We're going to talk about what you felt then and what you've been feeling since then. Feel free to say what you need to – good, bad, or ugly. Okay?"

Todd started this round, too. "I'm mad. I'm so angry that someone could just come in here and kill someone. I'm so mad at what he's done to us. I'm so sad for Gabrielle's little girl. And I'm proud, too. I'm proud of all of you." Again, he thumbed tears from the corner of his eyes.

"I hate him. He should be put in a closet and shot!"

"I feel responsible. I didn't stop him. I just hid and I should have done something. I should have tackled him or something."

"I feel guilty. I'm sorry, Jason, you begged for help and I just stood there."

"It's okay, man," Jason responded.

"Me, too. I didn't do anything. I just ducked."

They each contributed to the discussion. They were beginning to bond as they realized that they shared common thoughts and emotions. Abigail was pleased. She could see from the expressions on the ministry team that they were engaged and praying.

Abigail asked them to answer one question. "If you could change one thing with the exception of bringing Gabrielle back to life, what would that one thing be?"

"I would change the schedule so that I was here instead of Gabrielle."

"I would have tackled him."

"I would have gotten her out the back door."

"I'd want a couple of sheriffs in here ordering lunch when he got here." She was serious, but it brought a few cheerless laughs.

They continued with this step. Abigail noticed that they were getting more comfortable with expressing themselves with each level. That in itself was very healing.

"Okay, let's switch gears a little and talk about another issue. "What symptoms are you experiencing? What changes have you noticed since the incident?"

Jason jumped right in and said, "I couldn't get the taste of blood out of my mouth until I got counseling on Friday. But I'm still having trouble falling asleep at night. It's like my brain won't shut up."

"Me, too,"

"I jump at any loud noise."

"I can't watch television programs or movies where people get shot and killed."

"I've been having panic attacks."

Lynda L. Irons

"I don't care about anything. I mean, I just flunked a test and I don't care. Well, I do care but I don't."

"I can't concentrate on my homework. Shoot! I can't even sit still long enough to study."

"I thought I would have to go to the emergency room because I had trouble catching my breath."

"Nightmares."

"Yeah."

"I feel like I have the flu."

As they elaborated on their symptoms Abigail could sense that each one was beginning to feel less isolated as they realized that they were not the only ones with physical, mental, or emotional fall-out.

Abigail continued to facilitate. "As you heard, there are a wide variety of symptoms any one of you can experience. You are normal. You're all experiencing expected things from this unexpected incident. I'd be worried if you didn't."

She moved to the next step to help them understand what is, what has, and what might happen in their minds and/or bodies. She taught them about the effects of stress and what to do about it. She taught them about the fight-or-flight response and the effect of adrenaline on the body.

"Give yourself permission to have those normal reactions to the abnormal situation. Some things that you can do to help yourself is to exercise and eat a healthy diet. Write in your journal or talk with friends and family. Try to go easy on sugar, caffeine, and alcohol. They just make you more tense." She was pleased that they were tracking with her and nodding agreement.

"Now, if you are concerned about physical symptoms, go see a doctor and rule out anything that might come from something besides this incident. If you can't get past any aspect of this in a reasonable amount of time, see a counselor. Take care of yourself. You have been traumatized. It's okay." She could tell that these were new concepts for some of them.

"One last question in this step." Abigail looked at the group tenderly. "Can you think of even one good thing which has come out of this incident?"

"No way! Gabrielle's dead."

"Yeah! Her baby has to grow up without a mother."

Abigail just nodded and prayed that someone would reflect a more positive reaction. It usually came after the strong negative ones. She waited for a painfully long minute.

"I think that it's good how we're getting closer. I mean, I don't just think of you guys as co-workers, more like friends."

"Yeah, we've bonded."

"I don't look at people the same. Like, some people really have it rough. I'm a bit more sensitive to that."

"I don't take life for granted anymore. It could be over in a second."

They continued to express more positive than negative answers. Even the most negative among them were able to find at least one little good thing.

"These folks have come here to support you and to listen to your story. They'll pray with you if you like. There are probably some things that you couldn't say in the group and we want to give you that opportunity now."

Lynda L. Irons

They all indicated that they would participate so Abigail had the ministry team spread out in the lobby. She encouraged the employees not to be shy, but to join anyone who was there. It was amazing how they paired up effortlessly. God was at work!

"I'm going to call us back together as a group in about twenty minutes," Abigail informed them before she retreated to the counter and stood by Charles White, the regional manager.

"I am impressed," he said. "I was afraid we'd have to close this store."

"These are some terrific kids. Todd Bell is amazing. He really cares about them."

"He's a good man," he affirmed. "Did I hear that Gabrielle had a daughter?"

"From what I understand she's just a toddler."

"I wonder what'll happen to her with her mother gone and her father in prison."

They lapsed into silence and waited while the ministry team listened and prayed with the traumatized employees. Lots of napkins were taken from the dispensers and used to dab tears. Finally, it was time to wrap it up and Abigail called the employees back to their circle.

"How is everyone doing right now? Can you give each other some feedback?"

"I'm feeling relieved. I thought I was going crazy. I'm glad that I'm okay."

"Yeah, I thought I was the only one who was feeling stuff."

"I feel like a big weight lifted off. This was the first time I talked about it."

314

They each gave positive feedback and when they quieted, Abigail spoke again. "I want to talk about one more aspect of healing. I think one of you mentioned that the man looked like he was demon possessed. I don't know if he was possessed or oppressed, but there really is a spiritual realm and there really are demons. When these kinds of things happen, those scuzzie uglies are attracted to the people and places where violence happens. They're legalists and squatters and I want to make sure that no one here is getting picked on by the demons because of this incident. Is everyone okay with me asking God to cleanse this place and everyone that's here?"

Jason was definitely on board and vigorously nodded his head. All the others followed his lead and consented.

"Let's pray. Holy God and Father, we come before Your throne of grace today on behalf of The Taco Tower and all its employees. We ask that You would cover this place with the cleansing blood of Jesus Christ which washes whiter than snow. Evict any evil spirit that was brought here because of the murder so that no one who works here or dines here will be oppressed in any way. We ask that You would heal all the broken places in each one here and bless them with peace. We pray this in the name of Jesus, amen."

The quiet group looked expectantly at Abigail.

She smiled and said, "I think we're finished here. You guys are heroes in my book. Thank you everyone. Mr. Bell, do you have anything?"

"For those of you who haven't heard yet, Gabrielle's funeral will be on Wednesday at the Harper Funeral

Home. We will re-open on Friday. Check the new schedule before you leave."

Charles White stepped up and cleared his throat. "I just want to tell you what a terrific bunch of employees you are. I have an announcement that I just cleared with corporate. All the proceeds from our sales on Friday, Saturday, and Sunday will go to a trust fund for Gabrielle's little girl! Spread the word and get ready to build a lot of tacos!"

Whoops and shouts echoed off the walls. Tensions were broken. Purpose and joy were restored in a large measure. The employees and ministry team mingled and celebrated for a short while and then one by one and in small groups The Taco Tower emptied leaving Todd Bell alone to lock up. This time the atmosphere was different.

Radically different.

22

Wednesday, May 23

It seemed that all of heaven was mourning. The skies dripped sympathetic tears from heavy gray clouds. The light rain seemed to be an appropriate accompaniment for a funeral that somehow touched the entire county and beyond. Reporters from the larger metropolitan areas converged on Harper's Funeral Home along with hundreds of local citizens. The entire Ministerial Alliance team was in attendance as well. Deputies were dispatched to direct the traffic and escort the funeral procession to the cemetery.

Gabrielle attended the Kingston United Methodist Church as a little girl but Craig had forbidden her from going anywhere but work. Her mother still attended that church sometimes so Rev. Benjamin Morgan was asked to officiate at her daughter's funeral. He preached a message that included the plan of salvation. He also made a brief reference to the interdenominational team that ministered to the traumatized employees a few days before. It was a message of hope. It was a message of unity.

He concluded, "On behalf of Gabrielle's family, I want to thank all of you for your show of support. We are asking that just the immediate family and their guests come to the brief grave side service. Please join the family at the Kingston United Methodist Church for refreshments. Feel free to make your way over there now. I have one more announcement. As you know, Gabrielle worked at The Taco Tower. The

317

management there is donating all of the proceeds from Friday, Saturday, and Sunday to establish a trust fund for Gabrielle's little girl."

The sounds of approval rumbled through the crowd and he saw smiles breaking out of somber faces like shafts of sunlight punching through an overcast sky. Reporters added this item to their stories.

The brief graveside service was concluded without delay and the family drove to the church. The basement was filled to capacity. People spoke in hushed tones. It was made known that anyone in need of prayer was welcome to go upstairs where the Ministerial Alliance members were available. There was healing. There were salvations.

The sting of death was felt but the diabolical delight of the heinous celestial beings turned to fury as they realized that their schemes had backfired. Unbelievers were not becoming more entrenched and embittered towards the Great Enemy; they were turning to Him. People considered their own mortality. Redemption. Restoration. Recompense. The scheme to make all things work together for evil had failed again.

On Thursday afternoon, Todd had the entire crew show up at The Taco Tower to do prep work. He figured that some of them would still be shaken up by the events of the past week and he wanted to give them the opportunity to be able to ease back into their jobs. The place had been cleaned and cleared of any evidence that a murder occurred there only one week before. It had been more than a physical clean-up; the spiritual atmosphere had been cleansed as well.

318

The over-all mood made it seem more like they were getting ready for a party than for work. At one point, however, Jason noticed that one of the other crew members was staring at the floor by the closet. He walked over to her and asked, "Are you all right?"

Kristin was startled out of her thoughts and quickly dabbed at her eyes. "Yeah, yeah. I'm good. Thanks."

"It's okay, you know."

"How do you do it? I mean, you had it the worst," she said.

"I *was* a mess and still am sometimes, but I called my pastor and we got together with my counselor the next day. That lady that led the thing on Monday. Abigail Steele. God showed up and I got a lot of healing."

"Maybe I need God," she mused.

"We all do," Jason replied. He was suddenly nervous because he recognized this as a great ministry opportunity and he felt so ill-equipped. *Jesus, what should I say to her?* He quickly had a thought. "Do you want to meet Him?"

"You mean God?"

"Yes."

"How?"

"Let's go to Mr. Bell's office. He has his Bible in there and I can show you what it says."

They walked together to Todd's office. Jason rapped lightly on the door and explained why they were there. Todd broke into a big grin and invited them to have a seat. Jason was relieved when Todd grabbed his Bible from the far corner of his desk and took the lead. He explained salvation to Kristin and then asked her if she wanted to make that decision.

"Uh, yeah," she said. "I really need to."

Todd led her in a prayer of repentance and of receiving Jesus Christ as her Savior. It was beautiful to see the transformation in her countenance. She laughed and wept at the same time.

"I, I don't know what just happened, but I feel so light I think I could fly!"

"You just got saved." Jason joined in the laughter. He spontaneously gave her a hug.

Todd was dabbing at his eyes, too. "Listen, Kristin, it's important to be in a good Bible-believing church. If you don't have one or if you don't feel comfortable there, you're welcome to come to mine. We have a pretty good young people's group. Jason can talk to you about his church, too."

"Okay," she said uncertainly. Her family rarely went to church; they mostly just went on Christmas and Easter. Since they did not insist that she attend, she usually chose to spend Sunday mornings sleeping late.

"Celebrate and then tell someone what you just did and then you two get back to work." He stood and fist-bumped her before she and Jason returned to their duties.

Someone had cleaned two of the five-gallon food-grade buckets and started to do the lettering and affix enlarged pictures of Gabrielle and her daughter onto them. Slots were cut into the lids. Posters were made that would inform patrons about the proceeds. With all the busy hands, the work was soon finished. The crew headed out and Todd did his final check and locked the place up for the day. He was praising God for the way He was redeeming the ugly, difficult events of the past week.

"Mom! Dad!" Jason exclaimed as he burst through the kitchen door. "Guess what!"

"What?" Paul and Cassie harmonized as they responded together.

"Kristin got saved today. It was the coolest thing! She was staring at the floor where Gabrielle got shot and I said something to her and she asked me how I'm doing so well and I told her that God helped me, I mean, along with Pastor and Mrs. Steele and she said that she thought that she might need God, too, so I told her I could help her with that and then we went to Mr. Bell's office and man am I ever glad that he took over and he showed her verses in his Bible and led her to the Lord!" He blurted it all out in one breath while gesturing excitedly with his hands.

"Oh, that's wonderful," Cassie replied with a big smile. "Which one is Kristin?"

"She's kind of new. I think she's a senior. She has long, dark hair and stands about this tall." He flattened his hand at a ninety-degree angle and held it shoulder high.

"I'm so proud of you, son," Paul added.

"Thanks. But actually, I kind of wimped out." Jason hung his head briefly. "I mean, I got the first part right, you know, talking to her. I was going to ask to borrow Mr. Bell's Bible, but I really don't know what I would have done except show her John 3:16. Mr. Bell just knew what verses to go to and how to answer her questions. I really need to get to Bible College and learn this stuff."

"Why don't you ask Mr. Bell for those references? You can study them on your own later. You never know when another opportunity will come up."

"Good idea. Thanks Mom!" With that, Jason grabbed an apple from the basket on the counter and bounded out of the room.

Paul smiled broadly and Cassie dabbed at tears of joy as they hugged. "Thank you, Jesus," Paul whispered. They were profoundly grateful for the transformation in their son.

Todd Bell expected a busy day, but he was amazed at the turnout on Friday. The media had gotten the word out with feature articles and special reports. The community responded. Indeed, people came from near and far. They wanted to *do* something, something tangible. Cars were wrapped around the building continuously keeping the drive-through busy. Others came in and lingered because they just wanted to be there to support the cause.

In fact, some of the crew's relatives and friends pitched in and cleared tables and emptied trash. It was a community-wide celebration as they reclaimed their lives from the grip of tragedy and gave something tangible back. The trust fund for Gabrielle's little girl was well established by the end of the first day. Customers paid for their meals and then threw large and small bills, coins and checks into the donation buckets.

Max was on time for his appointment with Abigail and Pastor Spalding. He was beginning to look forward to unraveling the mysteries of his life.

"How are things since last time?" Abigail asked as she took her seat.

"I feel a lot calmer inside. I think some of my life is starting to make sense. I mean, my anger and resentment towards my parents. Even some of my fears." He briefly hung his head. "I hate to admit it, but I have more fears than I'd like to admit."

"Excellent start!" Abigail rejoiced. "We'll get at the fears but I have a question that's been lingering since you got healed. You said something like the death demon is not done with you yet."

"Yeah, I remember. After we got rid of Mot."

"Do you think the death demon was the spirit of pharmakia that drove Max-to-the-max? Or do you think there's some other back-up death demon?"

"I'm not sure."

"It just seems like you've had brushes with death a time or two. Like something has been trying to take you out all your life either medically or through the cult."

"Yeah, now that you mention it," he said thoughtfully. "My parents said that it was a miracle that I lived at all. I guess I was pretty sickly from the get-go."

"Are you an only child?" Abigail thought that he was, but wanted to confirm it. She had what she called a Holy Spirit hunch.

"Yeah. Their first baby was stillborn. Mom said that she was afraid to try again after me because of how rough it was. She couldn't stand the thought of losing another child."

"I understand. Are there any other miscarriages or stillbirths or maybe even abortions that you're aware of in the extended family?"

He thought for a moment and then said, "I don't know for sure, but one time I heard my aunts talking and one of them said that they were all cursed because they all lost their first babies. Something about Grandpa – well, I guess he'd be my great grandfather. They said he made his daughter drink something to make her lose a baby because she was pregnant before she and grandpa got married. I was just little but I remember that she used a cuss word."

"Oh?"

"Yeah, she said something like Grandpa wasn't going to have no bastards in his family."

"Well, let's open with prayer and ask the Lord to take us to the root of this death-demon issue."

"Sure."

"Holy Father we ask that Your Spirit would direct Max's spirit to take us to the innermost place where the secret of this death demon lies. Whatever thought or memory or…"

Suddenly, Max growled, "He's mine! You can't have him."

"Oh, dear Lord," Pastor Spalding said softly under his breath. Praying and wondering how Abigail would handle this situation, he momentarily wondered what his fellow seminarians would think if they were to encounter this kind of very non-Baptist prayer session. He almost chuckled but he was brought back by the guttural sounds Max was making.

He tried to anticipate her warfare strategy. He remembered that she would never answer a demon's question because that put it in charge by having her answer to it.

Abigail was not surprised that a demon manifested. "Ah," she said calmly, "you must be Molech."

Max's body briefly shrank back in shock at her words which confirmed her Holy Spirit hunch, but the demon quickly renewed its tirade. "You got no right to be interfering here," it snarled.

"I'm not interfering here. You are. Max belongs to the true Lord Jesus Christ of Nazareth by his own testimony, therefore, you are an interloper."

"He gave me the right."

"Oh? And just when was that?" Abigail did not want to have a dialogue dance with this demon so she went right for the jugular. "Was that before he was formed in his mother's womb? Because if it was, I'll just have to agree that the covenant that was previously ratified with God Almighty to give one of His own to Satan would have to stand and I'll back off and let you go your merry way and kill Max."

She was met with a sinister glare and a throaty rumble.

Abigail's tone remained cheery with a slight edge of sarcasm. "But both you and I know that that was not the case so, as I said, you have no grounds to either kill or torment Max Berryman."

Not having a good retort, the demon scrambled for some purchase on the cliff that was rapidly crumbling beneath it. "He gave me the right!" it roared.

"Who and when and where?" Abigail wondered if "he" was Max or his great grandfather.

"I am not saying another word."

"Then I will take that as a negative. There is no right. If you cannot produce any evidence, then you must go. Now." Her tone was no-nonsense and firm. She maintained eye contact at all times.

The demon was clearly agitated. His desperation was increasing. Suddenly he scowled and blurted, "Under the tree by the bridge. He sold his soul to Satan. He negated whatever arrangement he had with... with..." He would not or could not speak the name of his own creator. Exasperated, he said, "Max negated the covenant and he's mine."

"No. An eternal covenant previously ratified cannot be set aside in time by a minor while under duress. In the name of Jesus the Christ, back off. Max! Max, you need to take control. Max!"

Max shook his head as if he was shaking off sleep. "Yeah, yeah, I'm here. What just happened?"

"You didn't know that a demon took over for a while?"

"Cripes! Not another one," he said as his shoulders sagged.

"Sorry. I hate to tell you this, but between the generational junk and your involvement in the cult, we'll probably run into a bunch of them before we're done." She quickly reassured him, "There'll be an end to this. But you have to take control. Your life is your jurisdiction and if you don't want demons around, you have the right and authority to send them packing. In fact, you have more authority than I do. Or even Pastor Spalding."

"Really?"

"The only thing a demon can do is to deceive us into believing that it has a right. Look," she paged through her Bible and paraphrased Colossians two verse fifteen. "It says here that when Jesus had disarmed the demons he made a public display of them because God had triumphed over them because of what Jesus did on the cross."

"Huh. Makes sense."

"So, this demon said that it had the right to kill you because you sold your soul to Satan under the tree by the bridge. I also believe that it had an easy entryway into your life because of your great grandfather. It sounds like he forced his daughter, your grandmother or one of her sisters, to abort a child."

"Ooh." Max hung his head as he recalled the tree incident and then tried to comprehend the impact of his great grandfather's words and deeds.

"Let's take care of the generational spirit first."

"How?"

"Are you familiar with the books of Ezra and Nehemiah and Daniel in the Bible?"

"Not really." Max blushed as he took a quick glance at Pastor Spalding.

"Most people aren't. But these godly guys, that had those books named for them, all stood and confessed their sins and the sins of their fathers. You can do the same thing. Confess the sin of abortion on your grandfather's behalf. If we confess sin, God cleanses. You 'fess up and I'll pray in agreement. Okay? It doesn't have to be fancy."

"Uh, sure," Max said uncertainly. "I'm not good at this but here goes. God, I confess the sin of abortion that my great grandfather made my grandma do in

Jesus' name, amen." He looked up at Abigail and said, "That okay?"

"Yes. And Lord," she added, "I pray in agreement. We plead Your blood over that event and all subsequent infant deaths and ask that You would demolish any and all strongholds that have been established in the family lines and send all foul spirits – especially Molech – associated with it to a place where they would never be able to oppress Max or anyone ever again. Your Word says that no longer shall the fathers eat sour grapes and the children's teeth be set on edge. We ask that You would completely cut off any generational aspect of this event. Please complete and correct anything we prayed inadequately, amen."

Max looked up expectantly. "Now what?"

"Are you sensing or thinking about anything?"

"Not really."

"Some people do; some don't. Let's go after the other thing by the bridge. Can you tell me what happened?"

Taking a deep breath, Max described the black night in which he was taken to a ritual with his so-called friend, Levi. He described the fire and the chilled atmosphere, the drumming and the chanting, the robed people and the victim. He described the terrified young man who had a noose around his neck and the rope which was strung over a gnarled branch.

"I guess he was a Christian, you know. I got the idea that maybe he wanted to see if the cult was for real. It was almost like he thought he could convert them or something; then he realized it wasn't just a bunch of kids writing graffiti and sacrificing animals and he was in way over his head. They told him that he had seen too much. He would have to die or he would have to kill someone else and join them."

Max choked as he continued his narrative. "The next thing I knew, someone grabbed me from behind and put a noose over my head. They strung me up next to where he was standing. I could hardly breathe." Max was having a difficult time talking. Voice rising in pitch, fighting tears, doubling over onto his knees with his arms folded over his head, heaving deep, racking sobs, Max's muffled words came out incoherently.

Abigail and Pastor Spalding exchanged glances and shrugged. Neither one was able to clearly understand what Max was saying. Abigail began to rack her brain for clues. It had to be some kind of double-bind. They waited in silence until Max's sobs subsided. He finally sat up, wiped his nose on the back of his sleeve and snuffled softly.

"What happened next?" Abigail prompted.

"Oh, God!" Max moaned miserably. "They started to pull on the rope but then they let him have another chance. He looked at me hanging there and said that he knew he was saved but he, he…" Max gave in to the weeping again.

"Take your time, son," Pastor Spalding's fatherly voice encouraged him.

"He said that he wasn't sure that I was. He looked me in the eye and told me that he'd die instead of me and that he hoped I could get out and get right with God someday." Tears coursed down Max's cheeks. Reaching for a tissue, he blew his nose and then continued, "They jerked on his rope and we hung there. I don't know why I didn't die. All I remember is hearing them chanting something like cursed is he who hangs from a tree. When I came to, the kid was dead and they were telling me that I was cursed. That I killed him. That I was a murderer. It was on me and even that kid knew that I was damned."

Max dissolved in tears again.

"What did you say to yourself at that time? How did you process it?" Abigail asked. Her maternal heart broke for him, but her counselor's mind knew that he needed truth to set him free.

"I don't know," Max searched his memory. "I guess I just agreed with them that I was cursed so God wouldn't want me. I mean, I didn't argue and the kid was dead and I was still alive." Max absent-mindedly rubbed his throat.

"Okay, let's get this memory healed. Do you still believe that you are responsible for his death? Are you a murderer? Are you cursed?"

"Not really. I mean, I don't think I'm responsible, but I do feel like a murderer."

"Why?"

"Because if I hadn't been there; if I hadn't been a part of that cult…"

"Max, Satanists are like Satan. They kill, steal, and destroy. They're liars," Abigail said evenly as she looked him in the eye. "You're dealing with the best. They know how to use any given situation to the max. Pardon the pun. Let's start with the curses."

"Curses?"

"Yes. When they called you a murderer and said you were cursed and it was on you, they cursed you. They judged you. It's time to renounce those curses."

"Yeah. What do I do?"

"In the name of Jesus…" Abigail gently prompted.

"Oh, yeah. God, in the name of Jesus, I renounce the curse of being a murderer. I am not cursed, either, amen." He looked up at Abigail to see if that was adequate.

"Father, I pray in agreement and ask that You would cover not only the words that were spoken against Max that night, but also the activities. We plead the blood of Jesus the Christ over the entire ritual and every stronghold that was established by it. We ask that You would send every foul spirit with their entire hierarchies that are associated with Max to a place where they cannot afflict him or anyone else ever again. Heal and seal these broken places and fill Max with Your Holy Spirit and blessings and truth. We pray this in the name of Jesus the Christ, amen."

"I feel a little calmer."

"Are you a murderer? Was his death your fault?"

Max looked at the door and bit his lip as he sighed. "I'm not sure. It's like I know it here," he indicated his head, "but it still feels true here." He balled his fist and thumped lightly on his chest.

"Let's go back to the memory and ask the Lord to manifest there and bring you truth."

"Sure."

"Jesus, You're the same yesterday, today, and forever. You were there. As Max focuses on that memory, we ask that You would let Max see You, hear You, or sense Your presence as You bring him truth. Is it his fault? Is he a murderer?"

Max had his eyes closed as he focused on the despicable memory once again. After several minutes he opened his eyes and gave Abigail a faint smile. "No, I'm not a murderer. I saw Jesus in the memory this time. He was standing between that kid and me with His arms around both of us. It was like I was watching it from a distance. He put His finger between my neck and the noose but He couldn't do that with the other kid."

"What does that mean to you?"

"That the nooses were rigged. There was some kind of collar in mine and it would only go so tight. Those guys are the murderers. I was set up. I'm not a murderer."

"How do you feel now?"

"Um, maybe a little guilt."

"Why?"

"I should have done something. Maybe I should have died instead of him."

"Let's ask the Lord about that. Are you willing to let Him take that guilt?"

"Sure."

Abigail prayed and then waited for the report.

"I heard Him say, 'It's not your fault.'"

"Do you believe Him?"

"Yeah. I'm good." Max looked at Pastor Spalding and gave him a weary smile.

"One more detail," Abigail added. "You need to renounce Molech. I think it's still hanging around."

Max winced at the mention of the name. "Right. Um, God, I renounce Molech and all his pals in the name of Jesus. I don't want them in my life and he has no right anymore. Amen."

"And, Lord, I pray in agreement. We ask that You would bind Molech and all the other spirits in that hierarchy together – especially the spirits of murder, abortion, calamity, hell or Hinnom, poverty, vagabond, and fugitive spirits. We also ask You to heal the body memories. Complete and correct anything we prayed inadequately and fill with Your Holy Spirit where these things have been. Amen."

"Ah, that's better," Max reported. "I feel like I can breathe again. Thanks for praying about the body memories. I could still feel that rope."

They were all in agreement that the session was over. Max expressed his gratitude and left after making another appointment. He glanced at his watch and then hurried out so he could get back to work at his father's dealership. He had a debt to repay.

"Whew!" Pastor Spalding let out a breath. "That was something. I wasn't sure how this was going to end up when that Molech demon showed up."

"Me either."

"Really?" Pastor Spalding was shocked. "You sit there so calmly and act like you know exactly what's going to happen."

"I'm only calm because I know that God's got it. I just need to listen to Him and to Max. I think the Holy Spirit uses my experience to help us out, too. I just know that Molech is that heathen god that the Israelites sacrificed their first child to, so when Max said that his aunts and mom all lost their first child, Molech popped into my mind. Working with post-abortive women, I've pieced together other demons that run in the hierarchy. It's probably where the spirit of murder came in."

Lynda L. Irons

"Oh, so if anyone invites any one of the demons in a hierarchy into their life, the others kind of have an open door."

"Exactly!" Abigail was delighted that Pastor Spalding was grasping the principles. "If someone makes a suicide attempt, then murder or Molech or poverty or any of the others can dominate the person's life. Or even future generations like in Max's case."

They continued to debrief for a short while and then went their separate ways. Pastor Spalding went to his office to review his notes and ponder the implications. Abigail headed home and spent the remainder of the day with Lee and getting ready for their trip on Monday.

23

Sunday, May 27, Pentecost

Amy was nervous about meeting Carrie Sue, but she trusted Abigail. She was getting more comfortable with Lee and was glad that Abigail had invited Earl and Jan over for dinner after church, too. She was up and about more often. Next week she would be nearly finished with her fourth month. She was astounded to think that her pregnancy was nearly half way completed. She was beginning to show and she was grateful for the maternity clothing that Abigail had given to her on Mother's Day.

Since Amy was able to be up for extended periods of time, she insisted on helping Abigail as much as she could. She volunteered to make the salad while Abigail was at church. "And yes, I'll make sure the roast doesn't burn."

"Thanks. And if you'd put the double-bakes in around eleven-thirty, I think they'll be ready about the right time."

"Go on. Don't worry. I'll set the table and everything will be great."

"Thanks," Abigail said as she opened the front door. She heard Lee's toots and grabbed her jacket as she was leaving. "And don't worry, I think you'll like Carrie Sue. She's probably just as nervous as you are."

Lee met Abigail on the front porch and gave her a hug and a kiss before escorting her to his truck. Even though they had spent a considerable amount of time together it seemed that they never ran out of things to talk about. This morning they talked about their upcoming trip.

"I'm looking forward to meeting your family," Lee said.

"I think they'll like you. Just don't believe everything you hear. My brothers are prone to exaggeration."

"What time are we leaving in the morning?"

"It's about a six or seven-hour trip so I'm thinking that if we're on the road by six we'll get there right about noon their time. We gain an hour heading west."

"Works for me. I'll be ready."

"You sure you don't want to take my truck? Better gas mileage."

"But I have the extended cab. We won't have to worry about locking stuff up in your box."

Entering the foyer of the church, Abigail was immediately hailed by a distraught Barbara Berryman.

"Abigail, Max is gone! He didn't come home last night. We're afraid that something happened to him. He's not answering his phone."

Paul was standing next to her with deeply furrowed brows. "You don't think the cult had anything to do with this, do you? We thought about calling the sheriff, but remembered what you said about some of them being involved. What do we do?"

"Who can we trust?" Barbara was trying not to break down.

"Oh, dear." Abigail went through a mental check list of possibilities and dismissed everything except the fact that today was Pentecost. A ritual day. Last night would likely have been another ritual night. *Oh, Lord, please no. Please let him be safe from the cult.* "He's working so hard to get his life straightened out."

"What should we do?"

"I'm not sure that there's anything we can do but wait and pray. How about if we do that right now?"

"Yes, yes," Paul said. "Would you lead us?"

"Sure." Abigail reached for Lee's hand and took Barbara's hand while Barbara and Lee reached for Paul's. "Lord, we thank You that You know exactly where Max is. Lord, we pray that You would set the captive free if he is in the clutches of the cult. We ask that if there is any other reason he did not go home last night that You would send someone to find him or bring him home on his own. Father, we ask that You would give Paul and Barbara peace that passes understanding. We pray this in the name of Jesus, amen.

Just then the muffled melody of a cell phone was heard. Barbara opened her purse and checked the face of the phone. "Max! Max! Are you all right, honey? We've been so worried!"

The tinny sound of a distant voice could be heard for a couple of seconds as Max answered her.

"Okay, baby, we'll be right home." Barbara disconnected the call and started to tug on Paul's sleeve. "He's home. He said he needs some help. He got beat up but he's okay."

"The cult?" Abigail asked discretely.

"He didn't say." With that she and Paul rushed out the door.

"We'll call you later," Paul added as the door was closing.

337

Lynda L. Irons

"Well, that was a timely answer to prayer," Lee observed.

"It sure was." *Thank You, Lord!*

They settled into their usual pew with Cindy and Gary and Carrie Sue. They had a minute to greet each other and then the service started.

"Good morning!" Pastor Spalding's enthusiastic voice rang out. "Before I get into my message, I want to thank everyone who supported the folks at The Taco Tower the last couple of days. I heard a report that the trust fund for Gabrielle's little girl has exceeded anyone's expectations and they still have the rest of today to go. Her mother cannot be replaced, but at least that little one will be provided for. Praise God!"

Several amens were heard and some people clapped. Soon they quieted and looked expectantly at Pastor Spalding.

"Today I want to preach out of Luke fifteen. You are all familiar with the story of the prodigal sons. One of them left the family farm and the other stayed and worked, but they were really both prodigals. Neither one honored their father. And, by the way, Jesus was telling this story to the tax-gatherers and sinners *and* the Pharisees and the scribes who were represented by the younger son and the older son respectively. Folks, if we are honest we would admit that each one of us have fit into one category or the other at some time in our lives."

Reluctant nods were seen throughout the congregation as they followed his teaching. He continued to read the passage and point out various details that added to the story.

338

"Now, I want to throw a bit of a monkey-wrench into this story." He paused with a smile and a twinkle in his eye. "I've always been taught that the younger son was truly repentant and actually came to his senses as he humbled himself before his father and offered to become a hired man. But what if the prodigal was still a prodigal? What if he made up his speech just to manipulate his father into feeling sorry for him? I mean, the young man was starving to death. He'd do anything for a full belly. If he was truly repentant, why didn't he offer to be a slave and not a hired man? After all, he squandered his entire inheritance and didn't deserve one thin denarius more. Would he eventually have demanded a raise so he could get more money out of the old man so he could go on with his loose living again?"

Pastor Spalding had them thinking. He then went on to make comments about the older son and finally closed his message. "Folks, if you find yourself somewhere in this story, come on down and pray with someone. If you're a truly repentant prodigal or you're trying to manipulate God into filling your belly – getting you out of your misery, come pray. If you're just playing church like the older prodigal, come get real with God. It's time to possess your birthright, your inheritance. Don't wait for the wedding feast of the Lamb. We need to turn on the music and dance now. We need to eat and be merry with our Father's provisions now."

After they had been dismissed and the worship team was playing softly, several people went up to the front for prayer. Among them was Jason and a pretty young lady who was dabbing tears from her eyes.

339

Abigail got Cindy caught up on the latest word on Max. "I suspect that something happened with the cult, but at least he's alive. Paul said they'd call and let me know what happened."

"I'll be praying," Cindy said.

Lee was giving Gary an update on his animals. "There shouldn't be anything that has to be done. They have all the water and feed they'll need for a couple of days. If you'd just check on them to make sure they're okay, I'd appreciate it."

"No problem. Bryan is begging me to take him out there. Maybe I'll throw him on one of the horses and let him ride a little."

"Yeah, and I really need to give him that ride on the tractor. We'll do that when I get back."

Max had taken a shower and washed off most of the filth. The dirt and blood, ashes and the smell of fire came off with soap and water, but he could not scrub away the taintedness. He was lying in his bed with pain so deep that he could not have summoned tears if he wanted to. Shame. Confusion. Anger. *What's the use? What's the point? Maybe I am cursed. They're right. God doesn't want me. I'll never get free.* Emotions and thoughts swirled as he relived the previous night's events until he fell into a fitful sleep.

"Max! Max, honey, we're home! Where are you?" Barbara burst through the front door ahead of Paul. They hurried down the hallway and found the door to his bedroom wide open. Max was curled into a fetal position on top of the covers, what was left of his hair was still damp, uncombed and fanned across his face.

Moaning, Max stirred and uncurled.

"Oh, baby! What happened?" Barbara was on her knees at the side of the bed tenderly putting strands of hair into place. "Oh, Jesus!" she exclaimed as she saw the top of his head.

"Son, are you all right? Where else are you hurt?"

"They got me, Dad. I don't know why I went to the park after work. Levi was there and that's about all I remember until... until... Oh, God! It was awful." Max broke down and covered his face with his hands as the thoughts of his wretchedness assailed him with gruesome reality.

"Max, what happened to your hair?" Barbara looked at the blistered area on top of his head which was surrounded by singed hair. "Paul, go get that burn ointment from the medicine chest. Are you hurt anywhere else?"

"I can't say! I can't say." Max rolled over and faced the wall. He could not utter the words.

By that time Paul had returned with the ointment. "You can tell us anything, son. What happened?"

"I can't. I just can't."

"What about your counselor? Should we call her?"

"No! I don't want to talk to her about it either."

"What about Pastor Spalding?"

"I don't know. Maybe."

"Church is still going on, but we'll get a hold of him as soon as we can. Will you let me put this ointment on your scalp? It looks pretty sore."

"Sure." Max extended his neck so that the top of his head was more accessible for his mother. He did not realize how painful it was until the ointment began to soothe the angry blisters.

341

Carrie Sue pulled up beside Lee's truck and it was not long before Earl and Jan came up the driveway as well. Amy had the table set and the food was ready to be served. She had even gone out and picked a bouquet of wild flowers and put them in a quart mason jar in the center of the dining room table.

"Carrie Sue, I'd like you to meet Amy. Amy, Carrie Sue."

The two women looked at each other and were not sure if they should shake hands or wave or hug.

"Hi," Amy said with a shy smile. "I guess you got me and twenty chickens to put up with for a couple of days."

"No problem."

"Amy, this is the lady that helped me find the maternity clothes."

"Oh, cool. Thanks. I'm really starting to need them now." Amy put her hands over her belly and turned to show her profile.

"You look really cute in those clothes, Amy," Jan chimed in.

"Thanks."

"Is anyone hungry?" Abigail asked.

A chorus of yeses resounded and the group made their way into the dining room. Abigail and Amy brought the hot dishes and set them on the table. The awkwardness of the initial meeting soon wore off and the conversations flowed.

After the dinner was over, Lee brought Carrie Sue's suitcase to the upstairs bedroom for her. Earl and Jan left shortly after that. Earl said that he had an appointment with his easy chair – his way of saying that he needed his Sunday afternoon nap.

"You just make sure that you call us if you need anything," Earl said.

"Any time," Jan added.

"We will," Amy and Carrie Sue said in unison.

After they left, Carrie Sue and Amy drifted out to the back where Amy introduced Carrie Sue to the chicks. They were about five weeks old and Abigail was almost ready to put them in the coop she had prepared, but she wanted to wait until she got back so it would be easier for the ladies to take care of them. The phone rang as she and Lee were relaxing in the living room.

"Hello?" Abigail had recognized Pastor Spalding's number.

"Abigail, I need some advice," he began.

"Sure, what's up?"

"Max is back home. Apparently, he got abducted and taken to a ritual. Paul called me a little bit ago and wants me to come pray with Max. I hate to say this, but Max definitely did not want to talk to you. I'm afraid I'm in way over my head."

"I'm glad he's still alive."

"Me, too, but what do I do?" Pastor Spalding was feeling as if he was thrown into the deep end of the pool off the high dive. And he did not know how to swim.

"Okay," Abigail was thinking and praying as she formed a response. "I suspect that the reason he doesn't want to talk to me is that they probably raped him or did something sexual to him that is too embarrassing to talk about with a woman."

343

Pastor Spalding sucked in his breath but said nothing.

"Listen for the verbal assaults. What did they say to him? How did he process it? You know, like how we've been doing. You'll probably have to break direct and indirect unholy unions, soul ties, and flesh links from any sexual stuff. And then check for other kinds of trauma and body memories."

"Uh huh," Pastor Spalding muttered as he scribbled down some notes.

"Remember to put off and put on."

"Okay, it's coming back to me. Listen, if he's okay with it can I call you if I need to?"

"Absolutely. He's probably been reprogrammed or they tapped into some programmed part of him. We can take care of that Friday. You don't have to do a counseling session. Even if you don't get to any of the specifics, he'll be fine. He just needs to know that he's still loved and especially that he's not hopeless. I'll be praying."

"Thanks."

"Hoo boy," Abigail said softly as she hung up.

"Sounds like trouble." Lee pulled her to his side. Abigail leaned into him and rested her head on his muscular shoulder. "Yes. Max is back home, but something's wrong. We need to pray for Pastor Spalding. He'll be fine, but he's nervous."

They spent some time praying for Max and Pastor Spalding and then talked about the up-coming trip.

"All of a sudden July 7 is coming up really fast!" Abigail sat up straight. "Do you realize that we still have a lot of stuff to do before our wedding?"

"Yep," Lee said calmly and pulled her back to his side. "It'll be fine. You have your purple dress. Cindy has hers, right? Me and Gary have our black leather vests and our purple ties. What else do we need?"

"You're right. We are pretty well set. I was just thinking about little details like the rest of the stuff for the church reception. I guess we don't have anything to do for the reception at the restaurant."

"Nope. And I have our honey-moon plans nearly completed. We're good!"

Amy and Carrie Sue were having their own discussion on the back deck. The most often used words were, "You too?" as they compared their stories. Having lived in the relative isolation of being raised in a cult family, they each thought that they were the only ones who tried to escape; that their experiences were just because of a local band of Satanists. But in other ways they thought that everyone was a Satanist since they went to church with them and patronized stores that employed them, lived next door to them and were related to them.

Lee sighed and said, "I need to get out of here and get packed. I want to stop by to check on the critters."

"Yeah, I have some last-minute things to do, too. I want to make sure Carrie Sue is settled."

They got up and hugged. Walking to the back door, Lee said goodbye to Carrie Sue and Amy before heading out to his truck. Amy needed to get back to bed so Carrie Sue and Abigail had time to talk for a while before the phone rang again.

"Hello?"

"Abigail," Pastor Spalding said, "I just wanted to let you know how things went with Max."

345

"How is he?"

"He's pretty shaken up and really hurting. I think that some part of him got him to meet Levi. That's where things are a bit blurry, but he remembers some stuff."

"How bad?" Abigail asked, dreading the answer.

"Well, you were right about them raping him. He's feeling pretty angry and humiliated. It was really hard for him to come out and say it."

"Were you able to process it with him?"

"Yes." Pastor Spalding was triumphant. "It was amazing. I tried to remember how you prayed about memories and we muddled through it. Jesus showed up and Max said he feels clean again."

"Excellent!"

"We didn't get to the burns on the top of his head, but I think he'll be okay until we can work with him again on Friday."

"Burns?"

"Yeah. Apparently, they were taunting him. Somehow, they knew that he was done with Satanism, or at least most of him is. They were mocking Pentecost and said that he needed to have a flame of fire on his head if he had the Holy Spirit."

"So, they burned him?"

"He said they put something on his head and lit it. He's got some nasty burns on his scalp and a lot of his hair was burned off. Looks bad."

"Wow! That's a twist I haven't heard before."

24

Monday, May 28, Memorial Day

Lee and Abigail were on the road by six o'clock in the morning. Neither one had slept very well in anticipation of their trip. Lee had his thermos of coffee and Abigail had her thermos of tea. Sometimes they talked. Sometimes they rode in companionable silence. Most of the time they held hands, that is, unless Lee needed to sip his coffee.

They were already nearly half way to Abigail's father's house before the Ministerial Alliance members started to gather at the church. The weather was cool but sunny. It promised to be perfect weather for the parade and the possibility that people would come in for ministry. Streets were barricaded along the parade route and there was a sense of anticipation in the air.

The Ministerial Alliance members, along with supporters and participants, started the day with prayer. They stood in a large circle, held hands, and several of them prayed short, informal prayers.

School bands could be heard warming up in the distance. The rousing drumming added to the festive atmosphere. People in lawn chairs lined the sidewalks as clueless children watched and waited. American flags fluttered and veterans saluted them. They remembered.

Lee followed Abigail's directions and listened to her talk about the area with which she was once so familiar. Her parents had moved from the home in which she and her brothers were raised to another one in a nearby subdivision. Dad still lived in the house that was now too big for him, but he was not ready to give up his lawn and garden, garage and shop. He liked having enough space to accommodate visitors. Soon they were off the main highways and winding down secondary roads. Abigail pointed to a Catholic church on the right and told Lee to turn there.

"We're about three blocks away." Abigail was simultaneously excited and nervous. She was proud of this new man in her life. He was handsome and intelligent. He had a great sense of humor. He was sensitive and decisive. Above all, he was Spirit-filled and loved the Lord. She was sure that her family would like him, too.

"There!" Abigail excitedly pointed at a mailbox. "6801. Rooze. That's it."

"Huh, I didn't even think about your maiden name. Rooze."

"Yep, I'm an all-American European mutt. English, German, French, Dutch, and some East Prussian way back there somewhere."

Lee turned into the driveway and pulled up behind the pale-yellow Impala. There were a number of other cars in the driveway and along the street as well.

"Looks like a crowd," Lee observed.

Abigail saw her father on the front porch and did not wait for Lee to open her door. "Dad!"

"Hey, you made it. What time did you leave this morning? Perfect timing! We're almost ready to throw stuff on the grill." They embraced on the sidewalk and then her father held her by the shoulders at arm's length and gave her his assessment. "You look happier than I've seen you in a long time."

"I am, Dad." Abigail smiled back and then turned to Lee who was standing a few feet behind her. "Dad, this is Lee Norris, the man I told you about."

The men advanced toward each other with right hands extended. "Well, Lee, it's nice to meet you. You must be some kind of special guy to turn this stubborn lady's head."

"I don't know about that sir, but I do know that she's turned mine."

"You don't have to call me sir; that's a bit too formal. You can call me John."

"All right, John it is."

They went inside and by the time they got to the back yard, the entire clan was excitedly surrounding Abigail and Lee. Introductions were made and Abigail was able to get caught up on some of her brothers' lives. She was amazed at how much her nieces and nephews had grown. *How long had it been?* Abigail had pretty much dropped out of family life after she lost her husband and sons. It was almost too painful to be around intact families for a long time and then she just got out of the habit. They did not pursue her either.

After an initial awkward phase, the conversations became more playful. The teasing and bantering, bad puns and old stories began to flow. Lee was enjoying the experience. He was able to have some serious conversations as well as some light-hearted ones. Abigail's family accepted him as readily as Lee's family had accepted Abigail.

"Hey, sis, don't you have a birthday coming up pretty soon?"

"Friday."

349

"Thought so."

With that, the family started to sing the traditional birthday song complete with one of the most wretched off-tuned endings that sounded remarkably like a pack of howling dogs.

"Thanks," Abigail said shaking her head, "that was truly pitiful."

After the laughter died down, a cake was produced, candles were lit, and a card was placed in front of Abigail.

"We didn't know what you needed, so we just pitched in and got you a gift card."

Abigail was touched by their thoughtfulness. Rising from her chair, she went around the room and hugged every member of her family. Family. It felt good to reconnect.

It felt good, that is, until John Junior sidled up to her and gave her one of his patented joint-dislocating side-hugs. It had been so long that Abigail forgot to brace herself for his assault. "Ow!"

"Sorry, did I hurt you?"

"You always do."

"So, toughen up!" He tried to joke it off and make it her fault as usual.

"I'm right on it," Abigail replied evenly as she rubbed her shoulder. Her mind automatically started to scroll back through numerous such interactions over their lifetime. *Bully!* She was brought back to the present by his less-than-light slug on the same shoulder.

"Anyway, I'm glad you finally found a guy. You've been an old maid too long," he remarked as he turned and rejoined the party.

Abigail was stunned. Hurt. And angry. *Old maid? I'm a widow!* It was a typical cold-hearted, thoughtless big brother remark. Fortunately, she did not have time to dwell on it. It was time to cut the cake.

Amy and Carrie Sue were getting along very well. They traded stories about Abigail and some of the things that went on in their sessions. Amy was very curious about what it felt like to be fully integrated after spending a lifetime being dissociated. Carrie Sue explained it as well as she could and encouraged Amy to keep pursuing the healing.

"There were times I just wanted to quit. It seemed like there was just so much programming and so many memories and that I was just hopelessly crazy."

"Yeah, I can relate. I spent too much time lying to Abigail and being evasive. I think she knew all along, but she just waited until I was comfortable enough to open up."

"And here we are at her house. Amazing. You know I lived in your bedroom for a while?"

"Really?"

"Yeah. Let me tell you a wild story," Carrie Sue said. She then began to describe her harrowing experience as she escaped from a ritual at a nearby site and breaking her foot in the process, being mad at God and how He healed it. Amy especially liked the part about Carrie Sue's protector, David, punching Zorroz.

Gary smiled as he watched Bryan's excitement. He chuckled at Bryan's ultra-serious expressions and body

351

language as he tried to imitate Cousin Lee. He wore his boots and took long strides as he helped carry rations of sweet feed to the horses. Gary had fired up the four-wheeler and they had ridden down to the pastures to check on the horses and the heifers. Gary let Bryan steer and only had to correct their path a couple of times. Bryan was like most children who believed that they had to constantly be turning the steering wheel left and right in exaggerated motions.

Tuesday morning was blessedly quiet at the Rooze house. All the chatty adults and boisterous grandchildren had gone back to work or school. That left Abigail and Lee with uninterrupted time with her father.

"Coffee?" John Rooze held up the pot and offered it to Lee and Abigail.

"I'd love some," Lee said.

"No thanks. Do you have any tea bags?" Abigail asked.

"You still don't drink coffee?"

"Nope. Mom tried to get me to drink it once but it just made me queasy. I figured that there was enough stuff that I didn't have to learn to like already out there."

"So, tell me about your plans. You sure you're not rushing this? You've only known each other for a couple months now. And just how did the two of you meet?"

Driving home after their lunch with John Rooze on Tuesday, Lee and Abigail had a lot to talk about. They reviewed some of the conversations that they had had with various family members. They laughed at some of the stories. They both basked in the warm glow of the family's approval for their marriage.

"It was good to meet your family. Quite a group."

"You could say that."

"What's the matter?"

"Oh, I was just remembering why I don't visit them very often."

"Does this have anything to do with Junior?"

"How'd you know?"

"I was watching you. It seems like all the sparkle left your eyes after he talked to you. What did he say?"

"Oh, he just said that he was glad that I finally found a guy and so I won't be an old maid anymore."

"Really?" Lee was astounded. "He said that? Doesn't he know that you're a widow?"

"That's Junior. I guess he forgot all about his deceased brother-in-law and nephews."

"I'd like to turn this truck around and punch him out!" Lee's face was flushed and Abigail could see his knuckles whiten as he gripped the steering wheel.

"Not worth it. That's pretty much what I grew up with. Criticize. Blame. Belittle. Nothing anyone said or did was right. Dad called me stubborn. What about him? He can be a widower and it's no big deal, but I'm stubborn because I'm not remarried... or whatever they expected."

"I had no idea."

"That's not even the worst thing Junior's ever said."

353

"Dare I ask?"

"How about at the funeral? Four caskets and he comes up to me and says, 'Celebrating Halloween's wrong. Do you think that if they hadn't been out on the devil's night they would still be alive?'"

"Now I really do want to turn this truck around! Is he planning on coming to our wedding? 'Cause if he is, there'll be trouble."

"Not worth it, Lee. Seriously. I'm not going to sin in response to his sin."

"Yeah, you're right." He sighed and changed the subject. "It's after six, do you want to stop for something to eat?"

"Not unless you do. I'm kind of anxious to get home and see how the ladies did. I made a big pan of eggplant lasagna and there should be some left. In fact, I wouldn't be surprised if all they ate was a tiny square each."

He chuckled as he envisioned the ladies dutifully trying the dish. "Sounds good. It seems like your survivors have limited diets."

"Yeah, now that you mention it," Abigail said thoughtfully as she scrolled back through the eating habits of other survivors, "a lot of foods are triggers because of color or texture. Like catsup looks like blood. But I think a lot of them have mothers who were not exactly 'Susie Homemakers' so they were left to fend for themselves."

"Makes sense. Well, I can wait until tomorrow to check the critters. Gary would have called if there was a problem. The guys should be putting the finishing touches on the house and then there's the inspection."

"Oh, that's right! You have to move this week." Abigail had put that item on the back burner while she focused on this trip and the wedding plans.

"I'm afraid I'm going to have to stay with Gary or Grandpa unless that inspection gets done in record time. Meanwhile, I need to finish packing."

Lee carried Abigail's suitcase into the house while she gathered her thermos and a couple scraps of trash. Amy and Carrie Sue were excited to see Abigail but were a bit more reserved about Lee. They had been abused by so many men over the years. They had finetuned radar for angry men with lust problems and would have discerned anything in Lee if it was there. They were both protective of Abigail and were both pleased that he passed their test and had their approval.

Carrie Sue heard them coming and opened the front door. "Hey, welcome home! How was the trip?"

"Great! It's good to be home. How did everything go for you two?"

"It was really good. Amy and I got along just great. It's nice to know that someone else really, really understands."

"We're going to grab some supper. I assume you two have already eaten."

"Yes. And you'd be so proud of us. We both tried *and* liked the eggplant lasagna."

"Excellent!" Abigail smiled and then exaggerated a worried expression, "You saved us some, didn't you?"

"Plenty."

Abigail and Lee heated up some supper. Amy and Carrie Sue sat in the kitchen and chattered about their time together and the little problem with the chicks.

Apparently, the screen got moved just far enough for several of the chicks to escape.

"Yes, it's time to move those peepsters out to their own place. That will happen before the end of this week. I hope."

Wednesday morning already. Filling his thermos with the remainder of the coffee that he had brewed earlier, surveying the piles of items that had accumulated around his tiny apartment, Lee mentally assessed the size of the moving job. It would not be nearly as difficult as moving across country, but he still had much to do. Actually, he had everything to do. *First things first.* With that he headed out to the farm.

Abigail went down to her chicken coop and made sure that there was enough straw and wood shavings on the floor. Opening the barn door, she hitched the trailer to the four-wheeler and drove it up to the back deck. Loading the five-gallon water dispensers onto the trailer, she filled them with the hose. She had already placed the large feeders in the coop but needed to bring what was left of the fifty-pound sack of chick feed with her as well.

"I'll be back in a little bit for the peepsters."

"I wish I could see them in their new digs."

"I don't see why you can't take your time and walk down there. Your doctor did say that you can walk more, right? I'd give you a ride on this thing, but I think that might be a bit too bumpy."

"Thanks. I think I'll walk."

Amy started walking across the dew-glistened back lawn, through the wide-open gate, and down the gentle slope to the tack-room-turned-chicken-coop. Peering inside and taking a deep breath of the sweet straw and shavings mix, she felt peaceful and calm. *I could get used to this country life.* Her thoughts were interrupted by the arrival of Abigail on the four-wheeler.

"This is really nice. They ought to like it."

"I hope so. I need to keep them cooped up... er, sorry, bad pun... for three days before I let them out so they better like it."

"What for?"

"I'm not exactly sure. The book says something about that's how they know where to come back and roost at night."

"Huh. Learn something new every day."

Abigail transferred the items into the coop and then returned to the house for the chicks. She had a plastic storage box with a lid. Gently putting ten panicked, squawking chicks into the box, she secured the lid and put it into the trailer. After the slow but bumpy ride down, Abigail brought the box into the coop. Amy stood just inside the door while Abigail removed the lid and slowly tilted the box. Sounds of scrambling chicks were heard along with their alarmed little screeches.

"Chill! She'll think I'm killing you."

Amy laughed with delight as she watched the chicks calm down and begin to explore their new home. "Come on out."

Abigail tilted the box enough to force the chicks to slide onto the straw. "Move it, ladies, I need to get the rest of the gang." She was laughing, too. "Can you make sure they don't get out the door while I get the rest of them?"

"No problem."

They repeated the operation and soon the chicks were boldly exploring the coop. Abigail put the four-wheeler away and together they walked back up to the house.

"How do you feel?"

"Good. Really good. I think I actually feel calm. Maybe for the first time in my life."

"Praise God!"

After cleaning up the chicks' box and vacuuming the dust and bits of straw, medicated crumbles, and other debris that had accumulated in the utility room, Abigail told Amy that she was heading over to Lee's to help him move.

Lee smiled as he saw Abigail strolling up the lane and stopped what he was doing. "Hey there!"

"Good morning!" Abigail greeted Lee. "This is the day."

"That the Lord has made," Lee picked up the verse and they finished it together.

"What are you up to?"

Lee took a deep breath and said, "Well, first I'm cleaning this horse trailer out and then I'm going to find my tarps and head over to the apartment and pack it up."

"I've got all day. How can I help?"

"Grab a bucket and a brush." Lee had just hosed out the bulk of the residue from having transported horses and cows. It was time to apply the scrub brushes and soap.

They talked and worked and soon it was time for the final rinse.

"What's next?" Abigail asked.

"I need to let this dry out, so let's go find the tarps and make sure they're okay and then it's time to pack up."

"Are you saying that you haven't started packing yet?"

"I never really unpacked but basically I haven't done a thing."

"O-ka-ay," Abigail said drawing out the syllables. "We have some work to do, then."

"Yep."

"Do you have enough boxes?"

"Probably, but if not, the grocery store is right there."

Together they drove over to Lee's apartment. This was the first time Abigail had been in it. She surveyed the kitchen and estimated that it would take a couple of hours just to pack it up. It was always the most time-consuming part of a move.

"How about if I pack up the kitchen?"

"Works. I'll pack up the bedroom and start staging things in the living room."

"Works."

By noon Lee had his large desk and bedroom furniture moved into the living room. He had several boxes piled on the dolly and was wheeling them past the kitchen where Abigail had packed and labeled a number of boxes.

"You getting hungry?"

Abigail turned and said, "Now that you mention it, I think I am."

359

"Let's take a break and get something to eat."

They drove to the Sandwich Shack and had a leisurely lunch. On the way back, they stopped at the grocery store and picked up a few more boxes. Lee stopped by his landlord's house and made the arrangements for the final inspection, turning in his keys, and receiving his security deposit.

"I was hoping that everything would fit in the trailer, but I'm beginning to wonder now that I see it all stacked up here."

"You have the horse trailer and the one you put your tractor on, right?"

"Yeah."

"Why not put your furniture on the flatbed and cover it with tarps until we can move it into the house and put the boxes and other stuff in the horse trailer?"

"I was thinking the same thing."

Lee packed his suitcase with a week's supply of clothes and all his toiletries. The rest was packed into boxes. By the end of the afternoon they were nearly finished. Tonight, he and Gary would load up the trailers and store them in the barn. Tomorrow he and Abigail would clean the apartment.

25

Friday, June 1

Abigail was just finishing her breakfast when Amy sat down across from her. "I heard a rumor that today is your birthday."

"You heard right. Who told you? Carrie Sue?"

"She mentioned it. We got you something." Amy smiled as she shoved a wrapped gift across the table. "Happy Birthday! And I know it'll be happier if I don't sing," she added with a giggle.

Abigail laughed with her and said seriously, "Oh, you didn't have to get me anything." Abigail was touched. She knew that both of these women needed all their extra dollars. She still had a difficult time accepting gifts and felt a little tinge of anxiety.

"Come on; open it!" Amy was excited.

Abigail obliged her and tugged on the ribbon. Pulling the taped paper off the box, she took the cover off and peered inside. Carefully lifting a figurine out of the box, she was speechless for a moment. "It's perfect. I love it."

"We thought you would." Amy beamed. She and Carrie Sue had conspired to find something meaningful for Abigail to show their appreciation for all the hours she had prayed with them and others. Amy chipped in with some of her tax refund money and Carrie Sue was now collecting a small paycheck.

"*You* didn't go to the store, did you?" Abigail interrogated Amy.

"No. I was good. Carrie Sue did that."

"Good. I mean, I know you're behaving. Thank you so much. I will treasure this. In fact, I'm putting it on my dresser right now." The figurine of the praying woman kneeling with a Bible in front of her was soon sitting in a prominent position on her dresser.

Abigail finished her morning routine and headed to the church praying fervently that Max would show up despite his latest setback. Abigail knew how much damage could be done in just one ritual and assumed that there were additional parts of Max with which to deal. She sighed because she knew that Max would have a much longer healing journey ahead of him than he thought. *God, please grant him the grace to see it to the end.*

Max was a bit late that morning. It worried Pastor Spalding and Abigail, but it gave him the opportunity to get her caught up on the time he spent with Max on Sunday. They both felt relieved when they heard the outer door open and then click shut.

"Hey," a very subdued Max said, "sorry I'm late. Traffic."

"No problem," Abigail replied, "we're just glad you made it safely."

"I'm proud of you, son, for sticking with it."

"Thank you, sir," Max said as he slouched into his chair.

"Let's open with prayer and see where the Lord takes us," Abigail suggested.

Max bowed his head but he did not take off his cap. When Abigail finished the prayer, he looked up and said, "I guess I'm really mad at myself for going to the park. I can't figure out why I did that."

Looking Max in the eye, Abigail asked, "Does anyone in there know about going to the park last week?"

There was an awkward silence until Max asked belligerently, "Can't a guy go to the park if he wants to?"

"Absolutely," Abigail answered congenially, "I'm just wondering who's been programmed by the cult to meet Levi there on a ritual night so you can get your butt whipped."

"I ain't programmed!" He was clearly a dissociated part of Max. "I didn't get my butt whipped, either!"

"No," Abigail continued with a calm voice, "I suppose *you* didn't, but somebody did."

"We did not!"

"Okay, take off your cap and explain that."

"What do you mean?"

"The burns on the top of your head."

"I don't know nothing about that."

"I know you don't. Just like some part of Max who doesn't know about being drawn to the park to meet Levi. Your job is to get him there. Someone else gets to be abused. Can I talk to the one who got burned?"

"I'm outta here!" With that Max switched into another part who was obviously in pain."

"Hello. I'm Abigail. Who are you?"

"Pete."

"Nice to meet you. Thanks for coming out to talk to me."

"Didn't exactly want to. Got shoved out here."

"Who shoved you out here?"

"I can't say."

363

"Because you don't know or because you'd be in trouble if you said?"

"Trouble."

"Okay. I don't want to do anything that will add to your troubles. Are you allowed to talk to me or do I need his permission?"

"Uh," the part was taken aback by her directness.

"I ain't giving you no permission for nothing!" another part snarled.

"No problem. What kind of trouble would you be in if you did?"

"What do you mean?" he scowled.

"I mean," Abigail said patiently, "that I understand that there is a hierarchy. Everyone answers to someone in there. I just don't want to violate jurisdictional lines and get anyone into trouble. You're over Pete. Someone's over you."

"So?" he growled. He did not like the fact that Abigail knew so much.

"I'm just trying to get Pete and the others who got hurt at the ritual some help. Oh, by the way, is your name Peter?"

"You're freaking me out, lady," he sputtered. "How did you know?"

"Guess I'd call it a Holy Spirit hunch. Is there a little guy in there named Petey? The one who got sodomized?"

"Crap!" Peter was flabbergasted.

Pastor Spalding was sitting on the sidelines absolutely fascinated by the words of knowledge that Abigail was getting. He continued to pray for breakthrough and favor.

"Can we get them some relief? As their protector, you'd want them to get some help, right?"

He did not have a ready comeback. He could not argue with her logic.

"Look, I know that you've had a tough job trying to protect them, but it was kind of like they gave you a job, tied your hands behind your back, and expected you to do it."

"I guess," he said while trying to whittle the bitter pill down to a size that he could swallow.

"Let me help you."

"What can *you* do?"

"We can ask the true Lord Jesus to heal Pete and little Petey and then if you're good with it, you can all be integrated back into Max so that you can't be abused again."

"We'd like that."

Abigail spent the rest of their session accessing and ministering to Petey who was sodomized and Pete who had the burns on the top of his head. Peter surrendered his assignment and after healing and deliverance, the three were integrated. They were also able to minister to the one that was programmed to contact the cult and he was integrated as well.

"What happened?" Max asked after the integration. "I caught some of it, but I was blocked out of most of it."

Abigail gave him a quick review of their session and then she said, "Max, I have a feeling that you need to be prepared for the probability that there are a whole bunch more cult-loyal parts in there."

"What do you mean?"

"They accessed the Peters. That tells me that they have been around awhile. My experience tells me that there will be more."

Max groaned inwardly. "How many?"

"There's no telling. All I know is that this is very fixable. We'll just keep going until we're done. I know you must feel like it's one step forward and ten steps backward, but it's really not. Look at how much got done today."

"I'm proud of you, Max. Your history is your story and your test is your testimony. God is redeeming you and I know God will use you to help others, too," Pastor Spalding interjected.

"I don't know about that. I just want to be done."

"I don't blame you," Abigail said, "but remember that each step in a race is as important as the one that breaks the tape at the end."

Abigail and Pastor Spalding debriefed after Max left and then they parted ways. She finished her usual Friday afternoon routine with the exception of stopping at the thrift store to thank Carrie Sue for the gift. After putting her groceries away and eating lunch, she and Amy met for a long overdue session.

After opening with prayer, Head Honcho switched in and gave her an update. "We don't have Blood Avenger and his guys chasing the Man-slayers anymore so things are a lot calmer everywhere except level six."

"Has anything changed?"

"It's hard to tell. It just seems more intense and quite frankly, the constant noise is really getting to us."

"Did you ever get a chance to follow up with the top Fuchsya?"

"A little. She's still resistant, but something's changed with her. I think she's afraid of something or someone."

"I most certainly am not. And I'll thank you not to put words in my mouth!" Top Fuchsya stormed into the conversation displacing Head Honcho.

"Hello there. How are you?" Abigail asked pleasantly.

"Just fine; no thanks to you!"

"Oh?"

"I've got a *dead*-line to meet! Get it? Dead-line."

"Why the pressure?"

"Anybody ever tell you that you stick your nose where it doesn't belong?"

"Yep." Abigail smiled and then continued, "So what's the threat?"

"I just need to get a few things taken care of and you need to stop interfering." With that, Top Fuchsya disappeared.

"Who's here?" Abigail asked.

"Me again," Head Honcho replied. "Now what?"

"Not sure. This is tricky. We consolidated your area with your cooperation. Mayor gave us permission to take care of his town, but Joktan has jurisdiction over the six subterranean levels. Top Fuchsya's over all of you and then there's the original Fuchsya, wherever she is. I don't want to trample on that jurisdiction, but we need to find a way to resolve this."

"Yeah, the level leaders are still cult-loyal. Or at least they're acting like they are," he added.

"Do you still think that the buzz from the sixth level is because of the original person?"

367

"I wouldn't be surprised."

"Let's pray and see what the Lord shows us."

After a couple of long quiet minutes, Head Honcho said, "I know this sounds crazy, but I think the original Fuchsya needs to come out of there."

"I agree. Let's ask the Lord for a strategy." Once again, they prayed.

"Humph," Head Honcho grunted, "I just had a thought. The Lord sealed Apollyon and his people down there, but I don't think He sealed the original down there. She might be trying to come up but is being held captive somehow."

"Interesting. Let's keep praying." Abigail prayed again, "Lord, You said that You came to set the captives free. You said that You cut in two the cords of the wicked. You said that You have broken the snare and we have escaped. Would You free the original Fuchsya Amy Bolton from the abyss in level six right now?"

Head Honcho was immediately displaced as evidenced by the adjustment in posture. It was almost as if he had passed out. Amy's head flopped back against the back of the chair with her eyes closed.

"Fuchsya? Are you Original Fuchsya?" Abigail asked hopefully.

"Where *am* I?" she asked groggily as she peered out of eyes that were not accustomed to light.

"You're in my living room. I'm Abigail."

"Wow. This sure beats where I've been." Fuchsya straightened up in the chair a little, looked around the room, and stared out the windows. "Is that real?"

"Yes, it is," Abigail smiled. "Welcome to the top side."

"Thanks."

"You must have a gazillion questions. What can I do to help you?"

"I'm not sure. I know a bunch of stuff because all those parts kept integrating into me. I think that's why Apollyon is so upset. He couldn't stop my growth so he kept trying to keep me in the abyss. It really did feel like a bottomless pit."

"I'm glad you're out. Can I ask how old you feel right now?"

Fuchsya tilted her head one way and then the other before she answered, "I think I'm twenty-six."

"Excellent!" Abigail was excited. She checked the front of Amy's file for confirmation. "Your thirty-first birthday is coming up on June six."

Fuchsya shuddered involuntarily.

"What's the matter?"

"I don't know. I mean, when you said that I just got a really creepy feeling."

"Interesting. This year it would be six, six, o-seven. Last year would have been six, six, o-six. Hm. Well, maybe that has something to do with Top Fuchsya's comment about a dead-line," Abigail mused out loud.

"Well the brilliant counselor thinks she has it all figured out!" Top Fuchsya taunted.

"Welcome back," Abigail smiled at her graciously. "And no, not really, suppose you fill me in."

"What? And make it easy for you?"

"No. It'd make it easier on you."

"You're the one making it harder; not me!" Top Fuchsya protested with a sneer.

"Let's not argue about that right now. How does original Fuchsya's escape from the abyss affect you?"

369

Top Fuchsya's face contorted as if she were trying to swallow a mouth full of stones before she spat out her retort. "Stupid woman! I'm in charge of all levels!"

"Oh, so you've failed to keep her under wraps. You couldn't stop the integrations and her aging."

"Bingo!"

"So now it's Plan B. Kill her."

"Give the lady a prize." Top Fuchsya regained some of her boldness and clapped five times very slowly and sarcastically.

"But if you kill her, you kill yourself."

"Nope."

"How do you figure?"

"I just migrate to another body."

"So, you're saying that you didn't come from the original Fuchsya and that you're a totally separate person who just happens to be living in her body."

"Right."

"What if you're wrong?"

"I'm not."

"Who did you inhabit before you migrated to her?"

"Nobody. I was always assigned to her."

"If you say so. Do you mind if I talk to the original Fuchsya again?"

"Are you dismissing me?" Top Fuchsya asked indignantly.

"We seem to be at an impasse. Do you mind?"

"Fine!" Top Fuchsya huffed and disappeared.

"Original Fuchsya Amy Bolton? Can you come back out?" Abigail asked.

"I'm here." She looked more oriented this time. "Are you saying that she and I have the same name and she's part of me and she wants to kill me?"

"There's been a death-warrant out for you from the beginning, unfortunately," Abigail said sadly. "How much of your family history do you understand? How much of your personal history?"

"I'm getting a pretty good idea that my life was awful," she nearly sobbed. "Was I so bad?"

"No, you weren't bad. Not at all. Your parents and grandparents were Satanists. They were evil and did everything they could to take you out. But you survived and you've come a long way in taking your life back."

"I don't know about that. Seems like all the others did the hard stuff while I was ... was down there."

"That couldn't have been very pleasant either."

"I'm not sure if I want to take my life back even if I could. I mean, I don't know how to do anything."

"That's the beauty of dissociation," Abigail smiled and continued, "all those wonderful, capable parts of you got all those qualities from you. The Satanists depleted you through dissociation and now, as they return to their rightful places back inside of you, you'll be as competent as the parts are."

"I don't know about that."

"Trust me. I've walked several people through this. I'll have Carrie Sue come back over sometime and she can tell you first-hand what it's like if you want to."

"Uh, sure."

"Meanwhile, I think we need to ask the Lord to give you a safe place you can retreat to."

"I'd like that. I'm really tired."

Abigail prayed and the original Fuchsya was replaced by Head Honcho.

"They're really buzzing now."

371

"Let's ask the Lord to put up a sound barrier."

"Why didn't we think of that before?" Head Honcho asked as he rubbed his chin.

They prayed and he reported that it was finally quiet inside. Amy resurfaced and they discussed the emergence of the original Fuchsya. They also discussed the up-coming birthday threat. Abigail knew by experience with other survivors that the birthday rituals were some of the most gruesome. There were usually a series of warm-up rituals to "honor" the birthday girl as well.

Amy went to her room to take a nap while Abigail went down to check on the chicks.

"I'll open the door and let you out tomorrow," she promised. The chicks looked healthy and vigorous as they scurried around the coop. Some of them had made it to the lower perch and were proudly looking down at the others. Several of them were huddled in one of the nesting boxes. Others were busily scratching through the straw and wood shavings. They had lost their fuzzy yellow coverings and were beginning to sport their auburn and bronze, brown and ginger feathers on their heads and bodies that gave way to the white tail feathers.

"You're getting so pretty, ladies," Abigail said softly as she closed the door and secured it carefully.

She heard the blare of a horn as she was crossing the back yard and took a quick detour to the north side of the house to get a look at the road. All she saw was the tail lights of a maroon colored pickup truck that looked like it might be Charlie Fletchers'. She gave an involuntary shiver and then heard Lee's familiar toot-

toot and the crunch of gravel as his truck neared the other side of the house.

Reversing her steps along the back of the house, she rounded the corner and greeted Lee as he got out of his truck. "Hey, there. What was that all about?"

"I think that was our neighbor, Charlie Fletcher," Lee said. "He swerved over the double-yellows and acted like he was going to run me off the road."

"Oh, boy! Here we go again!" Abigail was a bit distressed.

"I just scooted off the road into your driveway and he flipped me off and yelled something as he went by."

"Lord, protect us!"

"Amen," Lee agreed. "Come here," he said and gave her a hug. Then he led her around to the passenger side of his truck and retrieved something from the floor.

"What are you up to?" Abigail asked curiously.

"Here," he said as he straightened and faced her. "Happy birthday." He handed her a bouquet of flowers with an attached card.

"Oh, they're beautiful. Thank you. You're so sweet!" She held them out to the side as she put her hand to his face while he bent to kiss her.

"Will you let me take you out to dinner tonight to celebrate?"

"I'd love it."

They decided that they would go to The Iron Skillet and enjoy some of Auntie Z's cooking. Maybe they would run into Abigail's friend and owner, Paula. Putting the flowers in a vase, checking on Amy, Abigail was soon ready to go.

"Oh, before we go, I want to call Earl and Jan and let them know that Charlie Fletcher is getting aggressive again."

"Good idea."

26

Monday, June 4

Abigail was fretting. It was June already and all she had done in her garden was make one quick pass with the rototiller several weeks earlier. Frowning at the vigorous weeds that took advantage of the situation, she resolved to get the plants that she and Lee had recently picked up at the farmer's market into the ground this week. But it would probably not happen today.

Today she was getting ready for the Ministerial Alliance meeting at Rev. George Bordman's Presbyterian church in Hawville along with many others – both human and those in the angelic realm. There was a clash in the heavenly realms that was unseen by the natural eye. Many attacks were thwarted; some were not.

Dennis Walsh woke up with a splitting headache. Paul Overton was running late because he received a call from a distressed church member. Don Wilmore had a flat tire. Clara had an unexplained power outage in her area. Traffic was snarled. Family members were edgy. Distractions abounded.

By noon, most of the Ministerial Alliance had assembled with several new participants joining them. The meeting got started a few minutes late to accommodate those who had been held up. Finally, George's raspy voice quieted the gathering and he opened with prayer.

Lynda L. Irons

"We're getting so big that we're going to do it buffet style today. Come on up and help yourself. These ladies made some wonderful casseroles and salads. Don't forget the drinks and desserts."

"Well, that's Biblical," Richard Morris quipped, "Paul said that he buffeted his body." He pronounced it "boo-fayed" and accompanied it with a hearty laugh that rumbled from deep within his chest. His laugh was contagious and it enhanced the light mood at the luncheon.

When everyone was nearly finished, Pastor Spalding cleared his throat and got their attention. "There's been a lot of activity in this area since we met last month. We had The Taco Tower debriefing and then there was the Memorial Day out-reach. I know that there has been at least one salvation after the fund-raiser weekend at The Taco Tower. One of the employees who goes to my church was able to talk to another employee. He brought her to the manager's office and Todd led her to the Lord! She came to my church on Sunday and got more prayer."

"Hallelujah!"

"Wonderful!"

"Praise God!"

"I had several families come back to church since the murder. I think it really shook up our communities," another minister reported.

"Same here. New people, too."

They continued to report changes and rejoiced at the good news. Pastor Spalding asked for someone to report on the Memorial Day out reach.

"People were really open to prayer. I was able to pray with several about health issues."

376

"I found that many of them were believers but they just don't go to church."

"Me too. I heard that a lot."

"I was surprised at how open the young people were."

"They're hungry."

They continued to discuss the positive impact of the out-reach and took time to prayerfully brainstorm about effective ways to impact their communities.

"The way I see it," Pastor Spalding said, "we have unbelievers who need the Gospel. We have believers who need fellowship. We have Satanists who need to be shut down and their victims who need deliverance."

"That about covers it."

"Mike," Pastor Spalding addressed Rev. Griffin, "have you had any more ritual activity at your church? And how about that elder?" He was referring to Russ Ranson but did not want to mention his name.

"Nothing that either I or my custodian noticed. I haven't seen Russ much lately. He seems to be avoiding me. Hasn't shown up for the consistory meetings either."

"Excellent. I mean about the lack of activity. I just hope and pray that he renounces Satanism." Turning next to Don Wilmore, he said, "Pastor Wilmore, how are things with your church since the Bynum family transferred?"

"It's been calm," he reported. "I think it helped that we prayed that jurisdiction prayer last time. I still haven't seen more than one little girl. Sad family. They don't seem to talk to anyone; just show up and leave as soon as possible."

377

They discussed setting up another community outreach centered around the Fourth of July celebrations. They decided to have the worship leaders of the various churches come to another meeting with pastors the following week. They wanted to put together an interdenominational musical group that included musicians and singers.

"Everyone would come to a good old Gospel sing!" Clara Bardwell said with conviction.

"I think you're right. It would cross denominational lines and appeal to the unchurched as well."

"We need a name."

"Yeah, something that goes along with the fishing nets," another agreed.

"Good idea."

"The Trawlers," someone else offered with a chuckle.

"That has possibilities."

More discussions followed and the logistics were hammered out efficiently. The sound of chairs scraping tile flooring ebbed and flowed as they broke into small groups again and prayed for the unsaved people in the community. After that they prayed for the believers who were disenfranchised or marginalized by churches for a variety of reasons.

"One last round of prayers today," Pastor Spalding announced. "Abigail Steele, would you mind giving us some prayer points about our Satanism issues?"

Once again Abigail's stomach momentarily lurched inside because of the unexpected spotlight. *Holy Spirit, show us how to pray.* "Here's what I'm getting right now," she said confidently, "we need to go back to the opening that the Satanists used to get into this region, that is, the area where we collectively have a measure of jurisdiction based on our residency here." New thoughts were pouring into Abigail's mind as she continued, "If our country was created as a Christian nation under God, then somewhere in this region, someone either actively or passively allowed for Satanism. I think we need to begin by confessing the sins of our fathers like Ezra, Nehemiah, and Daniel did."

"Oh, that's good," Robert Warrens commented.

"That makes sense."

"So," Abigail continued, "we're going after the so-called legal rights that the Satanists and demons have claimed in this area because the Christians abdicated their responsibilities of guarding and maintaining Christianity here by confessing the sins of our ancestors and whatever responsibility we have as the current guardians of this region."

Some of the groups were quiet; some were boisterous. All of them were sincere. Voices surged and abated.

"God, we are slaves to kings that we do not know because our fathers have committed iniquity and we have sinned just like them."

"Lord, Your throne is sovereign over all. Thank You for Your mighty angels who perform Your word. Lord! Commission them to work in all places of Your dominion."

"Have mercy, Lord! Save the Satanists."

"Transformation!"

"Encourage their victims. Set the captives free."

On and on the prayers of confession and repentance, praise and worship rose as sweet-smelling incense through the atmosphere, through the second heavens, to the throne of grace. Bowls were filled and answers were spilling back to earth. There was a reaction in the heavenly realms as angels were dispatched to aid the saints.

Abigail stopped at the thrift store on her way home to see if there was another maternity outfit available for Amy's upcoming birthday. She watched Carrie Sue for a minute before she approached her. It was evident that she was much more at ease here. It was also obvious that she was very popular with the regular customers and her co-workers.

Noticing Abigail, Carrie Sue greeted her with a hug. "Hey, what are you doing here?"

"More maternity clothes if you happen to have some still. I want to get something for Amy. It's her birthday Thursday."

"Yeah, there's still a bunch of things here. Come on, I'll help you."

Together they picked out another outfit that still had the tags on them. "The Lord must have reserved these for Amy. I can't believe someone hasn't snatched them up by now."

"You always have God-things happening," Carrie Sue observed.

"I'm not sure about always, but I sure am blessed." Abigail hurried home with her treasure and wrapped it before Amy woke from her nap. Then she changed her clothes and checked on the chicks. She had opened the door on Sunday afternoon and they had barely hazarded exploring much more than a few feet away from their comfort zone. Curiously scratching and pecking, bobbing and backing, they quickly adapted. She was pleased that they had all found their way back into the coop by dark. Today some of the bolder ones drifted a few more feet away in search of earthy treasures.

Walking to the door, they scattered in alarm. Abigail peeked inside and did a head count. "Just remember that there are raccoons and 'possums and other critters that like chicken nuggets," she chided them. "You make sure you get back in there before it gets dark."

Satisfied that they were fine, Abigail decided to mow the lawn. She walked past Dude's grave on the way to the shed and paused for a moment. *Lord, I sure loved that dog. Why did the Satanists get away with that?* Abigail firmly believed that no weapon formed against her would prosper so it baffled her when they did any damage at all. *Lord, I trust You. Vengeance is Yours. Go get 'em God!* Abigail satisfied herself with trusting God's sovereignty and went on to mow the lawn.

The riding mower fired right up and she immersed herself in the task at hand. It took her the rest of the afternoon to mow the orchard, the back yard, the north side and all of the spacious front lawn. She opted to leave the area on the far side of the driveway for another day. Inhaling the sweet smell of freshly cut grass mixed with a hint of wild onion, Abigail looked with satisfaction at the yard as she walked back up to the house.

"How are the chicks?" Amy asked from her chair on the back deck.

"Getting braver. I just hope they don't go too far into the woods, but I suppose they'll do it anyway."

"You could put up a fence."

"I thought of that, but it seems like a lot of work and expense. I guess we'll keep praying for their safety."

"Hey, I got the salad made. When's Lee going to get here?"

"How'd you know he was coming?"

"Duh! He comes every night."

"Oh yeah. He does, doesn't he?"

"When's moving day?"

"Should be this weekend. He's got most of the stuff in there already, but he wants Gary to help him with the big stuff."

Abigail sat on the top step and they continued to chat like old friends. Abigail asked Amy about her doctor's appointment that was coming up next week. Amy asked about the Ministerial Alliance meeting. The pleasant day drew to a close with a beautiful sunset painting the sky and lengthening the shadows.

The weather cooperated the next day and Abigail was able to finish the lawn on the far side of the driveway and rototill her garden.

"Oh, it feels good to sweat!" Abigail proclaimed out loud. She looked with satisfaction on the freshly tilled garden plot as she removed her gloves. Inhaling the earthy scent, she could envision the beans and tomatoes, squash and peppers, pumpkins and sweetcorn. Yum! Tiny apples were displacing the pinkish blossoms. Peaches and pears were close behind. The grape vines were finally putting out miniature leaves. It promised to be a bountiful year.

Tomorrow she would rake the garden. She couldn't wait to plant bean, squash, pumpkin, and corn seeds and put in the tomato and pepper plants. Then she would clean Thumper Bumper, her .22 rifle, and have it ready for the rascally rabbits.

Amy was getting more edgy as she neared her birthday. She was quite restless and had trouble concentrating. On anything. She avoided Abigail; a fact that Abigail noted and resolved to address later that evening. There was no sense in having Amy be upset any longer than she had to be so she called Lee and let him know that he would have to scoot immediately after supper.

Amy opted to skip dinner that night so Lee and Abigail ate in the dining room. She had proudly shown him all the progress she had made on the garden and lawn. They had wandered down to see the growing chicks who were about as tall as they would get but they would need to fill out a bit more.

Soon enough Abigail and Amy were seated in the living room. They opened with prayer and were surprised when Top Fuchsya showed up instead of Head Honcho.

"Hello," Abigail said. "What brings you here today?"

"Hell-o!" she replied with a sarcastic edge to her harsh tones. "It dead-line time! Don't you remember anything?"

"Oh, I haven't forgotten," Abigail replied pleasantly.

"So, are you the edgy one or is that someone else?"

"I am not edgy!"

"Right. So, what brings you here today?"

"I have a dead-line and you took Original Fuchsya away. You had no right to do that!" she ranted.

"I didn't take anyone away. We just prayed and asked the Lord to put her in a safe place."

"She's gone and you need to bring her back right now!"

"I will if that's what the Lord wants us to do."

"The Lord! The Lord! What a lame excuse!"

"So, who's telling you what to do? You're a Satanist so I have to presume that you follow your lord's dictates. Why are you putting me down for doing the same thing you're doing?"

"My lord is superior. He's the preeminent one and you might as well get used to that idea."

"I concede that he has some power, but he's not my lord so I'm not taking orders from him. I know you understand authority."

"Some?" she screeched. "Some power?"

"The only power he has is the power to deceive. If you believe he has the right to do something, he'll do it. He's a bully and a manipulator."

Top Fuchsya fumed for a full minute trying to gather her thoughts for a come-back. "You... you... you just don't understand." She was starting to sound desperate as her cheeks flushed to a full, ripe tomato red.

"What happens to you if you fail to commit suicide on Thursday?" Abigail asked patiently.

"Nothing!" she spat.

"No. I don't believe that. You're a bit too upset and persistent. Besides, if your assignment is to make her commit suicide and you fail to do so, you'd be the first one I know of that didn't get punished."

She pressed her lips into a line so thin they almost disappeared. Through clenched teeth she uttered her ultimatum, "Get her back here. Now!"

"They're really threatening you, aren't they? I can help you with that, you know."

"I don't need your help. I need her! Now!" she demanded, emphasizing each word.

"I'll tell you what: I'll pray and ask God if it's okay for her to come up if you promise not to threaten or intimidate her. She might take off on us."

"Fine. I'll back way off but I'll be watching and if you try something slick, I'll be back with a vengeance."

"She has a free will, or at least a freer will now, so don't blame me if she makes a decision."

Top Fuchsya grudgingly backed down and Head Honcho showed up. He and Abigail discussed the situation and then they prayed that if it was the Lord's will for Original Fuchsya to come out of her safe place that He would bring her out. After several long minutes, she emerged.

"Hello there. How are you doing?"

"I feel a little stronger than the last time I showed up, but I still feel a bit intimidated by life." She looked around the room uncertainly but then dared to look Abigail in the eye as she asked, "And who's that one that wants to kill me? Did I hear something about committing suicide?"

Abigail gave her a more detailed explanation of her system and some of the personalities that had all split out of her. She encouraged her to try to understand that Top Fuchsya was not bad but that she had a lousy job, that she was programmed and demonized so Original Fuchsya and the others did not have to do that job.

Original Fuchsya paused a moment and then said thoughtfully, "I think the fear of life… of living is about as deep as the fear of death."

"That's very common with survivors. I promise you; it will get better."

"Now what? What's next?"

"Do you want to take back your life?"

"I think that would be better than having one foot in and one foot out. And since I am still breathing I should probably go for it."

Abigail smiled at her emergent spunk. "Let's do it. I want to talk to you a bit about jurisdiction and the authority you have as the original person."

"Okay," she said uncertainly.

"Think about it like this. If everyone inside there came out of you, then they are all part of you. They *are* you. You are ultimately responsible for them."

"Ugh. I'm not sure I like that idea."

"Well, it kind of works for you and against you."

"What do you mean?"

"Let me give you an example. I worked with another survivor who had a very strong Christian original person come out one time and said that even though some other part of her was promiscuous, it was still her body that sinned. The promiscuous part was adamant that she was not going to change so the original one prayed and confessed the sin on her behalf. When she did that, it touched the promiscuous one and she was willing to give up her assignment and defect into God's kingdom."

"Oh, I think I see what you mean. So, if some part of me wants to kill me or cause me to commit suicide or have me killed by the Satanists, I can confess it to God on their behalf."

"Yes. And when we confess our sins, God is faithful to cleanse us from all unrighteousness. Including the strongholds and demons that come with the package."

"Can I do that right now?" she asked eagerly.

"Sure. Which part do you want to assume responsibility for?"

"That one that wants to kill me. Us."

"Top Fuchsya. She's in charge of everything that's left – the six subterranean levels and Head Honcho's prison area."

"Okay, here goes. Jesus, on behalf of the Top Fuchsya..."

"Shut up! You can't talk for me!" Top Fuchsya dashed forward and cut her off.

"Why not? She's the original and you're a part of her."

"I didn't do anything wrong. And I am not a part of her!"

"Then what are you so upset about? If there's nothing wrong and you're not a part of her then nothing will happen."

"I still don't like it. You're up to something."

"What's the harm? Why don't you let her finish her sentence?"

"Fine! But I'll be back!"

With that Top Fuchsya disappeared and Original Fuchsya came back into executive control. "Whew! She's something else!"

"Oh, you've got some characters in there," Abigail agreed with a soft chuckle.

"I think I want to change my prayer," Original Fuchsya said as she stared at the floor. "God, I want to confess my sin. I'm sorry that I get so mad at that Top Fuchsya part of me. I forgive her for her rudeness to me and everyone else and I forgive her for wanting to kill me. Amen."

"Amen."

"Now what?"

"Let's touch base with her a minute," Abigail said. She had a hunch.

"What do you want?" Top Fuchsya asked in a more subdued tone.

"Are you all right?" Abigail asked, not sure if this really was Top Fuchsya because of the change.

Top Fuchsya looked anywhere but at Abigail. She was trying to form words, but it was not because of anger, it was because Original Fuchsya's prayer and tenderness touched something deep inside of her. "I don't know."

"What's changed?"

"I can't believe that she's forgiving me when all I wanted to do was kill her off."

"Wanted?" Abigail caught the past tense of the verb.

"Yeah, I mean, I don't feel like I want to kill her now. Like the drive to do it is gone. I don't know what happened." A very puzzled Top Fuchsya pondered the change.

"Would that make you think that you might be a part of her?" Abigail probed gently.

Top Fuchsya heaved a deep sigh, kept her chin on her chest, but raised her eyes to look at Abigail as she said, "I guess so."

"What do you want to do now?"

"I'm not sure. I mean, I don't know what I can do. I'm so embarrassed. How could I not know?"

"You were blinded by the god of this world. Do you want to see what else he kept from you?"

"Yeah. Yeah, I mean, I can't go back. They'll kill me." She winced in pain and gasped, "I think we'd better hurry."

"Okay, then, why don't you do business with the Most High God and renounce Satan and Satanism?"

"Uh, sure," she grunted, "Um, God, I'm really sorry. I screwed up and I really want to be done with Satan and all his stuff and if You'll have me, I want to serve You instead." She looked up and it was obvious that she was in pain.

"Let me pray for you," Abigail offered. Getting the nod, she launched into her "sozo" prayer – saved, healed, and delivered – covering all the things in Top Fuchsya's assignment that created strongholds and gave demonic oppressors the so-called legal right to operate in her life. Putting off the old and putting on the new, Abigail prayed blessings upon this part of Fuchsya Amy Bolton.

Top Fuchsya sagged in the chair exhausted. "How can I make it up to Original Fuchsya? I didn't know. I'm so embarrassed. I thought I was right. How could I be so stupid?"

"Stop beating yourself up. Programming and demons do a number on you. What do you say we ask the Lord about what's next for you?"

Lynda L. Irons

"Yeah, sure."

They prayed together and they both sensed that it was not time for Top Fuchsya to integrate yet, but that she would receive a new name and a new assignment so that she could help with the internal work.

27

Friday, June 8

Amy's birthday came and went peacefully, at least it appeared so. She loved the new clothes and became totally bashful at dinner with all the attention from Abigail and Lee. She was accustomed to negative attention and a part of her, indeed, a number of parts of her, kept wondering when the double-bind would kick in. When would they have to pay for anything good that might happen? Nothing happened that night but they would remain vigilant. Ever vigilant.

"Hey, A," Abigail called out, "I'm going to check the chicks and then head out. You need anything?"

"Okay," Amy called back in a triumphant sing-song voice, "and if I need anything, I can go get it. I'm not grounded anymore." Amy had her appointment earlier that week and all restrictions were lifted. She should be able to look forward to an event free second half of the pregnancy.

"Right. Forgot. Just be careful." Abigail closed the door behind her and it was not long before she was going down the driveway thinking about the upcoming session with Max and Pastor Spalding.

She had just finished setting up the office when she heard Max and Pastor Spalding enter the waiting area. "Come in!" she greeted them. "How are you? Let's get started."

They settled into their chairs, opened with prayer, and waited for Max to start.

"I kept thinking about what you said about being prepared for a lot more cult-loyal parts. It kinda scares me to think that I don't know what's going on in my own head."

"That can be a bit alarming," Abigail conceded with a slight nod, "but we always have to remember that God's got it. He's intervened in your life a lot and He who began a good work in you will continue."

"Yeah, I guess. So where do we start?"

"Let's ask God."

They prayed and Max reported, "I'm getting the word, the name Maximillian."

"Is that your full name?"

"No, on my birth certificate I'm just Max."

"Okay, is there someone in there named Maximillian?" Abigail asked.

Max shifted in his chair and then announced in an authoritarian voice, "I am he." Looking down his nose at Abigail, he continued, "and why would you be summoning me?"

"Because your name came up. Apparently, you have something to do with the cult-loyal side of Max."

"That peon has no idea what he's up against," Maximillian said condescendingly.

"Suppose you fill us in," Abigail invited pleasantly.

Maximillian was incredibly arrogant and proceeded to inform Abigail and Pastor Spalding that he was a general, a five-star general. His ego was immense. He hinted that the military organization under him consisted of quite a number of elite personnel who were quite capable of carrying out assassinations and other covert operations. By the time he was finished with his oration and switched out, Abigail had gleaned enough information to conclude that she was right about Max's system. It was much larger than any of them had hoped. She was saddened for the young man.

"Max," Abigail began after he resumed executive control, "it sounds like Maximillian is the general of a fairly large army."

"Oh, boy." Max looked like he was just told that his leukemia was back.

Abigail abruptly looked at Pastor Spalding and asked, "Did you get the idea that it was kind of like an ancient Roman army?"

"Yeah," he replied thoughtfully, "especially after he said something about a cohort. And I vaguely remember that name associated with ancient Roman history."

"That's what I thought. The five-star thing doesn't quite fit, but the rest does."

Max looked confused as his eyes shifted from Abigail to the pastor and back again several times. He was afraid to ask and he was afraid not to ask. "What does that mean?" he squeaked in a whisper.

"Were you privy to any of the conversations I had with Maximillian?"

"No."

"Okay, then," Abigail said, "let's go with what we know. You dissociated when you were a little guy because of the trauma of the leukemia. That means that you have a high dissociative ability. You were also disgruntled. Apparently, Levi figured these things out and recruited you into the cult. You have very few cult memories because you were drugged and intentionally split and these other parts took over cult activities. Evidently, the cult managed to create quite a number of cult-loyal, demon-loyal parts. Maximillian is probably not the head of the whole thing, but certainly is one of the higher-ups."

"Why wouldn't he be the top guy?"

"He might be, but it would be a rare exception for the top one to come out. I'm thinking – and this is just a guess – that if Maximillian is a five-star general in an ancient Roman-style army he's probably got a Caesar of some kind over him and the rest of the cult-loyal level."

"Cripes!" Max gasped and folded his arms over his belly. "I felt that."

"Okay, we're onto something but don't get alarmed. Everyone has an internal system. Some have cities, some have buildings, others have castles with dungeons, prisons or hospitals... I've heard of all kinds of systems, even pyramids. But every one describes a hierarchy of some kind. And if we know generally what your system is like, we can work our way to the top better."

Max just blew out a long breath and sat up straighter.

"I know that this must be overwhelming to you right now, but it really is good news to know what we're up against. I am also encouraged that you weren't raised by Satanists. So, your original, core person is intact. They didn't get to you until you were a teenager."

"Well, I'm glad something is good."

"I'm not saying that they didn't do a lot of damage, but you have a lot of advantages that most of my SRA survivors don't. We'll get through this, Max. I'll work as hard as you do."

"Me, too, son," Pastor Spalding assured him. "You've got a great set of parents and a bunch of other people who'll be praying for you, too."

"Well, no matter what, I'm not going to let them win!" he asserted. "They've taken too much of my life and I'm taking it back."

Lee heard the crunch of gravel as a vehicle slowly approached the house. He was on the far side of the house checking on his heifers and started to head back. Breaking into a smile when he saw Abigail, quickening his pace, Lee soon enveloped her in a bear hug. "How's my warrior doing?"

"Oh, I'm fine," Abigail sighed, "I just feel bad for the client. He's got a longer row to hoe than he thought. I just *hate* what the Satanists do to these people! I wish I could find a short-cut. Pray some comprehensive prayer that heals it all. They've been through hell and back and then they have to go through the healing process on top of it."

Lee hugged her tighter. "Me, too, babe. Someday."

"Thanks," she said and then changed the subject. "So, what have you been up to today?"

"Oh, just checking the heifers. They're getting fat. Should be ready to have them bred on schedule."

"Why do I think that calling someone a fat heifer is not a compliment?"

"Cows. Just for cows." Lee laughed, grabbed her hand and led her into the house. "Come on, I need for you to show me how you want the furniture arranged in here."

They went from room to room and Abigail did not make any changes to the sparse collection of furniture. They discussed the timing of moving her things over to the house as well.

"Lee!" Abigail said with an "aha" look on her face, "we're going to own two houses. What are we going to do with my farm if we're living here?"

"I was wondering when you were going to ask that question. What do you want to do?"

"Well, what are the options? Sell it? But I don't really like the idea of giving up land that we might need to use. Rent it out? But I hear too many horror stories about bad renters. We need to pray about it because I don't know where Amy could go."

"I remember hearing you say that you always wanted to have a sanctuary for your SRA survivors. Maybe this is God's way of providing it."

Abigail's jaw dropped. "Of course! Oh, of course. Duh! Why didn't I see that?"

"Maybe because you're right in the middle of the forest and can't see the trees?"

"Oh, I'm excited. I'm really excited. You know? I'll bet Carrie Sue would love to get out of that apartment and live out here, too. She and Amy got along great." Abigail's mind was whirring as she thought of the possibilities. "These ladies were never taught how to cook or can or garden or sew or do much of anything."

"I can see the progress in Amy just in the time she's been with you," Lee added. "She's helping with meals and housekeeping. She's becoming a chicken farmer and who knows what else?" They chuckled together.

"Now, wait a minute," Abigail paused as another thought hit her, "let's think about this. I mean, if we're going to be married, I want everything to be all ours. I want my farm to be our farm and my truck to be our truck, ya know? I know some couples with pre-nuptial agreements and everything is either his or hers and it seems like they're almost planning on splitting up."

"Well, I can understand it if there are kids involved."

"Yeah, but there's got to be some way to provide for that. My kids are gone, and you have Lisa."

"I see what you mean. Lisa shouldn't inherit your family heirlooms and your siblings shouldn't get mine. We'd want those things to stay in the family."

"It's not like I have a lot of stuff, but there are a couple of things."

"But as far as this," Lee made a sweeping motion with his arm, "being our farm and our horses and our fat heifers, I totally agree with you."

"It doesn't seem fair. You have about eight times the land, a bigger house, a bunch of machinery, and all I have is ten acres and an ornery flock of chickens."

"I don't care. I want you. I need you. I love you. I want to spend the rest of my life with you. I want to grow old with you."

Her reply was muffled by his warm lips.

———————————

Sunday morning brought yet another surprise. Amy was up early and dressed in one of her new outfits. "I'd like to go to church with you guys if that's okay."

"Seriously?" Abigail asked with a huge smile. "I'd love it. Would you be okay with sitting by me and Lee and Carrie Sue and the McCord's?"

"Uh, sure, I mean, I could give it a shot."

"Do you want to ride with Lee and me or would you rather drive yourself?"

"I think I'd rather drive myself. That way I can boogie out if I need to."

"Works."

They finished getting ready for church and it was not long before they heard Lee's toot-toot. Amy was obviously nervous, but she headed to the door with her keys and back pack style purse. She followed them and parked next to them in the parking lot of the church. Abigail helped her navigate the crowded foyer and all the terrifyingly friendly people who wanted to greet Amy. She was still uncomfortable with interacting in a crowd.

Carrie Sue had arrived before them and she was talking to Cindy. Amy was greeted with smiles as she sat down next to Carrie Sue on the pew. Abigail leaned over to her and whispered, "I'll walk out with you if you think you need to leave."

Amy was obviously relieved and very grateful for the offer. She felt somewhat trapped sitting in the middle of the row of people, but she was soon able to focus on the music as the first chords were sounded. Not knowing the songs, she just stood or sat when everyone else did.

Pastor Spalding climbed the steps energetically and put his Bible on the podium. "Good morning!" he boomed. "It's so good to be in the house of the Lord today. I see some new faces here today. Welcome! I hope I get a chance to meet you before you leave."

Of course, the announcement about new faces caused people to turn and look for the new faces. Amy just held her head down and prayed for the moment to pass. It had never felt safe to be in the limelight.

"This morning I want to talk to you about compromise and standing firm. Let's turn to the book of Exodus starting at the end of the sixth chapter and let me fill you in what's going on here. The Lord told Moses to tell the Pharaoh to let the people go out to the wilderness to serve Him. God also told Moses that Pharaoh's heart would be hard and that he would resist, refuse, and renege every time which would give God the opportunity to prove to the Egyptians that God is the Lord. God had a strategy. Are you following?"

The nods and yeses assured Pastor Spalding so he continued to expound on the passages that described the ten plagues which came because of Pharaoh's arrogance. "He wanted the Israelites to compromise. Look in chapter eight verse twenty-five. He said they could worship God within the land of Egypt. Moses refused to compromise. A few verses later, Pharaoh said they could go to the wilderness but not very far away. Again, Moses refused to compromise. By chapter ten, Pharaoh was willing to let only the men go. Moses refused to compromise. The next compromise was to allow them to go but leave their flocks and herds behind. God was glorified because Moses would not compromise. But the Israelites complained because the Egyptians made their work a lot harder each time they stood firm."

Pastor Spalding paced back and forth with enthusiasm as he appealed to his congregation. "Folks, is there something that God has asked you to do and you find yourself wanting to compromise just a little bit because it would be easier? Is He asking you to go all the way into the unknown, wild wilderness of a godly life and you're being tempted to compromise because it would be easier to stay where you are or just venture out a little bit? I'm talking about your behavior or language or lifestyle or whatever it is that you know God wants to change in you. Stand firm, folks. God will be glorified! Come on down here if you need prayer. The prayer team is available."

He continued to close the service. Some went forward. Most headed toward the parking lot or the children's church area to pick up their children. Amy had made it through the service. She and Carrie Sue talked on the way out and they decided to go get a burger so they could continue the conversation that they did not want Abigail to hear.

"I'm not sure what I'm going to do," Amy said. "I've been homeless before, but now I have this baby to think about. I can't just live in my car again."

"That's too dangerous. You could stay with me," Carrie Sue offered. "It's just a one-bedroom apartment, but maybe when you get your job back we could find a bigger place together."

Meanwhile, Abigail and Cindy were talking about turning her farm into a sanctuary for SRA survivors.

"I'm not sure about legal or liability matters. I'll have to look into that."

"Maybe you could turn it into a non-profit."

"That's a thought."

"But, you know," Cindy said like the mother hen that she was, "Amy must be getting kinda nervous not knowing about her situation especially with you getting married in less than a month."

"Oh, you're right! I've been so busy with everything else that I didn't think about that. I'll have to let her know right away."

"I'm sure she'd love to stay there but she might be edgy about living there alone."

"Yeah," Abigail agreed. "Even with the Milner's and us close by, she'd probably be a bit nervous. She is a city girl, you know."

They parted ways. Cindy caught up with Gary in the children's department and Abigail found Lee in the foyer talking to some other men about heifers. Abigail walked up and touched his elbow.

"Ah, there you are," Lee smiled, "ready?"

"Yes."

"Home for lunch?"

"First I think we need to decide if we're kicking Amy out or inviting Carrie Sue in or what."

"Whoa! Wait. What's the rush? Of course they're welcome. I thought we decided."

"I just wanted to be on the same page with you. Besides, Cindy pointed out that Amy knows I'm moving out in three weeks, but I haven't said anything to her about letting her stay. I think I'd be really nervous if I were her."

"Good old Cindy. Of course."

"The two of them said that they were going to go grab a burger. How about if we find them and let them know what we've decided?"

401

"Let's roll!" Lee escorted Abigail to the truck, opened the door for her, and then headed to the burger joint.

Bells tinkled on the door and Carrie Sue looked up with surprise when she saw Lee and Abigail approach their table. "Hey, you stalking us?"

"Yeah. That's what we're doing," Abigail joined their laughter. "Mind if we join you for a minute? We have something we need to ask both of you."

"Sure," Amy and Carrie Sue said in unison.

"Okay, I have finally been thinking about what we need to do with my farm once Lee and I are married. We discussed it and we don't want to sell it or rent it out. Would the two of you consider living there?"

"Consider!" Carrie Sue exclaimed. "I'd love it!"

Amy was speechless. Her eyes misted and she barely croaked out, "Oh, thank you. Thank you. You don't know how worried I was."

"I'm so sorry, Amy," Abigail said. "I should have thought of this a long time ago. I mean, I did tell you that you could stay as long as you needed to, but I wasn't thinking about getting married back then. I hope you weren't getting worried."

"We were just sitting here trying to figure out how the two of us could swing a place together."

"Well," Lee said, "it looks like God figured it out for you."

28

Thursday, June 14, New Moon

Prinz was gone. His desiccated remains had been disposed of in a covert manner worthy of his status. The scrap for his position waged as Daggett and Darod pitted their natural and supernatural powers against one another while maintaining a façade of comradery. The corpulent Judge Roberts and the weasel-faced county commissioner Miller invoked powers and strategies to ensure favor. Zorroz, the sheriff, and Herrak, the prosecuting attorney, supported their respective leaders. Each man hungrily eyed the vacancy.

Xerxes, the congressman and regional master, had called for a region-wide ritual. Everyone was expected to show up. Since St. Mark's Episcopalian Church had been severely damaged by the tornado in April, they needed to select an alternate site for the ritual. This one would be deep in the remote woods closer to the capital of the state.

That night select children would be subjected to torments that were calculated to fragment their delicate brains and minds into hundreds or thousands of parts. Each part that was formed was identified and demonized, programmed and assigned a role.

The Satanists took advantage of the presence of the lake. A man dressed in white middle-eastern looking attire imitated Jesus. This false Jesus either ordered the drowning of the child or personally held the child under the water until the child was unconscious. The child would regain consciousness when the Satanists revived him or her.

"You saw who drowned you."

"Jesus is bad."

"Satan told us to save you."

"You belong to him."

"You owe Satan allegiance."

These children would be subjected to variations of these messages over and over again to drive in the point that God and Jesus are bad and that Satan is good. Christians are suspect; Satanists are benevolent.

That night several of the women were subjected to torment as well. As they watched their children being held under the water, limbs flailing and then gradually floating lifelessly to the surface. The mental anguish was worse than the physical torment as they were subjected to another set of customized double-binds.

"Kill that other woman's child and yours will live."

"This daughter or that son."

"You or your child."

Dr. Bacchus provided an assortment of needles. Blood was drawn from Xerxes and Luxor, Daggett and Darod, Zorroz and Herrak. Demonized masters. It was injected into the skin above the hearts of several victims in the form of pentagrams and Baphomets, broken crosses and crescents. Each of the hundreds of tiny injections came with a powerful hex driven by a massive demon. Blood tattoos. Blood oaths. Blood covenants. Layer after layer of programming and demons were installed to hopelessly lock the victim into Satanism. They were resigned to a lifetime of obeisance to their king and his masters.

Russ Ranson hungrily eyed the bound victims through seedy myopic eyes minimized by the thick lenses. He relished the festivities and lost himself in the power-enhancing, kingdom-advancing rites: the sexual perverseness, the gory communion, the deadly baptisms. He joyfully endured the pain and scorned the shame for the opportunity to embellish his status in the kingdom, not realizing that he was just as disposable as any of them.

Charlie Fletcher dutifully participated in the ritual. The demand on his life infuriated him. His escalating rage was taken out on the victims. He worked hard to keep up the appearance that he was fully engaged, but as soon as he could slip away shortly before three in the morning he headed home. An hour later his car careened down the last couple of miles to his home on York Creek Road.

That formerly quiet tenant that had lain dormant within him for so long made its presence known and Charlie heard himself growl as he passed Lee's farm and then the Milner's place and finally Abigail Steele's. He looked ruefully at his deformed hand and renewed his vow to exact revenge. In the remaining darkness of that night his neighbors heard his tractor belch and thrum.

The Rottweiler barked at the disturbance it caused. Partially gratified demons hounded their targets in an attempt to satisfy the insatiable. Broken cisterns. Always eating, never full. Always drinking, never quenching. Charlie Fletcher got their attention and the dog barked at the disturbance they caused.

———————

405

Lynda L. Irons

Amy had restlessly paced the floor of her room the previous night; she woke often, starting at the least sound, but by Friday morning she was calm again. It was considerably better now that Top Fuchsya had settled down, but the hammering waves of the fear of being lured or kidnapped or having some latent programming triggered kept pounding and left her hypervigilant day and night. *Will I ever get over this?*

Looking at her round belly, Amy caressed her growing baby with gentle strokes and promised, "I won't let them get you; I won't."

Amy finally heard Abigail shuffling around the kitchen and joined her. "Morning," she called out as cheerily as she could. Amy felt like she was a burden to Abigail and now she felt even more indebted because of the offer to live in the farmhouse with Carrie Sue. What other options did she have?

"Good morning," Abigail returned her greeting and then scrutinized Amy's face. "Rough night?"

"Not one of my better ones, but we made it through."

"Yes, you did! I know it doesn't seem like you're making much progress, but you didn't go to a ritual last night. Did you sense any programming or any parts that wanted to go?"

Amy scrunched up her face and ran her hand through the tangles at the back of her head before she replied, "I'm not sure what it was. I was jumpy but I didn't feel like I needed to go anywhere so I guess that's good. I don't know; maybe it… well, I think I was mostly just afraid that they'd come and get me. It was the worst around four o'clock this morning."

"Interesting. I have to meet with Pastor Spalding and a client and then if you're up to it we can work on some stuff when I get back."

"Yeah, I'd like that. Thanks. Hey, I'll check on the peepsters for you."

"Great! I'll get ready then and head out." Abigail finished her morning routine and headed down the road blowing a kiss as she passed Lee's lane. *Three more weeks and that'll be my home, too.* Abigail tried not to allow herself to get too distracted by the butterflies that were flitting about within her.

Pastor Spalding greeted her as they converged on her office simultaneously. "How are you today?"

"Great. Just trying not to get too distracted by the wedding."

"I'm just tickled for you and Lee. You two seem like you've been together forever. We probably need to talk for a few minutes sometime in the next week or so and hammer out some last-minute details."

"Good idea," Abigail agreed.

They heard the outside door and soon Max joined them. "Hey, sorry I'm late."

"You're good," Abigail assured him. "Any fallout from last time? Maximillian?"

"No, it's been quiet, but I had a rough night. I just couldn't sleep. I wanted to run but had nowhere to go so I just paced a lot."

"It was a ritual night. Maybe it was programming. Probably the cult-loyal ones were trying to get you out again."

"That's what I was thinking. I was afraid to sleep so I actually read my Bible a little."

407

"Excellent!" Abigail encouraged him. "Let's open with prayer and see where the Lord leads us today." She led the opening prayer and then looked expectantly at Max.

"I think you're right about that Maximillian guy. I mean, he hasn't shown up or anything, but it feels like he's just lurking below the surface."

"Have you lost any time?"

"I don't think so, but sometimes I'm not sure if I do or not. I'm pretty sure I can account for everything I did this week."

"Good. Let's ask the Lord what He wants us to do about Maximillian and Caesar and whoever else is in there."

Max suddenly stood up and imperiously announced, "I will not tolerate your conspiracies and disrespect!"

"There was no disrespect intended," Abigail said as she tried to pacify the personality. "Are you General Maximillian?"

"Who do you think you are, questioning me?" he asked as he paced to the door and back.

"I'm Abigail and if you would have a seat, perhaps we can sort things out."

"I shall remain standing."

Abigail noticed that his left leg seemed to be normal. He did not limp. "Do you mind if I ask you some questions? You said some impressive things last time we talked."

"Ask what you will."

"Who are the other two generals and what's the name of your Caesar?" Abigail sucker-punched him.

He stepped closer to Abigail and glared at her as he pulled himself up to full height, "I am not at liberty to disclose that information."

Pastor Spalding tensed in his chair and prepared to intervene if Maximillian threatened Abigail.

"Okay, I don't need their names, but it would be nice to talk to the Caesar."

"He will not be summoned for an audience by a commoner such as you. And a woman at that!"

"No problem. How about if I talk to Max again? Maybe we can talk again some time."

Sputtering at her impudence, General Maximillian disappeared. Max returned, limped back to his chair and sat down with a bewildered look on his face. "What just happened?"

"Maximillian, er, General Maximillian was here. He wasn't pleased when I asked about the other two generals and the name of the Caesar. But the way he answered me confirms that they exist."

"Cripes! What do we do with that?"

"Let's talk about the authority and responsibility you have as the original Max. It's within your jurisdiction to make decisions for and about the other personalities. It would be best if they were in agreement, but if they're not," Abigail's eyes twinkled, "sometimes we just need to ask for forgiveness later. It is for their good."

"How do I do that?"

"Let's review your identity. You are a born-again Christian. That means that when you got saved, you entered into the death, burial, and resurrection of Jesus Christ. That means that the certificate of debt that

409

consists of decrees against you have been nailed to the cross and have been taken out of the way."

"Okay, I'm following you."

"That means that your covenant with God that was previously ratified and that cannot be set aside cannot be replaced with another covenant."

"You lost me."

"You entered into covenant with God... what? Ten years ago?"

"Yeah, about that," he said and looked for confirmation at Pastor Spalding who nodded.

"And that put you into Christ – His death, burial, and resurrection – about two thousand years ago when Jesus died for you. So, any covenant or agreement that was imposed on you since then is bogus. It illegally sets aside the covenant that was previously ratified between God and you. So, no covenant between Satan and you or some Satanist and you can stand."

"All right, but how does that help us with Maximillian and Caesar?"

"They were forced to accept bogus assignments, covenants, contracts, callings, and so on."

"Oh," Max brightened, "I think I see what you mean. I can renounce their junk because it's bogus and I have the right to do it because I'm me."

"That's it!"

"Can I do that right now?"

"Yes, but first let's ask God to bind any demons associated with them and separate programs and stuff from them."

"Would you do that? I'm not sure if I'll cover it all right."

"Sure. Holy Father, on behalf of Max, we appeal to Your heavenly council, Your court where You are Judge and God of all. We ask for Jesus Christ to represent Max, the plaintiff, as his advocate and that You would call forth all defendants in this case: Satanists and demons alike. We ask that You would go back through Max's history and render a judgment on each and every bogus covenant or contract, assignment or calling that was imposed on him prior to his birth, while he was a minor, while he was impaired, while he was not in full control of all his mental faculties because of the dissociation. We ask that any part of him – his brain and/or his mind that has been so affected would be set free from satanic control as Max prays and assumes his rightful jurisdiction in directing his life. Lord, we ask You to complete and correct anything we pray inadequately, in Jesus' name, amen."

"God, I just want to say that I want my life back and that everything that was taken away from me be returned. I renounce all bogus covenants and accept only my covenant with You and Your covenant with me. Please help all the parts of me to be good with this and if they're not, would You please put them to sleep or whatever You have to do and take their junk away. Amen."

"Amen!" Abigail was pleased with the way Max was learning and applying the principles. "What are you sensing?"

"I didn't realize how noisy it was in my head until it got quiet."

They continued to talk and pray a little longer and then their time was up. Max proudly reported that he

411

had finally finished paying his father off for the things he had stolen. They finished their session and after Max left, Abigail and Pastor Spalding debriefed.

"It's so good to see him turn his life around. Less than a year ago he was plotting to kidnap Jason's little sister and kill you."

"He probably still has parts in there that are plotting."

"Serious!"

"Oh, yes. You saw the general today. He wanted to kill me. You should have seen the demonic daggers in his eyes."

"I had no idea."

"You must have had some idea because you tensed up there."

"You are observant. I don't know how you do it."

"God. Only God."

Carrie Sue had called the night before and cancelled her appointment with Abigail explaining that she was doing great. Abigail loved working herself out of a job and headed home early.

"Hey, A," Abigail called out when she got home, "are you ready?"

"Let's do it." She bowed her head and opened with prayer.

Progress!

Head Honcho reported that things were unusually quiet inside. "Almost eerie," he said. "It's kind of like when you go out in the woods and all of a sudden the birds and crickets shut up and you know that some predator is close by."

"Peculiar. Let's ask the Lord." They prayed for direction and then waited.

"It's me."

"Top Fuchsya?" Abigail guessed.

"Yeah."

"Are you the cause of the quiet or you know about the quiet?"

"I think I know. It has something to do with Apollyon's level. I think they may be about to explode or implode or something."

"Thanks. It's kind of what I've been expecting. By the way, how are you doing?"

She smiled sheepishly and said, "I'm okay... I'm just so embarrassed that I acted the way I did and gave you such a rough time."

"No problem. Today's a new day and you have a new job."

"I think I have a new name, too. I keep hearing 'Tiara' and it gives me kind of an excited feeling. What do you suppose it means?"

Abigail smiled with understanding. "Let me read a couple of verses that come to mind from Isaiah sixty-two." She tilted her notebook up against her chest and then paged through her Bible. "Here. *'And you will be called by a new name, which the mouth of the* LORD *will designate. You will also be a crown of beauty in the hand of the* LORD*, and a royal diadem in the hand of your God.'*"

"Oh, wow," the former Top Fuchsya said, misting up, "Tiara. I'm Tiara. I like it. God named me?

"Way cool. How about your new assignment? Any ideas there?"

"I think I'm supposed to team up with Head Honcho and help him help the original. I could use some of his savvy to deal with the levels."

"Have you talked to any of the leaders?"

"Nicholai was a bit suspicious at first, but we're talking. Achan, Beor, Jonah, and Judas are listening, but they're mad because a bunch of their people have defected and gone up to Nicholai's level. I think most of them have integrated already."

"That's great!"

"Apollyon? Now that's another story. Even though I'm technically his leader... I hate to admit it, but I'm a bit leery of him."

"Why?"

"I'm not sure. It's like he's gotten more powerful since he's been locked in."

"Maybe because of defections the demons are more concentrated in the ones that are left."

"Makes sense. Or at least as much sense as anything does to me right now."

"Let's ask the Lord what we need to do next."

"Sure."

They prayed briefly and then Tiara said, "I get the idea that I need to have a meeting with Nicholai and the other four level leaders."

"Okay, but what about Joktan?" Abigail was not quite sure where this was going but she trusted the process. Sometimes she was the last one in the room to know what was going on. "Lord, we trust You to arrange this meeting right now."

"I'm in some kind of a room with all of them," Tiara reported, "they're quiet and just looking around. Huh. There's no door. No Joktan either."

414

"Interesting. Can they hear me?"

"Yeah. They're listening."

Abigail introduced herself to the four personalities that she had not directly addressed before and then got down to business. "Tiara says that you guys seem to be angry because of all the defections. That right?"

Tiara relayed their message, "They say that I don't have any business making decisions anymore because I defected. They'll only listen to Joktan."

"Where's Joktan? He's the leader over all the subterranean levels if I remember right and we haven't heard from him in quite a while."

"He's not in our private quarters; I think he's down with Apollyon and all the level six people."

"Hm. Maybe that's were all the extra power is coming from." Abigail pondered that for a moment and silently prayed for insight. "Okay, let's see if we can figure out why they're so mad. Guys? Can someone let us know?"

"They're not going to talk," Tiara related.

"Let's ask the Lord to remove programming and demons from them."

"Ooh! That got their attention. They're screaming at you and, well, I won't repeat what they're saying, but they don't want you messing with anything. Nicholai's trying to explain that it's good but they're shouting him down."

"Tiara, what do you want to do on their behalf as their leader who is responsible for their welfare?" Abigail plainly laid it out for Tiara and the subterranean leaders.

"I want to help them so I'm going to pray," she announced decisively. "Lord, would You please take

415

Lynda L. Irons

out all their programs and demons and set them aside right now?" Tiara suddenly looked surprised.

"What happened?"

"The room got brighter. They're all just looking around kinda shocked but a lot less angry."

"Guys? Can we talk?"

"They said they're okay with it now."

Abigail began to negotiate with the four subterranean level leaders by explaining the big picture and the recent changes. They admitted that they were tired and that they were more than a little bit concerned about Apollyon and the sixth level activities. None of them had seen Joktan and the consensus was that he was locked down on Apollyon's level, too.

By the time they were finished with their discussions, they were ready to defect out of Satan's kingdom and into God's kingdom. There were some hold-outs, but the majority of them were ready for some peace and quiet. Abigail prayed her comprehensive 'sozo' prayer for all of them.

"Is anyone ready for integration?"

"They said that they want their levels to be like Nicholai's and have all the little ones and most of the others either integrate into Original Fuchsya or consolidate into the leaders. The leaders think they need to hang around to help."

Abigail was delighted to facilitate their desires. When she was finished praying, Tiara gave a report: their levels were cleared of all walls, all hiding places were eliminated, a central access portal was established, and all the young and vulnerable ones were either integrated or consolidated into their respective level leaders. It was a major turning point in Amy's healing journey, but it was far from over.

Lynda L. Irons

29

Sunday, June17, Father's Day

"Happy Father's Day to the dads and grandfathers out there! Let's honor them with a round of applause!" He paused until the room quieted.

"Now, I'm not trying to throw anyone under the bus here but how many of us have had a perfect father?" Making an exaggerated show of looking for a hand, he drew some smiles. "Notice that my hand didn't go up, either. Men have a tough job. We *have* to work to provide for our families, but we also need to spend time with our wives and our children. Who has been able to successfully keep all the balls that keep getting added to our juggling acts from falling to the ground? I know that I certainly haven't."

Some women patted their husbands appreciatively while a few who had been known to elbow their husbands when a good point was made assumed the locked-and-loaded folded arm posture.

"I know that most of us have had pretty good fathers. I certainly did. I also know that there are some here who grew up without a father. Death. Divorce. Abandonment. Some of you never knew your father. Some of you were mentally, physically, emotionally, or even sexually abused by your father. How do you run down to the drug store and pick out a Father's Day card for a dad like that?" He could see that this struck a chord with men and women alike.

"Let's take a run through the Scriptures today and see if we can pick up some good pointers from some good dads and watch for pitfalls that other dads fell into." He apologized once again for preaching from the book of Concordance with his tongue firmly planted in his cheek. He really was not sorry and he used his corny joke whenever he could. He got away with it because he was loved by his people.

He pointed out Adam's reluctance to take the lead in the Garden of Eden, he drew attention to Enoch who walked close to God and contrasted him with Lamech who tried to get away with murder. He emphasized Abraham's faith but added that his lack of it at a critical time caused a lot of trouble for his wife and his son, Ishmael, and how that conflict continues in the Middle-east today. David's failure to discipline himself and his sons led to incest and strife. He went on to underscore the lives of some of the kings and some of the prophets.

"Folks, we need to pray for the fathers in our lives. We all exasperate our children and act less than loving to our wives at times. We're all going to fall short in one way or another. I love Psalm 27:10. *'For my father and mother have forsaken me, but the LORD will take me up.'* Another translation says that *since* they've let me down, the Lord will take us up. So, if you haven't been properly parented... properly fathered... why don't you come down today and get prayer for that old wound? You may need to forgive him. If you want to come down here as families and pray for the father in your family, come down and bless him. Come down for healing or any other reason."

Pastor Spalding walked down to the front and began to pray with some of the families. Lee's father was gone. Abigail's father was distant. This was the

Lynda L. Irons

first Father's Day since Carrie Sue's father died last fall. Amy had no idea who her biological father was. There was a lot of pain in that pew.

Cindy whispered to Abigail, "See you guys at the house?"

"We'll meet you there." Abigail was always warmed by the sunny smiles from Lee's family. She really liked the idea that her best friend and soon-to-be matron of honor was going to be her cousin, too. Family. No doubt this family had its flaws, but it had always been very accepting of her and that was beyond wonderful.

Abigail waved as she got into Lee's truck. "Hey, don't you two remodel that house yet."

"How'd you know?" Amy giggled.

"Busted!" Carrie Sue laughed.

"Later!" Lee shook his head as he closed the door behind her and walked around to the driver's side. Soon they were humming down the road to the McCord's house and another family gathering.

"Did Lisa call you this morning?"

"No. I didn't expect her to with the time difference. She would have had to get up pretty early to catch me before church."

"Maybe tonight."

"Maybe tonight."

"Well, here we are!" Lee announced the obvious. He seemed disappointed not to have heard from Lisa and changed the subject.

"I see smoke coming from the back."

"All right! That's a good sign. The grill master is at work. I'd better go harass him. I mean, help him."

Abigail laughed with him and said, "I'll go see if I can help in the kitchen."

They split up and helped or harassed where they could. Soon they were sitting next to each other at the dining room table with the rest of the adults. Teens took over the kitchen table but some preferred the picnic table in the backyard. Chatter and chitchat, heart-to-heart conversations and hearsay kept the house anything but quiet.

"How are the wedding plans coming?" Grandma McVeigh asked.

"We seem to be right on schedule. A couple more details to finish."

"Less than three weeks."

"Getting nervous?"

"How many are you expecting?"

"Probably fifty to a hundred at the wedding. Not exactly sure how many will be at the reception at the church afterwards but it won't matter, we have enough finger foods to feed an army and if only half an army shows up, we'll just know what we'll be eating for a while. We have all the RSVP's for the dinner reception at The Steak House; there'll be about thirty of us there."

Eventually the crowd thinned as the families hugged, bid each other farewell, and gathered their dishes and children. Abigail and Lee said their goodbyes and headed out as well. They stopped at Lee's farm and even though they still wore their Sunday clothes, they decided to walk down to visit the horses. Meandering down the dry path hand in hand, they savored the tranquility of the moment.

The horses nickered and put on a show when they sensed Lee and Abigail's presence. Manes streaming and rudder-like tails floating behind them, the five horses eventually pranced and paraded to the gate.

"You big show off!" Abigail reached up to Buster's magnificent head and scratched under his jaw where he couldn't scratch himself. "You need a ride, don't you?" She carried on the conversation absolutely certain that Buster understood every word she said.

"We should take another ride one of these days," Lee said. "There's nothing urgent to do around here anymore."

"Easy for you to say Mr. Already-moved-in. I still have a bunch of stuff to pack and move."

"Just pack the essentials. There's no rush to have everything done right away."

"You're right. But I do want my bedroom and bathroom packed so Carrie Sue can move in. But, I agree that we need to take a ride. These horses haven't been out in a while and they're getting fat."

Lee looked at his watch. "It's only three-thirty. Why don't we get changed and go now?"

"Why not?" Abigail was up for an adventure.

The walk back up the trail was more purposeful. Abigail drove Lee's truck to her house and changed while Lee got changed at the new house. Carrie Sue and Amy were jabbering away on the shaded front porch when she pulled up.

"Where's Lee?"

"He's changing. We're going to ride. Want to come along?"

"No way!" Amy said and patted her belly.

"Not today," Carrie Sue added.

"Someday," Abigail teased as she deftly took the steps and swept across the porch. She quickly changed, grabbed a couple of water bottles and hurried back the way she came.

"Have fun!"

Abigail felt so small in the full-sized pickup truck. She didn't bother to adjust the seat or mirrors for the short trip so she craned her neck to make sure she did not clip her own truck as she swung around after the three-point turn.

Lee had two halters ready and was waiting on the four-wheeler by the time she parked the truck and slid out of the driver's seat. "Let's roll!" He patted the seat behind him.

Once she was settled, he torqued the throttle and they eased back down the path to the horses. The horses were less demonstrative with this visit. In fact, Sassy and Misty only looked up from their grazing long enough to acknowledge the intrusion on their grazing session. Buster put his noble nose into the familiar blue halter rope and let Abigail slip it over his velvety ears.

"Well, it looks like Lady or Sparkles today. Who's up for a ride?" Lee addressed the two horses who came up to the gate with Buster. He eased into the pasture and stood to the left of Lady, easily slipping his arm over her neck and putting the halter on her.

"Here's Buster," Abigail handed Lee the lead rope. "I'll ma'am the gate."

"Ma'am," Lee muttered under his breath. Deep dimples creased his cheeks as he grinned at her humor.

"Well, I'm not a man!" Abigail said with mock indignation.

423

"No. You certainly are not a man," Lee agreed as he quickly raised and lowered his eyebrows twice.

"Let's ride!" Abigail was flattered and flustered.

Lee easily swung onto Lady's back while Abigail climbed onto the four-wheeler to get onto Buster. They rode bare-back up to the barn where they groomed the horses and shook out blankets, tightened cinches and exchanged halters for bridles.

"Where do you want to go today?" Abigail asked.

"I was thinking that I'd like to ride the perimeter of our properties. I've been sensing something and I just want make sure that nothing's going on."

"Good idea. I'm getting a bit careless. I've been neglecting the surveillance cameras; maybe we can swing down there and check them out."

"Absolutely. Why don't we start by your place and then make the rounds over here?"

A light heel to Buster's flank started him down the trail that went directly to the end of her driveway. Neither one of them forgot Charlie Fletcher's brazen attempt to ambush Abigail on that trail so their alert eyes continually scanned near and far, front and back, left and right.

Amy and Carrie Sue were still on the front porch and waved as they walked the horses over the highest point of the driveway and headed through the open gate and into Buster's former pasture. He snorted and nickered in recognition and wanted to head straight to the tack room. He shied a little when some of the chickens scurried into the open door at the sight of the horses.

"Good instincts, ladies," Abigail called out to her chicks.

"They're really getting big," Lee commented.

"Maybe another six or eight weeks until they start laying."

"Can't wait! There's nothing like fresh eggs."

"Right now they're freeloaders, but pretty soon they'll be earning their keep."

They finished the circuit around the edge of the property, exchanged the SD card at the end of the field, and then headed to the York Creek end of Lee's property.

"Hey," Lee said, "I've got a hunch. Let's go up the creek and then check out the back side of Charlie Fletcher's place."

"Sure, why not? We have plenty of daylight." They lapsed into a contented silence, relaxed but vigilant, as they rode side by side on the horse trails that were widened by four-wheeler traffic. Soon they forded the creek and followed the irregular edge of the field. Stout shoots of corn had pierced the ground and were waving in the light breeze in the first field. The neat rows in the next field boasted freshly sprouted soybean plants that had recently curled out of their seed hulls.

Buster started to balk and Abigail felt the vibrations rumble from deep inside of him. Checking his focus, she saw the large rock in the field about thirty feet off the trail. Pulling up, she waited for Lee to come along side, "I don't remember seeing that there before."

"Me neither. I wonder where it came from." His trained eyes swept back and forth until he picked up a hint further up the side of the hill. "Look," he said as he pointed to a deeply gashed tree, "looks like it came from up there. It must've bounced off that tree."

425

"Let's take a closer look." Buster obediently responded to Abigail's nudges but kept his ears flattened.

"Could that be...?" Lee didn't finish his sentence.

"Oh, Lord! Is that what I think it is?"

They moved a few feet closer and were able to see the distinctive chiseled five-sided rock that was formerly on the top of the hill. Tender soy bean plants were crushed in the path of the rock. "Why would it be down here?"

"Are you curious enough to go up there and see if we can figure it out?"

"Nope. Neither are you," Lee said firmly. Nodding at her horse, he added, "and Buster sure isn't either."

They turned their mounts around and loped past the two fields, splashed through York Creek, and turned to the right. Lee still wanted to finish riding the perimeter of his eighty acres.

"What a fabulous way to spend a Father's Day!" Lee exclaimed as he breathed in the fresh air. He had a great sense of satisfaction as he surveyed the fields and streams, the stands of trees and the pond. He stopped Lady on top of a knoll and gestured toward the house that was visible from that vantage point.

"A living Norman Rockwell painting," Abigail sighed.

"We are blessed."

"We are blessed."

They finished their circuit and ended at the barn. After grooming Lady and Buster they led them back down to their pasture. Swatting Buster on the rump after she slipped off the halter rope, she said, "There ya go, big guy."

Lady was rolling in the grass before the gate was secured. "Come on, sweet, let's head up to the house. I could use some iced tea."

They were both dusty and sweaty but that did not stop them from walking with arms looped around one another's waist until they got back on the four-wheeler. They contemplated the implications of their discovery. Why would the rock be in the field? Who or what shoved it? Was it Charlie or someone else?

Suddenly Abigail stopped. "Oh, man! I got to talk to Amy right away!"

"What?"

"Ooh," Abigail furrowed her brows and huffed. "Confidentiality. I don't think it'll be a problem for Amy, but I need to ask her something in private first."

"Let's go."

Lee and Abigail drove up to her place and found Carrie Sue and Amy on the back deck.

"Hey, how was your ride?"

"Interesting. In fact, I need to ask you something in private, Amy."

"Uh, sure." She looked as if she were being sent to the principal's office.

"You're all right, Amy. I just want to maintain your confidentiality."

"Oh, I don't give a rip about that. My life's an open book."

"All right, then. Do you remember that time you had a part that freaked out about the stairs?"

"Yeah, it was that little one who saw the two different men on the stairs. One was a really old guy and the other one had a bandaged hand."

"Beard and braided hair?"

427

"Right."

"I'm pretty sure that would be Charlie Fletcher. Our neighbor down the road."

"I've been there," Carrie Sue interjected and looked at Amy as she added, "that's the story I told you about me escaping from the ritual at Charlie Fletcher's farm."

"O-oh," she replied as she started to make the connections. "Wait a minute. My little part saw someone that you know?"

The implications dawned on them simultaneously. They were probably at the same rituals with some of the same people more than one time.

"This is getting weirdly interesting. Why are you asking about this now?"

"Well, we took a little detour because Lee had a hunch about something and we took the trail that goes behind Charlie Fletcher's farm. That five-sided rock that used to be under the big tree up there is now in the field down below."

"What! That's crazy! I mean, you don't mess with stuff like that unless you have a death wish."

"That's what I'm thinking. It doesn't make any sense. That's what made me think about those two people that your little one saw. Wasn't it an old man? Prinz maybe? The high priest."

"Yeah, and we're pretty sure he's dead."

"And Charlie Fletcher fits the description of the other one," Abigail continued to brain-storm with Amy while Carrie Sue and Lee attentively followed their dialogue.

"Okay, I have a question. How did my little part know about these deaths? Did she get the info from demons or from God?"

428

"Good question. I'll have to think about that one."

"Yeah, 'cause if she got the info from a demon and it came true, then I wonder how the demon knew. I mean, it's kinda like the demon knew something that only God's supposed to know."

"Wouldn't that be a false prophecy?" Carrie Sue asked.

"Maybe they're operating within God's judgment," Abigail mused.

"What do you mean?"

"I'm thinking of that weird passage in Chronicles where Jehoshaphat and Ahab were going to fight together and Jehoshaphat wanted to hear from one of God's prophets but Ahab didn't because Micaiah never prophesied any good for Ahab. Ahab wanted to listen to his false prophets."

"Duh!" Lee injected with a wry grin. "Ahab was pretty wicked. Jezebel and all."

"Yeah. So, Micaiah said that he saw God on His throne and all the host of heaven were standing on his right and His left – indicating good angels and fallen angels, I think. And God was asking them how Ahab could be enticed to go to battle because God was going to use the battle to finally kill him off. He had done enough evil."

"I don't ever remember reading that." Lee said.

"Me neither," Carrie Sue added.

"Don't look at me. I've been a heathen all my life," Amy quipped.

"It's in there, but it gets stranger. It says that one said this and another said that and finally one said that he'd go and be a deceiving spirit in the mouth of all of Ahab's prophets."

Lynda L. Irons

"An angel?" Carrie Sue asked.

"I think it was one of the fallen angels. A demon. You know, if God had that council already established before Lucifer and a third of the angels fell, I think that even though their character changed, their assignment didn't. They still served on the council."

"That would make sense. Why would God send a good angel to do something that fits a demon?"

"Right. It says 'I will go and be a deceiving spirit.' And then God tells him to go and be successful. So maybe we have a similar situation here where the Ministerial Alliance and people in our churches and this area and all of us are praying about the cult activity in this area and God's working it out in His council."

"Whoa! That's amazing! And that would make a crazy kind of sense."

"A curse without a cause shall not alight, but the reverse is true, too," Abigail said.

"A curse with cause shall alight," Carrie Sue finished the thought.

"So, I still don't know if a demon told my part something or if God did."

"And we still don't know if Charlie is dead or not," Lee pointed out.

30

Wednesday, June 20

It was the last day of spring. The longest day of spring for the northern hemisphere was the shortest day for the southern hemisphere. For most of the world it was just another day to mark the passage of time, the passing of a season, but for another group it was not just another day. Gatherings at Stonehenge marked the beginning of the celestial sweep around the globe to celebrate this annual event. The day with the most sunlight cast the most darkness.

Intangible tensions in the atmosphere escalated and reverberated in tangible tensions on the earth. Sharks attacked. Dogs growled and snapped. Customers were rude. Employees and employers faced off about petty matters. Fender benders and feuds, illness and pain, frustrations and annoyances abounded. Satan's ubiquitous dark spirits delighted in the torment and abasement of the clueless dust and clay image-bearers of the Great Power.

Amy was restless and she knew why. She felt the increased drawing from the dark side like the pull of the tide. Inside it was as if Apollyon and Joktan and all the other cult-loyal, demon-loyal personalities were pooling their resources to batter the jagged shores of her life. *Oh, God, don't let them break through! Save them. Heal them. Deliver them.* Her simple prayers spiraled their way through the chaos and touched the very heart of God.

"Would you have time to pray with me today?" Amy asked Abigail over breakfast.

"Absolutely. Let me let the chickens out and we can do it right away."

"Thanks. It's a ritual night. I can feel it."

Abigail finished her breakfast and then quickly walked across the glistening dew-covered lawn. Not wanting to startle the chicks, she started talking as she got close to the door. "Good morning, ladies. It's another beautiful day that the Lord has made." Unlatching the door, she swung it open and fastened it to the wall.

"Chill!" Abigail laughed as they swarmed out of the coop, heads bobbing and wings flapping, clucking and cackling in the rush to be first to get to some mysterious destination that they soon forgot all about. They fanned out and began to scratch the dirt for edible treasures.

Amy and Abigail took their usual places in the living room. Having opened with prayer, Abigail reviewed the status of the internal system of personalities. The original Fuchsya was stronger with every integration. Tiara, the leader over the whole system was defected and on board. All but level six had renounced Satanism and were mostly integrated.

"It seems that everyone but Joktan and level six personalities are on board plus the hold-outs from the other levels."

"Right," Tiara confirmed. "That's everyone that I'm aware of."

"Let's ask God for a strategy for dealing with them." Abigail prayed and waited to see if Tiara would have something or if someone else would show up.

"Hey," the soft, shy voice said, "it's me, Original Fuchsya."

"Good to see you. How have you been?"

"Well, not real proud of myself. I guess with all the changes I kind of shut down and left everyone else holding the bag again."

"Don't worry about it. That's part of the process. You have some very capable parts that have been doing a great job. Don't forget, they got all that resourcefulness from you and as long as they have it, you don't. So, once you're fully integrated, you'll be amazing."

"Thanks," she replied without much conviction. "I hope you're right."

"I am," Abigail gave a semi-cocky smile and tossed her head in a way that brought a shy smile out of Fuchsya.

"I think I'm supposed to step up today and sort of make an announcement to the ones down on level six."

"Really?" Abigail was not expecting that. "What kind of announcement?"

"That I'm not a Satanist anymore and that any part of me that is, needs to quit right now."

"You go, girl!"

"I need a little help with wording it, though. I mean, I want to tell them that since I'm a Christian, I can't have any Satan-loyal parts. I want my life back."

"I think you've got it. You can ask the Lord to invade level six with His Holy Spirit and shut down programs and bind the demons and give the parts an opportunity to listen to you."

"Good idea. I'll do that right now." Fuchsya bowed her head and started praying, "God, I just want to say that I am a Christian and I want every part of me to be, too. Would You go to level six and shut down the programs and shut up the demons and make the parts listen to me?"

She waited a moment and then announced, "I want everyone to listen up. I know you don't think you have to listen to me but you do. You all came from me. You're all parts of me and it's all because of Satan and the cult. I'm telling you and the demons and the Satanists that they're not going to run our life anymore. The true Lord Jesus is. So, you guys can stay down there without your demons telling you what to do and think about it. I'll check with you later."

Abigail was amused and delighted by the announcement. "Good job!"

"Thanks. It feels better inside. Lighter."

"Excellent."

"I think I want to go rest now. I'm not shutting down, I just want Amy to take over for a bit."

"Good idea."

The relentless rotation of the earth pulled the day closer to its end. Abigail tried to put the chickens up twice, but each time she went down to shut the door there were still some stragglers because of the late sunset. Amy seemed peaceful and was settled down in the living room with a book of baby names. Lee had just left so Abigail decided to pack some more things in her office. *Books. So many books; so little time.* Abigail sighed and packed books she had purchased but had not found the time to read yet.

The persistent pull activated Satanists and they began their surreptitious journeys to ritual sites. Zorroz came with his wife and remaining daughter. The child had already been abused during the day. Her vacant eyes indicated a trance state and having been switched into a personality that was compliant. Soulless Sol they called her, laughing at the pun.

As the day progressed Charlie Fletcher felt the wrenching tug, too. His anger matched the draw. That ever-simmering, sometimes-boiling spirit of rage stirred and instigated. Charlie had no idea that Rage ran in the same hierarchy as Murder, Suicide, Hatred, and many more foul spirits. He did not know that they were fueling his tirades. He only knew that he hated his life and so he ranted vigorously against Zorroz and Daggett and Xerxes. *I'll show them! I'm done! No one gets me!*

He had wrestled with getting out of the cult more and more seriously. Ideas were circling around his head like bees but only one irrational notion landed. He had heard of others getting out by giving a sibling or son or daughter or grandchild to take their place. An atonement. Even if it were true, he had no one. No one, that is, except himself.

One attention-getting rational thought was that they would know of his treason. They would know that he had removed the pentagon-shaped rock. The next ritual assigned to his place would make that evident. *Make a plan. I have to make a plan. They'll take me out.* He knew it would be a brutal end when they caught up with him. It was not pure will power that moved him. It was sheer, icy terror that drove him.

435

Lynda L. Irons

The decision was made and an eerie calm descended upon him. Having gone through so much fear, he was now quite fearless. Resolute and determined, the iron clenching of his jaw and his steely eyes made him look formidable. If he would have stopped to look into his own eyes when he passed the mirror he might have been alarmed to see the flat stare of demons glaring back at him.

I have some unfinished business first. His deformed hand forced him to adapt fine and gross motor function. He flew into a rage when he dropped bullets or when he could not carry something. He raged as he chose his weapon. Large. Effective. Hollow points. Revving up the engine on his maroon pickup truck under the cover of dark, spitting stones with the abrupt start, he slowed only enough to make his right-hand turn. Quickly accelerating, adrenaline pumping, demons exacerbating, he roared down the road until he found the Milner's driveway. It was steep. When he got to the top, he hastily did a three-point turn, intentionally backing hard into the parked car.

Earl heard the racket and put his hand on Jan. "Don't move. Don't turn on the lights. I'll see what's going on." He was not as nimble as he used to be but he picked up his Smith and Wesson with a smooth movement and quickly walked to the side of the picture window in the living room. Just as he carefully pulled the edge of the curtain back, the window exploded into jagged splinters that peppered the living room.

"Jesus, oh, Jesus!" Jan screamed from the bedroom as a hail of bullets pocked the front of the house and blew out their bedroom window too. She could hear

436

the thud when Earl hit the floor. She heard the roar of the engine as the intruder bounced down their driveway to the road.

Blam! Blam! Blam! Charlie aimed at Lee's house. He continued to drive and shoot towards the fields and pastures until all seventeen bullets had been fired. He ejected the empty magazine and slapped his back-up into the gun. At the end of Abigail's driveway, he skidded to a halt, leaned out the window and let a hail of bullets loose. The sounds of shattered glass barely registered in his fevered brain.

Amy fell forward onto the floor clutching her belly.

Abigail instinctively dropped to the floor and curled up with hands over her head in her office. All the terror of that night in March roared back and momentarily paralyzed her. Only when she heard the vehicle spin out of the driveway and peel out like a drag racer did she dare move.

Scrambling to her feet, reaching for Walther, chambering a round, Abigail cautiously crept toward the living room. "Amy! Amy! Are you all right?"

"I'm good."

"Stay down. I'm going to shut off the lights, but I think he went down the road."

Across the road, Lee got up from his recliner and ran in a crouch out the back door with his weapon in hand. Hearing the gunshots further down the road, he groaned in his spirit. *Oh, Lord, not again! Please not again! Protect Abigail. Oh Jesus!* He raced back into the house, grabbed his keys, and flung himself into his truck. By the time he got to the foot of Abigail's driveway, the gunman had moved to the York's house, peppered it, and was gone as quickly as he came.

Lee accelerated up the driveway remembering to softly toot his horn so Abigail would know that it was him. Shattered living room and bedroom windows glinted and winked around the black holes and his heart sank once again as his mind went back to the last time he had raced up here after hearing gunshots.

The motion sensor lights illuminated Abigail as she cautiously pushed open the screen door and walked onto the front porch. "I'm okay. We're okay!" Amy was right behind her protectively covering her belly.

"Oh, thank God!" Relief was too mild a word to describe the feelings that surged through him. He rushed up the steps and onto the porch and nearly crushed Abigail in a protective hug. "Let's get married right now. I don't want to let you out of my sight!"

"Uh, sure." Abigail's humor popped up at the most absurd times. She turned to Amy and asked, "Would you like to officiate? We can get Earl and Jan to be our witnesses."

The comic relief was something they all needed to momentarily break the tension.

"Wait a minute!" Lee said. "We need to check on Earl and Jan. I think that shooting rampage started over there."

"You're right! I'll call them and you call the sheriff."

"The sheriff?" Amy asked incredulously. "What if he's behind it?"

Somewhere off in the distance they heard another gunshot echo and tensed as they visualized more windows being shattered for another neighbor.

"It doesn't matter. He can't sweep this under the rug. Amy, why don't you take some pictures? And tell Earl and Jan to take some, too. I need to check up on my critters. The horses were making a racket and I don't know if the S.O.B. got one of them or just spooked them. It sounds like he moved down the road so stay here with the lights off just in case he comes back. I'll be back as soon as I can." Lee was thumbing his cell phone to make the 911 call as he quickly got back into his truck.

"Be careful!" Abigail called out and then went to the phone. Looking out her darkened window she noticed that there were no lights on at Earl and Jan's house either. *They're probably thinking it's safer to keep the lights out, too.* Abigail counted the rings and became alarmed once she counted ten of them.

"They're not answering," Abigail said to Amy.

"That's not good. Can bullets go through a house?"

"We'll find out."

———————————

Martha York dialed the long-distance number that started with two zero two.

"Mom?" Richard was alarmed by the phone call at this late hour. He knew that his parents retired early.

"Son, your father's been shot."

"What! Is he okay?"

"No. The sheriff said the ambulance is on the way, but he has to come first."

"Mom, you're not making any sense. Why does the sheriff have to come first?"

"Your father's been shot."

"You already said that. Who...? Why...?"

"Can you come right away?"

"Sure, Mom. I'm on my way." Richard shook his head as if it would help the jumbled thoughts settle into some sort of sense. "Wait! Does this have anything to do with all the shenanigans you and pop have been telling me about?"

"I'm not sure, but I think so."

"I'm on my way, Mom. Mom, I love you! Keep your cell phone on you. I'll be in touch."

"I love you, too, Richie. Drive careful, now." She had not called him by his nickname since he was a little boy.

Not long after she hung up, the shrill wail of a siren was heard in the distance. It got closer and louder. The blue lights of the deputy sheriff's unit punctured the darkness and raced around the perimeter of the room casting odd shadows. It slowed down and entered the York's driveway.

On the hill above, Amy and Abigail moved to the bedroom, peered through the window, and were able to see the lights through the woods. Moments later the red flashing lights of an ambulance followed by a fire truck interrupted the already disrupted night.

"Oh, my, you don't suppose one of them got shot?" Amy asked.

"It doesn't look good."

"Here come some more." They heard more sirens in the distance.

"I wish Lee was here. What's taking him so long? I hope the critters are all right."

"Maybe we should put the lights back on," Amy suggested.

"Good idea. With all them around I don't think that maniac would come back. Besides, we need to cover these windows and I'm not going to walk around in this broken glass in the dark." Snapping on the light and surveying the room she added, "Look at that mess! I've got glass all over my bed!"

"I'll help you."

They busied themselves patching up the remains of the windows, picking up the larger shards, and vacuuming up the tiny slivers. Finding a flashlight, Abigail walked around the front of the house to see if there was any noticeable damage besides the windows. She did not see anything obvious except for some holes in the siding. *Where did those bullets end up?* Abigail wondered if they were imbedded in the house or if they were in her couch.

Lee checked his animals and found Misty hobbling. She was bleeding from a wound that had grazed her rump. "Come here, sweetie. You'll be all right." In his haste to check on them he did not think to bring a halter so he took his belt off and used it to lead her up the dark path to the barn. Putting her into a stall, he retrieved the first aid equipment. Lee took the time to snap a picture of it with his cell phone before he cleaned the wound and put antibiotic ointment on it. He'd bring her to the vet if it warranted further treatment.

"Hey," Lee said when Abigail answered the phone, "Misty has a surface scratch and that seems to be the extent of it."

"That's a relief. What about the cows?"

"They were way on the other side of their field so I'm not going to bother with them until the morning. I've got Misty squared away in the barn so I'm on my way up. Where'd all the sirens end up?"

"Next door. I have a hunch that one or both of the York's got hurt down there. Earl and Jan still aren't answering their phone."

"Maybe I should stop up there first?" Lee bounced the idea off of Abigail.

"I hate to sound selfish, Lee, but if you go up there now, the Keystone Kops might think you're the shooter and take you out."

"Good thinking." As much as Lee hated to think that their neighbors might need medical help, Abigail was right. The sheriff would come by soon enough.

By the time Lee got up to Abigail's place, most of the mess was cleaned up and the gaping holes in the windows were temporarily patched up with tape and plastic. The ambulance had left the neighbor's house. They were discussing what they should do next when the blue lights moved from there to Abigail's farm.

The officer took his time gathering his reports and other items before emerging from his unit. He saw Abigail and Lee waiting for him and called out to her, "Were you shot at?"

"Yes sir," Abigail replied. "Got my windows blown out and have some holes in the siding. I won't know all the damage until I can look at it in daylight."

"That's fine. Anybody hurt?"

"No, but could you check up on the Milner's next door? That's where the shooting started. I tried to call them but they aren't answering. They haven't put their lights on either."

"Ma'am, we don't need you telling us how to do our job."

"No, sir. I'm just concerned about them, that's all."

"Any idea who would want to shoot up your neighborhood?" He seemed to slow down this farce by deliberately talking slower and pausing between questions.

"No," Abigail lied. She actually could think of several good candidates, but she had no proof and she had no idea if this deputy was part of the cult or not.

"Wasn't there a shooting up here a few months ago?"

Abigail was grateful that her face was in the shadows as she blanched. She certainly had not reported Charlie Fletcher's shot at her or Earl's shot at Charlie. *Was he fishing around? What did he know?* She recalled that a unit went past them towards Charlie's place that night so someone in the department knew exactly what happened. "Oh, people are always shooting at coyotes and raccoons around here," she said as nonchalantly as possible.

Lee stepped forward. "I'm Lee Norris. I live across the road," he said as he gestured toward his house, "My house was shot at, too. I don't know if anything hit the house or not, but I have a mare with a flesh wound."

"Let me finish this report and I'll get to you in a minute."

"Yes sir," Lee said respectfully as he stood closer to Abigail.

The deputy asked a few more questions and then turned his attention to Lee. He made some superficial queries and turned to leave.

"I think it started with the Milner's." Lee turned and nodded towards the hill behind them where the Milner's lived. He caught the sight of blue lights up

443

there and was only slightly relieved that someone was checking on them.

"That's all I need." The officer cut him off, put his pen in his pocket, and began to step away.

"Excuse me," Abigail said, "did you catch the guy? I mean, if you didn't, he could come back. Are we safe?"

"That's classified." He abruptly turned and slid into his vehicle.

They watched him leave the property, turn off his blue lights, and head back up the road the way he had come.

With his FBI and Marine background, Richard York was accustomed to packing quickly and lightly. Tonight was no exception. Within minutes of his mother's call, he was on the road. Once he was on the interstate and set his black Suburban on cruise control at seventy-seven miles per hour, he called his superior.

"Landrum."

"Sorry to bother you so late, sir, but I just got a call from my mother. My father's been shot and she told me that I need to get there right away."

"By all means! Go! Take as much time as you need."

"Thank you, sir, I'm on my way. I'll keep you posted."

Counseling related E-Books by this author

I am a Cutter, Please Help Me
Yo Soy un Cortador Ayudana Por Favor
Emotional Abuse and Verbal Assaults through Lies, Vows, Curses, and Judgments
Battling Anorexia, Bulimia, Binge Eating, Health Food Obsession
Panic and Anxiety Attacks
Heaven or Hell – Have I Lost My Salvation?
Mad at God, Self, and Others
Dissociative Identity Disorder
What's in Your Family Tree? Battling Generational Curses and Familial Spirits
Spiritual Gifts – Discovering Your Spiritual Gifts
Seeing, Hearing, Sensing God through His Broken-hearted Children

Fiction E-Books series by this author:

Ritual Abuse – Autumn
Ritual Abuse – Winter
Ritual Abuse – Spring
Ritual Abuse – Summer

Watch for paperback editions of the above titles.